A club Nero Ser
CW01464738
Little Pretty Things
Dale V Mcfarlane

A Club Nero Series Novel - Little Pretty Things- Vol 1

Little Pretty Things - Vol 1, Volume 1

Dale v Mcfarlane

Published by Dale v Mcfarlane, 2024.

A CLUB NERO SERIES NOVEL - LITTLE PRETTY THINGS- VOL 1

First edition. October 31, 2024.

ISBN: 979-8227327765

Written by Dale v Mcfarlane.

Chapter 1
Prologue

6 Months Ago

Elliot entered the toilet at the court house and went into the stall he sat on the toilet seat twirling his ring on the chain taking a deep breath his hands shook he had to be brave today and get his life back the past 6 months had been torture .Therapy was helping thanks to Darians help on giving getting him the therapist even though group therapy was great he just wanted a one to one to which Malcolm had used previously especially when he wanted to talk privately to his therapist about personal matters that he couldn't talk to the group about .He also dredded facing his rapist will he ever get over it Malcolm said he would eventually. Group therapy Everyone was great he had got to know helping each other out which was great too and everyone got on well with each other and sometimes confided in each other .

Elliot did his business and came out of the stall and washed his hands. He looked in the mirror giving himself a pep talk "Ok let's do this " Deep breath and another pep talk right Elliot thought I think I'm ready now checking himself one more time .Doing his breathing exercises to calm himself before going back outside .

Elliot was about to open the door his phone dropped and went to pick it up "Oh i'm so sorry " A foreign voice a hand reaching for the phone to Elliot looked up dusty blonde hair looking up blue eyes and a cute smile and a nice dark blue suit They both stood up and he was slightly taller than Elliot oh my Elliot thought clearing his throat he is cute "My fault nerves ".

" Yes, it can be nerve racking. In fact , I'm only dealing with a parking ticket. " Elliot sniggered. He had a nice voice and wondered where from He thought he smiled at Elliot. " Good luck with that. " The door opened. Elliot's friend Patrick appeared and saw them talking. Elliot looked round Patrick looked at the guy and back at Elliot .Elliot kinda hoovered oh god I'm staring Elliot thought .But I can't seem to get my legs moving I feel I want to chat longer .

"Mate the lawyer wants to see you, " Elliot nodded. He looked round at the guy "Good luck " He said before Ellio leaves " Thanks you to " They both hoovered this time before Elliot left Elliot smiled into himself he is cute did he imagine there was a spark the thought .Chewing his lip oh my That's first in months since he had felt something in a good way he guessed .

" WHAT SERIOUSLY "WAS Elliot hearing right his attacker had pleaded guilty regarding the other guy also " Yes Elliot he will have jail time which you don't have to be here for " Brendan his lawyer explains which Elliot didn't want to be here for at all he thought I just can't believe it he thought .Was Grant influenced or did he decide himself to plead guilty .

" He will, " Elliot looked over at his sister. She smiled and nodded " Thank you so much Brendan. " Elliot shook his hand and said he could have his life back. Finally that's what he wants and maybe date again Elliot smiled thinking about that for the future .When the time is right and he feels ready to .

" LET'S GO HOME SIS "Elliot lays his arm round Carrie's shoulder "Gladly but don't you want to celebrate " Carrie thought is he ok about this it has been a lot over the past few months .

All Elliot wanted was just to go home and chill. Elliot sighed and slid his arm around his sister again " I just wanna go home " .Carrie nodded and understood her brother she was pretty whacked about it all to Carrie thought .And so was Elliot he seemed more Carrie thinks maybe to do with the court case too .

CARRIE LAY HER BAG on the kitchen table. Micheal came over to her. She looked up at him and smiled leaning into him. " I'm just glad it's all over Micheal " " I know " Micheal went over to the counter and put the kettle on .Yep definitely over thankfully and now Elliot can get back to normality and so can he and Carrie .Also the kids too.

" Do you think it's a good time to tell him yet? " Micheal looks round leaning against the counter. " Maybe I don't know he will find out soon though " .That's true Carrie thought .Looking down at her stomach touching her belly Carrie smiled and thought about their little miracle growing inside .

" Find out what " Elliot asked, coming into the kitchen looking between his sister and Micheal, they looked at each other Michael nodded Carrie came over to Elliot . " Jesus guys tell me " .Looking between his sister and Micheal it better not be Mum he thought I couldn't bear it if it was .So many times his mum took bad infections and they thought she wouldn't make it .

" You're going to have another niece or nephew " Wow Elliot thought more great news he was happy to hear about " Elliot " Carrie asked god was it too much she thought .Would Elliot think he would have to move out " That's great sis I'm pleased for you " .They hugged happy news for a change Elliot thought then smiled into himself they definitely been having a lot sex lately lucky sods .

" Ready " Patrick asked coming into the kitchen what's going on he thought is Elliot ok he thought " Where are you going " "Be there in a minute " Patrick left all Elliot wanted was a bit off normality go out with his friends for a bit drink have fun " I won't be late I just want a bit guys time is that ok " .Carrie patted Elliot's arm he needs some time with his friends which is totally ok .

" Of course it is isn't it Micheal " "You can't stop living your life Elliot " Micheal said patting Elliot's arm so true Elliot thought I have put that on hold for the past few months healing and therapy .

Elliot nodded Micheal was right and time to get living again but not sex yet until he got his all clear next month again was he ready to have sex again he didn't know " Elliot if your thinking we want you to move out you don't need to this has been your home since you were ten " .Got to move out sometime Elliot thought he and the the guys have been talking about it for a while now .

" Carrie I know besides I got to move out sometime I know I know what your gonna say I have thought about it for a while we can talk about it another time and sis I, happy about the baby "They both hugged Elliot also hugged Micheal he looked round at them before he left " There better be just one baby in there " Elliot sniggered they both looked shocked when he said that .

Carrie looked at Micheal, the shock on her face he sniggered and came over to her and lay his arm around her " Honey don't panic he's kidding " " I bloody hope so " Carrie looked up at Micheal shaking her head .One baby is definitely enough Carrie thought and she couldn't wait to go for her sonogram soon . And well if it is two they can work through that .

" YOU MENTION ABOUT moving out " Patrick asked while driving along the road Elliot looked over while texting Malcolm " Yea Carries pregnant again " " For real " Bailey asked in the back Elliot looked round at him shaking his head " Yes Bailey" Patrick looked in the mirror at Bailey busy texting shaking his head .Cant those two not keep away from each other .Patrick thought but Senora is good for Bailey she doesn't take any of his shit .

" Are you texting Senora again? " Bailey looked up, smiling . He moved forward in his seat. " Can you drop me off? "" Bailey, no besides It's Eliot's day. He needs us right mate. " Bailey looked at Elliot, " Sorry mate, I'm here for you." Bailey sighs sitting back on the seat that's me told he thought but my friend needs me right now .

“Where To “ “Honestly patrick can we just go to Wetherspoons " Elliot asked Bailey screwed up his face Wetherspoon he wants to just go there “ We can go anywhere you want Mate “ Bailey tutted Shaking his head reply’s back to Senora that he would see her later . Patrick was right Elliot needed him and Patrick right now and that’s totally fine .

GOOD HE THOUGHT THAT’S all he could manage. He felt exhausted and he just wanted to be with good friends for tonight and talk about stupid things then the guy from.Earlier came into.Elliots mind and he wondered how long it would take him to have sex again .And the guy from earlier he was sure he had felt something but wasn’t sure what it was or was it just his imagination maybe smiling into himself looking out the window while they drove along the street to their destination .

PRESENT DAY

Elliot belly laughed at Freya at her rage off about anything and everything. He shook his head and looked round everyone a bunch off him and group therapy friends had been meeting a couple days a week for the past 6 months since he started therapy . They were really good friends now and Elliot would be starting his new college course soon which he was looking forward to. He had been thinking of changing his course to social sciences, the same one that Malcolm had done .It's what he wanted to do now to help people like the job Malcolm and Sam were doing .Malcolm couldn’t praise his job enough same with Sam it’s what they have wanted to do for some time now .And it sounded like he enjoyed what he was doing to and at the drop in centre to .

Malcolm helped him out on which course to do for social work " Excuse me " Thomas stood up everyone looked up at him " What i,'m going to the bathroom " Thomas shook his head and left to go to the bathroom. "He is ok right " Freya asked everyone to look at each other Elliot took her hand she looked at him . " Freya were not his counsellors " " Yea your right " .Freya sighs Thomas has been struggling a little bit lately and everyone rallied round for him whatever he needed .Anyone to talk to or any advice but sometimes he got in his head which Freya could talk to him he felt he could confide in her better and the counsellors To .

" Right for more drinks' ' Elliot went up to the bar to order more drinks. The bar is busy as Elliot works his way through to order the drinks and gives the waitress the order while he waits. Someone bumps into him as Elliot is about to take a couple off the drinks back to the table .Shit he thought that was nearly over him mind you the bar is busy .He was about to rant at the person regarding nearly spilling the drink over him .

" So sorry " Elliot thought he heard that accent before and looked round it's the parking ticket guy Elliot cocks his head what are the chances he thought when the guy recognises him too . " Parking ticket " Christian snorts he remembered him he thought " You have a good memory " Elliot giggles into himself and blushes chewing his lip .Fucking hell why the hell am I blushing Elliot thought and he didn't think he would bump into him again what are the chances of that .

" How's those drinks coming? Thomas asks, looking between Elliot and Christian "Um here I'll get the other ones " Handing Thomas the drinks and going off to the table . " My group therapy friends " Christian screws his face Elliot smiles " We are raging at the world " .Christian grins looking over at the table and back at Elliot .And thought why is he raging at the world Elliot staring at Christian

.

Elliot exclaims Christian giggles again Elliot thinking I like that giggle " And how's that going " " Oh you know gets all the rage out " They both giggle Christian winces and hobbles a bit on his leg noticed by Elliot . " I sprained my ankle " " Shit are you ok " .Elliot looked down at Christians leg and looked back up at him .Oh did that Worry him Elliot thought I hope it's not too bad Elliot thought he felt his cheeks burning for thinking like that.And a little flutter which he hasn't had in a while .Looking up at Christian Who was grinning .

" Yes of course it's my fault turning the wrong way " .

A guy came over to Christian he looked round at him as he whispered in his ear Christian nodded and looked over at the table. "Better go oh and good luck with your rage at the world. " Elliot sniggered and nodded " Hope your ankle gets better " . Christian nods and goes over to his table as well as Elliot. I am smiling, he thought because he sure is hot .Elliot chewing his lip his cheeks feeling hot .

"Who was that he's cutie " Dana said Elliot smiled and blushed " Bumped into him at the courthouse before in the toilet " Everyone giggled Elliot blushed he had a warm feeling which he hadn't had before in a long time he thought he smiled thinking about it .Also his belly and his cock were doing things he hadn't felt in a while that's a good sign right Elliot thought .Biting his lip smiling into himself .

" Guys I have a tingle " Elliot Announced he bit his lip again "How long has it been " Freya asked he looked at her then immediately regretted what she said " Sorry i didn't " " Freya it's ok " . He takes her hand and they both nod and smile at each other .I feel really bad for saying something stupid Freya thought she had a mind blank moment Elliot brings Freya close to him hugging her and whispers in her ear . " Don't feel bad, ok " Freya nods. They look at each other Freya clears her throat and donuts Elliot they both giggle .I'm glad he didn't take it the wrong way Freya thought and I think he likes this Christian guy which is great too .

A half hour later Elliot went to the toilet. He looks for Christian looks like he has left Elliot though there goes my chance of getting his no which is a total bummer Elliot thought hopefully bump into him again .

AFTERWARDS WHEN ELLIOT got home and chatted to Carrie and the kids he went for get a shower he let the water flow over him shutting his eyes blue eyes dusty blonde hair came into his mind while Elliot soaped himself he smiled thinking about him is it fate that they meet again will it happen again who knows Elliot thought . I would like to see him again but who knows when in the future .

Elliot looked down he had a hard on oh thats been a while he thought since the rape he had been having bad dreams 6 months on Elliot thought maybe get back on the horse and start dating again .For definite but no app dates this time he hoped the proper way get back to clubbing again to he was ready to get back out there and date

HE STARTED PUMPING himself. It felt good thinking of his blue eyes. The smile Elliot held onto the tile pulled harder. He slowed down his breathing. I'm gonna cum soon leaning his head against the tile until he came leaning his head against the tiles smiling into himself that felt so much better he thought chewing his lip and giggling into himself. Shit have I got a crush? Maybe I should check online for him but I don't know his name immediately, regretting that . Or put his face on a database maybe Darian knows how to ask him whenever he sees him at work .

Elliot lay on top of his bed checking his phone and the door chapped. He looked round " Ok " Carrie asked " Ok " Molly came running into Elliot's room and jumped on his back Molly " Carrie sniggered as they pretended to fight .Molly giggling while Elliot tickled her " Uncle Elliot no " .

" I'm making hot chocolate want some " " Ok i'll be down in a minute " Elliot tickled Molly again she squealed Carrie shook her head then got up and ran back out that girl she thought .She so loves her uncle so does Jack they have a good bond the three of them. And hopefully when the baby comes they will bond .

" HOW IS EVERYONE " Carrie asked Elliot got up and lay his arm around her shoulder " Good " The baby kicked again Carrie feeling her stomach Elliot looked down to Carrie looked up at him she smiled " Will you come with us to the ultrasound " Elliot looked up in shock oh wow Carrie wants me there to " Really you want me there at the reveal " .

" Of course c'mon let's get some hot chocolate " .

BAILEY'S LEG COULDN'T stop shaking, staring at the pregnancy test Senora sat on the toilet seat staring at him. He looked round at her and back at the two tears leaning on the sink the alarm beeped that the time was to check the test . Bailey looked and looked round at Senora. She had tears running down her face shit he thought he picked up the test both positive " I'm sorry " Senora said what's she sorry for he thought he picked up the tests went over to her and knelt down in front of her . "Please don't cry baby " Senora picked up the tests looking at them, something that they will have to talk about. She thought they were ready for a baby. They were young,

Bailey 20 Senora a year older at 21 but some mothers were younger, having babies these days .

" Are we ready for a baby Bailey " Bailey got up and sat on the edge of the bathtub "Maybe , maybe not we can work it out right " Yea it's too soon to have kids but they can't change it now he thought he loves Senora she was an amazing person .He was so grateful when she agreed to go on a date with her that time she could have anyone but she wanted to be with him .

Senora looked at Bailey as if he wanted the baby she thought they had only been dating a year. This will test their relationship " You know i love you right " Bailey said Senora nodded he stretched out his arms to go to him.they hugged " i love you to " .I really do Senora thought maybe this will get him to grow up a bit just sometimes he needed reminding about stuff but she wouldn't change him .

" Babe we can work this out ok I love you and I'm sure we will be amazing parents " Senora sniggered wow that's some speech she thought " I So love you right now " Senora said Bailey reached over to kiss her .And they hugged I will try and be a good father Bailey thought and I will be a good boyfriend from now on to .

PATRICK WALKED INTO Neros when a few of the staff had arrived. He noticed he saw Jake up at the bar checking over orders. The place looked great. He thought " Looking for someone. " The person asked Patrick to look round at who spoke to him, a girl she smiled cute, he thought pretty eyes so he cleared his throat . " Im patrick " " Ellie " she held out her hand and they shook hands she blushed .she seemed kinda shy to Patrick notices taking him over to the bar where Jake was .

"Ahh Patrick you're here " Jake said Patrick looked at him and nodded " Place is looking great " They looked round the room Patrick nodded " Mr Fraser is in the office i'll go over stuff with you when you log in " Log in Patrick thought is it a new system they have now .Good idea especially for getting wages etc Darian has really thought of everything Patrick thought .

CAMERON IS ON THE PHONE to Malcolm in the office Darian had gone to Italy for business and would be back in a couple days Malcolm in Edinburg couldn't make Glasgow because of work commitments The door chapped Jake appears with Patrick " Call you later Love " Cameron snorts and what Malcolm says on the other end .

" Patrick how are you "Cameron asks standing up, they shake hands "Good thanks place is looking great " .It sure does look great Patrick thought he liked the decor Red and burgundy .It had a good feel to the place to which Patrick liked .

Cameron got up and went round to the table leaning against it " Yes it is the apartment ok " " Perfect " Cameron went over to the filing cabinet bringing out a folder ":This is the rota file " Cameron sounded a bit off regarding that Patrick thought " Did Jake mention the fob " " He did " .

" HIS HIGHNESS " PATRICK sniggered Cameron referring to Darian " Sorry he is so precise likes things in order you know " " I understand when will he be back " Patrick kinda got that when Darian interviewed him for the job

" Next week I leave for Edinburgh tomorrow Jake and Julia have been great running the new club " Thankfully they had stepped up to be managers for the Glasgow club and they were doing a great job running it so far Cameron thought.

ELLIE WAS SORTING OUT the Vfvgb ip area Patrick the tables she seemed nice he thought he wondered if she came from Glasgow his phone beeped off a text he checked who it was Bailey asking him to call when he had a minute what's up with him he thought did he and senora have another fight he quickly texted back . " oh it's Mr Lenzie " Ellie said Patrick looked at her and round at the person she said about " he's one the vips " " Right" Patrick looked round at him very well dressed look expensive his suit he thought a woman was with him .Very attractive and very dolled up to he seemed to be making sure she was ok all cuddly with each other Patrick could see .

Cameron came to greet Mr Lenzie Jake came over, they shook hands and Jake took them over to the Vip area then Jake went over to the Bar for the champagne to take over to the Vip . Another couple who arrived looked like a couple Patrick thought Cameron seemed to know .

" Looking great Cameron " Sydney said looking round the bar area he looked at Luca "Thanks guys " They went over to the bar and ordered drinks Patrick came over to order drinks for another couple that had come in . " Darian ok " "He is fine, gone to Italy on business back next week " .Luca and Sydney look a

" GREAT HOWS PHILIP " " Hes good Betsy Jean "

"Adorable " Luca said looking at Sydney Betsy Jean, now three years old, both of them loving fatherhood, it was the best thing in the world they both thought .And Possibly thinking of extending their family .

Patrick went out the back to take a quick break. He got out his phone to call Bailey ``Whats up " Patrick asked when Bailey connected the call sitting on his bed at home . " Patrick my life is over, Senoras pregnant " oh my god Patrick thought it can't be that bad he thought " Bailey seriously it's not the end of the world " . Mind you it will be for him but maybe it's a good thing to happen .

" You think I'm so im.scared to tell mum " Patrick sniggers, he can be so dramatic he thought it's not as if they just got together " Mate your mum will be ok besides you always at senoras you love her right " " Course I i do it's just too soon " .

" Bailey i gotta go see you tomorrow ok " " Ok " Bailey sighed they disconnected the call Patrick went back to work Bailey pulled the covers over him his phone dinged a text from Senora letting him know about the doctors appointment in two days .

" Bailey are you awake " His mum shouted at the bottom of the stairs Bailey groaned. What does she want? He thought " Bailey " , His mum knocking on the door and coming inside .Bailey pulled the covers down " what " " Are you hungry you didn't have your tea are you ok " .

" Mum I'm fine , just tired, didn't feel great when I came home " " Hope you're not coming down with anything " . There have been a lot of viruses going around lately .

Bailey shook his head and she looked round at him " Chippy or take away " Bailey smiled he guessed she couldn't be bothered cooking after her shift at the supermarket. " Take away " " Take Away it is how's senora " .

" Fine, " Sharon sniggered. I think she may have had a fight. She thought typical teenagers thought " not had a fight have you " " No mum " .

Patrick finished his shift. It was after 12 everyone was getting ready to go home. Cameron had left earlier. Patrick called for a taxi. Ellie was waiting outside with Jake and he was going to his car . " I'm getting a taxi Ellievwant me to drop you off. " She blushed, looked round at Jake and nodded " That be great thanks " .

Ellie was kinda quiet in the taxi he kept looking over at her she was texting " You from Glasgow " Patrick asked Ellie looked at him she snorted what did i say something wrong he thought . " Yes im from Glasgow " " Cool "Cool you idiot he thought awkwardly .

Ellie got out of the taxi when it arrived at her house she looked round at Patrick who was staring at her " Thanks " " Your Welcome " Ellie smiled and shut the taxi door then the taxi drove off he seemed really nice Ellie thought . Patrick smiled into himself shaking his head .

AT THE DOCTORS A COUPLE days later senoras pregnancy test still came up positive when she and Bailey went together in the car Bailey was quiet there sonogram appointment would be in a few days she thinks she might be 6 or 8 weeks Bailey held the leaflets the nurse gave them . Senora looked over at him and said they would have to tell their parents soon " Bailey it's going to be ok we will cope " " you think so " .

Senora took his hand and nodded her dad isn't that bad he likes Bailey they got on just like she got on with Baileys mum " The thing is Bailey I'm feeling a little left out " Bailey looked round at her what does she mean he thought she looked round at him then back at the road while driving .Why would she say that Bailey thought .

" Senora what do you mean " " The three of you go off god knows where I don't get a text I'm not saying you can't see your friends Bailey just a little consideration about other people , like consider my feelings you know " .

Jesus, he hadn't thought of it. Like that Bailey thought he went to take her hand Senora pulled away oh she's mad at him or is it hormones he thought " Are you feeling sick Senora shook her head what the hell is wrong he thought .

" What is so special about the club? "" What do you mean? " Senora sighed, shaking her head. She stopped the car outside Bailey's house and she looked around." Everyone I know is raving about club Nero. What's so special about it? "

" I dunno it's just a club Senora your " Senora got out of the car. What's she so mad about the club that he thought about getting out of the car to catch up with Senora .What is she so mad about club Nero for taking it out on me and considering that's a new thing too .

CATHERINE LOOKED BETWEEN Bailey and Senora they had just told her there news " Well I better get the knitting needles out then " Bailey looked at Senora then his mum she got up put on the kettle " Mum " " I'm not angry Bailey " she looked round at them folded her arms and smiled " Are you moving out then " Bailey looked at Senora she nodded " Eventually " " Ok well you better get used to him slacking off Senora " Catherine giggled so did Senora that wasn't funny he thought " Mum that's not fair " Don't worry I'm used to it Catherine " .Looks at Bailey what the hell are they both ganging up on me that's not fair .

Senora pinched his cheek and gave him a kiss " what about your dad " " we're telling him tonight " Bailey looked at her shocked no way he thought Senora looked at him " Bailey stop it dad will be ok " Bailey huffed Nope I'm not scared her dad he gets on with him .

THE NURSE SQUIRTED the Gel on Carries stomach Micheal held her hand while the kids and Elliot waited for the screen to show up the baby " Do you want to find out the sex off the baby today " " We do " Carrie said looking at Micheal the nurse scrolled round the scope everything looked fine she looked round at the family then looked back at the screen . “ Everything looks fine Mrs Mathews ‘ Good Carrie thought looking at Micheal " You are having a girl “ .

Elliot thought that’s great, Jack groaned, not another girl Molly was happy Carrie and Michael were pleased they were having a girl too and the baby was ok so Michel kissed her head .The kids whooped going over to Carrie hugging their mum happy about the news .

" Elliot " Carrie looking at him with a tear in his eyes " its great sis " " Mum can we name the baby " Molly asked Carrie sniggered while getting sorted looking at Micheal .Why not they thought but not a silly name .

" Well we could put names in a hat and decide that way " Micheal suggested a good idea Carrie thought "What do you think Elliot " Carrie asked he looked over yea good idea to " Brilliant idea " .The kids are gonna have fun with this Elliot thought.

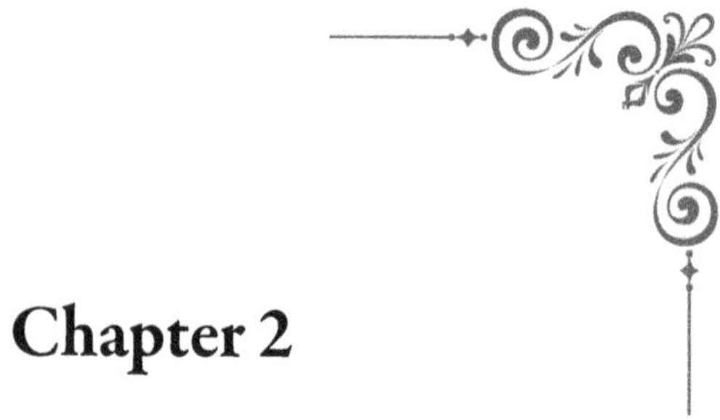

Chapter 2

Bailey sipped his cocktail at the Club Patrick listening to him vent about Senora Brandon, his work friend making drinks for members to take to one of the rooms. Patrick sighed and shook his head. Brandon looked over. That's the third cocktail Baileys had in the past hour he thought he also looked pissed off to .Patrick looked over at him and shrugged his shoulders. Maybe he should call Elliot or Senora to come for him but Elliot was with his sister Senora would be at work .I will have to cut him off at some point Patrick thought .

"Women Brandon there nothing but trouble " Bailey said he sniggered and went off to take the drinks to the private rooms " Is the boss in " " No Bailey there at the Glasgow club Jakes in charge " Bailey huffed I really need the loo he thought but I don't want to move then he decided to go after all . Brandon came back from the rooms and noticed Bailey had gone to the toilet " is he ok " he asked Patrick leaning against the bar " just his girlfriend there always fighting " .

" Glad I don't have that problem " Brandon said Patrick knew exactly what he meant then Bailey came back he overheard their Conversation " What's that " Bailey asked looking between Patrick and Brandon " Women problems " Bailey huffed a good looking guy like him the women should be flocking to him .

" I'm bi Bailey " " Oh ok " Brandon sniggered he leaned across his arms to Bailey he kinda looked shocked " Best of both then huh "

Bailey asked " Yes I do at the moment I have a boyfriend his name is Rory " Bailey held up his glass saluting " to Rory " Brandon shook his head . Then Jake appeared from the office he looked around the club which was filling up and noticed Patrick and Elliot's friend Bailey at the bar he came to visit from time to time Jake thought why doesn't he just work here when he is always at the club .He will ask him soon while he does a walk around checking to see everything was ok .

" Hey guys things ok " Jake asked Bailey looked over at him Jake acknowledging him " All good boss " Brandon said filling up his tray with more drinks to take to the tables " Bailey how are you " " I'm good Mate you " Jake could tell he had a few probably the cocktails he thought " Good " " Bet you don't have women problems " .What does he mean by that Jake thought probably having women problems Jake thought .

" Bailey enough sorry Jake he's just venting " " it's ok we all have to vent sometime " So true Bailey thought but I love my Senora he thought Jake went off to check on stuff " Patrick " " Yes Mate " Bailey flings his arms round Patrick's shoulders " I'm ready to go home now " Patrick giggles shaking his head he is definitely missing Senora .

SENORA WAS IN BED ASLEEP after her shift at work she felt exhausted Bailey had texted he was at the club again she thought she was going to wait till he got home then go to bed but she was so tired she went to bed instead hopefully he wouldn't be too late getting back .Because I'm not putting up with his shit tonight she thought .

The bed dipped Bailey lay beside Senora he lay an arm on her stomach " Baby are you sleeping " Senora turned to face him and opened one eye the smell of alcohol turning her . " I was Bailey, how much did you have to drink? " Bailey got up undressed to his boxers and he got into bed . " just three that's all " .

Bailey went for Senora's pj bottoms she moved his hand away he kissed her " Bailey im tired " Bailey looked down at her didn't she want to he thought " Baby don't you want to " Senora sat up he looked at her " Bailey it's not all about sticking it in and hoping for a quick release you know " Senora sighed what does the hell that mean is it the pregnancy that's making her feel like that Bailey thought .

Bailey screwed up his face. It isn't like he thought why is she being like this suddenly. What did I do wrong? " Can you get me a drink please " .Fuck sake Bailey thought huffing looks at Senora again .

Bailey got up,grumbling all the way to the kitchen, got Senora some orange juice and went back into the bedroom. Senora was asleep.Jesus he thought He shook his head and got into bed and moved closer to Senora snuggling into her.Kissed her cheek and they snuggled into each other .They can talk about it in the morning she is definitely mad at me about something.

IT WAS THE KIDS' SCHOOL dance recital a couple days later Molly was excited she kept going on about the new dance teacher Mr king Elliot went with them because Molly insisted he come see her dance recitals Which was fine by him sometimes he went with Carrie and Micheal to them . Darian , Cameron and Malcolm were there so they were so proud of Philip having a part in the dance recital to he was also excited about it .The kids all came out followed by the principle with another person that must be the new dance treacher Elliot thought he only saw the back off him until he faced the front Elliot got a shock it was the guy from the courthouse Principle Watkins introduced him his name was Christian king lochley . Oh wow he thought he was still hot looking Elliot shifted in his seat Moly was grinning she spotted her mum Carrie waved " He seems nice hot to " Carrie said she sniggered and Elliot shook his head .Well Yea he is hot Elliot thought he could see that .

Darian looked at Cameron and Malcolm so that was the new hot teacher everyone was going on about he thought no wonder the mothers were all encouraging the kids to take dance lessons Malcolm sniggered Philip looked over at his dads who all gave him a thumbs up for encouragement he smiled and did a thumbs up to .They were so proud of him and he was wanting to try dance class which was ok by his dads .Whether he kept it up they would just have to wait and see at least he went to rehearsals that wasn't to bad .

Christian spoke to the kids words of encouragement they were all engrossed in what he was saying all nodding then they got into their positions " Apparently this is just temporary for him " Alice said to Carrie she looked round at her " Really why is that " " Something about having an injury and only doing it as a favour Watkins is his uncle " .

Interesting Elliot thought listening to the conversation the music started the kids got into their positions and the dance started with Christians guidance they were doing really well Elliot thought then his phone beeped he checked texts from Patrick and Bailey wanting to know if he had wanted to go on a day out to Glasgow he texted back that he was in. " Ok " Carrie whispered. Elliot nodded and Jack looked bored. Carrie thought he wasn't interested in joining the dance class, just his football which was totally fine. Also, he liked his football more .

The kids finished there routine principle Watkins thanked Christian for stepping in and afterwards there was tea coffee biscuits for everyone Molly Came over to her mum she was so happy Carrie thought " Mum I want to be ballet dancer like Mr King " Carrie shook her head she is some girl she thought " Did you video it for dad " .

" I did honey " Molly beamed waved at Philip and Jacob then she went over to them Elliot kept staring at Christian while he chatted to some off the parents " I can see why all the mothers want their kids in the dance class " Malcolm said to Elliot he looked at Malcolm and blushed Malcolm sniggered him to he thought .He is definitely eye catching Malcolm thought that's for sure and what is up with Elliot with the blushing he seemed jovial which was good to see .

" How you doing " " Fine docs weaning me off the anti depressants, my anxiety not as bad " " Good to hear how's the counselling " They both walked over to the drinks table gathering themselves a coffee and a tea " Good everyone is great we help each other sometimes " .

That's good Malcolm thought he patted Elliot's arm Darian and Cameron watched their interaction he seemed to be doing better Darian thought happier Cameron looked at Darian he slipped his arm through Darians he looked at Cameron `` He seems to be doing better "Cameron says looking at Darian " He does' ' .Which pleased Darian he was glad Elliot was getting on with life now .

Eliot was grabbing Carrie a drink for her and Jack after his chat with Malcolm he was aware of someone near him he looked round at Christian staring at him he smiled " I thought it was you " " Hi Molly's my niece " Elliot pointed to Carrie and the kids over st the far side " Wow small world " Christian smiled Elliot smiled an awkward silence Elliot cocked his head . " So temporary then " Elliot asked if he could see from the corner of his eye Carrie watching him she was smiling Elliot wished she wouldn't stare. It's embarrassing .

" YES FOR NOW UNTIL they get a new teacher also I'm recovering from ankle surgery " " Damn That's not great " Elliot looked down he did have a foot brace on that he didn't notice before " Elliot I was wondering " Elliot looked at him how did he know his name ahh probably from Molly " Yes " .god my heart is fluttering Elliot could feel .

" Christian Mr, Mrs Norris would like to see you " Principle Watkins asked he looked between him and Elliot `` Uncle I'll be there in a minute " Principle Watkins went off leaving the two off them again " Can I have your no also would you like to meet for a drink lunch or dinner sometime " " I'd love to " Oh god that sounded to keen Elliot thought . Malcolm noticed them exchanging no good with him he thought get back out there also Cameron and Darian noticed too .Looking at each other happy for Elliot .

" Thank I will be in touch " Christian went off to chat to other people Elliot had a good feeling about him he thought he went over to Carrie she was grinning he shook his head " Mummy I've thought of a name for the baby " Jack said oh god it would be one these made up names again . " What this time Jack " .

" Semolina " Molly and Elliot giggled Carrie scruffed his hair up " Jack Mathews you're so silly " Jack laughed at his joke Elliot looked over at Christian again at the other end the hall chatting to a couple more of the parents he noticed Elliot looking and smiled .Elliot blushed and looks away I like him Christian thought it must be fate that our Chance meetings it must be a sign .

A COUPLE DAYS LATER Patrick, Bailey and Elliot went to Glasgow for the day Elliot and Christian had been texting for the past couple days they arranged to meet Saturday meet in town for dinner and drinks Patrick thought he looked and Seemed a bit happier which was good and especially arranging a date since it had been 8 months since . Bailey was miserable saying that Senora had a go at him then he just had to sort it out since he had half moved in with her and they had their sonogram soon hopefully that would cheer him up he just needed to grow up a bit more Patrick thought since he was about to become a father .

They went into forbidden planet to have a look Bailey said Senora wanted a pop vinyl so he went off looking while Patrick looked at the graphic novels and Elliot was in his own world texting while looking at the pops .He is in one those dreamy states Patrick thought he had said it must be fate that they have meet three times already it must mean something .Patrick was happy for his friend he deserves to meet someone new .

Patrick was looking, he saw a couple he liked " Mummy this one " " Which one " Patrick recognised the voice he looked round at Ellie with a little curly red hair girl Ellie " she looked round at Patrick she smiled ." HI " " And what's your name " Patrick asked, bending down " Ivy " Ivy hid behind her mum Ellie shook her head " Hi Ivy im Patrick " He held out his hand she looked up at her mum .

" Ivy it's ok Patrick is a work friend " She held out her hand and they shook hands. Ivy giggled. Bailey watched from behind Patrick at the cute interaction Elliot came round the corner and saw them talking whose she he thought his phone pinging of a text from Christian again he looked down and smiled . " There you are " Patrick said to Elliot he came over " Ellie Elliot " " Hi " Ellie said " Hi " .

" Ellie works at Nero's to " " Cool " Patrick looked at Ellie and smiled Ellie blushed " it was good to see you are you working the weekend " Ellie asked taking Ivy's hand " Yes I will be " They said their goodbyes Patrick watched her go over to the till Elliot sniggered Patrick looked round " What " " it's obvious Mate you like her " .Elliot grinned it's about time Patrick meet someone she seemed nice Elliot thought .Patrick didn't date much or anything else but Elliot and Bailey had always thought Patrick would have been the one to sleep around more than them .

Patrick huffed what's going on Bailey thought looking between the two of them " what did I miss " Elliot lay his arm round Baileys shoulder " Patrick likes her "

" No I don't " Elliot shook his head at the bullshit he thought he could tell by his body language he does . " I'm starving, are we getting food or what? " Bailey asked. They got their purchases and went to Tgi Fridays for lunch and a couple drinks while they were there .

" Are you going on this date then " Bailey asked Elliot it's been a long time since Leyton and a long time since he went on a proper date " I think I'm ready to date again I've got to get back out there right " Patrick patted Elliot's arm " You right Mate and if you feel he's an ok guy go for it right Bailey " . Bailey looked up after texting Senora " Yea what Patrick said " Patrick shook his head seriously this guy has got a baby head too .

" What about you " Elliot asked Patrick looked at him looking at Bailey to " What about me " " Ellie Mate " Bailey said sniggering " she's a work friend that's all " Elliot huffed he's got to get a girlfriend sometime" Get off my back guys l Elliot shook his head maybe he did like her but what could he do about it he thought .Besides they work together did she like me back Patrick thought while they eat their lunch .

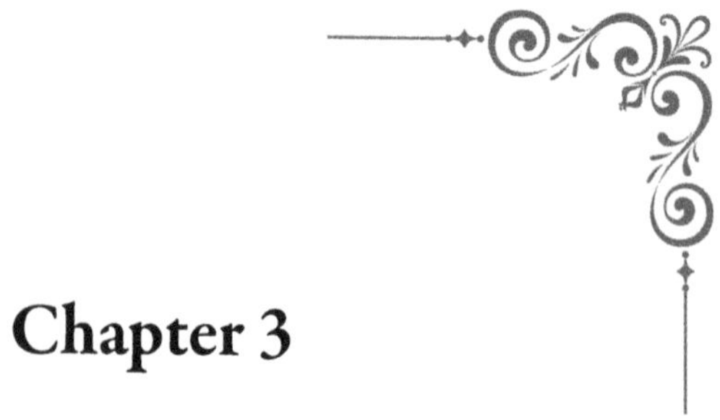

Chapter 3

Elliot tried on the fifth shirt. He sighed once again. He was nervous about his date with Christian he looked in the mirror again. Ok, that do black jeans, a tear at the knees white t-shirt and a bomber jacket . A whistle at the door Elliot looked round at Carrie he giggled "How do i look " " Yes it's fine " should i change again Elliot thought " i know what you're thinking " Elliot looked in the mirror at Carrie she came over to him .Lay her hand on his shoulder they look at each other in the mirror .Elliot leaned into Carrie smiling he is nervous she thought .

" You will be fine, you know what to do if not, " Elliot nodded. He hoped he didn't need her " Taxis here " Micheal shouted they were going to the club tonight Christian idea which was fine by Elliot .

" Have fun " Elliot said he got a text from the uber on its way in 5 minutes Carrie and Micheal left first the kids babysitter had the kids watching a dvd . Elliot looked in before he left and they were engrossed in the cartoon they were watching .Not bothered at all Elliot thought smiling to himself .

PATRICK SET UP THE tables while Julia , Ellie and Curt set up the bar area Patrick looked over at Ellie she looked up and smiled then carried on what she was doing Patrick phone dinged he checked the text which was from Elliot on his way to meet christian saying he was nervous but feeling good . Patrick texted back good luck fingers crossed it goes well too .I Really do hope it works out for Elliot he needs this he thought .

Ellie was checking in on her babysitter when Patrick came over she looked up at him they stared at each other " ivy's dad is he around " Not now " .Ellie picked up the tray to take up the vip shit he should have asked that he thought . Patrick " He looked round at Ellie and she bit her lip" " it's ok to ask about ivy's dad" " Sorry it just came out " . Dammit Patrick get a hold yourself and ask her if she wants to meet for a coffee sometime .

" She sees him though " " ok " there pinged from one off the rooms Ellie sighed and looked up " Again " Patrick asked he knew who it was " Have they not had to had enough to drink " Ellie said shaking her head .Jake overheard what they said and came over to them " Ellie ad the bill to the drinks tab ok with a note " " Will do boss " Ellie went off to do the drinks order Patrick carried on what he was doing " Patrick I'll be in the office if you need me " .

NICE OFFICE BAILEY thought while they waited for Darian to come in he looked over at Senora he went to take her hand she looked at him Bailey cocked his head " What " " Nothing just looking at you I love you " Senora tutted and shook her head silly fool she thought . The door opened Darian came inside on the phone Bailey and Senora looked up at him he nodded at them then disconnected the call and sat down at his chair . " Bailey , Senora what can I do for you " " Um well " .Senora and Bailey look at each other and back at Darian, Senora bites her lip and looks at Bailey again .

" We need to get our sex like back on track " Senora blurted out Bailey looked at her she looked at him then they both looked over at Darian " Senora " " Babe I love you but lately you're somewhere else

I'm pregnant Darian " .Senora looks over at Darian who is grinning . A young couple like them shouldn't be having problems listening to what they have to say .

" Congratulations " " Thanks this one is just like wham bam thank you mam "Senora wiggles her finger towards Bailey who tuts and sighs that's not true he thought Darian snorted Bailey didn't say anything he pouted " What is so great about your club Mr Longstrom "Fucking hell Bailey thought that's rude Well Darian thought no ones asked him that before " What do you want to know " " it's your hormones Hun " Senora huffed it's not her hormones she thought it's been like this way for past few months .Just not right between them sex was good before but lately no .

" Well what I'd like is for us to have good sex again " What the hell Bailey thought. What did she mean by that? Darian smiled their young still life in them yet but she probably thought something had to change . " There are workshops every month to check out on the website that caters for everything. Please come along and check it out " .

" Workshop " Bailey asked Senora sighed this bit needs to be kept up " Bailey likes spicing it up " Oh Bailey thought how can they make it spicier he thought looking at Senora and Darian aren't they having good sex he thought am I not performing well .

DINNER WAS GOING WELL with Elliot and Christian he was way to talk to he thought as they chatted away about most things Christian had ordered a chicken salad with a side order of fries and wings Elliot had the burger he thought it was a bit weird him ordering a salad Elliot had made a joke about watching his weight they both laughed it off maybe dancers have to watch their weight Elliot thought Christian did. After they decided to go to the pub for a drink the shelter people were out checking on the Homeless

Elliot noticed Christian noticed Elliot explaining to Christian about Malcolm .

They went to Wetherspoon for a drink. Elliot didn't want to drink too much alcohol because Christian had training in the morning and because it was their first date Elliot didn't want to get too drunk either .Christian mentioning his dance company and how he was enjoying working with the kids and his projects for the dance company and what they would be working on in the future .

Elliot mentioned his social work course he had started Christian asked him what made him go into social work Elliot explains how he likes to help people he thinks it is good to help out vulnerable people . Elliot wasn't ready to let Christian know about the rape until they get to know each other better Elliot couldn't believe how easy it was to chat to Christian they talked to much about most things where Christian comes from in South Africa Cape Town . Their music tastes what shows movies they were into .

Afterwards they made arrangements to meet Saturday to Christians place where he would make dinner. Elliot snorted, " You're gonna make dinner. Yes, I can cook. " Elliot cocked his head and smiled, "I will even make a South African dish .That sounded good. Elliot thought I would like that very much .

They waited for the taxis to arrive. They kept looking at each other, Elliot feeling nervous. " I had a nice time. " Christian said, " Me too. " Christian made the first move. He came closer to Elliot, wrapping his arms around Elliot's shoulders, bending down to kiss him. Elliot lay his hand on Christian back , melting into Christian time stood still. I don't want this night to end. Elliot thought I've got to behave myself and not jump right in .

" Taxi for Mathews " The taxi guy shouted Elliot looked round " That's me " looking up at Christian they bumped heads " See you Saturday " Elliot said then parting he looked round at Christian before he went into the taxi Christian waved.Oh god he is so sexy right now Elliot thought the taxi driving off .

Elliot lay his head against the seat and grinned as the taxi guy looked at him in the mirror " Good night then " Elliot looked up " The best " .

Elliots phone beeped a text from Christian Elliot smiled looking at the text .

Christian- “ Still feeling our kiss “

Elliot - “ Me To “ .

Elliot smiled. He was still feeling Christians kiss. I like him. Elliot thought but wanted to take it slow and not rush things, something they would have to talk about soon .And get to know each other Elliot had a good feeling about Christian feeling the necklace around his neck smiling to himself .Leyton would like him Elliot thought he would want him to move on .

SENORA AND BAILEY SAT in the bar area of the club. Nero Senora looked around the surroundings of the place and it didn't look bad. She thought Bailey looked at her. What's she thinking? He thought he touched her knee and she smiled . " What is it? " She asked Bailey, reaching over to kiss her " Just wondering what you thought”.

" Something like any other club have been to " Right Bailey thought she's not being truthful here Senora cocked her head looking at Bailey " Your thinking off poseidon club arent you " " No .no i wasn't” .Bullshit he thought she is I can give her what she wants Bailey thought if it’s a bit kink fine we can do that .Poseidon club is in the past this is the future she and our baby is our future .

SENORA GOT UP KISSED Bailey cheek and went to the bathroom Bailey watching her go into the bathroom Brandon saw Bailey with his girlfriend he was collecting glasses when he came over to Bailey's table . Finished with that " Brandon asked Bailey to look at him while he took their glasses' ' Thanks " "Another drink " .

" Same for me orange juice too " Senora saw Bailey talking to one the waiters quite good looking she thought when she got closer Bailey lay his arm round Senora waist . " Senora this is Brandon " " Hi " .Cute Senora thought she looked up at Bailey he cocked his head grinning at her .Laying his arm around her waist kissing her cheek .

Brandon nodded and went to get their drinks Senora put a leaflet on the table " 2k for a member that's pricey " She said Bailey picked up the leaflet " Elliot said that's everything to use in the club " .Really Senora thought she would have to check out more info for future reference whenever she comes back with Bailey .But my god that's a holiday abroad for that price who would pay that .

" No wonder he's opening up another club " She is being snippy now Bailey thought " Sorry my mouth runs away with me " Senora apologising Bailey smiled Senora batted him.away then giggled. " Bailey wilson " " What i didn't say anything " .They kissed Senora leaning into Bailey kissing her head .

Brandon came back with their drinks then left Senora moved closer to Bailey again she kissed his cheek just as his phone pinged Senora sighed Bailey checked his text which was from Elliot checking in his date went good all ok and meeting Christian on Saturday . " Elliot his date " Bailey looked up no Senora did she go to the bathroom again he thought another text came through from Senora he grinned sneaky he thought .

BAILEY WALKED ALONG the corridor looking for the room he shook his head chapped and entered the room Senora was sitting on the burgundy leather couch legs crossed Bailey stood for a moment Senora smiled Bailey went over to her he hovered over her she looked up as he bent down to kiss her . " Sneaky " Senora cocked her head and went to unzip Baileys jeans he took her hand she slapped it and went to stand up pulling down his jeans and sliding her hand inside Bailey hissed they looked at each other while she wanked him off .

SENORA THEN BENT DOWN she licked up and down his inside leg fuck that was good Bailey thought Senora took him in her mouth Bailey held onto her hair she looked up Bailey bit his lip and she went to stick a finger inside him. " shit Senora no not there " .No way anyone is going there Bailey thought Senora sniggered he looked shocked she thought maybe should have prepared him .

Senora stood up, she cocked her head again wiping her mouth, he went to kiss her " We want to spice things up right " " Yea but " Senora kissed him again cupping his balls again Bailey arched up Senora wrapped her arms round his shoulders looking at him leading him to the bed while they kissed .Oh no is she leading Bailey thought I like it she is certainly feisty tonight .

They crawled onto the bed, Senora discarding her underwear. She always had a great body. Bailey thought he reached up to cup her breast. Senora reached down to kiss him. Oh boy , he thought she was really taking charge tonight .Is it her hormones or something because she is looking really sexy tonight Bailey thought and those boobs are a bit bigger too .

SENORA EASED HERSELF onto Bailey he wrapped his arms round her waist he moved up kissing licking her breasts then getting into a rhythm " Fuck your so beautiful fucking me " Bailey said in between there kissing . Then Suddenly Senora felt nauseous. She put her hand to her mouth and had to run to the bathroom to throw up followed by Bailey .Ahh fuck he thought it's the morning sickness why sometimes last most the day to .

" Shit I'm sorry " Senora said in between retching Bailey, rubbing her back " Baby it's ok " Senora looked up at him then retched again " I so hate this " " I know " Bailey standing up getting a washcloth for her wishing he could take her sickness away for her .

After Senora felt better they got dressed she looked over at Bailey she was feeling sexy she wanted to take charge as he was disappointed she thought Bailey looked over at Senora looking at him . " Are you disappointed? " Bailey came over to her. They sat on the sofa and he lay his arms round her. " No, I'm not disappointed. It was fun except for trying to finger me." That won't be happening again Bailey thought .

Senora giggled, shaking her head as she reached over to kiss him " let's go home " Senora asked Bailey nodded taking her hand they giggled coming out the room just as Brandon was passing they must've had fun there all giggly he thought Bailey looked over at him just as he turned the corner .What was that about Brandon thought Bailey was being a bit weird earlier maybe talk to him about it soon .

In the taxi home Senora lay her head on Bailey's shoulder holding hands `` Bailey " "Mmm" Senora looked up Bailey looked at her " i didn't mean to diss Darians club he's an ok guy right " .She's feeling ashamed that she dissed Darians club now and yes he is a nice person once get to know him .

" Yes baby he is and it's ok he's not " Bailey stopped himself before he regretted what he was going to say " Bailey it's ok Mika was a long time ago " Bailey pulled Senora close to him i'll give her what she needs Bailey thought .That's in the past with Mika he was her future and their baby .I'm not gonna be like Mika treat her different .

ELLIOT ALSO TEXTED Patrick letting him know how the date went and had arranged to meet Christian on Saturday at his place good Patrick thought he was pleased that there date went well " Do you want to come with us for a midnight snack " Patrick looked round at Ellie while he was cleaning up " Sure that be great " Ellie smiles good she thought she didn't want to leave Patrick out .

The 24 hour McDonalds they went to was a good way to get to know everyone Patrick thought since they all worked together his work mates were nice in the Glasgow club and everyone pitched in to help out at the club Jake and Julia were great to work with too . And their experience helped to help out when they could throughout the night .They must have a good work friendship with Darian since Jake and Julia have worked for him for ten years .

" Have you got college this week? " Ellie asked Patrick. He looked at her. She had a bit of sauce on her cheek. He got his napkin to wipe it off. They looked at each other. Ellie smiled, " Thanks, " " No problem and yes I do, how is Ivy? " .

" She is good with her dads this weekend " " Good at least she sees him " Ellie nodded. That's one thing he had to step up to see his daughter and take turns each week day or weekend .Which was working out just fine. Ellie thought they had to get along for Ivy's sake, which they did .They did try at the beginning to stay together but things were not working. For them and they decided to split and co parent which was working out .

" we're gonna go now, are you guys ok to get home? " Gus asked Patrick and Ellie if they would get a cab back. It was after 3am to get home. Patrick thought he called for a taxi and he would drop Ellie off on their way home .Which she was grateful for Patrick was a nice person and got along with him even though he could be a little shy sometimes maybe that was the way he was with people .

" Do you want to come over to mine for Sunday dinner? " Ellie asked Patrick. That was nice of her. He thought when they got to her place " Sure that would be great " " cool I will text you my address. "

Just as Ellie was getting out the taxi Patrick stopped her she looks round at him " Your no " Patrick asked he handed her his phone for Ellie to type her no in Oh god I completely forgot that Ellie thought " Thanks See you Sunday " " See you then " Ellie waved just as the taxi drove off Patrick sent her a text with a smiley face Ellie giggled thinking that was sweet to do .

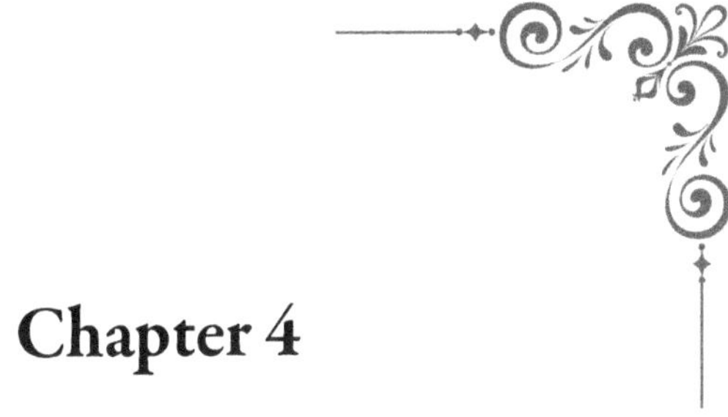

Chapter 4

Bailey and Senora had their workshop meeting at the club Bailey was surprised at the amount of couples that were there including Elliot's Sister and husband. It's surprising he thought Elliot didn't mention anything about them going to these workshops, that's their business he guessed .And thought they didn't seem the type to be into a bit kink .But it's surprising the amount of couples who want to spice up their sex life .

Malcolm came out to the bar to introduce the people that did the workshop Mika and Danielle what the hell Senora thought of her ex. She looked over at Bailey and his reaction . " Do you want to go " " Bailey why should we besides its been two years i've moved on " That's true Bailey thought he just didn't want it to be awkward for Senora with her ex .And true she had moved on from Mika not that they parted on bad terms the relationship just fizzled out .

Senora took his hand and squeezed it he reached over to kiss her Brandon noticed Bailey and Senora had come to the workshop to good on them he thought .The both them were a lovely couple " Babe there's a seat over there " Rory his boyfriend said he noticed seats behind Bailey and Senora Bailey nodded Senora smiled when they sat down they both looked round at Brandon with the other guy .Bailey felt kinda awkward he didn't think Brandon woulda a meet a person like Rory who was kinda more feminine than Brandon but they do say opposites attract .

" Hey guys Rory Bailey and Senora " Bailey nodded as Rory Senora dunked him and he looked round at her ." What " " Don't stare "What did she mean he thought Brandon sat forward " We are gonna go for a burger later if you fancy it " mm a burger Senora thought she nodded at Bailey " Sure that be great Brandon " .Senora looks at Bailey he sighed What's his problem she thought .

MIKA NOTICED SENORA in the crowd it had been a long time since he saw her that must be the new boyfriend the one with the mousy brown hair casual look totally different from what he thought he would look like .she looked good though a bit pale he thought and wondered if she was looking after herself . " Ready " Danielle asked him and he nodded . Cameron came out from the office over to Malcolm to watch the workshop too .Sliding his arm round Malcolm's waist they looked at each other Malcolm smiling up at Cameron .

Mika and Danielle introduced themselves and where their club was and what it was they would be doing a demonstration on s/m etc and what people were comfortable with and not comfortable with any questions that everyone wanted to know about s/m .

" Do you want a beer? " Christian asked Elliot while they were in the kitchen Christian went into the large fridge and brought out two beers. His kitchen was massive, Elliot thought . " I'd love a place like this " Elliot said while sipping his " expensive " Beer he asked Christian giggled "Not that expensive affordable Christian went over to the hob to check on the food ." Smells good " " Thanks " Christian looks round at Elliot he smiled and looked away then moved over to the lounge and looked out the window.

" Amazing view " " It is " Christian looked round at Elliot looking out the window then the oven dinged " Dinner is ready " .Elliot looks over at Christian at his kitchen Elliot smiles he looks good he thought .

ELLIOT HELPED TO CLEAR up Christian insisted he didn't need to help Christian moved nearer to Elliot standing beside him he placed his hand on Eliot's back he turned his head Christian kissed him. Elliot turned round to face Christian they looked at each other they kissed again kissing his neck Christian moved closer to Elliot opening his legs he helped Elliot up onto the counter .Elliot's heart beating faster looking at each other .

Christian half opened his shirt kissing Elliots neck again placing his hand on his crotch Elliot froze Christian looked at him searching for something that Elliot was ok " i cant "Christian could feel Elliot shaking Elliot moved him away getting up and going over to the window . Christian watched him Elliot looked round tears stung his eyes shit what did i do he thought .

" Elliot what did i do wrong " Christian wiped his tears away god he was so nice how can i tell him Elliot thought i really like you " will he think differently off me " it's hard to say Christian " " Come let's sit " Christian took his hand leading him to the couch taking his hand Elliot took a deep breath to calm himself. I've got to say it, I can't not, Elliot thought .

" i was raped " The world stopped Christian stared at Elliot what can i say he thought he has been brave enough to tell me and he was thankful for that " i should go if its to much for you to handle we can stop this right here " .

" No no i don't want you to go Elliot i'm grateful that you told me it doesn't change anything when " " 8 months ago reason why i was at the courthouse that day " seriously your ok with it ":Christian moved closer to Elliot he touched his face Eliot leaned into him ."Christian

I really like you I just need time and patience " Christian smiles I like him to and that won't change how I feel about Elliot .

" I really like you so there is no rush we can get to know each other ":Elliot let out a. Breath he was holding in he felt better less anxious about telling Christian " Believe me I really want to " Elliot wrapped his arms round Christian shoulders he tip toes up to kiss him they deepened the kiss then bumped heads . Christian looked down to sort himself Elliot sniggered Christian blushed.Dammit I had to go and get a hard on at a difficult time .

" Another beer " He asked Elliot nodded and he went off to the kitchen to get the beers Elliot sat on the couch looking out to the sky view Christian came back sitting beside Elliot they looked at each other . " My friends will like you " Elliot said Christian nodded "And I think my friends would like you to "

They both giggled well, which killed the tension between them Christian laid out his arm, Elliot moved to him Christian kissed his head. I just needed time; he thought there was no rush to be physical right now getting to know each other is good .

PATRICK HAD A GOOD dinner date with Ellie they chatted about most things he helped with the washing up which Ellie thought was cute they chatted what kind off bands music films tv they liked there were a couple movies coming up that he would like to see and if Ellie wanted join them at some point which she thought was nice off him to ask .

Ellie went into the fridge to get a drink for her and Patrick stood behind her when she shut the fridge door and turned he pushed her against the fridge bending down to kiss her she didn't resist he leaned into her she could feel his hardness against her leg . They suddenly frantically kissed Ellie and went for Patrick's jeans he pulled her against him lifting one arm up onto the fridge door Ellie pushed away " Wait wait I don't have any condoms " Shit Patrick thought neither did his hands behind his neck " Neither do I " .

Ellie snorted. Patrick pulled her close to him. He kissed her bumping heads. She looked up at him. " I like you Ellie. " " I like you too. " Patrick took her hands leading her to the lounge. They sat down. He looked at her. What's wrong, she thought he looked serious staring at Patrick . Doesn't he want to have me push it too far now she thought .

" Ellie there's something you should know " " God don't tell me you have a disease " Patrick snorted he shook his head she's funny he thought "No I don't it's „ I'm ," Fuck he thought just say it he thought Patrick took a deep breath " I'm still a virgin " . Ellie sniggered right that's some joke she thought was not funny. He looked at her and nodded as she moved closer to him . " you're not joking " Nope I mean I've had a couple girlfriends that didn't last too long though just not done that yet " .

" Wow I'm surprised I thought you would have girls flocking to you " " I wish " .

Seriously he was a good looking guy she thought she digged the dirty blonde hair look on a guy and his dress style to " I don't care whether you've not had sex yet that doesn't matter it's getting to know the person right " Ellie said Patrick smiled and nodded true I like getting to know people . " I'm a people person and I want to get to know you " .Ellie cocked her head and smiled " Ivy " .Patrick asked if he would like to get to know her if it's ok with Ellie he hoped .

" Don't worry about her and her dad. We split up two years ago. He's moved on with someone else. He sees her all the time . Just as long as he does his share she will be back tomorrow. ". " Take things slow " Patrick asked Elllie nodded. That's fine by her not to slow down. She thought she had ivy to think about so she had gotten hurt in the past because she introduced Ivy too quickly and she didn't want that to happen again .

“ Does Ivy like the zoo? “ Patrick asked, getting out his phone to check his schedule. “ She does, why? “ Patrick checked his work schedule and college days when he wouldn’t be in Glasgow and maybe arranged a day to Edinburgh zoo . “ We could arrange a day out if you want “ “ That be lovely Patrick “ .Ellie thought that was really thoughtful of Patrick to want to include Ivy that’s what she liked about Patrick .

AFTER THE WORKSHOP Mika came over to Senora while she was talking to other people Bailey watched them while he was talking to Brandon and his boyfriend “ How you been “ “ Good “ Senora looked over at Bailey she smiled at him he nodded “ I see your still with Bailey “ Senora looked at Mika “ He is moving in we’re having a baby “ .

Mika was shocked to hear the news a baby Bailey moving in he nodded he didn’t look impressed Senora thought she didn’t care one bit “ Congratulations “ “ Thanks " Bailey said coming over to Senoras side sliding his arm round Senora’s waist she looked up at him he smiled at her they both looked at Mika . “ Mika ready to go “ Daniele asked looking at Senora and Bailey “ Yes, let’s get our stuff Senora Bailey congratulations again “ .Bailey nodded and Senora looked at him "Oh he is being protective of his woman and it’s quite sexy Senora thought .” You know you are so sexy right now “ Bailey looks at Senora I Do he thought grinning he gives Senora a kiss on the cheek and squeezes her bottom Senora giggles .

BRANDON AND THE OTHERS opted for Nando’s Senora excused herself to go to the toilet after ordering Bailey get her usual drink Rory seemed Nice Bailey thought looked ok can be deceiving he thought Senora always said that . “ Is Senora ok? Rory asked

Brandon, huffing, Rory looked at him “ She’s pregnant Rory" " Oh I didn’t realise congratulations “ .

“ Thanks “ Senora came back looking better. She took a sip of her drink and felt better now she looked at Bailey with a silent understanding. “ Better “ Senora nodded and looked at Brandon and Rory “Morning sickness is s killer last all day “ .Senora sighed sitting back feeling whacked out .

“ I can vouch for that “ Bailey said “ I’d hate to be a woman “ Rory said Brandon sniggered shaking his head there meal came Senora was hungrier than she thought “ So how did you two meet then “ Senora asked in between eating her fries Rory looked at Brandon “ We meet on an app “ Brandon said looking at Rory “ Not Grindr “ Rory corrected Bailey sniggered .

" GRINDR IS JUST A QUICK fix " Rory said looking at Brandon " We talked for 2 months before we met didn't we hunt" Rory put his hand on Brandons both smiling at each other . " if you need parenting advice i have a six year old " .

Bailey nearly spat out his burger. He has a kid so he thought Brandon looked at him " Are you ok Bailey " " Yea yea fine " .

" Six " Senora asked Brandon to get his phone out looking for a photo. He handed it to Senora. A little curly blonde blue-eyed boy was his phone screen cute, she thought . " His name is reece i see him all the time his mum and i were in a year relationship she knew i was bi but things got complicated and we decided to split no hard feelings " .

" That's not so bad at least you see him " Bailey said Rory grinned he and Brandon have been together for a year and a half and getting to know his son has been great too and Reece loved Rory too and understood his dad had two different preferences . “ So why did you guys go to the workshop? Bailey asked Senora, glared at him. That's personal, she thought he shouldn't have asked . Brandon and Rory looked at each other " well since he works at a sex slash night club I just wanted a little bit of insight into s/m kink right babe " Rory asked, sliding his arm through Brandon's leaning into him .

" That you did, " Senora blushed at their affection. It's cute she thought about a year there trying out new things " So what about you guys " Rory asked leaning into the table Senora looked at Bailey he looked at her . " I've been a little bit neglectful, " Bailey confessed. Senora smiled and snorted, shaking her head. Brandon wondered what he meant, maybe he shouldn't ask personally .

"Oh honey that isn't good " Rory tutted Brandon snorted that's Rory he's blunt that's for sure " Ok ok let's get off everyone's sexy life " Brandon said hands up and reaching an arm round Rory " Sorry I tend to rabbit on " " That's ok " Bailey said he was beginning to like the guy he could see why Brandon fell for him.

Afterwards they went their separate ways Rory suggested they all meet and have a night out sometimes which they all agreed to which would be good and getting to know his work friend better Bailey thought . Rory and Brandon were ok with Bailey now he just wasn't sure by the first impression of Rory when they first met him and after talking to him.

Chapter 5

The day off there sonogram came Bailey held Senoras hand while the nurse rolled the scope around Senoras stomach and the machine came to life and there it was confirming there was a little person in her stomach Bailey couldn't believe it the nurse confirmed the dates that Senora had given she was 8 weeks pregnant. Good strong heart beat when they heard their baby's heartbeat and everything seemed good. When the nurse was checking Senora asked what remedy's she could use for the sickness. The nurse suggested ginger tea and ginger biscuits and normally the morning sickness would ease during the 6 months .

The nurse had given them their other appointment for a couple months time for follow-up and a suggestion on which midwife to check out and doctor recommendation which they should check out for and what her birthing plan she would like .

BAILEY SNIFFED WIPING a tear away looking at his photo Senora looked over at him while driving he's got emotional all of a sudden she thought was it because off the sonogram. " Bailey " He looked over at Senora she reached her hand out he took it " I'm such a woos " " Your not i got emotional to " Bailey looks round at Senora she is looking amazing he thought is it the pregnancy he thought. And seeing his baby on the sonogram it was real they are really having a baby .

CATHERINE BAILEY'S mum was ecstatic at the baby sonogram picture when they arrived back she cried while hugging them both then made tea . " Have you thought of a name? " Bailey snorted he hadn't thought about it or Senora . " Not yet mum " Bailey sighed, shaking his head too soon for names he thought they would figure that out when the time comes .

Elliot went into his mum's room at the hospice. She was sitting up on her chair asleep. He sat down her bag of juices and other stuff he and Carrie had always brought . He went over to his mum. He bent down placing his hand on her arm. Nessa woke up. Elliot stood up, kissed his mum on the head and she smiled .Glad to see Elliot he touched her face and gave her a kiss on the cheek .

" Ok mum " she nodded and coughed. The nurses had said she had a chest infection which was clearing. He got a hankie and wiped her mouth . " Carries coming later " Nessa grunted her speech was getting worse now Elliot's phone pinged another text he checked one from Bailey about the sonogram and Christian he smiled . The door knocked Avril once the nurses came into the room to check on Elliot's mum .

" How things Elliot "Avril asked while checking on his mum " Good " Picking up one of mums books there ritual when they came in to read a couple chapters off her book there mum loved reading when she could and when she got sicker she wasn't able to so Carrie , Elliot and Micheal read to her when they visited . " Cup tea Nessa " Her face beamed when Avril mentioned it then did a little cough again .

" Not as bad now her chest infection " Elliot asked Avril " sounding better we will get mum back into bed soon " Avril left then Elliot sat in his usual seat and got the page to where they last read from he looked up at his mum waiting for him to start . "Now where were we? " Elliot looks up at his mum. She is smiling. He thought she seemed happy today, which is good .

AFTER HALF HOUR CARRIE came in she had been shopping gave her mum a kiss on the cheek she had brought more books and a couple magazines the nurses arrived to put Nessa back to bed while Elliot and Carrie went outside " Senora and Bailey had the sonogram today " " Ahh did they how did it go " .

Elliot took out his phone brought up the picture that Bailey sent Carrie smiled thinking back to when they had first got there sonogram " I bet there excited " Elliot snorted Carrie looked at him " "What " " He is now was freaked out before " That's understandable Carrie thought most parents are when they find out they are going to be parents just like her and Micheal when they first found out they were having Jack .

He will be a good father Elliot thought smiling to himself someday I would like a family either when I'm with someone or on my own who knows what the outcome would be in the future .He wondered if Christian had thought about having kids in the future what did I think about that for they had just got to know each other recently .Some people bring up kids on their own maybe I can do that in the future Elliot thought .

CHRISTIAN IS AT THE studio working on some dance moves and exercises and strengthening his leg and ankle. He had been at the school for the kids to practise their dance moves. They were doing good and getting better even though a couple of the girls had said they wanted to be ballet dancers, which he thought was cute . Christian looked in the mirror Elliot standing watching him he looked round at him Elliot coming nearer " How long were you standing there "Christian grinned at Elliot leaning against the door " Long enough " .

Elliot looked at Christian up and down. He thought he liked what he saw Christian cocked his head and grinned " Are you checking me out? " Elliot sniggered and leaned against the bars folding his arms" " How is your mum" " Much improved she was exhausted by the time we left " .

" Good to know " Christian lifted his leg up onto the bar stretching. Jesus Elliot thought Christian noticed him cringing at his stretch " You get used to it , it strengthens your muscles here try it . Elliot snorted again Christian lifting his right leg onto the bar bloody hell he thought as he stood behind Elliot he looked round at Christian.Elliot Blushed he looked away Oh hell he didn't get hard Elliot thought . I wonder if any dancers do get hard ons when they dance with the skimpy outfits Elliot blushed thinking about that .

" RELAX YOUR MUSCLES and bend " Christian slid his hand down Elliot's Leg leaning into him he could feel his breath on his neck his hand sliding down his leg again and straightening his back " Relax your muscles in your back "Christians hand on Elliot's back oh boy he thought " Not so easy " .Elliot sighed Jesus he is gonna kill me with these stretches .

Elliot said Christian moves closer feeling his back. Elliot got tingles. He closed his eyes concentrating. " Once you get used to it it's not so bad. "" Huh you think " Elliot snorted seriously. dancers do this all the time he thought. I guess to practise like Christian does .

" Can you feel the burn yet " He definitely felt the burn on the back of his leg now and began to cramp up " Christian my leg is cramping " Christian lifted down Elliot's leg and rubbed the back off his calf which was feeling better the feeling was coming back . Christian looked up at Elliot he was biting his lip he stood up and touched Elliot's lips " You will bruise them " Feeling round his lips they stared at each other Christian moved in closer they kissed Christian slid his hand down Elliot's side .lifting up his t shirt Elliot shivered his hand was cold they looked at each other Christian kissed licked Elliot's ear . " Elliot is this ok " looking at him he nodded he could feel Christian hardness against him he looked down he was hard and looked back up at Christian he smiled kissing Christian again he groaned .Elliot didn't mean to groan it caught him off guard and tried to refocus .

CHRISTIAN LIFTED ELLIOT'S arm up unzipping his jeans looking at Elliot whispering to him " Do you want me to stop " Elliot shook his head he bit his lip again Christian touching his mouth he went to slide his hand back down . " Christian..the door " Christian looked over at the door and back at Elliot yes he should lock the door he thought didn't want to get caught Do wee .

He quickly ran over locked it looked over at Elliot leaning against the bar looking sexy he ran back over planting a kiss then kissing his neck sliding his hand inside Elliot's boxers " Tell l me it's not ok " Elliot nodded Christian carrying on wanking him off a flush on Elliot's neck Christian noticed he kissed licked his neck again . " Christian..I " Christian looked at Elliot again the ecstasy on his face he loved Elliot went to slide his hand into Christian pants he was all fingers and thumbs ." Christian no condoms fuck shit " .

Christian bent down slid down his boxers looked up " Me neither " He stood back up looked down Elliot was fully erect he smiled " We are just making out come " Elliot looked down and back up then pulled his boxers back up Christian taking his hand leading him into the showers .Oh a make out session in the showers very sexy Elliot thought grinning .

ELIOT LICKED AND KISSED all the way down Christian back he had a lovely back he thought his muscles from working out and for his dancing no tattoos Christian looked round while Elliot was rubbing his back and he kissed his back looking up at Christian he smiled reaching up licking his ear pressing into Christian.

Reaching his hand round palming his cock and starting stroking him Christian leaned into Elliot " So good " Christian said ." Mmm "Was all Elliot could think of to say while they made out in the shower. kissing Christian stroking Elliot making sure he was ok .I am definitely ok feeling safe with Christian making out kissing the water flowing over them while they made out .

DANIEL CHRISTIAN PA went to open the door. It was locked. Strangely, he thought it was not like Christian to lock the door. He got out his phone and dialled Christian no answer Daniel leaving a message asking where he was .This isn't like him Daniel thought no answer and dialled again .Where did he go home without him .

Shit Christian thought coming out of the shower room two missed calls from Daniel Elliot looked up as he put his shirt on what was wrong he thought when Christian went over to the door unlocking Daniel sitting on the stairs . " Finally what kept you " Christian looked round at Elliot and back at Daniel . " Sorry Daniel " Daniel saw Elliot looking at Christian shaking his head .Right they had been doing stuff Daniel thought, shaking his head and tutting he needed to be careful .

" Hi im Daniel his Pa " Daniel said looking at Christian smirking " Elliot " Daniel looked round at Elliot " Ahh the Elliot Christian mentioned " Oh he's been talking about him.Elliot thought smiling at Christian. Christian came over to Ellio to lay his arm round Elliot . Elliot smiled at him Daniel thought Christian looked a bit happier Elliot seemed nice .And it was good to see Christian happy for once

Elliot seemed nice he hoped it would work out for them but still needs to be careful .

" SOME THINGS WE HAVE to go over Christian " Christian looked at him and looked at Elliot " i'll get my bag " Christian nodded going into the shower area Daniel watched him go " We didnt " Christian said Daniel looked at him and nodded . " Feeling ok " Daniel asked Christian as Daniel brought out his filofax " Fine dont fuss Daniel I like him " . Christian smiles. I can see that Daniel thought and it had been a while that Christian had met anyone Elliot seemed ok with .

CHRISTIAN REACHES FOR Elliot's hand in the car on there way to get food Elliot takes his hand looking at Christian " About Daniel " " What About him " Elliot looks round at Christian " He knows about you also i get tested every few months i am.always safe " That was good of him to say Elliot thought and he was always to .

" So do it " Christian nods and looks over at Elliot squeezing his hand " Elliot " " I know what you're gonna say no rush right " Christian snorted even though they made out earlier having sex would be the next step . " Christian seriously i'm not "

" sorry i know i just want you to be comfortable " Oh " Elliot looks away looking out the window chewing his lip Christian touches Elliot's knee squeezes it Elliot looks round at him they smile at each other " Christian you don't have to worry ok " Christian nods concentrating on his driving he's so amazing Elliot thought leaning his head back while they held hands .Elliot smiles he likes It Christian making sure Elliot is ok and he is it's quite What's the word Elliot thought .

THAT NIGHT PATRICK and Bailey came round to Elliots for pizza and beer Christian had a dinner thing with his fellow dancers Elliot put music downstairs in his room while they sat on the floor chatting while they ate and drank. Elliot thought about Christian missing him already, he thought .

" Christian and I made out. " Patrick spat out his drink well. That's something he thought looking at Bailey. He shrugged his shoulders. " Did you have sex " Bailey asked. " Not yet, it was fun and exciting at the studio. " " Wow mate, well done! Patrick patted Elliot's leg and he sniggered , shaking his head. That's a step up Patrick thought .

" I kinda feel I've got myself back and not be scared of having sex again " " Good on you " Patrick patted Elliot's leg again the door chapped Carrie came in . " we're going for burgers, need anything " .Looking round the room at the guys they seem giggly, are they talking about guy things she thought .

" No sis were good " Bailey and Patrick held up their beers and pizza Carrie nodded " The hospice called mums ok the antibiotics are working " " That's great ." Elliot thought hopefully they will work since she had been a bit poorly lately. It has happened before when she had an infection .

Carrie left, they opened another beer and ate more pizza." Senora tried to finger me" . Patrick and Eliot looked at him and he blushed looking between the two of them . " It gets better once you get used to it " Elliot explains he sniggers " Nope not happening " .Definitely not happening Bailey thought even though she did like a bit kink before but doing it to him was a no no .

" i like Ellie i kissed her " Elliot and Bailey looked at him Elliot patted his leg smiling " Good for you go for it Mate does she like you " Patrick nodded the three of them laughed so hard their eyes watered .Well the three of them thought with their confessions it made them feel better .

" We are such disasters aren't we " Elliot said Bailey nodded. That's true he thought " Seriously Elliot if you like Christian and you know go for it " Bailey said he nodded he did like Christian a lot he thought .But we have to get to know each other and not jump on him not quick .

" If you need advice Patrick you know to ask right " Elliot said laying his arm round Patrick's shoulder the three of them moved closer to each other and hugged saying they love yous to each other .Patrick thinking he wanted things to work out with Elliot and Christian it sounded like he liked him . And he hoped he and Ellie would progress. I really like her, he thought .

I am definitely not doing other kinky stuff that Senora tried to do Bailey thought when she tried to finger me just was too weird for me and he hoped things will work out with Elliot and Christian sounds like he really likes him .

Chapter 6

Bailey reached up for the box in the store room. Why do these boxes always get put up in stupid positions? He thought he got it eventually just as he was coming down the steps Brandon came in for stuff and gave Bailey a fright and nearly fell. Brandon caught him round the middle . Everything went in slow motion as they looked at each other. Bailey's heartbeat went up and he swallowed. What the hell Bailey thought wriggling to get out of Brandon's hold .

" Are you ok? Brandon asked Bailey nodded and stood straight up " Thanks yea im ok i better get these out " Bailey went off what's wrong with him Brandon thought he was being weird Brandon went into the boxes and brought out the condoms for tonight to put in the rooms .Did I do something wrong maybe while he set up for tonight maybe I should talk to Bailey about it .

Christian looked round the club he whistled nice he thought he looked at Elliot looking at him he smiled Elliot suggested they go to club Nero so Christian could have a look around and they could spend time together Elliot thought Christian looked a little pale tonight he had said he was a little tired from working Elliot thought nothing off it . They went over to the bar. Senora was already there talking to someone with bleached blonde hair, his shirt up to his midriff earring and eyeliner that Brandon's boyfriend Bailey had tried to describe him .

Elliot hugged Senora and introduced Christian to Senora Brandon came back and made sure Rory was ok. He was fine now that Senora and the others were there and Elliot had said his introducing Christian Bailey came back and reached over to Senora. She held her hand out to him making sure she was ok . " What do you think? Elliot asked Christian what he thought of the club while sipping their cocktails " Not bad busy" Christian asked looking round " Always busy midweek and especially for non members night " .

" Which gets busier " Brandon said overhearing their conversation wow Christian thought Elliot had mentioned non members get discounts every week or just pay a small amount to use the facilities `` How much is the fee " " 2k " Wow that's a lot Christian thought .But if it that much to pay and Elliot told him what you could use while at the club which sounds not to bad Christian thought .

" YOU ARE GETTING EYEBALLED babe " Brandon said noticing member Mr Carson checking out Rory at the bar he looked round at him suite balding and totally not his type Rory looked back at Brandon `` Not funny "Rory tutted Shaking his head Bailey looked over at Brandon and Rory while he stuck his drinks Senora watching him he looked serious for some reason " Bailey " Bailey looked up at her she cocked her head he smiled back " Are you ok " . " Fine, just a little tired. " Senora sighed and shook her head. He was crazy to work a shift at the bar tonight especially when he had been working today and did not have much time to rest .He is a little cranky, she thought .And I was up in the middle of the night too which makes him cranky too .

" I feel sorry for him in some way " Elliot said about Mr Carson he wasn't a bad man he just came to the club for company " Why's that " Christian asked " His partner died last year " .That's sad

Christian thought maybe he is here for the company to talk to someone which is understandable Christian thought .

" Can I get you a drink? " Mr Carson asked Rory, Brandon tried not to laugh watching their interaction. " Can I politely decline? I'm sorry I'm taken. " Rory said he looked dejected. Brandon thought he did feel sorry for him .Rory looked scared Brandon thought I should rescue him should Mr Carson be harmless he just liked company that's all .

Darian came out of the office to have a look around the club. He thought Julia was up at the vip tending to some members. A couple people said hello to him. Darian noticed Elliot with his friend Christian he was right, he was good looking, and he looked happy while they chatted . Bailey's girlfriend at the bar while Bailey tended the bar and Brandon talking to his boyfriend Rory with Mr Carson.

" Elliot how are you? "" Good Darian this is Christian " They shook hands and he seemed nice. Darian thought he hoped it would work out with him. " Malcolm " " Malcolm is in Glasgow with Cam. He's at the other site while Cam has a book signing event something called" Book bonanza " .

" Cool l sounds good " " Going tomorrow for a couple days " .

Darian noticed Mr Carson looked a little wobbly on his feet while he chatted with Rory he excused himself to go over to them " Mr Carson how are you " " Ahh Darian I'm well I was just saying to this young man " Darian winked at Rory while Darian guided Mr Carson over to one off the tables . Ed from security came over to Darian saying to him to order Mr Carson a taxi .

" it's so sad he must be lonely " Rory said looking over at Brandon he nodded yes it was sad his partner for several years passing away Darian came over to the bar "He wasn't annoying you was he " " No no Mr Longsrome he just wanted to buy me a drink " Darians phone rang off he excused himself to take the call .Rory thought that was kind of Darian checking up on him Mr Carson just wanted to chat that was all .But my god he is handsome Rory thought and quite intense looking to .

" I can see the appeal " Rory said Brandon sniggered Rory looked at him what's funny he thought Brandon reached over to Rory " You are adorable " Rory blushed and looked away " Rory " Brandon asked Rory looked round at him Brandom whispered in his ear he looked at him and nodded grinning and blushed .Brandon kissed Rory on the nose and they bumped heads noticed by Bailey collecting the glasses quite cute he thought with Rory and Brandon's interaction .

Christian excused himself to go to the toilet Bailey came back over to the bar " Another drink " He asked mixing one for Senora `` Thanks " " Christian ok " That's what Elliot thought he excused himself to and went to the toilet just as Christian was coming back out . "Ok " He does look a bit peaky. Elliot thought " Yea fine, just my stomach is a bit dodgy, that's all " .That's not good Elliot thought I hope it isn't to do what they had earlier .

Christian went back to the bar while Elliot went to the toilet. Bailey was clearing some tables while Brandon was bringing orders over. He thought Bailey was being weird tonight and just couldn't place what was up with him . Bailey " " Yea " Bailey looked up at Brandon while clearing up " Whats up " " Nothing Man just tired clubs been busy and I've had a full shift at work to " Bullshit Brandon thought .There is definitely something up with him but I won't push it tonight .

Senora saw them talking while clearing tables while chatting to Rory and Christian Elliot came back from the bathroom Darian was talking to some members up at the vip he nodded at Elliot his silent understanding. Elliot smiles and Darian looks like he likes Christian Good. I like him touching Christians knee . Christian takes Elliot's hand kissing it Oh they are being all smoochy Senora thought it's cute when she noticed .

SENORA CAME OUT OF the bathroom into her bedroom Bailey was already asleep and lightly snoring she shook her head. I knew she thought he's exhausted from picking up the extra shift. At least he's off tomorrow he should just quit his job and go full time at the club she thought . She opened her side off the duvet, got inside and scooted over to Bailey's side and lay her head on his shoulder. She gave him a kiss on the cheek and he opened one eye . " You better not be taking advantage " Bailey croaked, Senora shook her head " Go back to sleep " Bailey lay his arm round Senora falling back to sleep snuggled into each other ." Love you" Bailey said first snuggling into Senora " Love you to " .

ELLIOT GOT A DRINK out of the Christian fridge and noticed that he still had the food he bought from the other day. Strangely Elliot thought he hadn't used it yet; it will be out of date soon if he doesn't use it up . He washed his glass and sat it on the side and then went into the bedroom Christian was already in bed, his arm around his head sleeping. He did say he was tired though Busy day Elliot smiled. He looked cute. He thought about going over to the bed and getting into the covers . He lay his head on Christian shoulder looking up at him " Your staring " Christian opened one eye looking at Elliot he smiled Christian reaching over to kiss him . " Tired, " Elliot asked Christian smiled looking at Elliot " A little. "" Christian " Christian looked round at Elliot. He bit his lip again. " What is it? " " I'm happy with doing anything we decide. " Christian smiled. He touched Elliot's face and his mouth, Elliot leaning into him, he nodded . " Let's go to sleep, " Christian said, wrapping his arm around Elliot. He liked this. Elliot thought no rush getting to know each other first, making out is good too .And they both drifted off to sleep hugging each other. I should talk to Christian about the food situation tomorrow.

" BRANDON „YOUR " RORY couldn't get the words out Brandon pounding into him one off Rory's legs up in the air a sheen off sweet on his chest Brandon bent down Rory looking up at him Brandon smiling what's he smiling for Rory thought " Honey what " " I just love your sex face " Now not the time for that Rory thought Brandon stole a kiss . He slid himself back inside Rory he was close to coming Rory pulling at himself " " Turn around " Brandon asked Rory going onto his side he turned his head they kissed again Brandon holding onto his back pounding into him again .

Rory screamed fucking hell he thought he's gonna kill me one these days he thought Brandon collapsed onto the bed taking off the condom and placing it in the bin Rory turned round to snuggle into Brandon He lay his arm round him " Ok " Brandon asked Rory looked up kissing Brandon again " Yes baby I'm ok not so hard next time " .Brandon sniggered looking round at Rory " " Love you " " love you to " .Rory sighed flapping the sheet because he as hot Brandon sniggered .

" Next time I won't be too rough " Rory sniggers Brandon touching his face they kiss Brandon laying his arm round Rory`` Brandon " " Mm " Brandon looks at Rory "Do you want me to " .Rory sits up placing his hand on Brandon's chest looking at Rory .

Brandon smiles touching Rory's mouth " I'm good let's go to sleep ok " They kiss again Rory moving closer to Brandon laying his head on Brandons chest feeling his steady heart beat .Brandon kisses Rory's cheek " Love you " Rory looks up at Brandon smiling at him " Love you to " .

Chapter 7

Christian went to snuggle into Elliot not there he opened his eyes looking round the room not there he sat up where did he go he thought then the smell of cooking wafted into the bedroom was Elliot making breakfast he thought Christian grinned that was the cutest thing Elliot could do for him . Christian got up, put on his robe and went to investigate .His stomach rumbled the thought of Elliot making breakfast .

THERE HE WAS IN HIS kitchen cooking breakfast singing to himself on his iPods as Christian stood watching him Christian smiled watching him for a few seconds then went over to Elliot wrapping his arms around his waist Elliot looked round at Christian. " Morning " Elliot said, taking off his iPods and turning round " When did you get up " "Not long. Besides, if these weren't getting used soon they would have to be thrown out as well as other stuff in your fridge ``.Elliot pointed to the fridge looking at Christian. Ahh Christian thought I had forgotten that I had stuff in the fridge to use .

Christian looked at the stove bacon , eggs , toast he nodded he had made a lot and had it would go to waste he thought " You have gone to a lot trouble Elliot " " Np problem sir I'll get the coffee or do you want tea " .

" I will make the tea also. I'll just have the toast and a little egg for it's training today " Shit Elliot thought that's right he didn't want to be too bagged up for his dance classes he bit his lip Christian notice. He came over to him touching his face . " Sorry I should've asked " " Don't worry it's fine " .Christian gave Elliot a quick peck on the nose and pinched his bum Elliot giggles .I should be more thoughtful Elliot thought but it was gonna go to waste if it didn't get used up .

They both sat down Elliots phone pinged and he checked who it was, which was Freya from group therapy. If he wanted to be picked up he quickly texted back saying he would make his own way there . Elliot looked at Christian he looked up at Elliot " Freya from group therapy " .

Christian nodded. Elliot held out his hand Christian squeezed his hand and smiled, " Plans for today. " Christian asked in between eating his toast. He made good toast, he thought , smiling into himself. Noticed by Elliot he must like my cooking Elliot thought that's good right .He hoped Elliot cocked his head staring at Christian .

" Group therapy first for an hour then hand in my essay at college visit mum witn Carrie you " Dance class with the kids lunch with my fellow dancers and Daniel and I have a few things to go over " .Christian took a few more bites of his toast and tea .Busy day for both us they decided last night to meet up after they were finished what they would be doing .

Elliot nodded and looked over at the fridge while buttering his toast he pointed to the fridge " Your food in the fridge is gonna go off you know it's a shame to waste " .Christian nodded yes he will have to sort that out hopefully some of it can be saved .I should be more wary of the dates and my housekeeper normally let's me know about that Christian thought .

" Don't worry I'll get onto it with my housekeeper. I'll let her know," Elliot snorted. The housekeeper thought Christian cocked his head . "Housekeeper " Elliot thought why the heck does he need that " She is amazing, you will like her and yes I need a housekeeper " .Christian giggles Elliot shakes his head he is probably right the size of the place he does need one .

" I hope so I've just had a thought. I could take some off it to take to group therapy. Malcolm will be there today. He could take some for the housing "" Ok if it's not too much trouble " .That's really kind of Elliot to do that especially if people are homeless and need to eat .And the volunteers mostly do the cooking at the drop in or bring it in .

" It's not " Elliot helped Christian clear up Christian wrapped his arms round Elliot kissed his neck leaning into him he turned his head they kissed " Do we have time " Elliot asks in between kisses " We will always have time " Elliot sniggered Christian slid his hand down to Elliots boxers he moaned as Christian stroked him .That's so good Elliot thought while Christian carried on what he was doing .

Elliot turned round Christian carrying on stroking him licking his ear "Shower " Christian whispered Elliot nodded Elliot took his hand and they ran to the bathroom for a make out session which made them both late but they didn't care.And they nearly didn't make it out the Apartment until they eventually had to depart in between making out .

IVY WAS SO EXCITED to go to the zoo with her mum and new friend she was nearly sick with excitement it was good that Ivy was getting along with Patrick Ellie thought that she hoped she would Ivy took her mom's hand while they walked along to see the other animals Bailey and Senora behind them hand in hand stopping every so often to look at the animals .And taking some photos of themselves or the the animals .

“ Mummy look at the penguins “ Patrick looked at Ellie looking over at the penguins with the keepers walking along. They stood to watch them. Ahh that’s cute. Bailey thought the keepers stopped at the crowd that gathered so that people could take pictures of them .And the penguins getting Fish too .

“ Dad the penguins “ Reece shouted looking up at his dad with Rory Brandon looked over and noticed Patrick with Ellie , Bailey and Senora no Elliot he was probably doing something else as they caught up with the crowd and the others Bailey was surprised to see Brandon with Rory and his son .They looked cute like a little family Brandon’s son is the spitting image off his dad .Bailey noticed and it looks like he and Rory get along to .

“ It's our ritual to come to the zoo. He likes to come not all the time though, “ Brandon explained Bailey wondered if he and Senora would do that with their kid. Bailey lay his arm round Senora. She looks at him watching the penguins. Is he ok? She wondered, I expect , so they will check in when they get home .Watching the penguins waddling along with the keeper to get their fish .

AFTER EVERYONE SAT together this have lunch Patrick gave Ivy a pound coin which she was chuffed about Ellie said to him he know has a best friend forever after giving her money Her and Reece sat together the canteen had the kids option which they had drawing pencils and paper and a couple puzzles to do which kept them quiet for a bit .And helped each other with the drawing which Ellie thought was cute .Brandon said Reece gets on with other kids and helped Ivy with her drawing .

“ Guys I have a show next week. Will you come along? Rory asked looking at Brandon he smiled at him “ What’s the show Rory

" Senora asked Bailey looking up from his phone looking between Rory and Brandon . " I do drag" " Really that's great I have a friend who does the same " .

Senora announced ahh Christopher who Bailey had met before was a nice person he thought " He does it very well " Brandon praising Rory he pretended to flick his hair " what's your drag name " Bailey asked Rory stood up Brandon sniggered knowing what was coming everyone was looking at him . " Miss Veronica sunshine darling " Everyone clapped. Patrick laughed at the antics Rory sat back down .Leaning against Brandon who had his arm round Rory's waist .

" Great name Rory " Senora said Rory pretended to be tipping his hat " Thanks honey " .Giving Senora a love heart sign to her she did one back to him they both giggled and noticed by Bailey .I wonder what his other friends and family think of what Rory does Bailey thought what am I thinking about that for Bailey thought .

" I've never been to a drag show before " Ellie said to Patrick he looked at her he had been to a couple with Elliot they were good fun " You want to go " He asked Ellie looked at Patrick why not she thought Ivy's dad could have her for the weekend ." Sure that would be great " .Ellie was pleased to know that Patrick would take her and Rory was a lovely person she could see why Brandon fell for him .And it was thoughtful of Patrick to ask .

" THAT WAS NICE OF HIM " Malcolm took a couple of boxes and tub food from Elliot that he could take to the shelter and food bank he sat them on the table " They were going to waste " .Elliot explained while Malcolm sorted the boxes out these would do for today's he thought thanking Elliot again .

" WELL THEY DEFINITELY will go to a good home " " I'm worried " Freya said when she came over to Malcolm and Elliot they looked at her " What is it Freya " .Malcolm asked Freya biting her lip looking at her phone .Why isn't Thomas responding to her messages and calls .

She leaned on the table teary eyed Elliot lay his arm around her shoulder " Thomas isn't responding to my calls or texts do you think he had relapsed " Malcolm hoped not Thomas was doing well past few months his time at rehab did him good with his bulimia and his friends rallied round to help him . " Freya, I'm sure Thomas will be ok. His support workers will check on him. " Freya hoped they would because she didn't want anything bad to happen to Thomas .He was doing so well the past few months .

Freya went back to the group Elliot got a text he checked it which was from Christian missing him heart emoji he smiled noticed by Malcolm Elliot looking up at him watching him . " Christian " Malcolm nodded he guessed the two of them were getting on great . " Going well "it sounded like they were getting on Malcolm thought " it is we're taking it slow I told him and he understands " .

" That's good c'mon let's start " Malcolm thought it was very brave of Elliot to tell Christian about his attack so early on he must have thought he could trust him and they got close quickly too .He just hoped it will work out with them maybe he has found his soulmate and it was a sign they were meant to be together .

AFTER GROUP THERAPY Thomas arrived not looking good at all. Everyone thought Malcolm Niel and Theresa took him into the office to have a chat while the others waited around to see Thomas before they all went home . They hoped he wasn't letting himself go again; they would rally round and help him out if need be .Just what triggered his relapse they thought .

SYDNEY , LUCA AND BETSY Jean arrived at the penguin enclosure its Lucas birthday and for a surprise Sydney and Betsy Jean decided to take Luca to the Zoo and for his birthday surprise was to feed the penguins to which he as grateful about even though Betsy Jean was having fun helping the keepers with the fish . Sydney and Luca took turns with help from the keepers and they were having good fun .

Luca thought this had been a great family day out he would Thank Sydney properly later sliding his arm round Sydney's waist Sydney looks up at Luca smiling at him . " Are you enjoying your birthday? Sydney asks while they watch Betsy Jean with the keeper . " Yes Love I am Thank you" " Good " .Luca kisses Sydney's head while smiling up at Luca .

Luca moves closer to Sydney he looks at him " Have I Any other surprises " Sydney shakes his head and looks at Luca again " Maybe " ." Dada " Betsy Jean shouts they look over at her " What is it honey " Sydney asks coming over to her " Dada name a penguin " .

The keeper explained he off the younger penguins didn't have a name yet and he wondered if they had wanted to name him " Pat , postman pat " The keeper snorted he guessed she had been watching postman pat " I'm so sorry she has a postman Pat obsession at the moment " .Luca explains going over to Betsy Jean bending down to her ." That's ok my little girl is obsessed with Frozen at the moment "

.

Oh god he is as well as Betsy Jean also she even had the Elsa dress and sometimes they had to put on Frozen but that was totally ok anything for there little girl Sydney thought while watching Luca and Betsy Jeans interaction with the penguins .

BAILEY WAS COLLECTING his and Senora drink at the cafe Brandon placed him on the counter looking over at Bailey he smiled Bailey nodded his head he looked tense for some reason Brandon thought ." Whats up " Bailey looked round at him picking up his drinks " Nothing why " .What's with the questions Bailey thought I'm perfectly fine no need to worry .Brandon has been constantly watching him for a while now maybe he should talk it out with him but not today .

" Just asking " " Dad can i get an ice cream " Reece had come over to his dad while chatting to Bailey Brandon looked down at him "Course you can " Brandon looked at Bailey " you've all this to look forward to " Bailey snorted Brandon looked at him Reece tugged at his dads jacket " What Reece "Brandon sighed this boy never stops " Can a have a drink to " .Brandon went into his pocket brought out change to give to Reece .Reece grinned taking the money to go get a drink for himself that boy an endless money pit but Brandon wouldn't change that he is my boy after all .

Bailey bent down to Reece. He went into his pocket bringing out 2 pounds, handing it to Reece Bailey looked up at Brandon, " A whole two pounds dad " ." What do you say? " .Bailey didn't need to do that but it was kind of him to do so .

" Thanks " " you're welcome you can get any drink you want now " Reece looked up at his dad he nodded then Reece went off to the drinks machine watched by Brandon thinking that was kind of Bailey to do that .

What's keeping them Senora thought Reece came running out with an ice cream and a drink going over to Rory " I got a whole 2 pounds Rory " " Wow amazing " Brandon and Bailey came back out " There was a que " Brandon said Bailey sat beside Senora finally she thought opening the can and taking a drink .Dying thirst here

Senora thought tutting What's with her Bailey thought probably hormones .

" Is your ice cream good Ivy " Patrick asked Ivy nodded. She reached over for Patrick too. Take some he pretended to Ivy giggles so cut

ELLIE AND IVY WAVED at Patrick when they went through the gates at the train station Patrick insisted she stay over at his apartment but Ellie had work tomorrow Senora and Bailey waited in the car park for Patrick. " Hes smitten " Senora said Bailey huffed Senora looked round at him.what's up with him she thought .Is Bailey not happy about his friend interested in someone Senora shook her head that's between them .

PATRICK WAS SMILING when he got in the car Senora and Bailey looked at him " What " " See told you " Senora shook her head laughing into herself she started the car Patrick sat forward " She is nice right " He asked Bailey looked at him " Yea Mate she does Babe what do you think ."

" I like her and if you like her we like her right Bailey " He nodded. Patrick sat back smiling and he hoped everyone liked her. Bailey shook his head and definitely smitten that he could see it but he is bound to be cautious because Ellie had a kid .

ELLIOT LEANED AGAINST the bed while he did some course work while on the phone to Christian who was having dinner with his dancer friends . " How were the kids? " Christian sighed leaning against the wall. They were a nightmare today, he thought but they

were good kids .And they were all trying but sometimes they would just get unruly at times .

" They were fine, how was your day "Christian sighed " Fine apart from group therapy, Thomas is in a bad way " Elliot sighed thinking about Thomas Christian could Tell Elliot was worried about his friend .

That wasn't good Christian thought he hoped the boy would be ok. His friend came to look for him. He had been gone for a while and he signals for 5 minutes Christian signalled he would be there in a minute .

" Got to go i'll see you Friday " " See you Friday " Elliot had asked Christian if he had wanted to come along to Brandon's boyfriend Drag show Friday night to which he agreed to Christian thought that was a nice thing to do .And it would be a date to which Chsrtian would be looking forward to .He had only been to me drag show before with friends .

Carrie was bringing washing upstairs Elliot came out of his room and saw her with the washing basket he went over to take it off her she shouldn't be carrying that he thought . " I'm fine Elliot " He sat it down and looked at Carrie " How is Christian " " Good where do you want this " .Elliot thought she shouldn't be carrying heavy things .

" Spare room Elliot i was thinking why don't you ask Christian over for sunday dinner " Elliot thought for a minute isn't it too soon maybe Carrie looked at him.while they sorted the clothes " To soon " she asked sitting down " No it's not that we haven't haven't really said what we.are yet " .I know I would like to be exclusive to each other Elliot had thought .

Carrie sniggers, they have only just met a few times but Elliot seems keen on him " But i will ask him over for sunday dinner " Elliot thought they are just getting to know each other and if they make it official it would be on their terms .And Yea why not bring Christian over for dinner that way he can get to know the family .

" Good cause we would like to know him, have you " Elliot laughed, he's not talking about his sex life with his sister " Not yet were we getting to know each other first " Elliot blushed looking away .

Good she thought take it slow and not jump head first Carrie was glad Elliot had found someone he was getting on with and now getting on with his life now and Christian seemed nice and by the way Elliot talks about him to it's like it was meant to be they have met .

Friday Patrick asked Ellie to come along to Rory's drag show and had planned to stay over with Patrick Ellie's ex would keep Ivy overnight. Senora was working at the hospital and she couldn't get a change of shift which was a bummer everyone thought . Christian and Elliot arrived together. His friends seemed nice Christian thought, making him feel welcome into their group .Which Elliot was pleased about, he wanted everyone to like Christian and Christian the same too .

" Shame Senora couldn't be here " Brandon asked yea it was a bummer Bailey thought Brandon's phone pinged off a text he checked it which was from Rory asking him to come see him Brandon excused himself and went through the back chapped on the door and went inside . Winston, one the other drag queens, was in the room to calm Rory. What's wrong Brandon thought , Brandon went over to him and bent down in front of Rory . " What's wrong? " Rory waved his hands. Brandon looked up at Winston, looking worried .Is he having stage fright Brandon thought because he has never had that before .

" honey never in a million years would this happen "Rory fanned himself to calm down " For god sake Rory tell me" .

Rory handed Brandon his phone for him to check the message his mouth dropped he looked up at Rory and back at Winston `` I don't believe it you got accepted for drag queen Uk " Rory squealed he stood up hugging Brandon he was so proud of him for his life dream .To be accepted for his favourite show Drag Uk Brandon couldn't believe it .Rory talked about it constant whenever it came on that's what he loves about Rory he goes for his dream and when Rory first thought about entering the next season Brandon had to convince him to enter .

" HAVE YOU BEEN HERE before " Christian asked Elliot " A couple times " Brandon came back Bailey wondered if Rory was ok he said he was with a big grin on his face Baileys phone beeped a text from Senora the Ward was busy with new patients sad face he quickly texted back sad face missing her .Sighing and feeling a bit bored now but he is here with his friends he should enjoy tonight .He knew Senora would be peeved off next time they would try get tickets to the next event .

The comparison came on introducing himself and the other acts Patrick took Ellie's hand she looked down and back up at Patrick they smiled at each other Elliot winked at him he was happy for his friend . Christian put his hand on Elliot's knee he looked at him " Ok " Elliot asked a Christian nodded then the compare started to introduce Miss Veronica Sunshine the music played to I am what I am then Rory made his entrance . That's my boy Brandon thought black wig multicolour dress made up to perfection everyone cheered and clapped .Rory going back forth on the stage singing everyone cheering .Brandon was so happy for Rory he loved the club and doing his act people also liked him which was good .

Bailey was surprised Rory looked amazing he looked over at Brandon he was beaming with pride for his boyfriend which was nice he thought supporting him then he did another song . After there was a Dj set before the other two drag artists came on then Rory would do another set .Not so bad after all Bailey thought Elliot asked him if he was ok Bailey nodded .He did look a bit peeved that Senora couldn't come but Bailey was still having a good time .

Rory got claps and cheers from everyone when he came over to sit with the others Brandon kissed his cheek and noticed Bailey cute he thought " Well how did I do " " Really good " Christian said .Rory giggled and went off what did i say Christian thought " Did i say something wrong " Christian asked Brandon " No he gets embarrassed sometimes don't worry about it " . Why does he feel embarrassed Christian thought he was doing a great job with his act?.

Elliot looked over at Patrick and Ellie chatting. They were all googly eyed with each other Christian noticed placing his hand on Elliots knee and he looked round at Christian. " I hope it works out for them " Elliot says Christian hoped so too and for the two of them also. `` By the way Carrie has asked if you wanted to come over for Sunday dinner " . Christian smiled, that's so sweet he thought and then Wham I'm your man came on the dj set ." I'd like that " The others got up to dance. Elliot laughed at them Christian took Elliot's hand and dragged him up to the dance floor .

Christian wrapped his arms round Elliot's shoulders they looked at each other Christian whispers in Elliot's ear " I want to be your man " Elliot looks at Christian surprised at his confession he smiled a tear forming Christian wiped it away they kissed jeers from everyone they both looked round at them Elliot looked at Christian again . " You are a silly bugger " Christian snorted many times. He had heard that word Elliot wrapped his arms round Christian looking at him as they swayed to the music . " I'd love to be your man " .Kissing Christians nose grinning at him .

Christian nodded, touching Elliot's face he leaned into his touch Bailey lay his arm round Elliot's shoulder " What's happening get a room you two " Elliot laughed bringing in Bailey closer " I think we just made it official " Elliot said looking at Christian wow Bailey thought that's amazing looking between them . I'm happy because my friend Bailey thought he deserves happiness after what he has been through .And Christian is perfect for him Bailey thought .

Patrick lay his arm round Bailey's shoulder looking between Elliot and Christian what's going on he thought " what's happening " Elliot looked at Christian and back at Patrick. " I think we're official now " Elliot said looking at Christian smiling at him woo that's quick he thought but if Elliot is happy " Just so you know you hurt him " " Patrick " Christian giggles pats Patrick shoulder " Don't worry i wont " .Elliot and Christian look at each other grinning he is so amazing Elliot thought .

" So when you gonna seal the deal " Patrick looked at Bailey shaking his head he looked round at Ellie she wasn't there where did she go he thought he looked over at the bar she wasn't there may be in the toilet. Is Ellie ok Patrick thought I hope she had enjoyed tonight ." Soon I hope " Elliot said whispering into Patrick's ear they look at each other nodding there

He waited at the toilet door as people came in and out he checked his phone no text the toilet door opened Ellie came out she looked like she had been crying he went to hug her she shrugged him off . " Ellie whats wrong " " Don't play me Patrick " What did she mean he's not playing her why would he .I like her and wanna date her .

"Ellie i'm not i have feelings for you " " i heard what Bailey said " shit Patrick thought idiot he didn't mean what he said Patrick took Ellies hand she looked up at him " Bailey didn't mean what he said Ellie he tends just to blurt it out " Ellie huffed looking away folding her arms ." Ellie " she looked at Patrick he touched her face and went to kiss her Ellie looked away . Bailey and his big mouth Patrick thought I'll have to ask him later .

Patrick pushed Ellie against the wall and she giggled. They kissed Ellie struggling against Patrick " Better " " Mmmm" Patrick took Ellie's hand to go back into the bar Elliot came to see what was taking them so long and he could tell they had a little fight . " I'll get the drinks " Ellie said leaving to go into the bar Elliot looked at Patrick "What happened " " She overheard Bailey it's sorted though " .Typical Bailey his mouth tends to run away with him at times .

" You like her right, " Patrick nodded. Elliot patted his arm shaking his head ";Don't rush into things ok " Patrick snorted he's normally the one giving him advice instead the other way round .And Yea there not rushing things they are getting to know each other .

" Mate I know and the same goes for you with Christian " Patrick pats Elliot's back he nodded and they hugged " Love you Mate " Patrick says Elliot nods holding onto Patrick " Love you to " .Patrick lays his arm round Elliot walking back to the bar and over to the others .

Senora was sleeping. She tried to stay awake for Bailey coming home but she was so tired she couldn't stay awake. Bailey quietly came into the bedroom and went over to Senora, bending down and kissing her cheek. Senora opened her eyes to Bailey smiling at her . " Tired baby " " Mmm" Bailey undressed Senora sat up rubbing her eyes she grinned at Bailey stripping down to his underpants he cocked his head Senora checking him out . He had a nice body not to muscly mind you he kept on about getting abs but he didn't need to . " I tried to stay awake " Bailey got into bed scooting over to Senora " How much did you drink " " Not a lot " He bent to kiss her so she could taste beer and chips .

" Rory did well " Senora asked while Bailey touched her belly rubbing it Senora looked down her bump starting to show " mmm he did and hows this little one been " Bailey talking to her belly Senora giggled he is being silly she thought " Fine " They kissed again Bailey moving his hand down further inside her jammie bottoms rubbing her spot she was wet Senora moaned that's nice she thought as he stuck another finger inside her he licked her ear .

" You wanna come baby " " Mmm There " Senora took his hand guiding him to the spot kissing frantically now he watched her biting her lip the flush on her face " Are you close "Bailey kissing her ear " mmm" Senora moved round she slid her hand down he was erect Senora mounted him easing herself onto Bailey he lifted up her pyjama top feeling her breasts . They were getting sensitive now with the pregnancy he licked the nub on her breast while they got into a rhythm. Senora lifted his arms up, he looked at her, they kissed and she bent down to lick his nipples .Jesus that's good Senora licked around his nipple and gave it a little bite that's Cheeky he thought .

SENORAS ORGASM RIPPED out off her Bailey holding her as he came to they both collapsed onto the bed Bailey held Senora she snuggling into him " I'm sensitive everywhere right now " Bailey snuggled her neck " mmm nice " Senora went to get up Bailey wondering why ahh yes off course her bladder because off the baby .She looks round at Bailey before she disappears into the bathroom Bailey smiling at Senoras little bump showing now .

PATRICK AND ELLIE STUMBLED through his apartment door all hands kissing he pushed her against the wall kissing her lifting one arm up they looked at each other . " Patrick are you sure " " God yes " Ellie went for his jeans Zip he took her hand leading to the bedroom Ellie pulled down Patrick jeans looking down she smirked well now looking up at Patrick they kissed Ellie palmed Patrick cock he shivered cold hands he thought .

She started stroking him, they bumped heads, that's good he thought " Ellie slow " She looked up at him then kissed Patrick helped Ellie to take off her top he then went over to the drawer to get the condoms Ellie got on the bed going into the covers . Patrick scooted over to her " Ellie don't cover up i want to see you " .

Ellie moved straddled Patrick her body looked amazing he palmed her breasts stroking them Ellie got the condom Patrick looked at her while she opened it then looked down at Patrick cock still erect . She put it on him wow he thought that's the most sexist thing he has seen he moved her onto her back kissing she reached up bringing him closer to her opening her legs for better access .

ELLIE REACHED HER HAND down to guide Patrick he lifted her hand before entering her making sure he didn't hurt her nuzzling into her neck and slowly getting into a rhythm " Patrick. .slow " he looked down at her he nodded Ellie wrapping her arms around his waist her leg up for more room there was a flush on her face he kissed her another push inside her .Ellie arched up oh god that's . Patrick still had not come yet he thought Ellie held his face he looked at her " let me go on top " They rolled round changing positions Patrick looking up at Ellie making sure the Condom was still on then eased herself on him .

Patrick reached up for her Ellie bent down to kiss him he felt her breasts licking and kissing them " Are you there yet " Ellie's face was flushed her belly fluttered as her orgasm loomed " mmm you " He was close to coming he jerked up " Fuck shit " Patrick said Ellie held his hand he closed his eyes while he came his orgasm ripping out off him . Ellie still felt him pulsate while her orgasm came and she bit her lip Patrick held onto her. Was it good for her? Patrick thought it was good for me .

They lay beside each other Ellie scooted over to Patrick he lay his arm around her kissed her nose " Are you ok " He was more than ok he thought that was amazing Ellie lay her head in his shoulder " I'm fantastic " looks at Ellie she sniggered they kissed again " You " He asked " I'm good " Patrick brought Ellie closer to him facing each other she touched his face " Ellie " " mmm " .

" I'M OPEN FOR SUGGESTIONS you know other stuff " she nodded she knew what he meant she kissed him again " Plenty time for that Patrick " " We could even get workshop "Wow Ellie thought looking at him she nodded she looked down at Patrick oh he's erect again wow he looked down to smiled at Ellie . " Wanna go again " Ellie giggled and slid her hand down he thought then Ellie slid down taking him in her mouth .

ELLIOT LAY HIS HAND over to reach Christian his side empty he sat up where was he Elliot thought rubbing his eyes he checked his phone for the time 2 am he decided to get up and went through to the lounge Christian was in the kitchen the fridge door opened Elliot smiled oh he's getting a sneaky midnight snack he thought . " Christian " he peeked over startled that Elliot was up; he was holding a trifle. He looked down at it " You caught me having a midnight snack " " so I see " .

Elliot went over to Christian dipped his finger in the trifle and licked his finger off the cream with Christian watching then Elliot went into the drawer to bring out a spoon and took a scope " Nice " Elliot smiled Christian nodded Elliot dipped taking a small amount off cream leaving it on Christians nose then licking it off . Christian moved Elliot against the table he kissed his neck sliding his hand down into his boxers kissing " Christian " he looked at Elliot " Want some trifle " Elliot scooped some onto his chest Christian looked surprised and smirked bending over and licking the remains off Elliots chest .

" Mmm Human trifle " Christian wiped his mouth they kissed again a sticky mess Christian did the same opening his boxers rubbing some off the trifle on his privates Elliot took Christian hand and licked his fingers staring at his mouth open that is hot he thought .And sticky but who cares it is fun Christian looks hot in a sticky mess from the trifle .

Elliot bent down sliding down his boxers licking off the trifle taking him.in his mouth licking up and down Christian closed his eyes holding onto Elliot's head . " Elliot " Elliot stood back up, his face covered in cream Christian sniggers as Elliot wiped his mouth ." Shower " Christian asked Elliot nodded and they ran to the bathroom.

They both soaped each other washing each other's hair getting the remnants off the trife of them kissing each other in between " Christian the kitchen " Elliot asked " Don't worry about it get it in the morning " .

Elliot cocked his head. I will feel bad if we don't clean up, he thought until they eventually left the shower and tidied up the best they could before going to bed.

Chapter 8

" Oh dear oh dear " Gloria Christian housekeeper shook her head what has happened in the kitchen overnight she thought while starting to do her cleaning Christian came out from the bedroom saw what Gloria was doing she looked up at him " Morning Mr King " " Morning Gloria sorry about the mess accident with the trifle we cleaned best we could " .

Gloria tutted, shaking her head mumbling to herself " Ready " Elliot shouted coming out from the bedroom he stopped when he saw the lady Gloria looked up and smiled " Gloria this is Elliot " "Hello .dear " .Gloria looked between Christian and Elliot so this is the young man he has heard about she thought .

" Hello " Elliot looked at Christian he lay his arm round Elliots waist "We are going out for breakfast Gloria " Gloria thought Elliot was handsome Christian did seem happier which was good they said their goodbyes and went off to get breakfast Gloria carried on with her cleaning and she had brought more grocery's for Christian to she went into the fridge she sighed the trifle was half eaten she scooped some off it out and out it in a plastic container.Hopefully it will keep Better that way she giggled into herself Mr King seems a bit more happier lately now that Elliot was around .

PATRICK WRAPPED HIS arms round Ellie's waist while she made breakfast while he distracted her with kisses she tried batting him off but gave up trying. He felt her bottom and she slapped his hand " Patrick do you want your breakfast " " MmmI'd rather have you " .

Ellie turned to him and they kissed and looked at each other " Are you sore? " He asked if they had made love 3 times last night until they eventually fell asleep Ellie shook her head and kissed her again . " Do you want toast with this? "" Yes please, I'll make the tea. " Patrick's phone beeped. He checked it, which was Elliot checking if he and Christian were going for breakfast. Patrick smiled. He was really keen on him, and he liked Christian to . " Elliot checking in with Christian going for breakfast " .Thats Nice Ellie thought the three of them look out for each other which is great and really close friends she liked that about the three of them with their close bond looking out for each other .

They sat down to eat there breakfast Ellie liked Christian to Elliot seemed to like him a lot " That's good they seem to be getting along " " They do I just don't want Elliot to hurt anymore " Ellie took Patrick's hand he lifted it up kissed her hand " You worry to much " Patrick sighed he knows that he does but he's his best friend and since the attack he needed him and Bailey more now . " I know but he's my best friend " Ellie nodded and drank her tea looking at Patrick " he's a survivor Patrick he had you , Bailey and other people around him " That is right he has he thought .

Ellie's phone rang her ex Brian she got up to take the call out in the hallway " Everything ok " "Yea don't worry a little one wants to know when her mummy is coming home " Brian looked down at Ivy sitting on the stairs that girl Ellie thought giggling into herself Brian handed the phone to Ivy . " Mummy, when are you coming home? " .

" I'll be home this afternoon honey ok " Ivy smiled looking up at her dad " ok mummy " then handed the phone to her dad and ran upstairs " I think she's bored of me Els " Ellie snorted she is definitely not bored off her dad she thought Ellie looked round at

Patrick doing the washing up . "You're exaggerating Brian see you later " .

Ellie went into the kitchen to help clear up, shaking her head. Patrick looked at her. He smiled and slapped his bottom again Ellie squealed " Hey " " Ivy was wondering when I would be home " . Ellie leaned against the table Patrick moved closer to her she looked up at him" What train will you get " " Oh plenty time " Ellie cocked her head " Besides got to get a shower first " Ellie sad they kissed Patrick smiled " I need a shower to " They both giggled Patrick took Ellie's hand they ran upstairs to the bathroom for another make out session .

BAILEY IS ON THE COMPUTER Senora went out to meet her friend Melinda for a girls day he was checking gay porn then he thought to himself why am I checking this maybe it just curiosity he did get an eyeful he did watch porn before two straight couples which turned him on but this he thought was something else which kinds stirred something but didn't know what . He quickly shut the computer, you being stupid he thought to himself ok time for a shower then tidy the house .I'm being stupid thinking these thoughts while he got ready to get into the shower .

Bailey let the water flow over him then shampoo his hair brown hair green eyes a vision off Brandon what the hell Bailey thought as he soaped himself he got a hard on fuck he thought one hand on the tile shaking his head he started stroking himself Brandon's face again he pulled harder the water flowing over him .Going with the feeling he was having am I attracted to Brandon he thought .

Why am I having visions of Brandon Bailey grunted c'mon come already he thought his orgasm was close another few strokes his orgasm came hard he leaned against the tiles until his orgasm subsided Jesus that was intense he thought I'm not attracted to

Brandon am I that just be weird . Am I bi he thought no it can't be that what's that other thing that people are that are attracted to both sex Bailey thought .Is it just curiosity Bailey thought he just wasn't sure besides these days there were different names and stuff . I should look up to letting the water flow over him again, shutting his eyes don't thinking of Brandon Bailey .

“ AHH MEL LOOK “ SENORA pointed to some baby clothes she spotted while browsing in one the shops little bootees Melinda came over to see what she was looking at they were nice “ lovely have you started getting baby stuff yet “ “ just bits the spare room we're gonna do it up soon “ Melinda snorted Senora looked at her what's funny “ We ” Melinda asked “ Yes “ Senora carried on looking at the baby clothes " Sorry hun " Senora looked at Melinda shaking her head .Bailey isn't useless she thought he is able to do most things and painting a room we can both manage .

" He is capable you know " Senora said Melinda snorted pointed to Senora belly she looked down " Yea he's capable alright he got you pregnant " " Mel " Melinda wrapped her arm round Senoras shoulder they both laughed then Senoras phone rang her dad .

" Dad " " Hey honey you guys free sunday " Harvey asked while chopping vegetables " I think so " senora smiled he probably wants us over to sample a dish she could hear ringing coming from the cafe he owns " Ok hows " Senora felt her stomach smiling " cooking along " .Senora looks at Melinda who rolls her eyes .

" Good good gotta go honey love ya let me know what time ;you will be over " " Love you to dad will do " did he mean this sunday or next she thought she quickly texted to confirm her dad

CHRISTIAN TOOK ELLIOT to Leytons grave for his monthly visit. He stood at the car watching him take his usual flowers and beer. Elliot had noticed Leytons grave had been tidied up. Elliot looked up at the grave stone and looked over at Christian and back at the grave stone . " I really like him Leyton he's been patient with me good looking right " Elliot sniggered laying down the flowers he opened his can took a sip " Cheers " Christian came over to Elliot when he stood up placing his hand on Elliots back making sure he was ok Elliot looked round at Christian smiled at him " He would've liked you " Elliot twirled the rings on the chain looking down at the chains .

LEYTON LOOKED OVER at Lucien while they watched Elliot and Christian at his grave Leyton sighed he just wished Elliot would move on properly now he thought Christian seemed nice he seemed happy that's what he wants is for Elliot to be happy with someone else . " Lucien " " He is going to be ok Leyton" Lucien looked round at Leyton he nodded " About " " Leyton I've told you " .Lucien sighed so impatiently at his words at times they just had to be patient he thought .

" I KNOW BUT " LUCIEN sighed they can't interfere he had told him countless times "Also I'm running out off favours Leyton " Leyton huffed looks at Lucien again he just wanted to see Elliot again and how he is with Christian " There is something wrong with him isn't there " Leyton asked but as usual Lucien can't say unless the big guy lets him . Also Lucien hasn't been himself lately Leyton thought he seemed distracted by something . Maybe to do with assignments he had been doing lately .

" I can assure you it will all be ok now we must go " .

Elliot looks over at the other graves feels for his rings a Christian wonders if he's ok going over to him " Elliot " Elliot looks up at Christian and back at Leytons grave " I'm ok Christian I just had a feeling " Lets go " Elliot nodded Christian lay out his hand for Elliot to take he took his hand and walked over to the car .Elliot looks over at the graves before he goes into the car it was a weird feeling he had earlier was it Leyton he thought . Elliot looks at Christian Then gets into the car Christian takes Elliot's hand they look at each other .

" I'm ok Christian " Christian smiles touching Elliot's face he leans into Christian touch then Christian starts the car driving off I hope he is ok he squeezes Elliot's hand while driving off hopefully he will tell him later .

" MUMMY " IVY RAN TO her mum when she came to her ex Brian's to pick her up Ellie bent down picking her up as Brian watched from the door " Did you have a good time " Ellie asked Ivy she nodded as they walked into the house Brian had Ivy's stuff all packed " Cup tea " Brian asked Ellie nodded " Daddy " " Yes baby " " Tv " Ellie sniggered she knew what was coming Brian went into the lounge switched on the tv for the program she wanted that keep her quiet .

" Good night then ' Brian asked while they drank there tea " Yes pretty good " Brian nodded Ellie cocked her head what's up with him she thought " How is martine " " Good Els it's been six months and I'd like To introduce Martine to Ivy " Their agreement together that they both shouldn't introduce ivy to anyone so quick before Brian had a girlfriend every few minutes months .Now that Martine seemed to be a permanent she hoped and wondered if its permanent .

" El i love her and well we want to go on holiday with Alice and i thought we could take Ivy " Ellie looked at Brian she had no problem with that he often took her away a few days away . " Ok fine by me " Brian smiled. Ellie got up and put the cup in the sink. " Ivy time to go, " Ellie shouted. Ivy came running into the kitchen .Over to her dad for a cuddle Brian picked her up sitting Ivy on his knee before they left .

Sunday came Christian came for Sunday dinner Molly was ecstatic that he had come for dinner. They sat round the dinner table There was so much food Christian thought Elliot looked at him wondering if he was ok he squeezed his leg Christian looked at him and smiled .Is Christian ok Elliot wonders or is he just overwhelmed by it all .Or maybe to do with all the food like he had said to Elliot before about the food situation they calorie intake for a dancers routine.

" Dig in, " Carrie said, helping herself while sorting out the kids' plates. She looked over at Christian as he piled his plate, " watching your weight Christian " Micheal asked Carrie, kicking him under the chair ." Oh no its " " Christian has got to watch what he eats right " Elliot said looking at Christian who nodded smiling at Elliot .

" Ahhh ok strict diet thing "Micheal asks I guess it's a dancer thing to watch their weight " Yes kind off " .Christian says Elliot squeezes Christian leg he looks at Elliot grinning at him .

" Mr King " " Yes Molly " .Christian looks round at Molly .

" What music is next week? " Carrie sniggers, that girl way ahead of herself she thought " Possibly rock music Molly " Molly screwed up her face looking at her Dad and mum . " is that to coincide with the ballet one " Elliot asked he remembered Christian telling him about it before . " Possibly still to organise" .

" Anybody, anymore ? " Carrie asked, clearing the table Micheal helped " Any spare " Elliot asked Carrie to look round " I'll put in tubs don't worry pudding anyone ``.Any spare food Elliot was taking to the Shelter he even roped the kids in to help to Christian thought it was a good idea he was doing a good thing for the homeless .

AFTER ELLIOT TOOK CHRISTIAN up to his room he looked around Elliot watching him in a nice room Christian thought a typical boys room had some music pictures up on the wall and one of Adam Lambert Christian pointed to it . " I went through a faze " Christian noticed a picture of Elliot and Leyton he picked up taken two years ago .Elliot came over to him Christian looked at him .Then lay his arm round Elliot's shoulders looking at the picture .

" lovely Picture what was he like " " Amazing he was so full of life he had a future then well " Christian wrapped his arms round Elliot's shoulders he looked up at Christian " i'm moving on Christian i won't forget him though ." Christian nodded and bent to kiss him Elliot slid his arms round Christian waist deepening the kiss then they bumped heads . " Making new memories now " Elliot said Christian nodded, touching Elliot face he leaned into his touch they kissed again.

" I'm ready " Christian looked at Elliot. This would be another step in their relationship. " Christian " " Yes I heard you are you sure " Elliot nodded moving closer to Christian " I'm more than sure I want to be with you Christian " .I am definitely ready for the next step no more feeling anxious about having sex again they can work up to it Elliot thought .

Carrie had come upstairs to see if the both of them wanted tea or anything else when she listened in on their conversation then thought not to disturb them she had thought they already had sex but not yet she was glad he waited till the right time she could tell they were both keen on each other . Christian was 4 years older than Elliot. That was ok at least they were kinda of a similar age. Am I babying him too much? Carrie thought he was my little brother. I'm just making sure he is ok .

She went back into the kitchen Micheal was putting the pans away he looks at Carrie " Ok " " Uh huh " Micheal hugged her she looked up at him " Did they need anything " " I didn't ask " Micheal gave her a quick peck squeezing Carries bottom she tutted and was about to move away Micheal stopped her . " What " Micheal raised his eyebrows Carrie tutted again batting him away . And going into the lounge where the kids were while Micheal carried on with putting the dishes away grinning to himself.

" MOLLY , JACK DON'T stare " Carrie said to them when Elliot went outside with Christian when he was leaving she hushed the kids into the lounge to let Elliot have his privacy ." Ahh But Mum " Molly said huffing sitting beside her mum to nosey those kids she thought .Let there Uncle have peace .

" Your sister is very nice " " She is the kids like you to " He liked the kids to Elliot's brother in law was down to earth to Christian thought and they made him feel welcome to " See you Tuesday " " See you Tuesday " They kissed Christian went into his Range Rover rolled down the window leaning against the window . " My friends are going to like you " Elliot smiled leaning into the window to " I hope so " They kissed again Elliot pulled away Christian rolled up the window started the car then drove off Elliot watching him drive off then going back into the house smiling .

" I like him " Carrie said Elliot was pleased to know that he hoped she would " i like him to " Carrie put on the kettle to make another cup tea " Elliot " He looked at Carrie she came over to him leaning against the table " I know what your gonna say and it's all good we have spoke about it you do know we can just cuddle up " Elliot snorted Carrie playfully punched his arm . " Good you know you can talk to me too" " Yes sis I know " .Hugging his sister then going into the lounge tickling Molly she squealed.

Chapter 9

Senora was preparing dinner going over what she was going to say to Bailey when she went to check for baby stuff online he had left the history up and didn't delete it she heard talking from the back door Bailey normally left his work clothes outside when he got home so as not to stink up the place . He opened the door and left his boots outside. Senora looked round when he came in looking over at her. He smiled , gave a heart emoji and giggled then went upstairs for his shower to wash off the day . " Baby " Senora looked round and he did a pucker kiss " Love you " " Love you to " . He then ran upstairs to the shower. Senora shut the kitchen door and the smell from the slaughterhouse wafted in .Making her gag. I don't know how he did it. Senora thought of taking a sip of her drink .It's not a job I could do, Senora thought after what Bailey told her about what happened at the slaughterhouse.

After his shower Bailey came downstairs Senora was still in the kitchen peeling the potatoes he went over to her wrapping his arms around her waist she tried shrugging him off he kissed her neck " I would've done them " " I'm able Bailey you better sort your stuff " .pointing to outside Bailey sighed she needs to stop being bossy he thought .

" I'll sort it later for dinner " " Chicken and I don't wanna be a nag but it's making me gag Bailey " Understandable He thought I would be the same with the blood etc .

BAILEY WENT INTO THE fridge for a drink. She's being weird. He thought it was the pregnancy hormones he thought after it was prepared they sat at the table to have dinner " Any protests today " " No thank god " .While they carried on eating I had to say something about what I found earlier Senora thought .

" Bailey " He looked at her Carrie stared at him " What " Bailey looks up at Senora she doesn't look happy he thought is it to do with work the baby maybe.

" I saw the history on the computer " Fuck he thought busted he thought he had cleared the history Senora lay her hand on his he looked up at her " You mad " " I'm not mad Bailey I was just a little shocked that's all I mean if you want to experiment with guys we can discuss it " Bailey nearly chocked on his drink was she serious he got up went over to Senora bending down to her . " I was just curious, that's all, not interested in being with a guy " .

Senora shook her head as if he was sure she thought oh god Bailey thought she's gonna cry now hormones again he wiped her tears away " it could be a pan sexual thing " Senora said in between blowing her nose and giggling what the hell Bailey thought are all pregnant women like this . " why don't we go to the club this week like we planned " Bailey suggested Senora nodded " is it because I tried to finger you " Bailey sniggered god she's adorable he touched her face and kissed her nose . " No baby it's not that and what the fuck is pan sexual ".

Senora sniggered this boy. Why do I love him so much? " Do you want to experiment with women? " Bailey asked because that could be sexy. He thought " No baby I don't unless you do " . He also sniggered, stood back up and sat back on the seat shaking his head . " we're a disaster aren't we " Bailey said Senora huffed " We will figure it out we just need to be honest with each other right " Bailey nodded she was right they do need to talk it over and see what conclusions they come to .Maybe a threesome someday they did discuss that a while back .

" By the way Patrick isn't a virgin anymore " Honestly isn't anything sacred with these gifts. I know they're there . Close and talk to each other most things " Bailey " what did I say now he thought he got up went over to Senora again holding out his hand . " what " he bent down to kiss her " Bailey not now besides we have the dishes to do " Bailey sighed he looked round yep they do . " won't take long "

Bailey saluted Senora sniggers " Yes Sister no problem " . I wish she thought someday she will get a promotion so now she is happy .

PATRICK HAD A SHIFT at the club Ellie would be working to and he would stay over at her place the club opened at 2 till 12 at the glasgow site midweek Jake was co manager tonight he noticed the two of them were all smiley and giggly with each other a nice site to see he thought good that the staff were getting on .They were getting on to well he noticed is something maybe going on between them .It reminded of him and Julia when they first got together and if Patrick and Ellie seeing each other that's fine .

He was on the phone to Julia in the office when the door chapped Patrick came in " Boss the keys " Shit he forgot to sit them out Jake came off the phone and into the drawer for the room keys . A box was sitting there " Jake " Patrick asked he zoned out there he thought Jake looked up at Patrick " Story yes keys " Jake handed them to Patrick before he went out the door " You and Ellie getting on " Patrick looked round he blushed and smiled " Yea we " .Patrick blushed chewing his lip .

Ahh Jake thought they were having a thing he thought just like he and Julia had at the beginning good on him Jake thought " Mum's the word "Jake rubbing his nose Patrick sniggered then left well there must be something he likes about her he thought . Jake opened the drawer again picking up the box and he smiled. Soon he thought then his phone beeped off a text from Julia, a picture message from her and he quickly texted back a love heart .

ELLIOT HEARD THE MUSIC when he arrived at the theatre Christian was rehearsing with the other dancers they had s show in a couple weeks and were picking rock music for it when he heard Bon Joni playing he went further into the theatre Christian and his friends were practising the dance moves . Elliot stood and watched their choreographer explaining what they had to do. Daniel beside her Christian saw Elliot and he smiled and waved. Daniel looked round when Elliot came nearer Christian coming over to him he looked sweaty Christian bent down . “Hi “ “ Hi “ He reached over to kiss Elliot everyone jeered, they both looked over at them giggling .

“ Patricia this is Elliot “ They shook hands Daniel nodded “ Pleased to meet you Elliot “ “ You to “a woman came over to Christian he smiled at her and looks at Elliot “ Oh Christian he is handsome hello I’m Helene “ “ Hi “ Patricia claps her hands for them to start up rehearsals again Elliot went to sit back down while the dancers got into their positions the music played again Bon Jovi again it’s my life played .Elliot likes the song from the band and all the other songs to were classics .

Amazing Elliot thought the way they glided along the lifting the girls up Christian looked great especially in his leotard and baggy shirt sexy after they finished rehearsal Christian came over to Elliot “ How did it look “ “ Good from what I saw “ Christian was pleased he wiped his face with the towel “ I’ll get a quick shower ok the guys are looking forward to seeing you properly “ “ Great “ Christian went to get changed after they would be going to a local restaurant for dinner with the cast .Elliot felt a little nervous about it but he wanted to get to know Christians friends and the same with them .

Daniel came over to Elliot sitting on the other bench he seemed ok Elliot thought for a Pa " Christian seems happier your around Elliot " He hoped so he thought " I hope he is " Daniel sniggers nods he looks at Elliot " Is this a warning Daniel " " No off course not " Elliot cocks his head then what's the problem he thought " Ready " Elliot looks up at Christian all changed into jeans ripped on the leg another baggy shirt and looking hotter than usual Elliot thought smiling at Christian he looks between Elliot and Daniel has he said something to Elliot Christian thought .

DINNER WAS GOING WELL Christian friends from the dance company were really nice, making him feel welcome as Daniel Elliot wasn't sure about whether he was warning him or something. Not sure he would talk to Christian about that . "What do you do Elliot " Helene asked Elliot liked her she and Christian worked together for about three years she is from Italy " I work at a club part time and I'm at college doing health and social care " Helene nodded looking at Christian and back at Elliot she leaned into him " He is happier now " Elliot smiled Looked over at Christian who was talking to Simon one the other dancers " He had talked about you constantly " " How Did you meet " Phoebe one the dancers asked leaning. Elliot snorted, shaking his head thinking back how they met . " We have met three times before " " Really " Phoebe asked looking at Helene " Not that way the first time was at the courthouse " .Elliot grins looking at Christian and winks .

Helene looked wide eyed and Phoebe was intrigued. " That's another story. The second time was at a bar where I was with friends and the third was at my nieces school " " ." Oh wow that's so romantic " Elliot snorted romantically he thought " it's like you were meant to be " Helene said the three of them looked over at Christian who looked round at them are they talking about me he thought . " What " Christian asked " Nothing was discussing how we met " Christian smiled, taking Elliot's hand and kissing it .

Elliots phone rang Carrie calling him he excused himself to take the call outside Christian wonders if something is wrong he thought . " Carrie " " Mum has had a seizure Elliot " .

Damn he thought he looked round at the table from outside " Elliot " " I heard you how she I'm coming over " " Elliot you don't have to, the doctor is coming in " No way Elliot thought I would just worry about her Elliot thought .

" I'm coming in " Elliot went back inside and told Christian what happened. He would come with him, which he didn't need. Elliot thought Elliot excused himself, apologising that he couldn't stay . Elliot looks upset. Helene thought I hoped he was ok when they both left .I hope it isn't serious everyone thought when they both left .

CHRISTIAN REACHED FOR Elliot's hand and squeezed it looking over at him Elliot was looking out the window " Elliot " " I'm fine Christian " Elliot looked over at him he shouldn't have snapped at him " Sorry I just worry about mum " .Elliot sighs why is he so understanding Elliot thought I hope Mum is ok .Christian has been amazing Elliot thought .

" That's understable " .

CARRIE WAS ALREADY at the hospice when Elliot arrived the doctor had been to see his mum and told the nurses to keep.an eye on her. Mhairi was in her bedroom with Carrie Elliot, went over to his mum and gave her a kiss on her head while Christian waited at the door watching .

" She is starting to come round a bit " Mhari said while she tended to his mum Carrie came over to Christian she looked round at Elliot holding her mums hand talking ro her . " Thanks for bringing him Christian " " No problem, need anything " .

" A good night's sleep " Carrie said rubbing her stomach Christian sniggered she must be feeling it now especially at 7 months Elliot looked over at them talking " Tea anyone " Mhari asked before she left Morag started to come round a little opening her eyes now and again Christian sat on the chair while Elliot and Carrie sat beside there mum talking to her .

“ You gave us a fright mum “ Elliot said holding her hand he looked over at Christian he was on his phone texting away Morag coughing she still wasn’t over the chest infection Christian got up explains he had to take a couple calls Morag groaned Carrie and Elliot looked at her . Her expression noticing Christian go out the door Elliot looked at Carrie `` That is Christian mum “ Elliot said Morag groaned again lifting her eyebrows Elliot knew what she was meaning .

“ Handsome right “ Elliot said Carrie sniggered Morag lifted her eyebrows again off her approval the door chapped Micheal came inside going over to Carrie then Mhari with the teas `` Oh you got plenty come to see you now “ Mhari put down the teas and went over to Morag to check on her and her temperature. “ Still a little high but that’s to be expected you had us worried there Mrs' ' .

“SHE CERTAINLY DID EH mum “ Carrie said Mhari left Christian came back inside after his calls he went over to Elliot he looked up at him “ You can go if you want “ “ it’s ok I can wait with you “ .That is so nice of Christian to wait which he didn’t need to Carrie thought looking at Elliot he was radiating tension which wasn't good are they both ok Carrie thought .

Patrick wrapped his arms round Ellie's waist when they stepped into the shower after work Elliot had texted him about his mum having the seizure he gave him words of comfort and reassurance and to let him know anything knew about his mum . Patrick kissed her neck she turned her head to kiss him she felt his hardness against her " How Elliot's mum " " The same " Patrick cupped her breasts rubbing the nubs Ellie whimpered that felt good she thought .Closing her eyes while Patrick nibbled on her ear .

Ellie turned to face Patrick wrapping her arms round his shoulders kissing he slid his hand down and rubbed her sex while Ellie held onto him then stuck two fingers inside her he licked and kissed her ear " Is that good " " Mmm Yes " while Ellie leaned against the tile she felt her orgasm looming they looked at each other . He stopped for a second and put the condom on Ellie leaned against the tile while Patrick guided himself inside her she held onto him then getting into a rhythm . Ellie turned round holding onto the tile while Patrick guiding himself inside her Ellie wiggled her bum Oh that's good Patrick thought he kissed her neck when he pushed into her Ellie groaned as Patrick got into a rhythm.

Ellie came on a shout Patrick stilled spilling into the condom he wiped Ellie's hair from her face they kissed as they came down from there orgasm " I can't feel my legs " Ellie said she felt wobbly Patrick sniggered Ellie giggled they kissed again " Good " Patrick asked Ellie nodded yes it was good they got out the shower dried off then got into bed for another make out session .

HANDS GRABBING HIS throat closing up Elliot was having a bad dream he kicked in the bed waking Christian he held Elliot until he was still mumbling Christian couldn't make out what he was saying . Elliot held Christian till he woke up giving him words of comfort " Christian " " Shh it's ok I'm here " Elliot sat up scrubbing his face Christian watching him " Do you need some water " Christian asked Elliot shook his head " Hold me " Christian held out his arms Elliot went to him giving him words off comfort again kissing his head he was probably feeling distressed because off his mum .

" Will she be ok Christian " Elliot asked looking up at him " She will not stress yourself or sleep ok " Elliot sat up looking over at Christian " I'm too scared sometimes " Christian took Elliot's hand kissing his knuckle he wished he could do something for him to take the pain away . Christian reached for Elliot and brought him closer " I'm here " . Elliot felt better with Christian beside him; he was so worried about his mum and hoped this time she will get better.

Eventually Elliot fell back to sleep Christian arms wrapped round him he was slightly snoring after a while which was good Christian thought .I will make sure I take his nightmares away Christian thought .And take him places he wants to go to I want to try and be a good boyfriend.

Chapter 10

Elliot moved over to Christian side of the bed feeling for him he wasn't there Elliot sat up rubbed his eyes looking round feeling disoriented he got his phone to. Check the time it was 8.30 shit he had college he lay back down fuck it's Friday no college Elliot groaned I feel so tired he thought sitting up in bed stretching yawned then decided to get up to see where Christian was .

Christian is in the lounge with Daniel having their usual breakfast meeting to catch up when Elliot appears still looking sleepy. " Elliot " Christian said "getting up, going over to him" " I'm going to be late I need to call Carrie " Elliot looked over at Daniel who was looking at them . " I called her Micheal and she had a comfortable night" " Oh but " .

Christian touched Elliot's face he looked up at him " No buts we can go later " why is he so damn adorable Elliot thought they hugged " Breakfast first ok " Elliot nodded Christian kissed his head " I'll go and get started " Daniel announced they both looked over at him getting up and going over to Christian office Elliot looked at Christian he looked at Elliot taking his hand leading him to the kitchen .

" What's up with Daniel " " Nothing why " They both in sink with making teas coffees Elliot putting bread in the toaster " Just a vibe do you want toast " Elliot looked at Christian him leaning against the work top " Don't worry about Daniel love " Elliot cocked his head smiling at Christian " Do you want toast " Elliot asked

Christian and yawned " Had mine coffee will do " .I do wonder sometimes Daniel worries to much about Christian Elliot thought while he made his breakfast .

Christian looked at his phone it had beeped a couple times Elliot looked at him " Rehearsals " He asked Christian nodded looked up at Elliot `` Yes but not till later " Christian came over to Elliot leaning over him they kissed he has a boner Elliot thought gently pushing Christian away looking down Elliot smiled shaking his head . "What " Christian asked he moved nearer to Christian " it's a shame to waste that " Elliot pointing to Christian boxers he looks down and back up smirking . He goes over to Elliot they kiss again " Christian if we don't stop we won't get breakfast " Elliot whispers then the smoke alarm goes off smoke coming out the toaster shit he's forgot about the toast them both running over to it flapping the tea towel until the alarm stops .Both giggling while flapping the towel around .

Daniel comes out of the office wondering what happened as Elliot and Christian were rescuing the toaster he shook his head. They have to be careful, he thought. Have they been flirty with each other it seems so Daniel thought then went back into the office to finish off what he was doing .Shaking his head while he replies to a couple emails .

Well that's killed the mood Christian thought as they cleaned up and putting another two slices of toast in he went over to the sliding patio doors to let some air in to take away the smell he looks over at Elliot carrying on with his breakfast making the tea and coffee. He smiled . Elliot looked over at Christian over at the patio doors staring at him as he checked him out he thought then carried on preparing breakfast Elliot grinning to himself .

Christian comes over to Elliot standing behind him leaning into to kiss his neck Elliot batted him away and giggled he then wrapped his arms round Elliot's waist " Christian " "Mmm" Elliot turned to face him while he eat a slice his toast " Are you frustrated " Bits off crumb falling from Elliot's mouth Christian wiped Elliot's mouth looked at him . " A little like I said no rush and when you said you were ready other stuff is fine for now " .

" I know I am a little frustrated to and well I do feel ready and want to with you " Christian felt touched by what Elliot said he kissed him he could take him away for a few days somewhere which they could discuss soon Christian thought " What are you thinking " Elliot asked when they sat down at the table eating the rest off his toast . " I want to take you away somewhere for a few days just the two off us " " I'd like that " Elliot took Christian hand and kissed it he smiled then got up kissed Elliot's head " I'll go shower " Elliot nodded smiling into himself a shower together sounded good he watched Christian go to his room he looked round and disappeared into the room smiling .

ELLIE WENT TO MOVE over to Patrick's side he lifted his arm up for Ellie to move into him he bent down to kiss her she opened her eyes looking up at him smiling " Morning " Patrick said kissing her again " Morning " they faced each other Patrick touched Ellie's face she leaned into his touch she could also feel his hardness .Ellie slid her hand down and started stroking him Patdick closed his eyes while Ellie carried on she then moved and slid down licking and kissing down his leg holy god that's sexy he thought she looked up Patrick watching her she palmed his cock then taking him in her mouth Patrick held onto her head as she carried on .

It wasn't long till Patrick came Ellie sat up wiped her mouth fuck did she just swallow he thought touching her mouth sexy as hell he pulled her to him they kissed tasting his cum . " That's amazing and sexy do you want me to " Ellie goggled then straddled him " I'm good I'm gonna brush my teeth " Patrick held her did a pouty face Ellie giggled again shaking her head then got out of bed into the toilet to brush her teeth .

Patrick lay his arms around his head Ellie came back jumped back into bed " it's after 9 " she said Patrick looked at her " And " " We can't lie in bed all day Patrick " Patrick grabbed her Ellie lay on her back wriggling " Who can't " Patrick stole some kisses Ellie trying to bat him away they both laughed . " Ok ok you win " Patrick said holding up His hands then stealing a kiss again .

Rolling round straddling Ellie Looking down at her she looks amazing he bent to kiss her " What about going out for breakfast " in between kisses good idea Ellie thought " Or order breakfast " Good idea Patrick thought " I like that but first " Patrick reaches over for the condoms Ellie held his arm he looks round at her .

" What is it? " " Let's have a shower. " Patrick smiles. Patrick smiles. He thought about getting up, taking Ellie's hand and going into the bathroom into the shower for a make out session twice before they eventually made it out to go for brunch by the time they got out .

Elliot and Christian walked into the hospice they had gotten flowers on the way there ones that his mum liked there was a buzz in the hospice Elliot noticed he looked at Christian what's going on he thought .before they got to his mom's room one the doctors a couple nurses running into her room Carrie waiting with Micheal his arm around her shoulder crying What's happened Elliot thought .

" Carrie " she looked round at Elliot and looked at Micheal and back at Elliot " Elliot your mum " Once the nurses came outside Elliot fell to the ground he screamed Christian held him everything went in slow motion Micheal ran to Elliot then everything dizzy Elliot feeling faint he was aware off shouting when he passed out .

" ELLIOT " CHRISTIAN sat beside Elliot lying on the bed he was coming round when he passed out Elliot slowly sat up in the bed holding his head Christian passed him.A drink of water he took a sip passing it back to Christian. " Christian Tell me it's not true " Christian came over to Elliot sitting on the bed taking Elliots hand tears rolling down his cheek Christian wiped them away . Elliot held onto Christian while he cried as the door opened. Micheal came inside and saw Christian and Elliot hugging damn he thought not Elliot to .

" Micheal " Elliot croaked, wiping his eyes. He sat up on the bed. The nurses asked if you wanted to see your mum and Carrie. Elliot looked at Christian and back at Micheal he nodded yes he would like to see his mum it didn't scare him like he would have thought it's too soon I'm not ready to let her go yet while Christian held Elliot .

PATRICK WAS GETTING dressed when Ellie came upstairs and stood at the door he looked over at her is something wrong he thought " Ellie what is it " " Elliot his mum " Oh god he thought what's happened he got out his phone to call Bailey who was in tears over the phone Elliot's Mum had taken another seizure which resulted a bleed on the brain .

ELLIE CAME OVER TO Patrick and they hugged poor Elliot. He thought why did this have to happen so quickly he thought he would get the next train back to Edinburgh soon ." This is not good Ellie, he will be heartbroken " .Ellie wrapped her arms round Patrick touching his face he shouldn't worry Christian is with Elliot .

CARRIE AND ELLIOT STOOD outside their mum's room holding hands she looked over at him he had to be brave she thought " Elliot " He looked round at Carrie red eyed Carrie lay her arm round his shoulders and squeezed. " Be brave ok " Elliot nodded shes right he has to be brave Carrie opened the door they went inside Carrie went over to her mum . The nurses did a good job in making her look nice Elliot stood at the door watching Carrie with their mum she looked round at Elliot holding her hand out to come to him .

Elliots legs couldn't move at first he took a step forward and took Carrie's hand she squeezed his she didn't look too bad Elliot thought Elliot lay his head on Carrie shoulder " it's going to be ok Elliot " He nodded . The door-chapped Micheal appeared going over to Carrie and Elliot all three embraced.

PATRICK HAD CALLED Darian with the news about Elliot's mom's passing. He was saddened to hear the news that he will order flowers for them he thought and thanked Patrick for calling him about the passing of Elliot's mum .

MICHEAL LET PATRICK and Bailey in when they arrived at the house Carrie was on the phone to some relatives to let them know while Patrick and Bailey went upstairs to see Elliot he was laying on his bed when they both went in and went over to him he started crying Patrick and Bailey comforted him giving him words of comfort ." It's not fair guys I wasn't ready to say goodbye " Bailey looked at Patrick them Elliot " Elliot I know it's not the right time to say but your mum was gone a long time ago " Patrick said Bailey nodded while Patrick wiped Elliot's tears he and Bailey had to be brave and strong for Elliot at this time of need .

“ I guess you're right “ “ Where did Christian go “ Bailey asked his phone beeped off a text which was from Senora “ He had some things to do he’s been amazing can you guys stay with me tonight “ “ Course we can “ Bailey and Patrick look at each other and nodded he needs us right now Patrick thought .We did stay over most times in the past .

After rehearsals Christian sent a text to Elliot saying he was thinking about him and he would be over later “ it’s so sad about Elliot’s mum “ Helene said, sliding her arm through Christians he looked at her then he kept thinking maybe he shouldn’t have left him at this vulnerable time “ “ it is “ .

“ I LIKE HIM “ HELENE says Christian smiles and nods that Is a nice thing to say about Elliot Helene slides her arm round Christians waist leaning into him “ I have a feeling you like him to “ .Christian smiles and nods “ I thought so I think he might be a keeper yes “ .I think so Christian thought they were getting along and other things were progressing to .

“ I think so Helene “.

Chapter 11

Brandon thought maybe Bailey should have taken time off for Elliot when he came into work the day after he had said if he hadn't he would have been driven crazy besides Senora was doing night shift tonight that was another factor to he would be on his own the club was only open till 12 tonight . " A beer , glass Chardonnay and a water " Bailey giving Brandon a table order and giving him empty glasses " Bailey " " What " Bailey looked up at Brandon then his beeper went for one the rooms he sighed and looked at it for the Order .

" Why did you agree to work tonight " " Because I wanted to keep busy " Brandon shook his head Olly one the other barmen made up the room drinks for. Bailey and he went to take it to the room, chapping the door letting them know their order was there .Maybe I should have given my shift up tonight. I'm not in the right headspace for it, Bailey thought .

Darian came out of his office going into the bar area busy with a steady stream of members which was good. He said hello to a few people and chatted for a few minutes. Bailey was taking orders he noticed he looked tired he thought . " Bailey shows Elliot and Carrie " Bailey looked at Darian while he cleaned the table " Holding up there devastated " " Understandable you ok " Bailey shook his head then went over to the bar Malcolm came out to the bar spoke to Bailey for a few minutes then came over to Darian . " He looks tired "

Malcolm said Darian nodded " Apparently he and Patrick had stayed over at Elliot's " .

Darian lay his arm round Malcolm's waist he looked at Darian and smiled Darian kissed his cheek " We should send flowers " That would be nice Malcolm thought then they both went to sit up at the vip area Sara one the staff came over with Darians whiskey and a beer for Malcolm they know me so well Darian thought they clinked glasses ." Love you " Darian said, reaching over to Malcolm " love you to " .

Later on while everything is winding down people are going home Darian and Malcolm went home and couple off the staff left Brandon would close up with Bailey everything was checked Bailey was in the store room tidying up and putting stuff away before he and Brandon left . Brandon appeared with a couple boxes he looked round at Bailey. He really needed to talk to him about stuff .Should I tonight or wait till after Elliots mum's funeral.

" Bailey " " Yea just about finished " He looked up at Brandon standing beside him " What " " Senora she texted me Bailey why you looking at Gay porn " Bailey stood up why the fuck is Senora texting him about there personal stuff he thought " None your business anyways we sorted that " " Bullshit " .Brandon thought he has been acting weird for a while now there is definitely something going on with him .

Bailey got cross he looked at Brandon he should stay out there business " Bailey if there's something troubling you talk to me " Bailey shook his head he went to move Brandon grabbed his arm Bailey looked down and Back up at Brandon . " Fucking let go my arm Brandon " " Language " Bailey snorted shook his head and went to move again but Brandon still held his arm .

" Why the hell you texting Senora anyway you wanna fuck her to " Brandon then pushed Bailey against the wall he was shocked by Brandon's reaction " No I don't Bailey " Bailey snorted " Let me go

Brandon " .im gonna punch him Bailey thought Brandon staring at him.

Brandon lunged at Bailey kissing Bailey he tried to push Brandon away Brandon had a hold on him " Try that again or I'll knock you out " Brandon kissed Bailey again this time Bailey didn't resist Brandon turned him round against the wall leaning into him sniffing his neck . " Brandon don't " Bailey turned his head Brandon looked at him " i'm not gonna do anything " .

Bailey turned round to face Brandon again he had a hard on fuck no way he thought as he tried to adjust himself Brandon looked down he smirked noticed by Bailey. " Rory and I are thinking about a threesome " Brandon looked up at Bailey open mouthed Brandon touched his mouth Bailey's breath hitched . Bailey looked away Brandon touched his face Bailey closed his eyes .Fuck sake he thought why did I go and have a hard on .

BRANDON UNBUCKLED BAILEYS jeans Bailey grabbed his hand they looked at each other " No " Bailey said Brandon went to kiss Bailey again he stopped him " I'm gonna punch you out " Brandon huffed carrying on with unzipping Baileys jeans .Brandon went to kiss Baileys neck he moaned sliding his hand inside his boxers ." You need to learn and control your language. " Brandon stroked Bailey's cock he closed his eyes, moaning ." Brandon fuck " Brandon looked at Bailey again they kissed tongues then Brandon pulled down Bailey jeans bending down he looked up at Bailey watching him he licked his inside leg Bailey bit his lip .

Brandon went to stick a finger inside Bailey, took his hand and shook his head. He got up stroking Bailey again Brandon kissed licked Bailey chin " Brandon stop i'll scream " " Shhh feel " Brandon carried on stroking Bailey he was close Bailey thought chewing his lip bloody hell he thought I can't believe this is happening. I should stop him but I'm horny and I can't stop it .

" Fuck shit " Bailey held his head on Brandons shoulder when he came they looked at each other Brandon smiling holding his hand up Baileys cum on his hand .Bailey wide eyed looking at Brandon hes not gonna is he Bailey thought that be just gross .Brandon sniggered at Baileys shocked face looks at his hand and at Bailey .

Brandon got a towel cleaning his hand while Bailey pulled his jeans up Brandon looked at him smiling he went nearer to him.Bailey walked backwards onto the wall again Brandon lay his hand on the wall cocking his head . " We need to sort that temper off yours " Bailey huffed he went for Brandon's jeans he grabbed Bailey's hand shaking his head ." We need to get home " .

BRANDON STOPPED THE car at Baileys place he as silent on the way home Brandon looked at Bailey he went to reach his hand out but thought best not to " Bailey " " I'm not gay or bi or pan sexual or what ever else " Bailey opened the car door Brandon stopped him Bailey looked at him " Fucking take your hand off me also I'm not the one you want for your three way " Bailey got out the car Brandon signed he just wished what was going on in Baileys mind he watched him go into the house not looking back .Brandon was the same in denial about his sexuality at the beginning Did Bailey enjoy earlier was he freaked out that's what Brandon wanted to know .

Brandon's phone rang Rory sounding exasperated " Hey baby " " Honey I just can't decide " Brandon sniggered he knows what's coming " I'm on my way home I just dropped Bailey off " Rory sat back on the bed looking at one his dress hanging up " you want a McFlurry " " Oh honey yes please " .Brandon hung up he shook his head a McFlurry always helped to decide he thought thinking of Bailey to Brandon grinning about earlier .

Bailey leaned against the door asshole he thought making him come I'll knock him out next time Bailey thought he went upstairs to change mumbling to himself getting out his phone he looked at it well it's not gonna ring itself is it he thought . Fucking asshole making him come like that while Bailey undressed not his pj bottoms .

Brandon drove along to get to the 24 hour McDonalds to get there McFlurry his phone rang Bailey he connected the call " Bailey " " Sorry for being an ass I well " " it's ok but you do need to curb the language " Bailey looked whatever at his phone my language he thought whatever he won't be touching him again either .Ever again while he sorted himself in the bathroom .

" Bailey " the line went dead he's just hung up on me Brandon thought that they do need to have a proper chat about stuff he could be the one to do it .And Rude much hanging up on him that's not good either. Is he feeling embarrassed about earlier Brandon thought mind you I did surprise him .

Bailey decided to have a quick shower before bed still mumbling to himself he went into the shower letting the water flow over him he shit his eyes vision off Brandon appeared when he wanked him off Bailey was hard again he let the water flow on his back he went to stroke himself imagining it was Brandon again him leaning against the tile pulling faster . Fuck what the hell is wrong with me I'm thinking about another guy he thought Bailey turned to face the wall holding onto the tile his orgasm ripped out off him again bloody hell that was intense holding onto the tile while his orgasm subsided .His head on the tile pull yourself together man and stop thinking stupid things .

BRANDON WENT INTO THE apartment a case in the hallway a couple outfits hanging up he sniggered seriously he thought Rory wasn't going to London until another 3 months for the drag Uk show Rory appeared at the bedroom door smiling at Brandon he went over to Rory they kissed he handed Rory's McFlurry to him they went into the bedroom where more outfits were ." Rorry seriously can't you just take all of them " He looked at Rory as he started to eat his McFlurry he looked up at Brandon .I wish I could Rory thought but I love all the outfits I just can't decide which ones to take with me .

". Could but that means a lot of luggage honey I suppose I could pick out favourites what do you think "" it's your decision " I suppose he's right but Rory wanted to make a good impression ' Bailey Ok" " kinda yea he's just upset for Elliot it's just so sad ": It is so sad regarding Elliot Rory thought while eating his McFlurry .

" I know I would hate to have a disease that cripples you like that " A dollop of ice cream fell onto Rory's knee Brandon moved to him he bent down to lick it off he looked at Rory he touched Rory's knee that was hot Rory thought he grinned and reached over to kiss Brandon . " If you're not too tired ," Rory asked, Brandon shook his head ." I'm not tired baby " Rory wrapped his arms round Brandon's shoulders he cocked his head they kissed then Brandon lifted up Rory's t-shirt kissed his neck and lifted up his own shirt taking it off

.

Rory lay down on the bed Brandon hoovered over him he went to pull down Rory's tracksuit bottoms " The lube " Brandon nodded he kissed Rory and got up going into the drawer for the lube and condoms he went back over to Rory . Rory watched him biting his lip that's hot Brandon thought .Touching Rory's lip Rory licking his finger god he was hard Brandon thought.

Rory straddled Brandon he reached up to him they kissed feeling each other Rorry licked Brandon's nipple he tugged at his nipple ring Brandon hissed Rory licked round Brandon's nipples .They both took turns to give each other blow jobs .

AFTER THEIR MAKE OUT session Rory falling asleep Brandon looked up at the ceiling and over at Rory's outfits he smiled his phone pinged of a text he lifted up his phone to see who it was . Bailey opened the text and he looked round at Rory still sleeping and then checked the text from Bailey .

Bailey " To wired to sleep what the fuck you done to me 😖� "
Brandon sniggered opps he thought shaking his head .

Brandon " Go to sleep 😴 talk soon ok � " .

Go to sleep he says fuck you Bailey thought typing out another text .

" Bailey " Fuck you 😖� " .

Brandon " Language � " .

Bailey sniggers, who does he think is a bloody Dom that can tell me to mind my language Just you wait I will get you back Brandon Bailey thought tutting trying to get comfortable in bed his mind racing with thoughts .About Brandon the way he was acting around Bailey all Dom like is he like that with Rory to .

WHAT THE HELL IS THE rustling moving furniture? Senora thought she was in a deep sleep. She went straight to bed after her night shift. She sat up and checked the time after 12 she decided to go inspect Bailey in the spare room which they would be using for the baby . He had put down old sheets to do the painting. " Bailey " He looked round at Senora looking sleepy. He went over to her and kissed her cheek .

: What are you doing " " well i thought i'd make a start Patrick is picking me up soon go get that colour paint you want " .Oh Wow Senora thought I didn't even have to ask about that .

Senora snorted that he had a brain transplant or something. She thought Bailey went over to the paint pallet picking one up " is this the colour " He asked a neutral colour fuschia " Yes something like that " .Bailey hummed looks around the room Yea that could work he thought .

Bailey wrapped his arms round Senoras waist she looked up at him " Still tired " " A little i'm gonna go back to bed for an hour " Bailey raised his eyebrows Senora sniggers Shaking her head not remotely interested in that at the moment Senora thought .

" Cool " A car horn beeps. Bailey looked out the window of Patrick's arrival with Elliot. Good, he thought he probably needed out for a bit .And maybe he could talk to the guys about his feelings lately but he wouldn't say anything about what happened with Brandon .They would just freak at him maybe try and subtly say something in conversation .

THE THREE OF THEM WALKED along the aisle checking the paint pots Elliot was kinda quiet Baileys phone beeped off a text he ignored it noticed by Patrick. " How's the funeral arrangements? " Patrick asked while Bailey checked his phone for a text from Brandon . " We are gonna sort that tomorrow a cremation Bailey is this the colour " .Patrick asked looking round at him .

Bailey looked kinda he thought one of the staff came over if they needed help " Yea looking for this colour " Bailey said the shop staff nodded going over the paint " it's for the baby's room were going for neutral " Shevnodded her head and smiled " i think everyone goes for neutral these days here is this it " .

She pointed to one of the paint pots. Yes, Bailey thought that's what we want Christian texted Elliot asking if he was ok and he would see him later Patrick lay his arm round Elliot's shoulder " Christian ok " " uh huh see him later " .Elliot looks over at Patrick he is such a good mate .Always making sure how we are which is appreciated .

" Good, do you think he's being weird? " Patrick asked Elliot about Bailey. They looked over at him, sorting the paint " No why " " Dunno just thought he wasn't himself. " Elliot snorted Baileys Bailey. It's probably because of the baby he thought .He does know if he needs to talk he will come to the both of them if needing advice .

" All sorted and got a discount to " Bailey said great Patrick thought his phone beeped Ellie texting he quickly texted her back " Going well with Ellie " Patrick looked up smiling " Good so far " .Bailey patted him on the back he was happy for his friend Ellie seemed Nice he thought .And they looked good together to he needs someone in his life Bailey thought and she seems a nice person .

After they went for Lunch and went back to the house Senora was impressed Bailey had managed to get the paint that they needed Eliot got dropped off back home to help Carrie sort out Funeral stuff . " Since Patrick's here you can start the decorating " Is she serious Bailey thought looking at Patrick and back at Senora she giggled Bailey huffed not funny he thought . Those two are unbelievable. Patrick thought " We can make a start on it next week I'll help " Patrick suggested a good idea Bailey thought . And it was kind of him to offer to help with the decorating .

ELLIOT LOOKED THROUGH some photos to scan for the order of service. He couldn't decide on which ones he and Carrie wanted a good one for the front and back and they had thought a slide off pictures on the tv at the crematorium would be good too . The date was still to be decided and they had called up a couple places regarding the tea for after some relatives friends had got in touch regarding their mum the phone never stopped even the neighbours had come in when they heard the news .

The bedroom door chapped Elliot looked up at Christian coming back inside sitting next to him on the bed they kissed he looked tired Elliot thought when he stared at him " I'm checking out some photos for the order of service " Elliot looked at Christian he nodded " Are you ok " Elliot asked placing his hand on Christian knee " Just a little tired with rehearsals and the kids I can handle " .

" Dont be doing to much " Christian did a salute Elliot nudged him the door chapped again Carrie this time " Cuppa Christian I've also made some sandwiches " " Thanks but I've already eaten cuppa would be good " Carrie looked over at Elliot looking through the photos they are yet to decide.Then left to make them tea .

" Any decision yet " Elliot nodded his head. Maybe they should decide together. Carrie left Elliot and noticed an overnight bag Christian brought. " I asked Carrie if it's ok to stay overnight. " " You don't have to. " Christian laid his arm round Elliot and kissed his nose. " I want to." Elliot laid his head on Christians shoulder. Why is he so calming? I like it, Elliot thought . And it would be great if he can stay overnight with him. I like it when he does .

MICHEAL WAS ON THE phone when Carrie came back down she put the kettle on and stretched her back Micheal came over rubbing her back she looked up at him he's been amazing all through this she thought " what do you think of my suggestion " " Go for it he will need to know right " Carrie nodded. She still kept in touch with her father who is now living in Dubai and working there with his fiancé Miriam Elliot but didn't keep in touch with his father . He couldn't get over him leaving during the time of her diagnosis of Huntington's disease they had separated. First Gerry did try and visit as best he could but his working away was the main factor .

" Elliot has to know I've contacted him " " Contacted who " Elliot overheard their conversation looking between Carrie and Micheal Christian stood back he wasn't getting involved " Elliot obviously dad will have to be informed I was going to run it by you first " Elliot huffed his dad didn't care he didn't even try with him " Did he care before no so on your head Carrie I don't care if he comes or not " .

" Let's not fight about this Elliot it was only a suggestion " " Exactly " Carrie went into the lounge in tears Micheal sighed following her inside a Christian went over to Elliot taking his arm leading him upstairs he held onto a Christian crying him rubbing his back . " I didn't mean to be mean " " I know it's ok everyone is emotional right now babe c'mon dry this tears now " .

Christian wiped Elliot's face. He was so cool he leaned on his shoulder " You are tired lie down and have a sleep ok " Elliot nodded he was tired Christian got up and brought the blanket over for Elliot. " Hold me for a little while " Christian got on the bed wrapping his arms round Elliot until he fell asleep which he needed he had been restless most of the night .

WHY IS IT SO BRIGHT? Elliot thought, opening his eyes to Leyton , staring at him a bright glow, a very bright glow all around him. Leyton smiled sitting down on the floor next to him Elliot looked round at Christian asleep beside him . " Don't worry he won't wake your dreaming Elliot " " Mum " .

" Don't worry she's fine a little confused but fine " Leyton touched the rings on Elliot's chain Elliot looked down and back up at Leyton " I've earned my stripes Elliot " What did he mean Elliot thought earning his stripes Leyton stood up " I have upgraded " His wings sprout out oh wow Elliot thought and the glow from them very bright to Leyton smiled then the wings disappeared amazing Elliot thought .

He bent down to Elliot " Yes yes I know " He spoke up to the ceiling who is he talking to Elliot thought " Elliot it's going to be ok be got to go some poor soul is dying " " But " .Elliot sat up its to soon I want to chat to Leyton more can't he stay longer .

" Listen, you love him. " Leyton pointed to Christian Elliot and soon he thought Elliot smiled. " Leyton " He looked round he was gone and Elliot woke up looking round at Christian Elliot smiled . Elliot reached over to Christian laying his arm over his stomach Christian lay his arm round Elliot's shoulder . Elliot thought will Leyton come back he thought " Elliot " " Mmm" he looked up Christian opened his eyes at Elliot looking at him " Ok " Christian asked Elliot nodded Christian kissed Elliot's head and Elliot reached for his phone it was still early only after 7 the kids would be getting up soon Carrie let them stay at home for a couple days because of his mum which was the right thing to do .

Eliot looked down at Christians hard and he smiled up at him he smirked cocking his head Elliot kissed him " Will lock the door " Elliot jumped up going over to the door locking it he looked over at Christian arms behind his head smiling looking delicious Elliot thought .Elliot grinned licking his lips well we can't let that go to waste can we Elliot thought .

Elliot straddled Christian bending down to kiss him sliding his hand down to his length " Elliot " " Shh let me " Elliot lifted up the covers and went down Christian giggled letting Elliot do his thing Christian shutting his eyes his hand over his mouth to stifle his moans .Mmm that's good Christian thought the covers bobbing up and down .

" Jack let uncle Elliot sleep ok honey " Jack was about to knock open Elliot's door. It was locked. Why's that? He thought " Mum uncle Elliot's door is locked " Carrie guided Jack away from the door she heard giggling from his bedroom. Oh she thought, are they having alone time? Carrie sniggered into herself when she got into the kitchen Micheal looked up while he sorted the kids cereal

. Carrie was a bit giggly to herself. Micheal thought "What's going on?".

" Elliot is still sleeping " Micheal asked Carrie " Uh huh " Micheal scrunched his nose as Carrie sorted her breakfast. Oh Micheal thought they were having intimate time he didn't ask anymore .Just as long they are not loud and being responsible.

LATER ELLIOT HUGGED Carrie apologising on his outburst about his dad " it's ok all forgotten about " Carrie touched Elliots face she looked round at Christian eating his breakfast Molly drawing at the table Elliot looked back at his sister . " He has been so patient with me " Carrie did wonder if they had been intimate yet " He's a keeper " Carrie said going into the kitchen Elliot following her going over to Molly he thought yes he is a keeper alright .

" What's that Molly? " Elliot asked, touching Christian arm . He looked up at him.and smiled. " It's for Nana. " Molly held up a bit of paper, drawing a sunflower with love for Nana on the bottom . That's so lovely he thought he felt touched " That's lovely Molly isn't it Christian " .

" Yes it is " Molly giggled then got up into the lounge over to her dad to show him her picture " The funeral director called yesterday we go see them tomorrow " Carrie said Elliot nodded he reached her hand out for Elliot to take " We have things to discuss about that Elliot " Elliot nodded it's hard he wasn't ready yet.to say goodbye " i know i'll come with you ".

Carrie rubbed her head with her 7 months pregnancy. It's getting hard now. She was feeling a little stressed and the midwife had said not to overdo things or her blood pressure would go up . " You ok sis " " Just tired this one was active last night " rubbing her stomach.

Chapter 12

The day off the funeral arrived Elliot sat in his room with his suite on looking down at the rings twiddling with them with his fingers he talks to Carrie about the coffin he didn't want to be one off the people to bring his mum into the crematorium one his cousins would take his place so that he could be with Carrie while Micheal was one with others . He heard car doors shutting, shutting the arrival of people and family . " Not yet Leyton, let me have you here just for today " Elliot said, talking to himself he didn't have the courage to take off the chain yet he needed Leyton near just for today then he would put them in the box for safe keeping .

Christian had come upstairs to see Elliot he heard him talking to himself before he went into his room something about the rings " Elliot " he looked up at Christian standing at the door his hands in his pockets Elliot held out his hand for Christian to come to him . Christian sat beside Elliot holding his hand " Your Aunty Mags arrived " Elliot nodded he lay his head on Christian shoulder he rubbed Elliot's back giving him reassuring words .

BAILEY LOOKED AT PATRICK when they came upstairs to see Elliot and saw him and Christian sitting on the bed. They both went inside, going over to them. All four of them hugged .This is nice, Elliot thought I needed their strength today .My favourite person and my best friends all said they love yous to each other .

Carrie held Michaels hand when the hearse arrived. The flowers were beautiful. They had wanted sunflowers on the coffin with the kids cards beside the coffin which was a nice touch. Everyone thought Carrie and Micheal would talk to the kids if they had wanted to go to Nana's funeral, which they did . Her dad had called saying he would be there he would see her at the service Elliot looked at Christian he squeezed Elliot's hand for reassurance he smiled at him .

" I'll go with Patrick " Christian said Carrie looked round at Christian overhearing what he said " Christian come with us your practically family now " Christian was surprised to hear that Elliot nodded as he had planned to go in the car with Patrick and Ellie Bailey and Senora would go in there . " You want me to, " Christian asked Elliot. He nodded and took his hand. " I'd like that.".

IT WAS A GOOD TURN out the hospice nurses came more family members and friends Carrie was surprised at the amount of people that turned up even Darian , Malcolm and Cameron came to which she thought was nice off the, to do so . Carrie spotted her dad when he arrived on his own she went to greet him Elliot didn't Christian look at Carrie with her dad talking in his car . " Let's go inside Christian " Elliot said he didn't want to talk to his dad he thought best not to say anything about it just yet .

Carrie came to sit beside Elliot while the others waited outside to bring his mum in " He is going to wait at the back " Carrie whispered to Elliot about their dad Elliot looked round at his dad sitting at the back Gerry nodded Elliot looked at Christian he squeezed Elliot's hand again .Letting Elliot know it's going to be ok Elliot nodded and gave a faint smile .I will talk to him but not yet Elliot thought I need to get through today first .

Their mum liked the tune ave Maria which was to be played for her coming in and the celebrant said a few words about their mum and her little quirks, her work life and her favourite things to do whenever she could until her illness .When Carrie and Elliot were born and there favourite things to do together when mum was able to .

DARIAN HELD CAMERON'S and Malcolm's hand . They looked at each other, a lovely service they thought the music was nice even the committed all music was lovely to and the tv with the family photos was a nice touch also .So sad Darian thought he couldn't imagine life without his two loves in his life or them to.

During the service Leyton appeared again next to his mums coffin laying his hand on her coffin Elliot touched the rings noticed by Christian he reached for Elliot's hand he looked round at Christian nodded squeezed Christian hand .He looked over at his mums coffin again she appeared Elliots breath hitched she smiled looked over at Leyton his mum looked different as if she was well again .Leyton reached out his hand to Morag he nodded and they walked off towards the window Elliot had a sense of peace it was as if his mum was saying im ok now I'm at peace now .

Elliot looked round at Carrie wiping her eyes. He took her hand and she smiled and nodded. He's collecting souls now Elliot thought he's taking her to heaven now that's what his upgrade is . Carrie squeezed Elliots hand reassurance she was ok. He nodded. I'm happy that he is doing this for our mum taking her to heaven .

" Goodbye " Leyton whispered in Elliots ear then was gone was that him gone for good now Elliot thought when he came to him the other day telling him he had upgraded now Elliot nodded his understanding Christian looked round at Elliot .he took his hand again Elliot looked at him nodded he was ok Christian good he thought .It's been a day for everyone Elliot was glad he had Christian in his life and helping him through his grief as well as Bailey and Patrick .

After at the tea Christian let Elliot talk to his dad in private Elliot thought well i guess i've got to talk to him sometime Christian sat beside Carrie , Micheal with Bailey Senora and Patrick Christian looked over at Elliot and Jerry talking outside. " Christian " Carrie said he looked round at her " Don't worry " " I know ".

Brandon went over to the buffet table Bailey watched him then got up to get his and Senoras food he hasn't spoken to Brandon since that night Brandon looked round at Bailey while he played his food "Lovely send off ": U huh ". Jeez, does he have to be so ignorant? Brandon thought at least to talk to me .Following Bailey round the table I guess he was pissed at me Brandon thought .

" Bailey we have to " Bailey looked at Brandon then looked over at Senora she was talking to Patrick, and Darian " We don't Brandon cant you leave me alone ". I have nothing to say to him. I'm not going there again, Bailey thought .Besides he has Rory why would he want me .

Brandon sighed, picked up a couple more sandwiches and sausage rolls and sticks one in his mouth " i cant " Bailey goes back over to Senora Brandon following behind . Sitting beside Darian " You want soup " Bailey asked Senora she shook her head " ok " Bailey asked her " You ok " She asked he shrugged his shoulders Senora touched his face he leaned in kissing her hand .It's been a day she thought he is upset for Elliot which is understandable .

" THE SERVICE YOU AND Carrie did a good job " Gerry said while they stood out on the patio looking out to the view " Yes mum would have been proud " Gerry nodded he looked at the people who had come to Morag's funeral and couldn't believe the turn out she had . " Miriam and I might be moving to Spain. I have an offer of a new job there "" That's great dad " .

" It would be great if you could come over. " Gerry looked over at Christian and wondered if he would be a permanent fixture. He didn't have a problem with Elliot's sexuality; he just wanted him to be happy. " Christian is he. " " We are taking things slow, dad . I like him a lot." Elliot looks over at Christian and back at his dad .

" Right, is he good to you? " Elliot looked over at Christian again and he smiled " Yes, he's been amazing, we're gonna go away in a few days. We just need time to be together and what with mum and " Understandable son " . Carrie came out to see if they were ok and if they were hungry to have something. Elliot went over to Christian with Gerry to introduce him proper Christian had got Elliot some sandwiches while they chatted .

Gerry seemed like Christian Elliot looked like his dad, a bit of a down to earth person telling them about his job and place in Spain, what he does there and that Elliot and Christian should come over to visit sometime in the future .

After they got home Elliot flopped onto his bed Christian stood watching him Elliot looked up " I'm so tired " Christian sat beside him on the bed taking his hand " You should get changed and go to bed " Elliot sat up scooting closer to Christian " I'm not that tired " " Elliot " Elliot pouted Christian sniggered shaking his head he took off his tie and jacket Christian got up to check his phone .Elliot watching him type away whoever had texted him .

" You can go you know " Elliot said Christian looked at him Elliot looked up at Christian while he undressed into his shorts and t shirt " I'd rather be with you right now " Elliot got under the covers Christian sat beside him again " Christian I'm fine besides you have to catch up on stuff right " Christian nodded he stood up and took his shoes off and lay beside Elliot laying his arm over Elliot leaning on his shoulder .

" What do you think of the log cabin then " " I love to go " Elliot looking at Christian smiling at him " Ok I can sort that' Elliot huffed looking up at Christian again ``.I can pay my half you know " .Christian hummed kissing Elliot's head shutting his eyes snuggling into Christian .

MICHEAL WAS MAKING tea when Christian appeared Carrie had gone to bed she was exhausted the kids went to Michael's parents overnight " Elliot's asleep " " Good cuppa " Christian sat his overnight bag on the table while Micheal made his tea " " Carries went to bed too " " I'm going to take Elliot away for a few days " .

" Great idea Christian it'll do him good to get away for a few days. "" We just need to spend some time together .Christian explains that yes it is a good idea for them to get away for a few days to recharge .

MICHEAL IS GETTING changed while Carrie sat up in bed watching him change " i think now decided on a name " Micheal looked round at Carrie he sat beside her on the bed . " You have " " Morag after mum, " Micheal nodded. Why not? He thought it's perfect. Micheal took her hand. " I like it, why not? " .

" Did Christian get away ok " " He did i just checked Elliot he is sleeping " Good Carrie thought he needs it especially having a busy week and it would do Elliot good to go away with Christian a few days too .She had also thought the same maybe when after the baby is born they could have a few days away when she gets a bit older to .

" I need something. I'm gonna go get a drink. "" You, " Carrie smiled, cocking her head. Micheal snorted, reaching over to kiss Carrie, " I'll be quick."

Micheal ran downstairs, went into the fridge and got a bottle of water to take upstairs. He sniggered into himself pregnancy hormones he thought then ran back upstairs. Carrie stared at him and smiled " You better lock the door " She said Which Micheal did going over to Carrie he bent down to kiss her she noticed his bulge in his shorts he looked down and looked at Carrie again . " My Mr Matthews you are ready " They both giggled. Micheal sat beside Carrie she reached up to kiss him he touched her stomach the baby kicked they looked at each other again .

Elliot woke up no Christian missed him. He sat up rubbing his eyes and checked his phone. It was after 7 wow he thought he had slept that long. He must have needed a text from Christian pouty face he wasn't with . He did have work to do which was fine he would see him soon his phone beeped a text from his dad to arrange to meet up for lunch which was fine .

Chapter 13

Wow amazing Elliot thought when they went into the lodge cabin they had booked at Loch lomond the view was amazing to it had all the mod cons even a hot tub and the little patio was cute all the other Log cabins were dotted around the area too. Christian came in behind him while Elliot looked around .The fridge freezer was stacked with milk drinks, beers , wine and an amazing breakfast pack. Even packed with dinner essentials if I wanted to use them even if they eat out at any time .

There was a welcome pack on the table. There was a town nearby which was good to get food or any other essentials Christian came behind Elliot wrapped his arms around his waist. Elliot leaned into him.." Happy " "Mmm thank you " Christian kissed Elliots cheek " Lets get unpacked " Christian lifted up his case Elliot watched him go smiling he went to touch the rings forgetting that he had taken them off and kept them in a safe place as well as Leytons shirt Elliot nodded to himself picking up his duffel going into not the bedroom.Thinking I have done the right thing taking off the necklace and time to move on proper .

Christian unpacking he looked up smiled at Elliot " Hot tub later " Christian asked sounds like a good plan Elliot thought " mmm sounds good " After they unpacked Elliot made them both coffees while they sat out on the patio admiring the view the weather was now warming up for the month off May and the weathermen predicted it to be a hot summer . Elliot looked over at Christian on his phone, most probably looking at where they could visit. He looked up at Elliot " There is a restaurant a mile away we could check that out " .

ELLIOT REACHED OVER to Christian reaching out his hand " That would be great " Elliot's phone pinged of an alert her sighed getting up Christian looked up at him " Pill time " Christian took Elliot's hand he looked down at him " Hopefully soon you won't have to take them anymore " Elliot nodded he hated taking the anti depressants but since the attack the nightmares he had been having the doctor had preceded them on a temporary basis . Even Malcolm took them for a while and got weaned off them until he didn't need to take them anymore ." I know Elliot went well into the bedroom and brought out the pills he had to take. He would make arrangements to book his doctor appointment when he gets back home.

BAILEY KISSED SENORA pinched her nose she batted him away when they decided to have there night out at the club to have some couple time she had her orange juice Bailey a beer Brandon appeared to get some drinks orders he's doing that on purpose he though he still ignored Brandon's please to talk it had been a couple days since the funeral now .Bailey excused himself to go to the toilet " Brandon " Senora said he looked up at her while filing the tray " i was worrying over nothing we talked it over " .Senora smiled Brandon nodded was it over nothing Brandon thought cause Bailey is still being weird he thought .

" GOOD GLAD YOU GUYS are ok " Bullshit he thought something had to be done " Rory not here tonight " Bailey came back Brandon went to take the drinks to the customers Bailey touched Senoras leg reaching over to kiss her Brandon noticed he's showing off he thought . Brandon went back over to the bar and served a couple people Senora went to the toilet Brandon came over to Bailey " Another drink " Bailey looked up at Brandon Julia came over to Bailey there room was ready giving him the keys .Bailey grinning What is he grinning for Brandon thought shaking his head .

Brandon was seething Bailey looked at him again he stood up bending over the bar " I am gonna fuck her good till she screams " Brandon couldnt believe he had just said that Bailey walked away Senora appeared he lay his arm round her shoulder leading to.the back rooms .Asshole Brandon thought he is just showing off now .

" Brandon are you ok? " Julia asked. He looked at her. He nodded and Carried on. I'll get him back for that. Brandon thought, shaking his head, carrying on mixing the drinks .Julia went back to what she was doing if Brandon wanted to talk. He knows what to do .He seemed peeved about something Julia thought I should ask him about later .

IT'S A BEAUTIFUL VIEW of the water Elliot thought when they decided to go into the local town for dinner Christian looked at him looking out to the water Eliot looked back at Christian watching him then the waitress came over to take their order .Is he checking me out again Elliot thought smiling back at Christian while they look over the menu .He is giving me the sexy vibes Christian thought grinning into himself reading over the menu .

“ I'll have the muscles and the chicken salad with that to please " Christian ordering muscles Elliot thought and a salad to " Any starter " " No thanks and can i have the wine menu so i'll have sparkling water to " Elliot stared at Christian while he ordered he was sexy he thought .Biting his lip god I'm Horny Elliot thought shifting in his seat .

Well isn't that sexy Elliot thought staring at him.while he ordered " And for yourself "The waiters asked Elliot " The steak with fries no starter might have a pudding " Elliot looked at Christian when he said it " A beer to " .Christian took Elliot's hand kissing it Elliot blushed .

Elliot reached over to Christian" Do you know that muscles are an aphrodisiac ,: Christian grinned leaning over to Elliot " Yes i do know that " Sneaky Elliot thought grinning The waitress came back with there drinks Elliot sniggered Christian looked at him the waitress was ever so nice they both thought .I think she knows we're on a few days break smiling to herself .

" You've had them before then " Elliot asked with his chin on his hands " love in south africa " Elliot took a sip of his beer he had got a glass for the wine so he also took a couple pictures in the restaurant. And off both of them I also like this place Elliot thought.

Their meals came, they chatted about most things, especially if the loch ness monster was real or not. They both laughed about it Christian gave Elliot a couple of his muscles, not too bad he thought his steak was good to just perfect the way he likes it .Christian told him more about South Africa and some saying phrases he discovered a barbecue is a brain there . Same as Australia they call it a barbie Christian was getting used to some Scottish slang too .

" IM.STUFFED " ELLIOT rubbed his stomach Christian huffed, shaking his head. He didn't finish any more of the muscles as there were a lot of them . " Pudding " Elliot asked Christian if he couldn't eat anymore " We could have a share one " .Elliot asked I'd rather have him for Pudding Elliot thought chewing his lip .

" Ok we can do that " They ordered the sundae for sharing in 2 spoons helping each other with the sundae and giggling in between they were having the best fun and got brain freeze from the sundae they were having .It was good to see Elliot happy Christian thought he didn't want him sad and was happy to hear he and his dad had a good meet up and wanted to meet up when they could in the future .

AFTER DINNER THEY TOOK a walk along the beach taking photos Elliot took a photo of Christian doing one of his ballet poses. It was a great picture especially with the backdrop of the sun going down. There were a few people walking along the shore line with their dogs or just couples taking a stroll while they walked holding hands just perfectly Elliot thought .Looking up at Christian while they walked along hand in hand .

SENORA COLLAPSED ONTO the bed arms splayed she was spent Bailey moved over to her he bent down to kiss her she smiled up at him " You feel good baby " " Mm yes " Bailey lay beside her Senora lay against his shoulder she was all wet and sticky from there sex session she looked up him " You well and truly came loads babe " " mmm " Bailey lifted up the covers Senora was comfy and didn't want to move Bailey kissed her head .Yep still got it making my girlfriend happy I will make her happy whatever she wants .And we can discuss any Kink she wants to do Bailey kisses Senoras head she hummed .

" LET'S GET A VIBRATOR tomorrow I know you Like it " Bailey asked and thought why didn't she have them at home " I know I kept meaning to get a new one and yes we can go to the shop and get one " Senora got a little flutter on her stomach was that the baby just moving now that she was nearly four months they did say she would get them sometime . She rubbed her belly noticed by Bailey he moved down looking up at Senora "I felt a little flutter " Bailey rubbed her belly Senora sniggered looking down at him " Hey you in there it's daddy don't give your mum a hard time now " Senora sniggered. Bailey kissed her stomach Bailey moved back up gave Senora a kiss .

" Bailey Wilson " Senora sniggered, they both looked down. Bailey was hard again. Now he thought looking up at Senora they both giggled they kissed " Home " Bailey asked Senora nodded yes definitely home feeling her belly noticed by Bailey he smiled taking her hand and kissed it .

BRANDON WAS COMING through the back to the rooms with champagne and glasses for one the rooms when Senora and Bailey arms round her came round the corner giggling they stopped when they saw Brandon he smirked they definitely looked like they had a good time he thought lucky them . " Goodnight Brandon " Senora said as he looked round at them he nodded then disappeared round the corner ." I love you " " Love you to " .Bailey bends to kiss Senora gosh he is so amazing Senora thought and I'm loving it .

ELLIOT AND CHRISTIAN fell through the door off the log cabin kissing Christian moved Elliot against the door kissing his jaw his ear Elliot was breathless pulling at Christian jeans lifting up his shirt slightly they looked at each other Christian touching Elliot's face . " Are you sure " " More than sure " Christian took Elliot's hand leading him to the bedroom they helped each other with their shirts Elliot looked at Christian perfection he thought his defined abs not too skinny for a ballet dancer he thought . Elliot traced his hand along Christian stomach and bent down to kiss it while he unbuttoned his jeans sliding his hand inside he looked up at Christian watching him while Elliot stroked up and down his shaft Christian closed his eyes Elliot moved down further sliding down Christian jeans and boxers while still wanking Christian off .

ELIOT LICKED THE INSIDE of Christians leg and went to take Christian in his mouth moving up and down his shaft Christian holding onto Elliot's head Elliot moved back up they kissed again Christian moved over to his case and brought out the condoms and lube he looked over at Elliot naked as he stood at the fire waiting for him .The light from the fire illuminating Elliot, Elliot bit his lip god he is so sexy right now Elliot thought .

CHRISTIAN WRAPPED HIS arms round Elliot's shoulders they kissed they moved closer together Elliot kissed licked Christian ear " Carpet or bed " Christian asked Elliot giggles looking down at the rug it would be a shame to ruin it he thought giggling to himself. " Bed " .Christian grinned and kissed Elliot " Carpet burns wouldn't look good "

CHRISTIAN LEANED OVER Elliot he looked up at him he reached up to kiss Christian them scooted up the bed Christian worked his way down kissing all the way down he started stroking Elliot cock looking up at Elliot open mouthed he bent down taking him in his mouth licking sucking up and down his shaft . Christian went to stick a finger inside Elliot. He clenched Christian looked up at him and scooted up to him .Shit did I hurt him? He thought of Elliot's face .

" What is it? "" I'm ok , sorry " Christian kissed him. They bumped heads. Elliot nodded. He sat up and bent over for the lube and Condoms, handing them to Christian. Just a slight glitch he thought they stared at each other Elliot nodded .

CHRISTIAN SQUIRTED the lube on his finger looking at Elliot he nodded Christian bending down to kiss Elliot he opened his legs for better access Christian stroked him.again with the lube kissing and started to massage his balls that felt good Elliot thought tingles down his back . Then Christian slid his finger inside Elliot moaning it felt good he thought Christian making him.feel good tingles . " Oh " Elliot said Christian looked at him Elliot bit his lip he was feeling good they kissed again .

CHRISTIAN LIFTED ONE of Elliots legs he put on the condom he kissed and licked the inside of Elliots leg he moved nearer to Elliot he guided the tip off his cock at Elliots entrance Christian held onto one off Elliots hands and gently pushed inside him they kissed . Christian wanted to be gentle with Elliot getting into a rhythm " Christian harder " Elliot asked he looked down at him " Are you sure " Elliot nodded Elliot opened his legs wider Christian slid back inside Elliot moving his arms up to Christian shoulders he did a thrust and another .

" Fuck that's good " They got into a a sheen of sweat on Elliot's chest he was close to coming they kissed again tongues Christian did a couple more thrusts he stilled nuzzling into Elliots neck until he came he grunted while Elliot held onto his neck a single tear running down .Oh god did I hurt him Christian thought touching Elliot's face .

Christian looked at him shit is he crying he wiped his tears away " Did i hurt you " " No Christian im happy it was good " Christian took off the condom discarding it in the basket he moved closer to Elliot laying his arm around him . " I'm glad it was you Christian " " Your welcome " Elliot looked at him he giggled .They kissed again then snuggled into each other .I am glad it was Christian Elliot thought smiling himself snuggled into Christian.

A LITTLE WHILE LATER sitting out in the patio snuggled into each other with a blanket over them enjoying the cool night weather " Christian " " mmm " kissing Elliot's ear " I don't feel him anymore " Elliot looked at Christian he did notice he didn't have the rings round his neck anymore " Leyton " Elliot nodded " He said his goodbye at the funeral I didn't know what it meant at first but I do now ".

" I did wonder when you zoned out for a bit and the rings " Elliot looked down at his chest and back up at Christian " He earned his wings he was the one that took her to heaven " Christian touched Elliot's face he leaned into his touch " He must've guided me to you Christian " " Really you think so " Elliot nodded he was at peace now regarding Leyton he knew he wouldn't see him again and maybe it was time to let him go fully and not visit his grave to much . He wouldn't forget Leyton he was his first love and maybe Leyton was right he did love Christian he was falling in love with him that's for sure .

" Yes really " They kissed again Christian wrapped his arms round Elliot his chin on his shoulder " Cold " Christian asked Elliot shook his head he wasn't cold Elliot moved off Christian all in his glory Christian looked at him up and down and looked outside the nest lodge next to them . Elliot went over to the jacuzzi, turned it on, looked round at Christian he went into it Christian got up, went over to the jacuzzi Elliot's arms splayed over the back Christian got into the jacuzzi too .

He went over to Elliot facing him they kissed again Elliot moved Christian round he slid his hand down palming Cock `` Care to christen the jacuzzi " Elliot whispered while moving his hand up and down his shaft Elliot kissed his neck Christisn held onto to Elliot as he carried on wanking him off . " Fuck that's good " They stare while Elliot wanks Christian off Christian came all over Elliot's hand all he thought about at that time the jacuzzi will need cleaned . " You good" " uh huh " all Christian could say coming down from his orgasm .

Elliot giggled damn they didn't bring the towel out with them all they had was the blanket on the ground they both decided to get up quickly cover themselves and ran inside into the bedroom falling onto the bed giggling . They kiss Elliot and move to straddle Christian him holding onto Elliot looking up at him " What is it? " Christian asked Elliot, smiling bending to kiss Christian " Nothing just happy to be here with you " .

" Same " " Good " Elliot bends to kiss Christian chest he looks up at Christian watching him Christian is hard again Elliot grins he reaches over for the lube looking at Christian again and the condoms he rips one open lubes up Christian and puts the condom on him .

Elliot eases himself onto Christian him holding onto Elliot's waist he bends to kiss Christian getting into a rhythm holding onto the bed Christian slides his hand down Elliot's chest he rocks his hips Elliot groans shutting his eyes going with the motions . Christian reaches up, holding onto Elliot kissing his neck. It tingles when they are close to coming Christian lays Elliot down, licking his chest and moves back inside him thrusting .

Elliot swears Christian thrusts again Elliot bites his lip Christian kisses him again chasing each other's tongues Christian feels something warm against him looking down at Elliot's cum coating him " Oh god "All Elliot could say Christian Looking down at him they giggle at Elliot's unexpected release ." Sorry " " Nothing to be Sorry for Love " .

CHRISTIAN KISSED ELLIOTS neck and chin he thrust once more before he came Elliot's arms wrapped around his back they kissed again Christian moved onto his back Elliot moving over leaning his head on Christians shoulder he kissed Elliot's head Elliot hummed . " Happy, " Christian asked Elliot, looking up, smiling " Very happy."

Bailey was amazed at the sizes and different makes of. The vibrators in the Anne summers store Senora giggled at him every time he picked up one and even asked about other things he saw which were but plugs nope not for him he thought he could hear Ellie and Patrick giggling they were over at the underwear section he shook his head . " Can I help you? " one of the store staff asked Senora, looking at Bailey's shocked face. They had been looking at a rampant rabbit, one which Bailey did like .

" YES WE WERE THINKING of this one " Senora said pointing to the purple colour rampant rabbit size the girl smiled " " Good choice it's popular " Senora looked at Bailey he nods the girl takes the box looks round "Anything else "" Still looking ``.They both said in unison looking at each other smiling while the store girl took the purchases over to the till .

" Nice colour this one " Patrick said while they checked out the underwear that Ellie was going to take she also got a small vibrator to which Patrick so loved the boys browsed while Senora and Ellie looked at more stuff " Ellie when you were pregnant with ivy when you start feeling her " Ellie looked round at Her that's so nice off Senora to ask she thought while she picked up the tingle lube " Oh about the three to four month that's when I got the flutters have you got them " .

" YES THE OTHER NIGHT it happened we're finding out the sex next week " " Great . " That's great to hear Ellie wondering if they wanted to find out the sex or a surprise .

Bailey and Patrick got a text from Elliot a picture message off the area they were staying it looked nice they thought they looked at each other and smiled " Our boy looks happy " Bailey said Patrick nodded patted Bailey shoulder " Who does " Senora asked Bailey held out his phone off Elliots picture message he looked happy she thought . Which was good Christian was a lovely person he was good for Elliot.And hoped it would work out for the both of them Elliot needed it after the past few months .

" WE NEED BATTERIES to hunt, " Rory said when they entered the shop. " Sure, " Rory looked round at Brandon. What's up with him, he thought ? Then Rory spotted the underwear grabbing Brandon's arm, leading him to the underwear. " Hey guys " Senora spotting them coming into the shop fuck Bailey thought thats all he needs he thought . " Oh hi honey how are you? "" Good " Rory hugged her. Brandon nodded. They seemed a bit weird with each other. Senora thought maybe it's her baby brain she thought .

" Good you guys " " Good browsing Rory is going to London next week aren't you " Brandon looks round at Rory smiling at him Rory slides his arm round Brandon's waist noticed by Bailey .

Rory nodded he was nervous excited to be going he thought it's what he has wanted for a long time Bailey stared at them while he made the purchase then went over to them . " We're going for lunch if you want to join us, " Senora asked Rory, looking at Brandon. " Thanks but getting reece later another time " .

" Sure that would be great " They left, leaving Brandon and Rory in the shop. Rory lay his arm round Brandons whispered in his ear "What colour " Brandon smiled and shook his head looking at Rory he pointed to the red pair .Rory looking at the underwear section was a good choice he thought ." Even better with you in them babe " Brandon whispered to Rory he blushed Brandon kissed his cheek .

ELLIOT SNIGGERED WHEN he got the picture message from Bailey regarding the rampant rabbit Elliot turned his phone round to show Christian he shook his head while he drove to the next town to do some sightseeing. " That boy has no filter " Elliot said shaking his head " Does that appeal to you " Christian asked he looked round at him yes Elliot had used a Vibrator before and it was enjoyable that time " Elliot placed his hand on Christian knee he took his hand and kissed it " i'm up for any suggestions Mr King " Christian nodded good to know Elliot went to feel him up not now he thought laughing Elliot leaned over to kiss his cheek .Christian sniggers Shaking his head I will end up crashing he thought taking Elliot's hand he looks round at Elliot looking at him " What " " Nothing I just like looking at your face " Christian smiles lifts up Elliot's hand and kisses it again " Good to know " .Grinning while they drove along to their destination listening to Rag n bone tune .

SENORA WAS WORKING nights again Rory had gone to London for a couple days to.meet up with the other drag uk contestants the producers to he was nervous about going and nearly didn't go But Brandon talked him into going he would be fine he had called to let him know he had arrived at the swanky hotel that that network put them up. If Brandon was able he would have put in a couple days' holiday and be a support for Rory but he will be fine he just hoped it would go ok and he won't freak out while away .Brandon did think about putting in for a couple days holidays to go with him but thought it What Rory needs to do for himself .

After work he parked at one of the disused car parks they were in the back of the car Bailey grabbed onto the back seat " Oh Brandon no not there oh " Brandon worked his way back up licking Bailey's neck he closed his eyes ." Did you like that " " Fuck no its " A slap on his bottom Bailey glared at Brandon what the fuck was that for he thought he did it again .I will slap him to Bailey thought trying to dominate me which he won't .Does he do that with Rory fuck why am I thinking that he thought .

Brandon kissing his back and whispered again " You want me to fuck you big rabbit " Bailey turned pushed Brandon down his jeans and Boxers were half down and he was all in his glory . " No go area " Bailey pointed down to his bottom area Brandon sniggered what he was laughing at Bailey thought . " You might like it " " I bet I won't " . Bailey held out his arm on Brandon's chest. What's with him Brandon thought .

Bailey hoovered over Brandon he looked down at his length and grinned " There must be a better way than the car Bailey " He looked up at Brandon this was the only way he thought he shook his head licked his lips Brandon was hard so was he . Bailey started stroking himself Brandon watching lifting up his shirt he bit his lip that was the hottests thing he saw Bailey strokes his cock from root to tip him slowly breathing .Brandon still watching while Bailey wanking himself off biting his lip Holy shit it's hot .

Brandon at that point wanted him he sat up slid his hand down and started pumping Bailey kissing his neck his jaw Bailey arched he was close to coming " Brandon ..i ..no ..fuck " At that he came and flopped down Brandon got the wipes and wiped his hand Bailey watching him Btandon looked at Bailey and thought what are they doing . " What's wrong "Brandon asked he has gone silent on me again " Nothing just thinking ": Fuck that was hot Bailey thought I'm kinda all sticky now blushing looking away .

Bailey pulled up his boxers and jeans Brandon was surprised by this and did the same they got back in the front Brandon driving Bailey home they didn't talk on the way home again " Bailey " Brandon looks round at him " You wanna fuck us both " What a stupid thing to say he thought no he didn't Brandon touched his knee Bailey looked at him shaking his head he got out the car came round to Brandon's side he rolled down the window . " Don't get feeling ok we're just fooling around " And at that Bailey left to go back into the house what the hell did that mean he thought it's not like that yea there just fooling around .Brandon shook his head grinning Bailey what is it about him that I find kinda cute in some way .

ELLIOT AND CHRISTIAN in the log cabin were watching a movie on Netflix curled up on the couch drinking wine. It was an ok movie. Eliot thought him leaning against Christian this was just perfect. He thought after their day off exploring Elliot turned his head and they kissed " You are adorable " Elliot said Christian smiled and kissed him again . " Elliot " "Mmm." Elliot stretches out his legs .

Christian took Elliot's hand he looked round at Christian " Be my boyfriend " Elliot smiled didn't he already ask him that before when one the wham songs played a while ago " "Elliot " " I heard you make it official like " Christian nodded Elliot kissed him a long kiss this time Elliot looked at him " Let's make it official but not official right got now cause the guys " Christian sniggered shaking his head he knew what Elliot meant by the guys because they would be mad at him they f it came out on social media which was totally fine .

" No problem we make it official when we get home " Elliot moved round to face Christian wrapping his arms around his shoulders " it's fate that we meet" " Three times " Christian exclaimed Elliot pinched his nose he was healing him in some way he felt . " Do you think Leyton will be happy? " Christian cocked his head, touching Elliot's face and kissing his nose . " He will " Maybe I shouldn't talk about Leyton so much Elliot thought he looked at Christian " You don't mind me talking about him "" Of course not he was part of your life before and well you haven't really properly healed from it " .

" I feel as if I have though " Christian moved up towards Elliot he sat on his hunches he lifted his t shirt half way up a slight kiss bruise just below his shoulder Christian kissed it " Are you gonna give me another one " Christian sniggered looking up at Elliot smiling " you want another one " Christian holding up his shirt a kiss bruise on his peck by Elliot he looked at him . Elliot traced the bruise with his finger pretty well. He thought Elliot moved off Christian moving along the couch Christian watched Elliot bite his lip .

Christian moved over to him touching Elliot's lip sliding his hand into Elliot's boxers Elliot licked his lips arching up while Christian Stroked him Christian bent down to kiss Elliot pulling his cock harder . " Christian..i " Christian licked kissed his neck and whispered " I know " They looked at each other. Elliot reached his arms up to Christian shoulders , His face flushed and mouth open . " Oh god " Elliot said when he came holding onto Christian they kissed again .A bit quick Elliot thought but that was fine .

"Good , " Christian asked. Elliot smiled, touching Christian face . He nodded Christian got up, went into the bathroom to wash off Elliots cum and went back into the lounge, snuggling back into Elliot on the couch. I should sort myself out to Elliot though but I'm comfy .

Elliot looks up at Christian he smiles holding hands while he lays his head on Christians legs. Elliot thinks we are never gonna be able to keep our hands off each other. They still had a day and half off their stay and he was having the best time so far he was having the best sex he had ever had he thought smiling into himself while they watched the movie .

Chapter 14

Bailey was painting the baby's room he and Senora found out last week for their sonogram appointment. They are having a boy which they both ecstatic about. They have thought about various names for the baby. Senora was out with Melinda for their lunch catch up .While Bailey sorted out the baby's room he had the radio on, singing away to the tunes while painting .

Bailey sniggered into himself and thought of an idea he put the paint brush down and got his phone pulling down his joggers taking a snap and pulled them back up sniggering to himself getting the no to send to .Asshole he thought sending the message with a message attached.

Bailey " You want this you gotta earn it " He hit send to Brandon sniggering into himself see how he likes that he thought then carried on with his painting turning the music on Calvin Harris tune singing away to the tune shaking his head then Thought shit will he get turned on by it sniggering to himself .

Reece ran over to the swings while Brandon sat on the bench his phone pinged off a text a picture message came up from Bailey Brandon looked up smiled " Dad look " Reece shouted Brandon looked up at him on the shoot " I see buddy " Brandon looked at his phone off Bailey's picture message . Well he thought it was nice he looked back up at Reece now over at the swings " Dad push me " Brandon quickly texted Bailey back before he went over to the swing .

Brandon “ Earn it do I “ He hit send then there was a cry he looked up at Reece on the ground holding his knee Brandon ran over to him tears running down his face his knee bleeding “ You didn’t watch me dad “ in between sobs Brandon tutted over dramatic he thought bringing out a tissue to wipe up the little bit off blood . “ There it’s not too bad is it “ “ it’s sore “ Brandon shook his head helping Reece up .

“ Can you walk on it “ Reece did manage to walk on it he looked round at his dad “ Mum is gonna be mad “ Brandon shook his head ruffling his hair no she won’t he thought he opened the car door Reece jumps onto his car seat at the back Brandon gives him another tissue for his knee till they get home . Brandon thought about the picture message he got from Bailey which was very bold of him . Reece wondered why his dad was being a bit weird today which wasn’t normally like him probably missing Rory Reece thought .

BAILEY HUFFED WHEN he got a text back from Brandon smirking he shook his head “ Hello I’m home “ Senora shouted Bailey came to the top the stairs brush in hand Melinda appeared “ Melinda “ “ Bailey “ Senora snorted Bailey came downstairs to rinse out the paint brush and noticed more baby stuff .Jeez how much stuff do we need Bailey though .

Senora brought out a blue sleep suite showing it off to Bailey he nodded his approval his phone pinged of a text he would check it later he thought Senora looked at him . " Probably Patrick or Elliot " He said Senora nodded and Bailey Carried on sorting the paint brushes " I would give the paint a couple hours " He said and went out the back leaving the paint brushes to dry .

Senora made her and Melinda tea while they went through their purchases Bailey went upstairs to take a shower and changed quickly texting Brandon back before he got into the shower .

Bailey " yes definitely earn it like beg 😜😄 " Bailey went into the shower to get rid off the paint smell hopefully the smell from the paint. Will wear off soon .

Beg for it Brandon thought when Bailey replied yeah right he thought sniggering "Daddy what's funny " Reece asked in the back " Nothing buddy just a funny text from.a friend " Reece huffed Brandon looked at him in the mirror he shook his head . " I wish Rory was here " Reece said in a huff. So do I. He thought " He will be back next week. I miss him too " .

" IT'S NOT THAT BAD honey " Marnie Brandon's ex said to him while she put the plaster on she looked up at him Reece huffed " Daddy wasn't watching me " Reece looked at his dad that little shit he thought Brandon ruffles his hair " Can I go and play my game "Reece asked looking between his mum and dad "Go on then " .

REECE GOES UPSTAIRS and looks round at Brandon " Love You dad" " love you to buddy " Reece runs up to his room to play his game Marnie goes over to the kettle puts more water in it she looks round at Brandon leaning against the sink. "What's up with you " Marnie asks Brandon, looking up at her, what does she mean " Nothing why " Marnie makes them both tea as she sits at the table and slides over the biscuits . "Are you cheating on Rory? " Brandon nearly chokes on his tea. What the hell he thought " No I'm not and I wouldn't do that to him " .

" Good Brandon Chris has an offer off a promotion " " That's good " Marnie gets up to shut the door and sits back down " We haven't said anything to Reece yet it's in Spain " " Spain right well that's something we gotta talk about right "

Marnie reaches for Brandon's hand he nods if it's to be this way then that's ok he thought Reece would adjust he thought " Brandon it's not what your thinking " "What do you mean " A little whimper came through the baby monitor Marnie got up went upstairs and came back down with her 5 month old daughter Evie she sat her on her lap with her blanket round her sucking her thumb . " she's starting to teeth now " Brandon did notice her little cheeks were red which brought him back to when Greece started teething .

" Marnie what did you mean " Marnie looked up at him then adjusted Evie on to her other side " us three have to agree speak to Reece about it to I've been looking to transfer to the hospital in Malaga to and well rather up rooting Reece to another School over there he can come over to us in the holidays " .That wouldn't be to bad Brandon thought it's something they all would have to agree on .

" Have him full time you mean I don't see the problem since I see him all the time anyway " Marnie nodded she looked down at Evie she had fallen asleep again looked back up at Brandon " I know it won't be for a while though you would be on board with it " .

" He's my son of course I would Marnie " .Good Marnie thought since Reece was born They had settled into a routine which worked out just great which suited all of them the past six years he was a good father to Reece which all Marnie wanted especially on the holidays they co parented that to .

" THEY BEEN OUT THERE a while " Micheal said watching Elliot and Christian they had arrived home ten minutes ago Elliot leaning on the car Carrie shook her head she looked out to " Micheal come away from the window don't make it obvious " Carrie sniggered Micheal went over to the sink washed his cup he looked over at Carrie folding baby stuff nappy's for her hospital bag . He had thought she's nesting now from before when they were having Jack and Molly he went to wrap his arms around her waist when the door opened .

" Hello I'm home " Elliot's face beaming coming over to Carrie hugging her she looked at him he had a bit off the sun while he was away those few days he looked happier she thought " Have a nice time " Carrie asked Elliot smiled and nodded " Amazing time with my boyfriend " Micheal looked round at the top off them Carrie was surprised but its his life she thought. She hoped Christian would be good for him

" Congratulations, " Carrie said, patting his back. Elliot sniggered, " We made it official while away, what's this you're doing? " Elliot asked, pointing to the table Carrie looked over . "Just sorting stuff for the hospital " .Carrie went over to the table to sort out the pile that was to go in the bag for the hospital .Is this the nesting stage he had heard about from the last twice before she went to the hospital.

" Ok I've got some washing to put in, I'll sort it later " Elliot picked up his bag and went upstairs. He's going to do his own washing well. That's the first Carrie thought what Christian did to him while she thought . And he didn't need to be asked to sort it .

Elliot sat down his bag on his bed, he looked over at the photo of him and Leyton he picked it up touching the picture " Look after mum " He sat the picture back down his phone beeped he checked it a text from Christian Elliot smiled opened up the text .

Christian " Miss you already ☹ x " .

Elliot sniggered he was only gone half hour. He would see him in a couple days and texted him back while he lay in his bed .

Elliot " miss you to 1😊😗 x " .

PATRICK, ELLIE AND Ivy were in the supermarket picking up food for a picnic they decided to have since the weather was good and go to the park so ivy could play around and they could go a walk his phone beeped Patrick checked it Elliot checking in he was home now he and Bailey would see him soon he texted him back he would call him later .He sounds happy Patrick thought the break would be good for him and Christian .

" Mummy ice cream " Ivy asked Patrick to look up ice cream for a picnic Ellie thought she looked at Patrick ` ` Why not we can have ice cream too?' Patrick said looking at Ellie she shook her head he should learn to say no .We don't want to be spoiling Ivy too much. She thought he had got to learn to .Not to give in to her .

Patrick went over to Ellie while she picked up a bottle of coke he leaned into her " Are you mad at me " " No but you should learn to say no " Ellie smiled looking at Patrick he cocked his head really he thought and sniggered Patrick whispered in Ellie's ear " I can't say no when it's you " Ellie giggled shaking her head she pinched his side " C'mon let's get these bought " Ellie said Ivy took her mums hand leading the way to the check out as they were turning the corner Patrick bumped into someone .

He was about to make his apologies when he recognised the girl from school he knew " Megan " Patrick asked and she smiled. It had been a long time since Megan and her family moved to Australia. She looked amazing. He thought Ellie watched the interaction between them while she was at the till .Did Patrick know this person Ellie thought .The girl was very pretty Ellie thought maybe it's a school friend who he has not seen in a long time .

" Patrick hi how are you " " Good I'm with Ellie that's Ivy her daughter we're going on a picnic " Patrick pointed to Ellie over at the till Megan nodded and smiled looked at Patrick " You look great how's everything " " Good everything is fine " Patrick said looked over at Ellie smiled at her " Early days but it's going great Baileys having a baby you know Senora Roop "

" Vaguely yea wow that's amazing I take it there together now " " They are Elliot's mum not long passed away he's with Christian now nice guy he's a dancer and teaches to " .Megan nodded and smiled sounds like everyone is doing ok she thought which is great Megan had thought of calling Patrick to meet up but decided. Against it .

Just then a guy came over to Megan she introduced him to Patrick Declan who she meet in Australia she was home to see the family and her Nana who wasn't to well for a while she did hear about Leyton through friends she kept in contact with when she went to Australia she will be meeting up with them while visiting.

They got into the car Ellie stared at Patrick he looked over at her " what " " well friend from school then " Ellie smirked Patrick blushed shaking his head " We were 15 she was my first crush we hung out a lot I was devastated when she and her family moved to Australia " Patrick started the car and ever since no other girl he meet wasn't like Megan until he meet Ellie " . He did chat to other girls onIce but nothing had come of it till now .

ELLIE SNORTED PATRICK looked at her what's funny he thought he went to take her hand " I would have loved to have seen you at 15 " Ellie asked I'll get her back for that he thought shaking his head " Thanks well I thought I was pretty handsome " Ellie snorted again she reached over to kiss his cheek Patrick smiled as he drove along . Smiling to himself yep I think I still have it mind you it was good to see Megan she looked great he thought .

IT WAS BUSY AT THE park with couples with dogs and children. Either taking a walk along the path or just hanging around some children playing in the children's areas Ivy went over to play for a while and made a couple friends like she normally does whenever Ellie takes her out to the soft play .

" You are amazing " Patrick said Ellie looked round at him while they sat watching Ivy play with the other kids " Am I " Patrick nodded, reaching over to kiss Ellie " Eugh Mum " .

Ellie looks round at Ivy standing watching them Ellie shaking her head " Honey what did we talk about " Ivy pouted looking down Patrick got up went over to Ivy bending down to her . " I like your mum very much Ivy " " You do " They both look round at Ellie Patrick smiled .Ivy was being shy she thought and hoped she would be ok about her and Patrick .

He looks round at Ivy again " And I like you too and I hope you like me too " " U huh " Ellie thought at their interaction " " Momma 5 more " " Yes honey 5 more " .Ivy grins gives Patrick a hug that's so sweet Ellie thought .

Then Ivy Ran off up the shoot again Patrick went back over to Ellie he took her hand and kissed it " That was cute " Ellie said Patrick smiled and nodded " your cute " .Ellie blushed Patrick taking her hand Ellie leaning into Patrick while they watched Ivy on the swings .

Patrick has been amazing since they started going out he was so good with Ivy and she wasn't fazed by him " What you thinking about " Patrick asked looking round at Ellie " Not much " Patrick kissed Ellie's nose they look over at Ivy on the swing another girl on the other swing chatting away which was cute to see .

Chapter 15

Patrick, Bailey and Elliot meet up for their usual meetup pub lunch day which they do twice a week if need be and their daily check in to Patrick thought Elliot seemed happier since he had his few days away with Christian he looked a bit browner too .Since the weather was heating up for the month of May.

" Guys i have news " Bailey stopped before he bit into his burger he looked at Elliot he looked between Bailey and Patrick " Christian and i are official " Elliot bit his lip Patrick looked at Bailey he shrugged his shoulders looked at Elliot grinning .

" Mate that's great right Bailey " " He better not hurt you " Elliot snorted Patrick rolled his eyes seriously. Time and a place Bailey Patrick looked at him " What i'm serious' ' ." Ok ok got it Elliot said . " Also were " .Elliot bit his lip blushing, noticed by Bailey and Patrick.

" Elliot you don't have to " Patrick touched his hand. He knew what he was going to say was that he Christian were intimate. Elliot nodded. Bailey grinned that he was happy for his friend . " Bring it in " Patrick said, opening his arms wide and all three of them hugged, patting each other . "Love you guys' ' Elliot said with a tear in his eye. . Oh god my boy has finally had Sex again Bailey thought grinning I'm happy for him now that Christian is

They sat back down. Bailey reached over, wiping his tears away as well as his own " what we like eh " Bailey said all three of them giggling. " I saw Megan. " Elliot and Bailey looked at Patrick. " The

Megan " Bailey asked, " Yes, Megan, she was in the supermarket visiting family. Her Nanas are not well to " .

" When you were with Ellie " Elliot asked Patrick nodded "Oh wow he thought imagine bumping into your first love " How did she look? Bailey asked while stuffing into his burger " She looked good with her boyfriend too " .

" Will you guys come to Christians show? Elliot asked Bailey's phone, beeped a text from Senora about the ikea delivery " i'll be there" " Me to " Patrick and Bailey said god he thought ikea is a flat pack he shook his head at the boys

" What's up? " Elliot asked. " I think it'll need three of us to sort the ikea flat pack out" " What she bought now? " Patrick asked Bailey, shrugging his shoulders ." Micheal said it's Nesting Carries been like that for the past two weeks " can't be that already Bailey thought she's only three half months or maybe it could be her way off wanting things done before their son comes .

" Guys also I don't feel him anymore " Bailey looked at Patrick they looked over at Elliot " Leyton " Bailey asked Eliot nodded " When since Mate " Patrick asked Elliot sat forward leaned on the table " At Mums funeral he came to me before that said he earned his stripes I didn't understand it at first but I know mum will. be ok" Bailey sniffed Elliot and Patrick looked at him " Sorry that's just " God what's wrong with me Bailey thought what Elliot just said am I coming out in sympathy for Senora he thought Patrick patted Baileys back shaking his head .

SENORA WAS CONFUSED by the flat pack and she looked over the diagram twice and still didn't have a clue. While she sat on the floor of the baby's room she heard a car door opening and shutting the front door opening " Hello it's only us " Bailey shouted up then Elliot and Patrick appeared . Senora looked up Elliot and Patrick looked at each other then went over to Senora to look over the flat pack then Bailey appeared. Senora smiled up at him saying that's good of the boys coming to help she thought Bailey did look a bit peeved off about it she thought .

" Let's have a look then " Patrick said " what was I thinking " Senora announced Bailey sniggers went over to her and kissed her cheek " Baby it's ok we will sort it " Touching Senora's face she leaned into his touch cute the boys thought .Patrick and Elliot grinning looking at Bailey and Senoras interaction .

" To be honest Carrie was like that too so you're not the only one did it look nice " Senora nodded leaning her head on Bailey's shoulder " Oh tell Senora who you saw " Senora looked at Patrick he would rather forget it he probably wouldn't see her . " Megan " Patrick sighed while looking at the instructions " Megan , how did she look " .Senora asked looking between the guys .

Patrick sniggered while he read the instructions " Really well over visiting friends her nana isn't well her boyfriend was with her " " Wow " Is this supposed to be a baby changing thing Patrick thought as they carried on helping each other with the flat pack why is it not easy to sort .These Ikea flatpacks can be confusing and god knows why she didn't just get other stuff from the supermarket which would have been easier .

Carrie sat at the kitchen table wiping her eyes.and blew her nose Elliot just came home and came into the kitchen and saw Carrie had been crying. Oh no he thought she'd been thinking about mum. Elliot went over to her and scooted the chair over to her . " Sis what is it? " Carrie pointed over at the sink he looked over and there it was the urn with his mum's ashes damn he thought he had forgotten they would be picked up this week . " I didn't think it would hit me this bad " Elliot wrapped his arms round Carrie " I know any idea what we could do with her ashes " .

Carrie wiped her nose with her tissue and looked over at the ashes again " Not yet you " Elliot shook his head they would think of something " I'm sure there have been plenty of places we had gone to I did hear something about some ashes. Can be made into necklaces " .

" Really well that's one idea " .Elliot had seen it somewhere online about it which he would look up again and thought about it a while back something that he and Carrie could look into and something they could treasure in the future .

A couple days later Bailey and Brandon lay in Brandon's bed in his apartment Sheet half off them Bailey's legs sprawled out over Brandon's Bailey lifted his head and smiled at Brandom asleep his nipple ring glistened in from the window looking sexy Bailey chewed his lip sitting up watching Brandon his breathing a Steady flow . Bailey smiled looking at him he then got up collecting his clothes he looked round at Brandon should he waken him before going into the bathroom to get changed he came out a few minutes later Brandon still sleeping Bailey looked at him one more time Bailey smirked biting his lip he did think about waking Brandon he then left quickly sending Brandon a text .I will let him sleep Bailey thought if I did he wouldn't leave Brandon had some sexual appetite that's for sure .

SOME MOMENTS LATER Brandon turned to Bailey his side empty Brandon sat up where was he was lifting up his phone a text from Bailey saying sorry Brandon huffed didn't wake him thanks Bailey he thought .Brandon shaking his head that's sneaky now sitting up in bed he looks round at the window I will get up soon. Bailey reply's back Brandon stretches lying against the headboard I sho

---

RORY WAS COMING OUT of his car all excited to see Brandon. He was home a day early. He wanted to surprise him and the news about the London trip he noticed Bailey coming out of Brandon's apartment building going over to his bike. What's he doing at Brandon's apartment Rory thought as Bailey drove off .Not seeing Rory maybe to do with work he thought .

" HONEY I'M HOME " BRANDON stopped stirring his coffee in the kitchen when he heard Rory's voice. What the hell he's home a day early he thought he went out to the hallway Rory laden with bags beaming he set them down his arms out. Brandon went to him and they hugged " Rory what happened? " Brandon asked Rory to kiss his cheek ." Nothing honey i missed you and well there wasn't anything else to do ".

Brandon looked over at the bags he's had a shopping spree Rory looked round at them " i bought presents oh i saw Bailey coming out everything ok " .Rody went over to the bags bribing them over .

" yea work stuff keys and something about a flat pack that he and Senora couldn't work out " " Oh ok anyway help me with the bags honey " Brandon shook his head that's Rory all over he thought always buying things. Which he doesn't have to do but I wouldn't change that Brandon thought .

They left the bags in the spare room Rory got presents for Reece and Brandon and stuff for himself hopefully that Brandon would definitely like to . Rory wrapped his arms around Brandons shoulders and they looked at each other " You will come to the taping won't you " " Of course I will know that " Rory smiled .Maybe I should stop asking so much

They kissed and hugged again; this was the first time they had been apart. They both hated it before Rory went to London they discussed moving in together Rory was already half moved in anyway with half his stuff at Brandons and some Brandons at Rorys .Like they have been doing the past few months I love this man Brandon thought .

" Let me show you how much I missed you " Brandon said, taking Rory's hand leading him to the bedroom Rory giggled. He definitely missed him then Rory stopped. Brandon looked at him as if something was wrong and he thought " Rory what is it " . Rory lays his arms round Brandon's shoulders kisses his nose Brandon wrinkles his nose shaking his head .

" Nothing babe " Rory kissed Brandon again they smiled at each other and Rory took Brandons hand leading him to the bedroom " We have make up to do " .Brandon smirked lightly smacking Rory's bottom wrapping his arms round Rory's middle kissing his neck Rory giggling .

ELLIOT COULD HEAR CHRISTIAN and Daniel arguing when he arrived at Christians what's up with them he thought when he walked into the apartment Daniel saw him first and walked away into the office Christian came over to Elliot hugging him ." Christian what's happened? " Elliot asked Christian looked at him touching Elliot's face " Just stressing about the event that's all ." I hope that's all Elliot thought, maybe he was overthinking stuff about Daniel .

" Are you sure we don't keep secrets, remember " " Yes love us dancers get a little jittery before the event " Elliot shook his head. He needs to stop stressing, he thought he took Elliot's hand Christian looked at him " Are you sure " Christian lay his hand round Elliot's neck " Yes come let's make dinner I've prepared half off it " Elliot snorted what he means is Gloria had prepared half off it . " What " " nothing oh I brought that wine you mentioned " .

Elliot placed the South African wine Christian had mentioned a few times on the breakfast bar. Red and white good choice Christian thought Elliot went over to the stove. The smell of cooking was delicious, he thought. Christian came behind him wrapping his arms round Elliot's waist he leaned into him " Missed you " Christian said kissing Elliot's ear " it's only been two days Christian " .Elliot giggles leaning into Christian .

" A long two days' ' kissing Elliot's ear again " Christian Daniel' ' Turning to face him Christian cocked his head they kissed Christian pinched Elliots bottom he giggled a cough they looked round at Daniel standing at the office door what's his problem Elliot thought he looks cross .Whatever it is hopefully he and Christian can sort it Elliot thought .

" I'm off now, I've left notes in the office, emails are done " " Thank you " Christian said Daniel nodded as Christian carried on checking the food . Elliot followed Daniel out " Daniel about Christian " Daniel looked round at Elliot . " it's about the reporters that's all he doesn't like them much " .Daniel sighs Yes Christian mentioned before he doesn't like his private life invaded . Which is understandable I wouldn't like that either but most celebs either like the paps or don't all depend if you get to know them from various events .

" Right i get that i'll talk to him ok " " Sure thanks " They were both about to part Daniel looked round at Elliot `` You know ive never seen him happier " Elliot smiled and nodded that was a nice thing to say he thought . " I certainly hope so ". Yes Daniel thought he could definitely see Christian a little happier lately now that Elliot was around and hopefully he would be a permanent fixture in Christians life which he needs right now .

RORY AND BRENDAN LAY in bed after their love making twice Brandon lay his arm round Rory as Rory held his hand Brandon definitely missed him he thought " Ok " Brandon asked Rory looked up at Brandon they kissed " More than ok baby " . Rory snuggled into Brandon he kissed Rory's head he hummed .

" Good " Brandon kissed Rory's shoulder " Honey bout Reece he's ok about staying with you " Rory turned to face Brandon leaning on his elbow " Yes he is and he has missed you " .Brandon touches Rory's face he kissed Brandon's hand .

" I've missed him too " " About the threeway are we in agreement about the person? " Rory sat up a little Brandon too before they had discussed having a three way but in the club only which they agreed upon . " Definitely babe and the rules we agreed upon " Brandon kissed Rory he leaned Brandon " Yes honey we go this week " .Brandon nodded and laid his arm round Rory him snuggling into Brandon again .

" Mmm we go this week i love you "Rory says first " love you to " Brandon kissed Rory again he felt Brandons hardness against his leg " Oh honey " " What " Rory giggled as Brandon moved Rory onto his back Rory looking up at him " Babe we don't have to if you don't want to " Brandon said bending to kiss Rory feeling his hardness again .

Brandon reaches for the condoms and hands them to Rory he looks at Brandon " you want me to " Rory asks even though they sometimes say " You're in charge this time " Rory grins bending to kiss Brandon you bet I will Rory thought.

CHRISTIAN AND ELLIOT on the couch Christian holding onto Elliot them making love blankets half round them Christian kissing Elliots chest a sheen of sweat over them " Do you feel good love " " Mmm" They kissed Christian slid his hand down stroking Elliot licking his chin pulling harder Elliot hummed closing his eyes .Letting Christian Do his thing .

" Christian " Elliot was close they moved positions Elliot laying down Christian put on a fresh condom.He looked down at Elliot deliciously naked Christian moved over to him lifting up one leg guiding himself inside .Elliot lifted his arms up Christian held onto one getting into a rhythm then kissing .Christian touching Elliot's face taking his time loving him .

Christian still came Elliot holding onto him while he came to Christian rolled off Elliot discarding the condom and wrapping the blanket over them kissing again Christian touching Elliots face they didn't need words to express how they were feeling Elliot was sleepy snuggled into Christian . " That was good " Elliot said sleepy snuggling into Christian he kissed Elliot's head " Good to know " .

" Can we just stay here? Elliot asked Christian smiled. I wouldn't mind that he thought I'm comfy " Course we can " . Touching Elliot's face they kissed Christian wrapping the cover over them Elliot laying his head on Christians shoulder . " I love you " Christian said Elliot was sleepy and hummed .

Gloria opened the door off the apartment the next morning and walked in and saw the dishes weren't done. She tutted oh that boy she thought oh that's right Elliot was staying over last night that's ok going nearer into the apartment shaking her head oh dear oh dear she thought and blushed at the sight before her .

Gloria stopped noticing clothes on the floor oh my she thought as she got nearer into the apartment Christian and Elliot were laying on the couch a blanket over them asleep. " Mr King " Christian stirred opening one eye Gloria looking down at him shit he thought he went to move and realised nothing on . Elliot stirred " Sorry we feel asleep Gloria " Elliot looked up oh damn he thought Christian looking down at him smiling and looking back up at Gloria .She didn't look happy they both thought .

" I got tidy up " Shit Christian thought they never got round to doing the dishes they both looked over at Gloria they looked at each other and giggled how were they gonna get to the bedroom Elliot snorted well this is awkward Christian and Elliot looking at each other .

THEY WRAPPED THE BLANKET round themselves and ran to the bedroom Gloria shook her head as she nearly caught an eyeful . Elliot went to go over to the bed, giggling Christian following him and caught him arms round Elliot's waist "Shower "Christian asked " Off course Gloria " . Elliot giggles this has been an eventful morning so far .

" she will be ok " I hope so Elliot thought the poor woman looked embarrassed. I would be to Christian peeking his head out from the bathroom grinning " Showers Ready " Elliot giggles shaking his head "Coming " .

Chapter 16

Bailey and Senora are having their date night at the club Patrick and Elliot are on shift at the Edinburgh club this week Christian was visiting friends and had meetings regarding the recital which was in a few days and Elliot's niece was excited from what Elliot saw from rehearsals people were going to be amazed .He felt so proud for him and hoped everyone would love the recital .Especially Molly who constantly had been going on about it for a while now .

Brandon and Rory came into the club and went over to one the tables to the person they knew Senora looked over at them so they were having their threeway now Bailey looked over to all three of them so they were having their threesome after all he thought .Senora looks at Bailey looking over at Brandon and Rory What is he thinking Senora thought .Looking round at Brandon and Rory chatting to the other guy .

" There having their threeway then " Patrick asked Bailey looking at him " Looks like it " Malcolm appeared going into the ice bucket Julia went over to Brandon giving him his key ." How's Darian Malcolm " Elliot asked Malcolm looking up at the ice bucket down " He is fine he just needs to learn to rest " . "What's wrong with him? " Senora asked, taking a sip of her orange and lime. "He has that bug going around and driving us a little crazy " Malcolm sniggers and notices Brandon with Rory and another person . It looks like they were friendly Malcolm grins .

" So they decided on the threesome then " Malcolm said everyone looking over at them " They sure did " Patrick said adding drinks to his Tray Cameron appeared from the office going over to Malcolm saying hello to everyone " How was he " Malcolm asked Cameron " He said he doesn't feel as bad as he was now I said we would be home in an hour " " Good " .Malcolm thought and he better be resting and not doing any work or they will be having words Malcolm thought .

" You don't need to worry everything is good " Julia said when she came over with her clipboard " I know but we were going a bit stir crazy at home right babe " Julia snorted she knew fine what they meant polly had the bug to and was feeling better also . " He is not the best patient " Cameron explained looking at Malcolm he nodded that's true .

" You ok? " Malcolm asked Elliot. He looked at him and nodded while he sorted out a couple cocktails. " Good Christian recital soon he's nervous about it. " " I bet he is looking forward to seeing it. Did you get the email regarding the course " .

" I did thanks " Malcolm patted Elliot's back he had hoped Elliot would get into the health and social work course. It's what he had wanted to do since he dropped out of his engineering course and the bar work at the club would do for now till after the summer whenever he would hear back from the college .And if he had wanted to do volunteering work he just needed to ask him .

Julia handed Senora and Bailey their keys Brandon and Rory with friends had already gone into their room since it was midweek the club wasn't that busy there was a steady stream of members coming and going or had just come in for a drink which some normally did .Or Just a mid week catch up before the weekend since some the members had made friends with other members .

Bailey went to the toilet and was coming out when Brandon pushed him back into the cubicle which startled Bailey ' What the fuck Brandon " " Rory saw you coming out the apartment " Fuck he thought have they been rumbled he thought Brandon shut the door of the cubicle " it's ok I explained that you were there for work keys and flat pack in case he asked " .

" Right whatever " Bailey went to move Brandon kissed him Bailey batting him off ' I'll go first " Bailey shook his head Brandon left an idiot he thought then he went out and washed his hands Jesus that guy Bailey thought .And thought what Brandon had just said about Rory .

" Finally " Senora said sitting on the couch waiting for him " Sorry baby must've been the curry she was looking amazing with her baby doll outfit on her stomach slightly jutting out she Sexy tonight oh he thought the paddle biting his lip as Senora twirled it round her fingers smirking at him . " Baby be gentle will you " Senora cocked her head Bailey came over to her leaning over Senora she looked up at him he bent to kiss her . Bailey's stomach lurched, he covered his mouth and ran to the bathroom to throw up followed by Senora " Bailey " he threw up again oh no Senora thought he had come down with this bug with great timing .

" Shit babe I'm sorry " Bailey rinsed his mouth and sat on the toilet seat he was pale Senora felt his head he was hot " I'm calling an Uber we're going home " " Ahh damn I'm sorry " .Baileys stomach lurched again feeling bad that there night was now ruined Have I caught this bug he thought .

" Bailey it's fine " .

Patrick helped Bailey into the Uber. He definitely didn't look good. Elliot thought looking at Senora she looked concerned. "He will be ok " Senora looked at Elliot and nodded "she's gonna have to do her nurse duties the next two days," she thought . "Thanks for helping " ." No probs update me ok " Elliot asked looking at Bailey in the taxi poor soul looked ghastly .

Bailey flopped onto the bed Senora shook her head helping to take his shoes off " I'll go get the paracetamol " Bailey grunted Senora went downstairs to get water and paracetamol and went back upstairs Bailey was changed and in bed she left the water and tablets beside him and sat beside him on the bed .Men why do they over drama things Senora thought Bailey snuggling into the blankets .

" How do you feel now " " My head hurts and stomach feels like it's been hit by a bus " Senora snorted. Bailey looked at her " You Better not get sick " As if she can't. Senora thought most days she went without being sick. Some things made her stomach turn . " You looked sexy tonight, " Bailey smiled. Senora patted his hand . " Easy, tiger, have a sleep. I'll be up in a while and take the paracetamol, " Bailey nodded, reaching over to take the tablets and water .

Her phone beeped Elliot and Patrick asking how he was. She texted back saying he was still a bit sickly and in bed and being a bit of a drama queen Elliot and Patrick laughed at her text typical Bailey they thought hopefully he will be better in a couple days .And they also hoped they wouldn't get the bug that is going around .

MALCOLM STOOD AT THE bedroom door Darian sitting on the bed computer open Malcolm shook his head also the dogs were asleep on the. Bed to " Darian Longstrom"

" He looked up and smiled as the dogs woke up wagging their tails. Malcolm came over to the bed " I know I just " ." What's going on here then " Cameron asked at the door Malcolm looked over at Cameron he then took the computer off Darian " Malcolm " Darian said sighing " you're supposed to be resting right Cam " Cameron nodded " I know but I feel better and " .Cameron folded his arms and sighed why can't he just rest and forget about work he thought .

Malcolm reached over to Darian he looked at Malcolm `` Stop right there everything is ok right Cam " Malcolm says looking over at Cameron ` ` It is Malcolm's right you should be resting " Darian looks between Malcolm and Cameron he sighs and nods " I'll take the dogs out for there last walk c'mon you two . Frank and Bluebell wag their tails panting, jumping off the bed to follow Cameron .

" Dad I feel sick " Philip says coming out of his room he did look pale. Cameron thought Malcolm came out to the landing bending down to Philip feeling his head look up at Cameron . " He's hot " Darian comes to the door oh no not Philip now he thought . Cameron gets the leads for the dogs while both Darian and Malcolm in the sink get the essentials for Philip .

Darian tucks him back into bed Malcolm brings the bowl incase Philip is sick Malcolm takes out the amount of calpol to give to Philip As he snuggles into Darian n the bed " How do you feel now buddy " Malcolm asks " My tummy hurts a little " " The medicine will help that " Darian says Philip nods Darian and Malcolm look at each other . Reminding them it's not the first time Philip didn't feel well and one of them had to stay with him then took turns with him .

" I'll stay with him " Darian suggests Malcolm takes Darians hand he squeezes it Malcolm nods and gets up the front door opens Cameron coming back with the dogs he looks up at Malcolm at the top the landing going into there bedroom Frank bounds upstairs into Philips room and jumps onto the bed to lay beside him knowing he wasn't well . Bluebell bounds into her cage and lays down with not a care in the world. Cameron sniggers, shaking his head and quite right to Cameron though she probably knows Philip isn't feeling well Frank just wanted to be his comfort .

He goes upstairs and looks in on Philip who is sleeping with Darian beside him, also asleep Frank at the foot off the bed so he wouldn't have their little family any other way he thought Malcolm lays his chin on Cameron's shoulder as he looks round at him . " C'mon let's go to bed " Cameron says taking Malcolm's hand and no sexy time for them tonight they both thought but that's ok they thought they will make time over the weekend hopefully .

Chapter 17

A week later the day off the showcase recital the newspapers were there interviewing the kids from the school who were taking part as well as the performers to Christian was nervous about it the day before worrying if it would come across ok Elliot kept telling him to not worry so much that it would be fine Brandon came along with Rory and Reece as Christian had been giving out tickets to the showcase recital . Everyone packed into the theatre. It was a good crowd Elliot sat with his sister , Jack and Micheal with Patrick Ellie Bailey and Senora Darian had arrived with Malcolm , Cameron and Philip who were feeling loads better after the viral infection they had and Bailey too . Who was feeling so much better than he did a week ago was the worst few days ever in his opinion .

Micheal.got out the video recorder Molly insisted her parents take a video so she could look through it after Elliots phone beeped a text from Christian he could see them all from the side Elliot smiled . Quickly texting him back with words of encouragement. With a heart sign Christian smiled looking up and peeking out he could see them three rows from the front . " Christian " He looks round at Helene and nods " Ready " " Yes lets get sorted " And they go off to warm up a bit and have a group huddle before the performance.

Everyone got in a huddle wishing everyone good luck. The kids had a pep talk. They looked amazing and little fairy imps there were good too . " Mummy " Ellie looked down at Ivy who was munching into her crisps " Yes Honey " Stealing a crisp from Ivy's crisp packet Ivy giggled .

Ivy looked up." When is it going to start " Ellie looked at Patrick who looked at Elliot " Soon Ivy is excited " Elliot said Ivy shrugging her shoulders Ellie snorted Elliot shook his head " she isn't bored is she " Elliot asked Patrick he shook his head. Definitely not bored Patrick thought just like everyone else waiting for the recital to start .

" Elliot " Ivy said Elliot looked over at her while she munched into her crisps " I'm excited " She said giggling hugging her mum " Good to know " .That kid is so cute Elliot thought and Patrick was smitten with her he could see .Ellie shook her head at what Ivy Said Elliot smiles at Patricks interaction with Ivy and thought someday I would like to have a kid .

CARRIES BACK ACHED probably from the seats she thought everything at the moment was uncomfortable Micheal looked round asking her if she was ok she nodded Micheal lay his arm around her rubbing her back noticed by Micheal's mother .Yes not the most comfortable at the moment Micheal's mother thought .And thought Why didn't Carrie bring a cushion with her .

THE MUSIC STARTED PLAYING, the lights dimmed, the music started, all the dancers stood under a white light, then more dancers came on, the setting looked good, everyone thought and the dancers and everyone else were doing a great performance .

During the performance Carrie had to go and pee. She couldn't hold it in because the performance was going well. The kids were doing great and the aerial acrobatics by the man and woman were good . Elliot was mesmerised by Christian performance . That's my man he thought amazing and sexy too in his leotard and white shirt and so sexy with his performance .Patrick daunted Elliot on his side regarding Christian performance man he thought that guy can dance.

Carrie sat in the cubicle toilet as she was in labour. She thought not now or maybe she was imagining it then a contraction hit her oh shit ok i'll call Micheal or text him she sent him a text while doing her breathing .Why did this have to happen now Carrie thought .Especially during Molly's recital I hope she won't be mad Carrie thought .

Micheal checked his phone and he excused himself. What's up Elliot and his mother thought while they watched the performance is he going to the loo now Elliot thought . Micheal chapped the women's bathroom door and went inside. I do hope Carrie is ok, Michael thought .Is Carrie ok Elliot thought when Micheal left to check on her .

" Carrie " " In here " Carrie opened the door Micheal bent down as Carrie puffed " Honey are you sure " Carrie didn't have to.say anything he could tell Micheal got his phone and dialled his mum's number and told her what's happening . Winnie excuses herself what's going on everyone thought as Elliot's phone pinged off a text from Micheal . " Mate what's going on " Bailey asked now that the interval was on Micheal letting Elliot know that he was taking Carrie to the hospital .

Elliot stood outside as Micheal and Winnie helped Carrie into the car they would take Jack with them and if he could look after Molly and take the videos wow he thought they didn't expect this Elliot's phone rang from Christian he connected the call . " Elliot I heard is Carrie ok " " Yes Babe she is don't worry Micheal and Winnie are with her " .Elliot looking round at Michael helping Carrie into the car Elliot bit his lip I hope they make it to the hospital in time .

“Good Elliot gotta go I’ll see you later “ He disconnected the call Elliot was about to go back inside Daniel appeared “ is your sister alright Elliot “ “ She may be in Labour “ Wow Daniel thought isn’t she a week or so early “ I must get back good so far isn’t it “ “ it is “ .That was nice of Daniel to come and check on them see how Carrie was .

WINNIE AND JACK WAITED at the waiting area while Micheal was with and the midwife she was checking over Carrie and informed her that she was 3 centimetres dilated well that back ache she had must’ve been the early stages of her Labour and the midwife confirmed that can go from front or back which Carrie didn’t have with Jack and Molly . Carrie opted for the gas and air. Winnie came into the room with Jack who was worried about his mum hugging into his grandma .

Micheal reassures him that it’s ok mums having the baby tonight it might be two hours or so Winnie would pop in to see how things were progressing and take Jack for a drink or if he wanted to go home maybe stay with his nana tonight which was totally ok by Jack he often stayed at his nannas overnight and get spoilt .

The whole theatre was a standing ovation for the performance. The kids did well off the story that Christian and the rest of the cast came up with. Elliot was so proud of him the expressions off the dance choreography was amazing. Just as everyone was leaving and Elliot hung around for Christian to finish his interviews Micheal texted Baby Morag Ida Matthews was born 8 pounds 10 just 20 minutes ago, amazing he thought and a good weight to Micheal would take photos later for them to see .

“ Uncle Elliot “ Molly stood with one the teachers he bent down in front of her “ Your baby sister was born 20 minutes ago Molly mums ok “ Molly's face beamed she hugged her uncle I’m a big sister now " Can we go see mum " " We can let's just wait for Christian first ok " Molly nodded looked over at her teacher " Let's get you changed . Then Molly " Molly went off with her teacher ." Wow I can't believe it " Senora said Elliot looked round Bailey's arm around her waist .

" I know she was complaining about her back being sore for a couple days " Elliot explained baby Morag just didn't want to wait any longer Elliot thought and that was totally ok it was going to be a full house with the new baby now .

Later as they all said their goodbyes Christian finally Elliot thought " I'm so proud of you " Elliot said to him wrapping his arms round Christian waist he smiled Elliot kissed his cheek " Thanks How is Carrie " " Good and if we take Molly to the hospital and a wee look at my new niece then we can still make the after party " .Elliot said smiling at Christian them holding hands while they walked to the car .

" I don't need to go to it " " You sure " Christian nodded strange Elliot thought he would have thought that Christian would have wanted to go Helene came over to them before they left " Congrats Elliot Christian are you sure you don't wanna come to the after party " " I'm sure Elliot needs me right now .Do I Elliot thought it's not really an emergency or does Christian not like after party's much which is fine if he doesn't .

MOLLY SAT ON THE BED beside her mum looking at her baby sister Elliot and Christian had brought flowers for her and sat them at the window sill Micheal lifted up Morag so Elliot and Christian could have a proper look at her a full head off hair amazing Elliot thought he looked at Christian while Micheal handed Morag to him .Elliot has tear in his eye while holding Morag she is beautiful he thought he looks u at Christian watching him .Mummy " " Yes darling " .

" I don't think I want to be a ballet dancer anymore " Well that's surprising Carrie thought she looked at Micheal he shrugged his shoulders Elliot looked at Christian then looked down at Morag she did a little pump Eliot giggled ill not be doing nappy duties . " Why is that Molly? " Carrie asked Molly, looking at Christian and back at her mum . " My feet hurt too much " .Carrie sniggers and looks at Michael he shrugs his shoulders she did complain that her feet were sore a couple times .That's ok Micheal thought I think it was just the fascination that Molly was curious about the dancing then it will be onto the next thing she will want to try next .

Elliot looked at Christian and wondered if they did or was she exaggerating Elliot went over to the cot and lay Morag down " When are you getting out " Elliot asked " Probably tomorrow or next day how was it " Carrie asked Christian " Good went well, as expected I may have had a little mishap with A step hopefully positive feedback" .If there was a fault Elliot didn't notice he was just taking it all in .Mishaps or did a wrong step he didn't notice if he did .

Chapter 18

Bailey was adding the drinks to his tray it was his second late shift on its the weekend and the club is always busier than Jake was co manager tonight his shift on at the Edinburgh club Brandon came over to the bar he had been busy taking drinks to the rooms " Bailey " " Yea " Bailey looked up at Brandon who was adding stuff to his tray " Could You help me with something after we've done these " " sure " . Bailey looks over at Brandon is he ok he thought he doesn't look happy or am I just overthinking Bailey thought .

THEY WENT INTO ONE the rooms to stock up for the brief that was given Brandon brought a box in from the store while Bailey stocked up " What's the brief again " Bailey asked Brandon handed him the brief on what Mr winterman asked Bailey shook his head and then carried on what he was doing . " Bailey " " Mmm " Brandon came over to him while he was stocking up " Bailey " " What " Bailey sighed. He looked round at Brandon. What is it he wanted? He thought Brandon was staring at him " I'm going to ask Rory to Marry me " .

Wow Bailey thought good on him he nodded but why is he telling him he looked at Brandon again " Ok good it's your life " " Bailey I " A chap at the door Jake appears. Looking round the room Brandon and Bailey look round at him . "How we doing guys " " Nearly finished Jake just the petals to go on the bed " Jake nodded and checked his watch and looked up at Brandon and Bailey . " Great Mr Winterman will be here in an hour I'll check back later " Jake left Bailey went over to the bed fluffing up the pillows . " Bailey " Bailey sighed looking round at Brandon " What " " Are you mad " Bailey snorted what is he mad about it's his life he thought besides were just fooling around and he loves Rory .

" Fuck no you love him right " Language and yes " Brandon held onto Baileys arms he looked down and back up at Brandon " Bailey I want your permission to ask him " Bailey snorted again shaking his head this guy seriously wants my permission. "Are you for real Brandon were only fooling around " Bailey was about to move Brandon stopped him Bailey stared at him " Will you come with me to pick the rings please " .

" What the fuck Brandon " Bailey moved to finish off preparing the room why the hell would he want me to come with him to pick the rings shaking his head he turned round before he left the room " Ok I'll come with you " Brandon smiled and nodded " Thanks " Then Jake appeared again with a refresh off drinks tray as well as champagne for Mr Winterman leaving them for the boys to sort .

Elliot yawned while he went round the tables to pick up Empty's and went back over to the bar where Christian was. He looked at Elliot and shook his head, smirking. Elliot noticed and reached over to him . " Excuse me Mr King " Christian moved over to him smiling " Are you tired babe " Elliot cocked his head smiling " A certain someone kept me awake most the night and another certain someone was up twice in the night too " .Elliot grinned and god knows why Christian was up those times during the night was he feeling ok Elliot thought .

Christian giggled pointed to himself Elliot shook his head " Get a room you two " Bailey said Elliot looked at him why is he so cross looking he thought " what's up Mate " Bailey leaned against the counter " oh heat to warm to cold sleep " Bailey said sighing sorting out the bar area .

Elliot sniggered and guessed what to do with Senora with her pregnancy understandable Elliot patted Baileys back he will be fine just wait till the baby's born he will be even more grumpy than he is right now pregnant women can be weird and the weird cravings are the same with Carrie .

Later after his shift finished the late shift came in at 3 till 12 tonight Elliot sat in the kitchen with Carrie it had been a week now since Morag was born she was a delight to the family even though she was a week and a half early and no after effects . Elliot had her on his knee to give Carrie a break. Morag already had her nap. The kids were not long home from school after Micheal picked them up and had gone to get a take away tonight .

" Ok there " Carrie asked as she was sterilising the bottles Elliot was giving Morag her bottle Carrie looked round at them Elliot was smiling down at her talking to Morag Carrie smiled . " it suits you " Elliot looked up and scrunched his nose " Do you want me to take over " .Carrie asked ping it did look like he was doing fine with Morag .

" I can manage sis can't we missy " Carrie sniggered and went back to what she was doing " You would make a good father Elliot. He looked over at Carrie; he had thought someday he would want kids . " Someday I will get plenty of practice " . And that is far into the future having his own kids .

Christian came downstairs. He had been on the phone to Daniel and a facetime chat with his fellow dancers he overheard the conversation about kids he also had thought about having children in the future with the right person .Has he met the right person he thought Christian smiled into himself he and Elliot were getting on great . Maybe they needed a chat about the future and he also had thought about having children with someone or by himself .

Christian went into the kitchen bent down to touch Morag's face he looked at Elliot he patted his back and sat on the other side "Business done " " it is we have a couple interviews coming up all good " Elliot felt Morag let off uh oh has she filled her nappy he thought thanks Morag he thought .

" Oh Morag you haven't " Carrie came over picked up Morag yep definitely needed changed and took her away to change Christian leaned over to Elliot `` You do know if you ever have kids you would have to change a nappy " Elliot giggled shaking his head he reached over he kissed Christian. " You're adorable" " i am " Christian asked they kissed again Christian touched Elliots face .

" Get a room you two " Carrie said coming back in with the monitor she had put Morag down for a nap she sniggered going over to the kettle putting it on the front door opened Micheal coming back with the takeaway at last everyone thought . Molly came in the lounge jack from his room, everyone tucking in to get what they wanted .

The food was left in the middle off the kitchen table to let everyone pick what they want Christian looked round everyone he.felt blessed to be part of Elliot's family " We still need to decide what we're doing with the ashes " Carrie said pointing there mums ashes sitting up on the window sill Elliot looked over we do he thought .They have been putting it off for to long now but he and Carrie were not ready to get rid off his mum's ashes just yet and they did need to think where to scatter them .

MEGAN AND JAKE WALKED into Neros. She looked round at Jake. He looked at her very impressively. They both thought great decor was the place they had heard since she came home to visit . Jake placed his hand on Megan's back guiding her over to the bar where Julia was sorting out drinks. She looked up at the couple who came over to the bar . " What do you want to drink hun " " A cocktail cosmo please " Jake smiles, kissing her cheek and sits on the stool Jake's arm round her waist .

That's an Australian accent Julia thought as Ben made up their drinks. Jake picked up a business card to check out the website for more info . Patrick came through to the bar. He had finished his shift and he was going to Ellies for dinner after work. He noticed Megan and her boyfriend at the bar. He thought what are they doing to her ? This is gonna be awkward. Megan noticed Patrick when he came over to the bar . " Patrick " " Hi how you guys hear about the club then " .

Megan looked at Jake and back at Patrick " Do you work here" " I do and the one in Edinburgh " What a coincidence Megan thought looking at Jake and back at Patrick`` Are you still. Doing construction for your dad " Patrick looked at his watch and looked at Megan " Yea part time look I sorry I'm meeting a friend `` .Patrick looks at Megan then Jake she does look good tonight he thought .

" That's a shame isn't it Jake it would have been great to catch up before we go back another time " " Yea sure another time enjoy your night " Patrick walked off Megan watching him she leaned over to Jake and kissed him " was i bit full on " " No baby you wasn't "Jake smiled maybe she was but Patrick seemed a bit of with her she thought as if he couldn't get away fast enough .Did I come on to strong Megan thought while sipping her cocktail .

" HARD SHIFT " ELLIE asked when Patrick arrived Ivy's dad was helping her into her jacket he was taking her overnight " Not to bad " Patrick looked over at Gerry a car horn beeps the arrival of Gerry's girlfriend Ellie bent down Ivy hugged her " Have fun " " luv you mummy " " I love you to " of. They went into the car Ivy waved as they drove off Ellie had got taken away for her and Patrick . He sorted it out laying it out on the table for him and Ellie to pick at. Ellie looked at Patrick. He was kinda quiet, she thought, while they picked through their take away . " What's up " She asked Patrick looked up " Nothing why " Ellie folded her legs picking away at her take away " Weird mood " Patrick snorted she is moody is she coming on her period he thought Ellie huffed Patrick got up bent in front off Ellie ` ` Pmt " Ellie nodded pouting Patrick held out his hand Ellie took it she smiled .

" Do you want chocolate " He had heard pms symptoms chocolate helps Ellie nodded and smiled Patrick got up went into his bag he had a bar chocolate in his bag and handed it to Ellie gosh he's so kind she thought " You have earned a reward " " That's good " Ellie got up went upstairs to the toilet and back after a few minutes ` ` Sorry " She said biting into her chicken looking up at Patrick ` ` natural thing no need honey " " I wish I was a man " Patrick giggled shaking his head. He got up clearing everything up and went to bed with Ellie " shall we watch a movie there a couple new ones on Netflix " Ellie nodded, a good idea she thought .He is so wonderful most men would just ignore it while she snuggled into him.while they watched Netflix .

I wonder if she needs a hot water bottle Patrick thought while they snuggled in together the covers over them " Ellie do you need a hot water bottle " Ellie looks up at Patrick smiling at him " No I'm fine you're keeping me warm " That's good to know Patrick thought kissing her head .

Chapter 19

Brandon looked over the rings in the jewellery shop Bailey was late he had texted he was on his way what's keeping him Brandon thought he sighed there were a couple nice ones he liked to choose from he just wanted the perfect ring for them " Sorry I'm late " Brandon looked up at Bailey puffing red faced Brandon smiled shaking his head has he been running " Can I help you " The lady shopkeeper asked looking between them smiling .

" Looking for engagement rings "Brandon asked the lady who smiled coming over to Brandon and Bailey Brandon came over to Bailey " What happened" " Oh Patrick about an ex on the phone for a half hour about her tell you rest later " Brandon nodded and the lady shopkeeper sat out some rings to look . " Have you the lady's size? Bailey snorted. She looked at him. Brandon went red, he tutted glaring at Bailey " My boyfriend, " And the lady shopkeeper went bright red, " Oh gosh I'm ever so sorry sir." Well at least she apologised I won't make a thing of it Brandon thought .

Brandon smiled as she went to change over the rings " it's ok no need to apologise and he's here for support " pointing to Bailey she nodded Brandon picked out a couple possible rings asking for Bailey's opinion he also liked a couple Brandon's choices until he decided on a white gold pair . " What about you? " Brandon asked Bailey. He looked at Brandon as the lady boxed the rings "Nope , not yet I'm starving where we are eating and way into the future with me and Senora " .Weird Brandon thought don't they want to get married at all Well that's up to them when they decide to get married .

Brandon shook his head, maybe Bailey was ready to settle down yet who knows he thought they came out the jewellery store Brandon felt confident he had made the right choice in the rings and was quite pleased with himself about the rings was Bailey ok about it he thought I should talk to him about that ` ` Burger or pizza " Bailey asked " I don't mind where we go " .

" Pizza then " Bailey asked Brandon nodded and smiled Bailey cocked his head staring at Brandon and he wondered why he was staring at him " What is it " Nothing c'mon let's get food ." He is being weird again Brandon thinks while they walk along to get to Pizza Hut .

" When is Rory back " " Next week " Bailey nodded Brandon had mentioned he had gone to an adventure outreach camp for disadvantaged kids for his job which sounded good he thought Malcolm had also mentioned the same thing the other day he was doing a good thing for the kids to which Bailey thought digging into his burger .Thinking must be a rewarding job that Rory does helping out the kids .

" Brandon " He looked up at who spoke to him, a friend of Rory's Kenny with a friend Kenny looked Bailey up and down and acknowledged him " Bailey from work Bailey Kenny " " Hi " Bailey said Kenny staring at him " When is Rory back " " Next week " .Kenny hummed nodding unusual to see Brandon with a friend he is normally with Reece or at work he thought .

" Hun we better get going " Kenny friend said Kenny nodded " Good to see you Brandon " " You to Kenny " off Kenny went with friend thank god Brandon thought Kenny can be annoying sometimes and nosey " Friend of Rory's "Bailey asked " Mmm " Brandon looked at Bailey then bit into his burger " When do you see Reece " .Is Brandon pissed off about that Kenny guy he didn't seem friendly Bailey thought .

" Tomorrow Marnie and Chris will be going over to Spain next week to look at houses for a few days I'll have him all week " Bailey hummed his answer glancing at Brandon now and again " You got a week off " " Will do " Brandon looked at Bailey what's up with him he thought . " Well then better make the most of it then won't we " .Bailey said smirking what's with him Brandon thought.

Bailey cocked his head raising his eyebrows smirking Brandon looked from side to side he knew exactly what Bailey meant smiling at him " I guess we do " Brandon grinned they looked at each other then they both got up putting their leftovers in the bin and headed for the car park .Got into the car Brandon touches Baileys knee Bailey takes Brandon's hand off his knee . What's that about Brandon thought glaring at Bailey then started the car driving off Bailey grinning .

BRANDON LICKED NIPPED at Bailey's inside leg stroking him at the same time he looked up at him all flushed Brandon moved up to kiss Bailey still stroking him he looked down as he stroked from root to tip Bailey's cock twitching and slick from the lube . " Brandon "Bailey croaked "Mmm " Brandon looks up at Bailey he reaching over for the condom he wants to fuck me he thought Bailey handing Brandon the condom Bailey biting his lip .

" You want me to put it on " " No it's for you "Bailey said chewing his lip did Brandon hear him right for him he wants me to Bailey sat up looking at Brandon " I want to " " Are you sure " Bailey nodded biting his lip again Brandon touched his lip he is looking sexy right now " I want you to break my cherry " Brandon snorted he knew exactly what he meant . " I trust you Brandon and I want it to be you " .Brandon felt touched by that and wondered why .

Brandon touched Bailey's face and nodded. He reached up to kiss him. They deepened the kiss, Brandom moving round to straddle Bailey. He looked up at Brandom as he reached over for the lube . He looked at Bailey watching him even though they made out most of the time Bailey did him he was adamant Brandon wasnt to go further with him . Brandon wondered why he changed his mind which was totally fine .

" Brandon " Brandon looked at Bailey a quizzical look on his face " What is it " Brandon came over nearer to Bailey he kissed him " Nothing " Bailey reached up for Brandon to come nearer him they kissed .Brandon squirted some lube on his finger looked at Bailey he went to turn round Brandon stopped him . He lifted one of Bailey's legs up reaching over to lick his nipple . " Breath " Bailey nodded Brandon slid his hand down and went to flick a finger inside Bailey he clenched at first . Oh that's a bit weird Bailey thought Brandon bent to kiss Bailey again adding more lube to his finger .

Bailey then relaxed Brandon flicked his finger in and out they looked at each other and kissed the tingles in his back down to his groyne was intense Bailey thought Brandon licked his ear Bailey moaned as he heard the rip off the condom . He looked at Brandon taking out the condom and putting it on he hovered over Bailey looking up at Brandon . " Ready, " Bailey nodded. Brandon lifted up Bailey's hand pressing him into the bed while easing the tip of his cock at Bailey's entrance. It felt weird at First, Bailey thought as Brandon teased his entrance with his cock .

Bailey arched up Brandon going in further " Breath Bailey " He was being gentle Bailey thought in between puffs Brandon went in further getting into a fuck Bailey thought he thought he was on fire Brandon kissed him tongues Bailey reached up to Brandon bringing him closer to him matching his strides he was flushed beads off sweat on his brow and chest tingles all over him .Brandon going slow to give Bailey time to get used to him .

Brandon stilled for a minute to let Bailey compose himself and eased himself inside again lifting one off Baileys legs for better access he impaled him Bailey screamed shaking his head from side to side he was close to coming Brandon to chasing kisses Bailey was on fire Brandon stroking him to his cock twitching .Fuck I'm on fire Bailey thought Brandon kissing him making sure he wasn't hurting him to much them all flushed and sweaty .

Brandon nuzzled into Bailey's neck he still came into the condom he grunting Bailey came over his hand Brandon moved off Bailey lying together all sweaty and stated . " Bailey " Brandon lay his arm on his head Bailey looked round at him " mmm " Bailey turned to him slightly wincing " Ok " Bailey nodded then Brandon's phone rang he sighed isn't he going to answer that he thought . The phone rang again and Brandon got up. It was Rory who went outside to take the call .

" Sorry babe had shopping ok " " Honey it's amazing here we should bring reece here " That sounds good Brandon thought Reece did go to an adventure park before and enjoyed it with his mum and from school before . Rory sounded happy and excited which pleased Brandon. He looked round at the door while listening to Rory .

BAILEY WENT INTO THE shower soaking himself he winced a bit. Hopefully in a couple days he will be ok as he let the water flow over him then the shower door opened. Brandon came in and Bailey looked round at him . " Brandon " Brandon pushed Bailey against the tile and he looked up at him . " Sore " " A little " Brandon hummed, placing his hand on the tile " You will be fine " .Bailey snorted, he looked down and back up at Brandon Shaking his head, Brandon moving closer to him . Does he want to again Bailey thought looking at each other?

BAILEY LOOKED DOWN again at Brandon grinning that guy is a beast he thought Brandon touched him.Bailey looked up at him wide eyed " Brandon " " What " Brandon bent down and took Bailey in his mouth he leaned against the wall holding onto his head shutting his eyes while Brandon sucked him off .Shit I'm still sensitive Bailey thought closing his eyes leaning against the tile . Letting Brandon suck him off Bailey bit his lip I'm gonna cum again soon he thought .

It didn't take him long to come again. He was exhausted lying on the bed Brandon sniggered, shaking his head . " im spent you are a beast " looking round at Brandon grinning " Why thank you " Brandon sniggered again. Bailey sat up leaning on his arms . " Stay over " Brandon asked Bailey huffed " No way you won't let me sleep besides i've stuff to do " . Bailey went to move jeez I'll need another shower looking round at Brandon smirking at Bailey he shook his head .

BAILEY STOOD UP BRANDON wrapped his arms round Bailey's waist he looked up at Brandon there was a moment between them it was Bailey that moved first that was kinda weird Bailey thought Besides were only fuck buddys " Right i better go "Bailey said first going to move " Ok yea sorry " .Brandon sat up in bed pulling the cover over him .

BAILEY WENT TO THE door and he looked round at Brandon still in bed watching him. Foot sticking out " See you " Bailey said first he is being weird Bailey thought " See you " Bailey went out and leaned against the door what the fuck is wrong with me he thought he took a deep breath and went the lift . Leaning against the lift Nope not catching feelings for this guy he thought .Besides they do have their significant others.

Bailey got to his bike he looked up at the building then started the engine he looked back up at the building stop thinking silly things Bailey thought then driving back home not knowing what the outcome of the next few months will be for him.and others do I want to see other guys should he and Senora have a three way like they had discussed before .

ELLIOT PUT MORAG'S dummy back in when he heard her crying Carrie must have fallen asleep Micheal came into the room he had taken the rubbish out and had forgotten to take the monitor ."

Thanks " Micheal came over to take over " No problem she's asleep now " They both looked down at her " Carries sleeping " Michael said yawning " She needs it " . Elliot said they were all tired since Morag had been up a couple times in the night since they brought her Home.

Elliot went into his room Christian was in the bed on the wrong side Elliot shook his head he gently shook Christian he opened one eye " " What is it "" You are in my spot " Christian sat up looked round oh right Elliot sniggered and sat beside him.. " Baby you ok" " Fine " Elliot got into bed and snuggled into Christian he lay his arm round Elliot kissed his head Elliot looking up at him . " I should've gone home " Elliot looked up at him " Comfy "Elliot asked grinning Christian rolled over to Elliot they faced each other " Maybe " . Christian smiled. He does look a bit tired. Elliot thought I do hope he isn't overdoing it .

ELLIOT KISSED CHRISTIAN then Elliot turned round Christian lay his arm round Elliot they giggled again " Christian " He looked at Elliot his face flushed " What is it " " Cuddle me " . Christian smiles, laying both his arms round Elliot kissing his head " That Better " Christian asked Elliot hummed "I'm very comfy now Elliot thought . He heard light snoring coming from.Christian he has fallen asleep Elliot looks up at him he is so cute when he sleep Elliot lays back down leaning against Christian shoulder. I won't wake him. He needs his rest just now since Christian has a couple projects and the troupe will be travelling to a couple overseas trips soon .

MEGAN CAME INTO NERO'S looking round for Patrick no sign she went over to the bar Julia was sorting out the beer cabinet humming to herself ' Excuse me " Julia turned round ahh the girl from the other night she thought ' Yes can i help you " .

" Is Patrick on tonight I'm a friend from.school " " His night off Ellie over there will know more " Megan looked over at the other person Julia pointed to the blonde girl that was with Patrick at the supermarket that time they met very pretty. Megan thought she thanked Julia and went over to Ellie .

" Hello " Ellie looked up at the person oh she thought the girl Patrick mentioned and bumped into from school " Megan right " Megan nodded and smiled " I was wondering if you could let Patrick know i'm going back to Australia soon and if you and he wanted to meet for lunch a drink or whatever " .Megan smiled at Ellie ok fine she thought could be ok to meet up before she went back to Australia . Which would be ok with me Ellie thought but it's up to Patrick whether he does or not .

" Ok i'll let him know " Megan got out her phone to exchange numbers Megan smiled looking up at Ellie " Thanks Ellie " Ellie nodded then Jake came into the club to get her " i'll be off now nice to see you again " Then Megan went over to Jake looked round at Ellie and waved before they went out.Strange girl she thought then carried on with clearing the tables shaking her head thinking she had got a strange vibe from Megan she would have to talk to Patrick about that .Did he think the same maybe or was it just the way she is with people Ellie did think .

Chapter 20

The start of July came the weather was getting hotter as predicted and the summer holidays started Marnie had come over for a few days to take Reece over to Spain to spend the summer holidays with his mum he would be turning seven while away Brandon had arranged to celebrate his birthday when he comes back his little sister was getting bigger now she would be 8 months now . Marnie and Chris' job was going well which was good Brandon thought he told Marnie his plans to propose to Rory when they go on holiday they planned to visit New York and San Francisco and after that Rory will be in London to film drag Uk Brandon will go with him this time . Rory was pleased Brandon would be able to make it this time and to support him which Brandon had been doing since the beginning of their relationship .

Rory half moved in when Brandon asked him but he wanted to still keep his apartment for other spare clothes Brandon had thought they could get a bigger place Rory had said they should think about when they come back from holiday for definite he was excited to be moving on with Brandon he so loved that boy . They had fun together and liked doing most thin

Baby Morag was thriving and at 2 months Carrie and Micheal thought it might be a little early to take her on a plane so they decided on a Uk break away now that Micheal would be home for at least six weeks and he and Carrie could also have a couple days away themselves she and Elliot still didn't make plans to scatter there mums ashes and she still was kept on the windowsill for the time being until they properly decided .Every morning they said hello to their mum whenever getting up or coming home It freaked out Michael a couple times and wished they would put the ashes somewhere else instead up in the kitchen windowsill but understood why they had wanted to keep her up n the windowsill a bit longer.

Elliot and Christian had also planned a break away also Christian parents had planned to visit him whenever they come over for there trip they planned they were nearly 3 months into their relationship Elliot was mostly at Christian or Christian at Elliot's Carrie thought the both them were joined at the hip the way they were with each other the honeymoon period as everyone calls it . She had thought it was pretty cute how they were in sync with each other every time Christian Came over to visit .

PATRICK DID MEET UP with Megan with her boyfriend and Ellie that night before she went back home to Australia nothing else came back off it she had just wanted to catch up on any news from other friends . Ellie was just overthinking silly things and she and Patrick were seeing each other more. They had dinner dates with Ellie's friends and met each other's parents . If Patrick wasn't with Ellie he was with Elliot and Bailey and they all had meet ups to Christian had them over for dinner to get to know Elliot's friends .

SENORA WAS NOW SEVEN half months and now on Maternity leave recently she as finding it hard at work and decided to take her maternity leave sooner which everyone thought was a better idea the baby's room was ready just the pram and carriers to get which Baileys And Senoras Dad would be getting soon . Bailey thought it was a kind gesture from Senora's dad and they were getting along better to Senora's surprise .

Senora lay across the couch so comfortable she thought in her bottom's loose t-shirt her fan beside her flicking through Netflix to see what's on the house had been tidied. Bailey came downstairs and saw Senora on the couch he smiled going over to her sitting on the coffee table . " Do I look sexy? " Senora asked. Yea he thought she's still sexy with her bottoms on loose t-shirt he bent over to her kissed Senora " Baby you are still sexy " They both giggled and the baby kicked her stomach " Even he thinks his mummy's sexy " . Cute Bailey thought, feeling Senora's stomach she looked up at him.

Bailey looked at his watch Senora looked at him " Won't be late ok " Senora snorted right she thought which means he will be but that's ok she rolled her eyes he cocked his head " Excuse me " Bailey shook his head Senora pouted " love you " Bailey bent to kiss Senora she is definitely comfy there he thought " love you to " .

Bailey set off in the bike to his destination got off at the hotel sent a text of his arrival went into the lift got out at the floor to the room number he chapped after a few minutes it opened by Brandon he pulled him inside against the door kissing him " Whoa there tiger " Bailey said as Brandon went to take off his clothes and pulling at Baileys he looked at him . " What "Brandon asked cocking the his head smirking " Not even a hi how are you " Brandon snorted .Bailey went to move Brandon lunged at him kissing him lifting up Bailey t shirt and off " Fuck sake Brandon " " Language " .Brandon slapped Baileys bottom he scowled at him then laughed shaking my his head showing his dominance today both stripping Brandon walking them to the bed .

Later laying in bed Brandon holding Bailey's hand he looked at Bailey thinking he thought " Bailey " " Mmm" Bailey looked round at Brandon " Whats up " Bailey sat up folding his legs looking at each other ." What time is your flight? " Brandon ran his hand down Bailey's leg .

Brandon lay on his back looking round at Bailey " 7am " Brandon groaned he and Rory will be travelling to New york in a couple days he hates early morning flights " Hungry " Brandon asked Bailey smiled and nodded reaching over to Brandon sliding his hand down Brandon grabbed his hand ." What " " Food " Bailey pouted Brandon grabbed Bailey pulled him down kissing him . " Brandon stop " Bailey giggling " Ok ok lets get food " . Brandon tickling Bailey again then bent to steal another kiss making Bailey breathless they look at each other again . Bailey sat up right this time they had to move to go and get food " c'mon let's get moving then " Bailey said first getting up Brandon slapping his bottom Bailey glaring at him breathless . He reaches over grabbing Brandon bottom and then slapping it they both giggle then eventually they leave the room after another make out session .

ELLIOT WENT INTO CHRISTIANS room after they had a shower he picked up his shirt looking around for his jeans he noticed a picture album sitting out on the side board Elliot was curious to see some pics and did wonder why the photo album was out . He went to pick it up to look through it flicking through some of the family pictures. Elliot came across one particular picture where he had to look twice Christian and two other guys. The other one was Grant, his attacker. He put his hand to his mouth and to stifle his scream he felt sick, his heart beating. What the hell he thought he knew him but how .

Elliot took a photo off the photo and put it back on the sideboard. He felt anxious and scared about how he was going to get out here. Should he confront Christian about it or maybe talk to Patrick and Bailey about him first he had to calm himself and not let

Christian See he was upset .Calm yourself Elliot thought taking deep breaths don't get a panic attack now .

Christian went into the bedroom Elliot wasn't there he smiled as he was playing with him he thought he went out to the Lounge Elliot was over at the window looking out Christian went over wrapping his arms round Elliots waist. " There you are "Fuck Elliot thought don't flinch and let Christian See your upset" Here i am " .

Elliot turned his head Christian lay his head on Elliots shoulder " Ok " Christian asks Elliot nods and smiles Christian phone beeps he sighs checking it Daniel.waiting for him.they had a couple meetings to attend to . " You better not let him wait " " i know but i'd rather be here with you " .Christian kisses Elliot's cheek hugging him . I would rather he not go either and talk to Christian about the family photo .Say something Elliot thought but I can't get the words out.

" Christian " " Ok ok I'm going " Christian held his hands up backing away he cocked his head " Wait up for me " " I will besides we won't be going for drinks later " Elliot had his group therapy session tonight Christian had a couple meetings for the dance troupe and to go over a possible tour coming up later in the year .Is Elliot ok Christian thought he seemed kinda offish I will talk to him later about it .

Christian looked over at Elliot before he went out. Maybe it's because the group therapy session sometimes he was off fish with them before or is it something else hopefully they could talk about later . Christian looks at the door when he goes out. I'm just being silly about it then gets into the lift to get Daniel .

Elliot let out a breath when Christian left sliding down the window head in hands fuck what am i gonna do he thought i cant go to group therapy tonight now . The club I'll go there he thought.Patricks working tonight I'll go talk to him .Elliots hands shook, he clutched at his chest and found it hard to breath. I have to get out of here, he thought but I don't have the strength to get up .

MELINDA MADE THE TEA while Senora and Lindsay shared out the pizza and chips. Senora's back hurt a little. She sat down. Lyndsay looked at her and she was washed out. She knows how that felt twice when she had her children . " Back sore " Senora nodded rubbing her back " i know how you feel hun " laid out her hand Senora took it and nodded .

" He is being secretive " Senora said Melinda looked round Lyndsay looked over at her " What " Senora asked looking between them " Look Baileys Bailey he won't change it's probably nothing and it's your hormones i can vouch for that " Lyndsay said she had plenty experience in that field .Am I being over active Senora thought maybe it is my hormones .But I do have a feeling something isn't right .

" We've not had sex for a couple weeks " Melinda snorted. Senora looked at her. What's funny she thought " Hun it's not that bad Ryan and i didnt have sex when I was seven months and it was 3 months after that " .Maybe that's what Senora thought I do want to have sex but Bailey grossed out because I'm getting bigger is it because off the bump or what .

" Did Ryan still find you sexy at this stage? " Lyndsay snorted. She remembered back when they were having their first he found it a bit gross having sex at seven months but they managed it .

" We compromised, yea it Can be a bit of a struggle but there are other ways to " That's something to think about Senora thinks we should talk about that they did other things before .

ELLIOT CAME INTO CLUB Nero he looked around for Patrick he couldn't see him then he came through from the back Elliot went over to him . What's wrong with Elliot Malcolm thought he looked upset talking to Patrick " Malcolm " Darian asked from the vip area he looked round at Darian`` Elliot looks upset " Darian stood up.he was with Patrick calming him down what's happened Darian thought .Has he had a wobble have he and Christian had a falling out .It's not really my business Darian thought but Elliot is obviously upset about something .

" ELLIOT , PATRICK SOMETHING wrong " They both looked at Darian Elliot had been crying. He looked at Patrick and Back at Darian shaking his head Patrick lay his arm round Elliot he was shaking looking at Darian .It's too hard to explain. Elliot thought the man I love is keeping a secret from him .

Darian paced the floor in the office looking at Elliots phone in the picture Patrick sitting beside Elliot arm round his head in hands " i don't understand i just don't " Elliot said shaking his head Patrick shook his head . The door-chapped Ed came inside and went over to Darians computer to type in a few things. What came up is that Grant Campbell and Christian are cousins .What the hell Elliot thought did Christian know about Grant Elliot thought .

That's the connection they thought " Has he been playing me Patrick " " i don't know Mate " .He needs to calm down Patrick thought getting worked up and where the hell is Bailey to not answering his text or phone .He is seriously pissing me off lately with his weirdness I will have to talk to him .

Bailey got out his phone while he and Brandon sat out in the beer garden a text from Patrick so it said shit i've got to call him it's there signal for anything wrong he excused himself to call Patrick. Is something wrong Brandon thought Bailey sounded worried when he went to call Patrick back .

" What happened? Bailey asked Patrick leaned against the wall outside the office. " Mate it's really bad " Bailey looked round at Brandon Bailey chewing his lip " Bailey" " Yea I'm here I'll be there soon ok . Bailey disconnected the call from Patrick Jesus Patrick thought he was about to tell him something else when he hung up on him fucking asshole .

After the call Bailey went back inside he had to go something bad had happened Brandon offered to give him.a ride back but he refused he would get a cab get there himself Bailey didn't say anything else when he left did say it's Elliot Brandon hoped he was ok he will text Bailey later .

CARRIE WAS IN THE LOUNGE. She had not long put Morag on her lounger. when the front door barged open and shut loudly she heard Elliot talking running up the stairs what the hell is going on she thought . Carrie went out to the hall as Patrick was going upstairs " Patrick " he looked round at Carrie and back upstairs " Um it's bad Carrie let me talk to him first ok " .Oh no Carrie thought they had a fight . I do hope it's not too serious. I should let Patrick talk to him first .

" What's bad oh have Elliot and Christian had a fight " The front door chapped and opened Bailey appeared as Patrick went into Elliot's room Bailey was about to go up Carrie stopped him " Bailey what's going on : " i um dunno " shrugging his shoulder then excused himself and went up to Elliot's room .Dear god boys and there troubles Carrie thought going back into the kitchen to sort the washing out .

“ I'M HERE WHAT'S GOING on “ Bailey went over to Elliot laying his arm around him god he looks awful he thought Patrick looked at Bailey where had he been he thought “ Elliot gave him his phone off the picture Bailey looked at it looked at Patrick then Elliot “ Where was it “ “ in a family album in his bedroom just sitting there " Elliot got up went over to the window Bailey and Patrick watching him Bailey and Patrick look at each other then thinking was it deliberate that the photo album was left out .

" Maybe you need an explanation Mate " Bailey asked and they do need to talk it over for Christian to explain " It's his cousin Bailey " What the hell Bailey thought when Patrick said that it's so messed up the bedroom door chapped Carrie appeared " ok " looking between the boys Elliot has been crying "No Carry it isn't " Oh no she thought they've had a fight maybe that's why Patrick and Bailey are here to talk about it .

" Need anything " " Carrie not right now " Carrie shut the door and went back downstairs Micheal was in the lounge with the kids he looked up at her " I think they've had a fight " Micheal sighed everything was good with them Elliot hopefully will sort it he thought .Carrie looks back upstairs if he needs her to talk then he can I just hope they can sort it out .He did sound really angry Micheal looks over at at Carrie thinking she shouldn't worry to much if Elliot wants to talk he knows he can .

AFTER HIS MEETING WITH Daniel Christian texted Elliot before he met up with the other dancer friends to go over the routine no reply from Elliot when he checked must still be in his group therapy session Helene thought Christian looked worried when they took a five minute Break. " It's Elliot he was being weird today "Christian sighed checking his phone for the millionth time " What do you mean " . Helene asked coming over to Christian if maybe he is overreacting to nothing Helene thinks .

" Not Not sure Helene not sure whether it's his antidepressants he's getting weaned off them can give mood swings " Helene Patted Christian back telling him not to worry so much she hears poor Elliot she thought she hoped it would be ok soon .Maybe it is to do with his antidepressants Christian shouldn't worry about it so much .

SHIT SENORA THOUGHT when Bailey called regarding Elliot she had gone to bed and was reading Bailey had said he and Patrick would stay over or he would come home let Patrick stay he would let her know Senora told him to stay with Elliot so if she needed him she would let him know. Good he must have been so worried over what happened the boys will make sure Elliot will be ok she hoped.

Miriam from group therapy called Elliot Patrick spoke to her saying he wasn't well and he just forgot to report that Elliot had cried himself to sleep with Patrick and Bailey holding him . Brandon texted Bailey asking how things were he had texted back it was bad but would talk to him about it soon Elliot needed them right now. Jesus Brandon thought it didn't sound good when he replied back to Bailey. I do hope Elliot will be ok .

RORY UNPACKED AND RE-packed for the millionth time he stood in the bedroom right he thought that should be enough clothes to take. I'm not gonna re pack again Brandon came into the bedroom he sniggered typical Rory there's always just in case . " Rory you have finally decided " He looked round at Brandon and nodded. Brandon came over to him and lay his arm round Rory's waist he leaned into Brandon sighing he needed to keep calm Brandon thought . " What is latest with Elliot moving away from Brandon "Rory asked while re packing again " Doesn't sound good, hopefully it will get sorted " .Rory sighs and Brandon thinks he should deal with what he has in the case .

" Wonder what it is " " Not our business babe c'mon let's sort the tickets and passports " Rory kisse Brandon's cheek he's such a good boyfriend he thought I love him so much what would I do without him he thought .Rory smiles looks round at the cases again " Rory " Rory looks round at Brandon standing at the bedroom door . " I know I know " .

Rory comes over to Brandon, slides his arms round Brandon's waist looking up at him " I promise I won't repack again " Brandon giggles he gives Rory a peck on the cheek and squeezes Rory's bottom " c'mon you let's check the passports and tickets " .

" HELLO, I'M HOME " Christian shouted when he came into the apartment, no answer huh strange he thought going into the lounge no Elliot he also went into the bedroom not there to and bathroom his stuff was still around he noticed what's going on with Elliot he thought no answer from his text . Christian looked around the room and spotted the family photo album sitting out not in its usual place . He went over to it which was in its usual place he opened. The oh fuck lightbulb moment the photo off him and his cousin Grant which Christian was going to get round to he will have to explain to Elliot about that . But Christian didn't leave the photo album there, did he or did I forget to put it back, strange Christian thought and it was something Christian was going to talk to Elliot about dammit Christian thought I have to see Elliot .

Carrie answers the door to Christian not like him to chap the door and not come in she thought they have definitely had a fight“ Can I see Elliot “ “ What is going Oh Christian have you guys had a fight “ Christian looks down at his feet if only it could had been that he thought “ well I “ He looks up at Carrie she staring at him shit how am I going to explain this Christian thought chewing his lip .

“ I don’t want to talk to him “ Elliot said at the top of the stairs with Patrick and Bailey beside him he’s been crying Christian thought “ Look I’m keeping out of it but you both have to talk “ Carrie looks at Christian he looks up at Elliot again “ Elliot please let me explain “ .

“ NO CARRIE DONT LET HIM IN HE KNOWS THE RAPIST “ Micheal comes out from the lounge when he heard the commotion and grabs Christian taking him into the garden Carrie is dumbstruck what the hell she thought Patrick and Bailey take Elliot back into his room to calm him down . Elliot sitting on the bed grabbing Leytons jumper hugging into it Bailey and Patrick look at each other .Fuck they both thought I hope to Hell he isn’t having a breakdown Patrick thinks . Bailey sits beside Elliot and looks up at Patrick. What do they do? “ Mate don’t you think Christian needs to explain “ Bailey says .

Elliot glares at Bailey and looks up at Patrick he shrugs his shoulders “ I can’t right now “ Elliot gets up still hugging into Leytons jumper Patrick looks at Bailey giving Patrick a faint smile .

MICHEAL WATCHES CHRISTIAN break down head in hands oh god I’m going to have to be peacemaker here he thought Micheal sits on the Garden chair next to him “ Micheal I was going to tell him I honestly didn’t know till recently he’s my cousin “ “ Ahh " Damn Michael thought he looks round at Carrie watching from the door looking worried . " That picture was taken 6 years ago at my other cousin's wedding. Grant has been getting into all sorts over the past years. Michael I have to explain this to Elliot " .

“ I understand Christian but don’t you think he needs time to process this “ I guess Micheal could be right Christian thought at least Micheal hasn’t thrown me out just yet . Christian sighed and held his head in his hands shaking his head watched by Micheal .

“ THERE STILL TALKING “ Bailey says watching from the window he looks round Patrick still giving words of comfort to Elliot “ I still don’t want to talk to him “ Patrick looked up at Bailey he shrugged his shoulders looking out to the garden again Micheal and Christian talking Michael patting Christian back .God this isn’t good Bailey thought Elliot was doing so well he was happy and Christian was amazing .

" Why can't I be happy because once I thought I met the most amazing person? I can't stand this pain. It isn't fair. Elliot cried again Patrick hugged him fuck Bailey thought i hate this he thought going over to Elliot he sat beside him all three them embraced giving words off reassurance hugging I really want him to be happy Bailey thought . Patrick and Bailey look at each other again. We have to do something for Elliot but what .

CARRIE CAME OUTSIDE while Micheal and Christian chatted. Micheal looked up at Carrie and shook his head. Carrie came over to them and sat down . " Christian why don't you go home " Carrie said he wiped his eyes looking at Carrie " Carries right Christian give each other space " . Micheal looks at Carrie. He knows she isn’t happy about the situation with him also but she is right he should go home and maybe in a couple days they will talk .

" I suppose you're right, I'm sorry about all this. " Carrie got up and went over to Christian he looked at her and nodded, " Elliots ok for now he has his friends Christian like I said , give each other space, ok ``.Maybe I should Christian thought, chewing his lip, he nodded , Carrie is right, will try again soon .

MICHEAL WATCHED CHRISTIAN drive off, Bailey came downstairs on the phone to Senora he was on his way home " i'm off Patrick is staying over Elliots asleep " .on his way out of over to his bike what a horrible mess poor Elliot he thought looking up at the building shaking his head he hoped all this mess will get sorted.

" Thanks Bailey goodnight " Bailey waved, got to his bike and drove off. Micheal went into the lounge Carrie looked up from tending to Morag " I think I've had enough off drama " Micheal sniggered when he came over to Carrie they hugged . " I'm sure they will sort it out " " I hope Micheal Elliot is different when he is around happier " .Which is true Carrie thought Christian was good for him since his arrival into his life .

SENORA SAT UP IN BED she sat her phone down after Bailey called her poor Elliot she thought she hoped she hey would sort it out she got up did her business in the toilet and went back to bed she got her book out the drawer started to read it when she heard the bike engine the arrival off The front door opening and shutting and Bailey ran upstairs he stood at the door Senora put her book down. Bailey Shaking his head, looked tired, Senora thought .

Bailey came over to her kissed her rubbing her belly " How is he " She asked Bailey got up took off his jacket " Bad babe " Bailey looked round at Senora she smiled " Patrick's staying over it's just a mess " Senora took Bailey hand he looked at her " its for them to sort it out ok " Bailey nodded Senora placed her hand on her stomach with the baby moving Bailey smiled touching her belly to feeling the baby kick .

" I'm gonna grab a drink, want anything " " Orange with Ice please " Bailey went down to the kitchen, got himself a drink off coke first then made up one for Senora he texted Brandon to let him know what's happening with Elliot and Christian Elliot was a mess .

Bailey " Elliot's devastated Patrick's with him " Bailey sat his phone on the side as he sorted a couple snacks for Senora his phone beeped. Bailey looked down at the text from Brandon .

Brandon " ok hopefully they can sort it good Patrick's with him " Me " to Bailey thought sticking his phone in his pocket " Can you bring the jammies dodgers to " Senora shouted Bailey shook his head giggling into himself going into the cupboard to get the jammie dodgers . She certainly has a craving tonight Bailey thought she stocked up on them before . Bailey looks down at his phone reading the text from Brandon again and sighed right let's get those jammie dodgers up to her sniggering into himself .

Bailey sat down Senora's drink and munchies on her side he stripped down stuck on his jammie bottoms and got into bed Senora looked over at him " Do you think I'm sexy " She asked Bailey coughed while taking a drink he looked at her what a weird question to ask . " Of course I still think you're sexy " . Weird question: he thought she looks amazing with her pregnancy .

" Oh just asking, I asked Lyndsay how she felt when she was pregnant. She found it kinda awkward when she was seven months and Bailey reached over and kissed Senora touching her boob and squeezed. They were very sensitive at the moment . "Baby, stop worrying about your beauty and those boobs well " . Well yes indeed she thought they are a bit bigger since her pregnancy and yes sex can be a bit awkward right now but they did find other ways .

" You still want to have sex with me " Oh my god Bailey thought what's brought this on she's reading too many online things again he thought especially the blogs and the books he shook his head . " Senora, will you stop reading the blogs there putting things on your mind? " He was right, she thought it's silly really. Of course I still want to have sex with you and you know the other ways are good for your beautiful and sexy son growing inside you ``.She has got to stop reading those online blogs. It's driving her nuts and he too. I love her whether she is pregnant or not .

He bent over to kiss her and she smiled. He laid his arm round Senora `` Sorry it's just " Senora sniffed Jesus Bailey thought what the hell has brought this on " it's ok love you " Senora moved a little closer grabbing her pillow which she now used to get a better sleep " love you to You mean it right " .Bailey sniggered again reaches over to kiss Senora " Your beautiful and blooming " .Bailey touches Senoras face she smiled what a lovely thing to say Senora thought which made her a bit happier .

" Now can I have a jammie dodger " Senora sniggers Shaking her head handing him the packet Bailey taking one " I love you " Senora says first they kiss again " Love you to " .

And both dipping their jammie dodgers in there drinks silly woman he thought and her baby brain and Senora thought it was me thinking silly things and yes I should stop reading online blogs Bailey laid his arm round Senora kissing her head . " Let's get some sleep ok " Bailey suggests good ideas Senora thought I'm pretty shattered right now .

CHRISTIAN CAME INTO his apartment he leaned against the door shut his eyes this is a mess he thought all he wanted was to explain to Elliot about his Cousin he moved off the door headed to the kitchen going into the fridge. He brought out chicken salad milk, drank some of the milk, dug into the salad, went into the fridge, brought out a pie half-eaten with more milk till he gagged, went over to the sink and threw up into the sink . Fuck he thought why did I have to go and do that again retching again it's been a upsetting night .

Shit dammit Christian thought you have to stop this Christian thought he got out his phone texting Elliot how sorry he is he just wants to talk .Christian then goes into the bedroom lies on the bed all he could smell was Elliot Christian rolled up the covers to himself no answer to his text his stomach aching tears rolling down his cheeks texting Elliot again then Christian cuddled into the sheets all he could smell was Elliot he groaned this is torture I see him everywhere . Christian didn't bother changing, going into bed hugging the pillow, a good night's sleep I need, then trying to talk to Elliot tomorrow.

" CHRISTIAN " Elliot shouted in his sleep Patrick sat up beside him Elliot throwing his legs about Patrick held him until Elliot settled he opened his eyes Patrick comforting him " its ok i got you " . The door chapped Micheal opened the door Patrick looked up " Bad dream " Micheal asked Patrick nodded then michael left Patrick got up looked at Elliot asleep. Thinking I will have to sleep sometime soon to go over to the makeshift bed lying down, he looks over at Elliot still asleep. They would talk things over in the morning. He just needs to rest and have a good night's sleep hopefully .

Chapter 21

Three days off hell it's a wonder i've coped so far Elliot thought he was sick off crying past two days hardly coming out his room Bailey and Patrick came over texted to check in on him even Senora came round to see if she could do something but failed she did try convince him to try go back onto his antidepressants which he would try to do .Today was group therapy day Patrick picked Elliot up to take him to therapy he didn't look happy everyone thought Malcolm took him into the office to chat .See what he could do if anyone else from group therapy could help with any advice for him .

" I FEEL I HAVE TO GO and him but i'm afraid to i'm sick of crying feeling like shit " Malcolm sighed listening to Elliot rant " i've not taken my meds for two days i know its bad but i just wanted to feel something is that bad " Elliot looks at Patrick he gives a faint smile to Elliot and nods willing for him to carry on talk more . I want to feel again just want to see Christian let him explain but I'm afraid of Elliot .

Malcolm got up went over to Elliot bending down in front of him taking his hand Elliot looked down at Malcolm `` Elliot listen to me you have to take your meds I for one know what it's like to feel the pain and hoping that pain your feeling will go away you need to go to the doctor tell them how your feeling you can't bottle it up

Elliot " Elliot nodded he was right he had to do something about it . The funny thing was he misses Christian and that made it worse. He so wanted to answer his text messages but couldn't bring himself to answer them he just felt bad .

Malcolm went outside with Patrick to talk to him. Freya hung around. She wanted to know how Elliot was and saw Malcolm talk to Patrick. Then Elliot came out of the office. He just looked so sad. She thought she went over to him and they embraced. She couldn't stand her friend being hurt like that . " I'll be ok Freya. I just need to figure out how to face Christian "" I hope so you need to heal Elliot " .That's true Elliot thought I guess I gotta face it head on and be brave .Freya padded Elliot's back giving him reassurance god I don't wanna cry again nodding listening to Freya .

" Ready " Patrick asked Elliot nodded he said his goodbyes to everyone and went to the car his phone pinged off a text he checked which was from Christian again while Patrick drove them while Elliot read his text his hands shaking noticed by Patrick .

" Christian " I'm away a few days with the company business trip to Spain I hope your ok and that we can talk when I get back on Sunday " Elliot stared at his text Patrick looked round at Elliot staring at his phone " Elliot " he looked round at Patrick " I'm ok " " Home " Elliot shook his head his stomach rumbles he hadn't eaten much for the past two days " Food it is then " .Elliot looks down at his phone reading over Christian text again he smiles noticed by Patrick . Patrick wondered if it's a text from Christian at least he is looking at his phone now Elliot had just ignored it for the past few days .

GLORIA WAS IN THE BATHROOM cleaning, mumbling to herself. Mr King is so sad she thought and wondered why Mr Elliot wasn't around for a few days. Are they not talking? She went outside the basket and noticed a couple bloody hankies. Oh no , she was startled at what she saw. Should I say something about it, Gloria thought .Is Mr King Ill nothing has been said whether he is she thought maybe I should ask Mr Daniel .

" Mr Daniel " Gloria chapped on the office door Daniel looked up as Gloria came inside " Mr Daniel " Daniel looked in the wastebasket shit he thought shaking his head " Gloria left it with me " ." Is Mr Christian not well " .He is doing it again Daniel thought maybe I should talk to him about it .

" DANIEL THE FLIGHT times " Christian came into the office saw Gloria and Daniel talking what's going on he thought " Sorting them Christian um thanks Gloria I'll sort that " Gloria nodded then left looked at Christian before she went out Christian phone rang Patricia there choreographer Christian sighed and connected the call " Pat" Christian went out to the veranda to take the call . He didn't look good, Daniel thought ever since the incident three days ago. He hoped they could talk, he thought and he had to talk to Christian about his health so he was looking pale. Maybe I should talk to Pat .

CHRISTIAN WAS SORTING his case for Spain when Daniel came into the room Christian looked up at him " Gloria noticed blood on the hankies " Christian sighed carried on with his packing Daniel stood watching him " I cut myself shaving " Bullshit Daniel thought shaking his head " Daniel your my PA not my therapist " Christian stood up looking at Daniel that's a bit cutting he thought his phone pinged an alert regarding the flight times he excused himself to go back into the office .He thought what Christian had said to him Yes I'm his Pa but his health is his priority to isn't it .

Christian felt a bit light headed and sat on the bed water he needed fluids that's what it is he thought and went to the kitchen for a bottle water he took a few sips refreshing he thought " Sandwich or bagel Mr Christian " Gloria asked he looked round at her and smiled " Bagel please Gloria you make the best ones " Christian smiled maybe I should try eat something to Gloria mumbled something in polish then carried on what she was doing . I should try and get to know some polish words Christian thought. Sometimes I think she is swearing at me in Polish Christian thought .

Christian looked at his phone and still no reply from Eliot. Well, at least he's reading them. He thought he did wish he would answer just to let him know that he was ok. Then a text came through from a number he didn't know. He opened the text which was from Patrick Why was he messaging him Christian thought .Is Elliot ok I hope nothing bad has happened to him while he read Patrick's text.

Patrick " Hi Christian it's Patrick Elliot's gonna kill me sneaked his phone while he went to the loo just to say he's ok well I'm looking out for him Bailey and I . Don't worry he won't be and just so you know I'm neutral I'm gonna try and talk him into coming to see you he did mention you will be away . I will update you on how things are ."

Christian thought that was really sweet of him, though If Elliot had caught him he would be annoyed at Patrick Christian giggled into himself thinking about it chewing his lip he sent a reply back to Patrick .He felt better knowing Elliot was ok and that his friends were looking out for him .

Christian " Thank You Patrick much appreciated " ..

Christian felt a bit lighter than knowing Elliot will be ok then he heard the arrival of the team Simon knocked on his bedroom door Christian locked up " What is this you're not ready yet Simon said standing at the bedroom " " I am just adding a couple things' be out in a minute ' .Simon left Christian sighed carrying on with his packing .

Helene came in with Champagne no not this time in the morning he thought he went out to the lounge Simon and Anya pouring champagne into their glasses `` Darling it's always eleven o'clock somewhere right " Yes Christian thought it's nearly twelve o'clock why not pour champagne into his glass . Daniel watched from the office shaking his head. He better eat something or not get tipsy before the flight. Helene is always drinking. She better be careful while Daniel carried on sorting out the itinerary .

BAILEY WAS HAVING HIS lunch outside with his work friends Patrick checked in letting him know how Patrick was going home tonight he had the club tomorrow night also told him what Malcolm said to get him back on his meds Bailey texted back he would check in on him later .He just wants his friend to be happy again I think they are in love Bailey thought for definite he could tell .

Senora also texted wanting a couple bits showing whenever he finished her cravings again he thought and another text from Brandon in New York saying they were having a good time seeing the sights . " When's the baby due now " Bailey looked over at his work friend Luke who had his face up in the sky enjoying the sunshine "Two months' ' Luke looked at him and nodded smiling at him .Luke was a good work friend Bailey and him got on which was a good thing Luke's phone beeped of a text he checked it probably from that girl he has been seeing for a while now .

" Ahh I can't wait for my annual leave " Another work friend Kai said coming out the building Bailey snorted shaking his head Baileys phone rang Patrick calling to check in Bailey answered it " What's new " He said exasperated leaning against the wall " " Bailey seriously " " Sorry Mate it's the heat and Senora not sleeping right " .

Patrick shook his head looking at Ellie while she was making the tea " I know I texted Christian letting him know how Elliot was he seems better Malcolm's told him to get back n his meds " Bailey rolled his eyes ok I guess I've to check on that to then he thought then a text came though he will check that when he comes off the phone . We don't have to babysit Elliot; he can make his own decisions. Yes, he has to get back on his meds .

" I was thinking we could go away few days see what Senora thinks I said to Ellie about it " " Ok will do " After he disconcerted from Patrick Bailey checked his phone a text from Senora she had gone to see Elliot and he had taken his meds finally Bailey thought he texted her back . Checked the time for another twenty minutes of his break. Hopefully I will get a bit of peace .

" Any jobs going at the club " Kai asked Bailey snorted "I know the feeling I hate my job too " I'll ask Kai " He sounds exasperated. Kai thought it was probably to do with his girlfriend's pregnancy " My sister was the same when she had her kids " .

Bailey looks up at Kai he screws his nose shaking his head " Your time Will come Kai " Kai snorts that he doesn't want kids in the future Bailey thought " I wanna go travelling for a bit before I settle down sow my oats a bit " .Kai winked Bailey shook his head laughing typical Kai he thought Yea he should do that go travel a bit .

ELLIOT AND SENORA SAT out in the Garden while they chatted baby Morag in her arms while Carrie did some washing Morag gurgled on Senoras knee Elliot smiled while Senora interacted with Morag . " He is going to be a good dad " Senora looked up at Elliot she hoped he would. Senora thought " I do miss him " . Senora knew what he meant. She touched his knee dont cry .Elliot smiled. I really do miss him and it suits Senora holding Morag .

" I'm ok with Senora . I will talk to him when he gets back. " Good now about going to the clinic. " Elliot sighed, looking over at Senora. " You know this is the longest conversation we've ever had . Jesus is it Elliot thought but it's nice to chat with Senora since she sees all sorts in her job .

They both giggled Elliot looked up at the sky and sighed " Will you come with me Senora " He looked at her she nodded Morag wriggled a bit then did a little pump then the smell hit Senora " She pump again " " I think she's done something else " Senora got up went into the house went to Carrie which Senora said she would change Morag besides it's practice when the baby comes .

" I'm here " Bailey shouts coming into the back door Elliot on his own looking at his phone he looked up and smiled at Bailey he looked ok Bailey thought when he came nearer to him " where's Senora " " Changing Morag " Bailey went over to Elliot patting him on the back . " Ok " Elliot shrugged his shoulders " You talk to him yet " Elliot shook his head Bailey lay his arm round Elliot " I will when he gets back from Spain " .

That's progress Bailey thought at least he's thinking about it " and I've taken my meds " " Good " Senora came back with Morag handing her to Bailey Morag looked up at him he stared at her " Well you better get the practice in " Senora fixed Morag head on Baileys arm and gurgled what's that he thought Elliot sniggers and playfully bops Morag nose she smiles . " She likes that " Elliot says Carrie comes out to the Garden to take Morag for her nap " a I was just bonding " Bailey whining while Carrie takes her away .

" I'm hungry let's go get something to eat " Senora stands up she looks over at Elliot " coming " Elliot nods Senora lays out her hand for Elliot to take them into the car Bailey texts Patrick the progress .

Bailey " operation get Elliot out a success we're going for a burger�😊" .

In the car Elliot sat forward while sorting his seat belt " Guys can we visit first " Senora looked at Bailey he nodded ""Sure ". I have to do this. Elliot thought of just one more visit before I decide what I'm gonna morning do about Christian I have to be free off Leyton now .

Patrick sat up in bed checking his text from Bailey good he was ok Ellie came nearer to Patrick wrapping her arms around his waist he turned his head " How's Elliot " " Bailey said he seems ok they've gone for a burger " Ellie kissed Patrick's shoulder he leaned into her " That's good you should stop worrying now " Ellie smiled cocking her head " I'll never stop worrying about him Ellie ",Patrick turned round moving Ellie back against the bed he kissed her " Sorry it came out wrong " .

Patrick hoovered over her he smiled bending down to kiss her nuzzling her neck Ellie giggles " Have you not had enough " Ellie asked looking up at Patrick he shook his head sliding his hand down flicking a finger inside Ellie bending down to lick her breasts while flicking his finger in and out her . " God your so fucking wet " Ellie bit her lip Patrick kissed her again working his way down licking and nuzzling the nub her breasts licking nuzzling her stomach until he got to her sex .

Patrick looked up at Ellie watching him, he got her vibrator from the side, flicked it on and teasing her sex with it, her face getting flush, He rolled it along the inside off her leg, Ellie moaned, the sensation getting intense, god she looked beautiful, he thought . " Patrick " Ellie was breathless Patrick flicked the vibrator in and out he licked at the entrance of her sex Ellie tensed up she was close her face squished into the pillow .

Patrick left the vibrator inside her watching her writhe with lust he bent to lick the nub off her sex Ellie screamed into the pillow her orgasm was intense she came twice oh my god that was amazing she thought Patrick nuzzling into her neck till she came down from her orgasm . “ You came twice “ “Mmm “ Ellie looked round at Patrick they kissed she tasted her cum from him . “ Good “ “ Very good “ .

“ Patrick what about you “ He looks round at Ellie kissing her nose “ I’m good “ Ellie looks down Patrick is still hard Patrick lifts Ellie’s chin she looks at him they kiss Ellie slides her hand down to stroke Patrick’s he groaned they kiss Ellie moves and slides down taking him in her mouth licking and sucking from root to tip . Jesus that’s good Patrick thought holding onto Ellie’s hair fucking her mouth I’m gonna cum soon Patrick thought . “ Ellie I’m close “ Ellie looks up grinning and starts pumping Patrick he lays back closing his eyes Ellie sits up still pumping him until warm jets of his cum covering her hand .

Ellie cleans off Patrick helping her they kiss “ Thanks “ Ellie grins kissing Patrick “ Your Welcome “ Patrick laid his arm round Ellie lifting up the covers snuggling into each other looking at each other “ I love you “ Patrick said first Ellie sits up he looks up at her . “ You don’t have to say it back yet .

Ellie smiles kisses Patrick “ I love you to “ Patrick smiles touches Ellie’s face I really do love this woman she is amazing laying his arm around her again snuggled into each other “ Are we officially in love then “ Ellie asks silly question Patrick thought they look at each other “ Yes I would say so “ .

Chapter 22

Brandon and Rory took a horse and carriage ride in Central Park they were huddled into each other enjoying the carriage ride they were 4 days into their trip a another couple days in New York then San Francisco " Happy " Brandon asked Rory he looked up at him " Happy " " Good " Rory lay his head on Brandon's shoulder it was good to get away from the stresses off home life and just enjoy their holiday they both needed it and New York is amazing the places they have visited so far .

" Any news from home " " Nope just Marnie texting about Reece there gonna go to Barcelona for a few days " .That's Good Rory thought he and Brandon should maybe try Barcelona next time it's a place they have always wanted to visit .Rory got out his phone to take a couple snaps on the horse carriage ride I am so loving this Rory thought and pulling funny faces to .

They stopped which meant that was there hour ride over the carriage guy looked round Brandon sat forward to thank him they hopped off holding hands while walked along the path off Central Park they stopped to take some photos from around the area they stopped Rory making a pouty face `` Brandon let's take another pic " Rory looked round Brandon was on my one knee holding out a ring oh my god Rory thought . Rory squealed oh my god his heart was beating fast and they looked at each other I'm not dreaming am I Rory thought.

" Rory Mcgregor I love you, your amazing person, will you marry me? " Rory had tears and people stopped to look at them. Rory looked round at the couple. People watching them went over to Brandon bending down Two rings white and gold Brandon took them out placed the ring on Rory's finger they looked at each other .Tears rolling down Rory's cheek I so love this man .

" Yes Yes I'll marry you Brandon " They kissed Rory took the other ring placing it on Brandon's finger a couple clapped congratulating them they both cried hugging each other then looked at their rings perfectly Rory thought " Good choice honey " " Why thank you I love you " " I love you to " . Brandon took Rory's hand and kissed it "c'mon let's go celebrate ":" Yes please " .Rory pinches Brandon's bottom .

Brandon giggled not that kind to celebrate he thought laying his arm round Rory " Food then that later " Rory pouted kissing Brandon's cheek "Even better honey "

Brandon took Rory's hand and took out his phone to take a photo of their rings " Brandon we tell people first " Brandon looks at Rory and nods tonight he will message his dad Rory his sister since his parents disowned him when he came out and he keeps in contact with his sister and a cousin . Brandon had thought maybe he should contact his parents sometime but that was up to Rory I would support him in his decision .

Brandon thought Rory looked sad he wrapped his arms round Rory's shoulders " Look at me " Rory looked up at Brandon " Don't be sad ok they might approve with the wedding " Rory stakes his head the only people who will approve will be friends with his sister. And my cousin . " c'mon let's get food " taking Rory's hand on their way to one the eating places Rory smiled thinking why do I deserve him he's so understanding and doesn't care what people think of me .And especially his sister and cousin who Rory keeps in contact with regular keeping him updated on family news .

CHRISTIAN LEANED ON the sink feeling dizzy. He looked up at the mirror so tired he thought he splashed his face with water. His phone pinged off a text he lifted it up, opening the text which was from Patrick an update about Elliot .Christian smiles leaning against the sink reading Patrick's text update .

Patrick " Elliot is ok gone to docs regarding his meds up the dosage he's going back to work seems more cherry " The text which was from.Patrrick. Christian smiles and nods. That's good news. I want him.to be ok Christian thought. I miss him so much right now and hopefully we can talk soon .

The bathroom door knocked " Christian are you ready " Daniel asked from the other side Christian sighed " Be there in a minute " Daniel shook his head leaving the room Helene came out of her room looked over at Daniel looking at the door she wondered what was wrong he looked serious. Is Christian ok? He did look pale the other day but he was not well .

" Daniel " He looked at Helene coming over to him " Is Christian ok " " yes i " The door opened Christian came out he looked between Daniel and Helene " C'mon you let's get the others " .Christian says smiling sliding his arm round Helenes .Daniel watches them he is putting on a brave face I do wish I could do something for him Daniel thought .

They all congregated in the lobby to meet up with the local newspapers for interviews before the showcase. In a couple days it was good rapport with everyone and with the news crew and interviewers .The place had a buzz of excitement and fans watching from afar were all excited to see them all .

" Pat " Patricia looked round at Christian he looked pale. She thought if he is ok I do hope he isn't coming down with anything they moved away to talk, noticed by Daniel. " Christian your pale what's wrong " " I'm sorry Pat i'm going to have missed this out i don't feel good " .leaning against the wall it has been a busy couple days Pat thought and with the possible tour coming up . It has been a lot for everyone. He probably just needs to sit this one out today and have a rest till later .

Patricia took Christian arms . Oh god she thought he might be coming down with something. She thought " Christian go back to bed. I'll get Daniel to get you something from the pharmacy, ok " Christian nodded. He felt bad but he couldn't stand or be around people any longer with the way he was feeling .Maybe he will feel up to it later Christian hoped .

ELLIOT AND PATRICK both collected the glasses while Bailey stacked his tray with drinks Elliot was getting a vibe from two guys who kept staring at him throughout the night which gave him the creeps . If they kept doing that he would have to say something because he really wasn't in the mood for any shit tonight .

One guy at the bar Bailey had noticed short black hair shaved in at the sides and it was kinda cute to keep smiling at him until he came over to him smiling at Bailey what's with people tonight Bailey thought .Is he checking me out Bailey thought because I am not interested .

" Another beer please a pink gin to and your phone number " Bailey snorted. The guy looked at him. He was kinda flattered by it though but no thanks totally no and Besides fraternising with the members were not allowed club rules .Bailey shook his head and smirked good try Mate he thought .

" I can get you the drinks but not my number. I have a girlfriend " He pouted while Bailey got him his drinks " Oh please really " Bailey looked up at Senora coming into the club he smiled she was wearing a black dress showing off her figure and baby bump . " That's her there Bailey pointing to Senora " The guy looked round at who Bailey mentioned, right enough he does have a girlfriend and was pregnant .Bailey went over to Senora to help her. She batted him away. I'm not an invalid she thought sitting on the stool at the bar .The guy who asked for his no was watching Bailey with Senora cute together he thought .

" I still look sexy right " Bailey giggled shaking his head he leaned over to Senora `` Yes baby your still and those baby's to " He pointed to her breasts in that dress Senora looked down Patrick giggled those two are unbelievable he came over to them while sorting out drinks . "What do you think Patrick does, my girl still looks sexy right? Patrick nodded and laughed " Definitely " .Patrick sniggered those two are unbelievable he thought .

" Why thank you even though it took me a while to try get the zip up I was determined to still fit into it " Patrick went to serve Bailey got Senora orange juice " By the way I got chatted up " Bailey nodding over at the guy who asked for his number he was with a couple other people Senora looked over she sniggered " Were you scared " Senora said and snorted not funny Bailey thought Senora patted his hand Sniggered she touches Baileys face . " Hey you guys see this,' ' Patrick said, holding out his phone while he was talking about a status update by Brandon and Rory on their engagement.

" That's lovely for them " Senora said it was Bailey thought he should be Happy with Rory he thought it's what he wanted Elliot went over to Ed who was by the entrance door they both went to the office where Darian was .Elliot spoke to Ed about the guys giving him the bad vibe .

THEY LOOKED AT THE CCTV watching the two guys Elliot mentioned nothing sinister Darian thought but if they were giving Elliot the creeps he should say something the three of them went back to the bar Darian went up to the vip to see how everyone was doing while checking the two men out he didn't recognise them as regulars probably come to check out the club .

" Elliot " He looked round it was one the guys he looked at his friend " I'm perry this is Mark Christian friends " Elliot remembered Christian mentioning his friends he sat his glasses down and went over to them " Sorry if we were creeping you out but Christian asked to see if you were ok " " Right I remember him mentioning you guys we didn't get round to meet you " . Christian didn't need to do that Elliot thought but I guess he just wanted to know if I was ok and he did wonder if Christian was too .

" That's right we were in Thailand for a couple weeks' ' Mark said Elliot nodded a sneaky bugger he thought "Everything ok' ' Darian asked when he came over to see if everything was ok " Darian this is Perry and Mark Christian friends' ' .Right Darian thought Christians friends that's not so bad after all Darian thought .And good of Christian asking his friends to check in on Elliot .

" Ahh pleased. To meet you both " The three of them shook hands so is Darian the guy that owns the club Mark thought very intensely he thought " you're the owner " Mark asked Darian and Elliot looked at him and back at Mark and Perry . " I am and Nero's in Glasgow has been open for 3 months now " . Great d he is a bit intense both Mark and Perry thought Christian did mention that .

" WE HEARD ABOUT THAT didn't we Perry " " We did "Perry looks between Mark and Darian he seems a bit intense they both thought .Darian excused himself going over to Cameron when he arrived " I better/ get back do you need more drinks " "Thanks we are just leaving anyway Elliot one thing talk it over with him " Mark said looking at Perry he nodded to " I am going to when he gets back " .That was kind of them making Sure he was ok which he was I think

Elliot thought I do miss Christian and when he gets back from his travels they will talk .

BAILEY SLAPPED THE bathroom door regarding the news about Brandon and Rory's engagement. Why did he have a pang of jealousy? He thought it's stupid they're just having a fling damn you Brandon but at the same time he was happy for them . We aren't anything but fooling around. Maybe we should Cool it off for a bit. Bailey thought Bailey splashed his face with water and looked at himself in the mirror giving himself a pep talk before he went back out to the bar .

A COUPLE DAYS LATER Senora met with her friends Melinda and Lyndsay for lunch Bailey was at work at the slaughterhouse Elliot doing the day shift at the Club he eventually texted Christian regarding meeting to talk Christian would be back in a couple days Elliot was kinda nervous and excited to see him. We have to talk it over, Elliot thought, see where it leads us .

Senora excused herself to go to the bathroom for the second time at lunch Lyndsay joked about it she knows how she feels constantly peeing Senoras back ached a little as usual she did her business and wiped . A bit of blood, what's what she thought, panicking a little. I'm not in pain apart from peeing a lot which is normal when she went back to the table, sat down and looked at the girls .

" There is blood in my pee " Melinda threw down her cutlery went over to Senora bending down while Lyndsay was about to call the hospital " Lyndsay don't can we just go there " Lyndsay nodded Senora had tears Melinda went to comfort her they both helped her up and to Melinda's car .Making sure Senora was comfortable .

“ is this normal “ Lyndsay looked at Melinda she didn’t want to scare Senora Lyndsay Patted Senoras hand reassuring her her back did hurt she had said it didn’t take them long to get to the hospital A and E department explained to the receptionist and within five minutes she was seen to . Melinda waited in the waiting area and Lyndsay went with Senora for support . Bailey will need to know what Melinda thought while she waited for news .

“ Miss Roop how are you, I'm Jean, what's going on? "" I had blood when I peed earlier. I'm seven months old , and my back is sore too. “ The nurse took down some notes that Senora had a twinge. The nurse looked at Senora then decided to check on her .Senora looks at Lindsay

" Let's see what's going on " The nurse lifted up the blanket a little more blood on her pants she did an internal examination " Miss Roop you are 3 centimetres dilated " " What i can't be i've seven weeks to go " Oh god Senora thought she had heard of babies being born early I’m not ready she thought .

Senora started crying Lyndsay came over to her comforting Senora " Miss Roop we have to get you up to Maternity " Senora looked at Lyndsay they held hands Lyndsay squeezing her hand then another twinge oh my god that was a huge one Senora thought .Gripping Lindsays Hand .

" I'm not ready, what if " Senora said to Lyndsay with tears running down her face " Senora stop panicking " .Bailey we have to call Bailey she thought .I don’t want him to panic so someone will have to call him .

BAILEY WAS WASHING off the blood from.his wellies outside his work " Campbell " Bailey looked up at his boss Arthur standing at the door what is it now he thought going over to him . " Answer your phone, hear the phone call " Bailey brought out his phone missing

from Lyndsay and Melinda . " Hello " " Finally Bailey Senoras having the baby you better get hear quick " Melinda said fuck no he thought Bailey looked up at his boss " ill be right there " .Oh god not yet Bailey thought please let them be ok .

" Go on then " His boss said Bailey got his things and got on his bike and drove off to the hospital don't panic Bailey thought it would be fine he hoped . Gathering his things with his work friends letting him know they are thinking about him Kai watched Bailey speeding off. I do hope everything will be ok .

DANIEL LOOKED ROUND the club looking for Elliot he then spotted him.carrying a tray going over to the bar Daniel went over to him Elliot looked up at him what's Daniel doing here he thought wasn't he supposed to be in Spain still . " Daniel " " Elliot can we talk " . Daniel looks worried. Elliot thought I hope Christian is ok .

“ Sure Julia, can I take a break? I need to talk to Daniel “:l Sure you were due one anyway “ They went over to the seating area to have more privacy. Elliot's phone rang again and he excused himself a second to take the call from Patrick. “ What is it?” “ Senoras in labour. " Jesus Elliot thought too early Patrick told him that Melinda and Lyndsay were at the hospital and Catherine and Harvey were on their way there .

“ Ok let me know if any update Patrick Daniel just arrived “ Elliot looked round at him “ What is he doing there “” Not sure Patrick “ After their call Elliot went over to Daniel he looked stressed Elliot thought “ Daniel what’s going on is Christian ok “ “ Your friend “ Daniel asked “ His girlfriend went into labour early “ .That's not good Daniel thought looking down at his hands .

⸻

" CHRISTIAN ISN'T WELL Elliot "Daniel looks up at Elliot " Ok is that the reason why he came back early " I wish Daniel thought he had to know how Christian is hopefully Elliot can talk sense into him " Elliot he's dropped out off the showcase I know I tried to talk him out off it there will be others , Elliot haven't you noticed the food situation " What the hell Elliot thought he was looking forward to the tour .

What does he mean Elliot thought? Does he mean watching what he eats and stuff he thought " Daniel spit it out what's going on " " Haven't you noticed his food habits how he's always saying can't eat certain things " . Elliot thought back he kinda thought that was just Christians habits and because of his dancing .

" I kinda thought it was something to do with his training are you saying that Christian has something like bulimia something like that " Daniel nodded fuck Elliot thought he's been blind to it why didn't he catch on and he just thought it was something to do with his ballet diets .What Dancers are like . Jesus Christian why are you doing this to yourself this is a lot of information .

" WE CAN COPE WITHOUT you, Elliot , go and see Christian I'll let Darian know what's going on " Julia said in the office when Elliot came to her he had to go even though he had only a couple hours to go . " Thanks Julia " .Julia Came over to Elliot he looked sad she patted him on the back giving him reassurance he nodded am I taking too much on he thought .

BAILEY RAN INTO THE hospital Melinda was waiting for him Lyndsay was with Senora up at the maternity ward they got into the lift to go up to Maternity said his name Melinda waited at reception when Bailey went into Senoras room the doctor nurse was around

Senora when he went in . " Bailey " " Baby I'm here " .Bailey going over to Senora hugging her .While the nurses were discussing with each other what to do .

" We are taking Senora to have a Caesarian right now " " Ok what's going on " Bailey asked while the nurse gave him a gown so he can quickly change if the baby was born right away they both could be critical after the checks the placenta had halfway attached and can be fatal for mother and baby Jesus Bailey thought how can that happen everything was fine two weeks ago at there last scan . Everything was a blur the next minute they were in theatre nurses doctor checking Senora was ok numbing her they held hands the nurses reassuring Senora they are doing their best .

THE SURGEON CAME OVER to them reassuring them that he will get their son out fast. Bailey rubbed Senora's face giving her words of comfort while holding his hand . She didn't want a caesarean. Senora had thought about a water birth and that was taken away from her . The nurse came round telling them that they were nearly there getting him out then a few minutes later he was taken over to the cot with the nurses checking on him .

Bailey went over to the cot they had oxygen on him " Bailey what's happening " Senora asked the nurses chatting looking round at Bailey`` Bailey we have to take him to icu to help his breathing " Bailey nodded then the nurses ran with him .Jesus Bailey thought it's all gone to fast he heard Senora crying looking over at her the nurse with her is the baby gonna be ok that's what he wants to know .I feel kinda helpless Bailey thought going over to Senora Comforting her reassuring her that the nurses know what they are doing.

ELLIOT STOOD OUTSIDE Christian room.he took a deep breath he looked round at Daniel watching him he nodded letting him.know he's with him if needed ok Elliot thought i have to do this his hand shook taking a calming breath he opened the door and went inside the room was in blackness a bulge in the bed .There was chocolate and crisp packets around the bed water at the side jesus had be been gorging himself Elliot calmed himself went over to the bed and bent down Elliot taking a deep breath be brave he thought .

" Christian " A mumble under the bed Elliot placed his hand on the bed willing himself to pull the sheet down " Christian " " I said leave me alone " .Fuck Elliot thought this is gonna be tough .He sounds croaky Elliot thought what is he gonna look like willing Christian to look at him .

Christian pulled down the cover and got a shock. Elliot was hallucinating . He thought it was really him. " Elliot "Elliot smiled. "It's me. " Christian coughed a cackle in his chest that didn't sound good, Elliot thought . Maybe a chest infection he would have to see a doctor about if he wants to see a doctor that's something they will chat about .

" Elliot i'm sorry i " Elliot got up and went over to the window to open the blinds so he could see Christian better he opened them the sun shining and going down giving a glow into the bedroom. Christian shielded his eyes. He didn't see sunlight for two days. Elliot looked over at Christian and was shocked by the look of him. It broke Elliors heart . He looked so pale it didn't look like Christian was brave , Elliot thought .

Elliot went over to the bed and sat beside Christian on the bed he took his hand and looked up at him his eyes were sunken in he looked a bit skinnier the bed was a mess with crisp and sweet packets he could see properly . " Christian Daniel told me " Christian lay his head against the headboard shutting his eyes. Shit Christian thought

I shouldn't have kept this from Elliot but it's hard I missed him so much I just couldn't cope with it .

" I'm so sorry Elliot. I tried to be honest at the court for a parking ticket. " Elliot placed his hand on Christian mouth and shook his head, taking his hand away . " I believe you Daniel said Christian why , why are you doing this to yourself and quitting the showcase, it's stupid " .Elliot sniffed don't get upset he thought you needed to talk it out but keep calm about it Elliot thought .

Christian coughed again Elliot picked up the water Christian sipped a little he sat up a little more " Are you back " Christian asked tears stung Elliot's eyes he nodded Christian reached for Elliot's hand he took it .That's something they need to talk about Elliot thought thinks and talk about stuff that needs sorting .

" Do you want to live Christian because I couldn't bear it to lose another person I love " Tears ran down Elliot's face Christian came closer to him reaching out for Elliot to come to him.. Elliot embraced Christian and shut his eyes, both tears running .

Elliot wiped his eyes looking up at Christian " You love me "Christian asked Elliot nodded Christian smiled touching Elliot's face " i love you to " They kissed bumping heads together they smiled . " Christian please for me i mean it " Christian nodded then Elliot stood up looking around the room .Right i gotta do something read up on stuff we have to talk it over .god we are a total mess Elliot thought m here for him I love him and I want him to get better .

" First we clean this up " waving his hand around Christian looked around the room yes we do he thought . " After that you need to have a bath, you stink " .Elliot points to Christian he gives a faint smile and nods. I'm glad to see him Christian thought but not like this . He didn't want Elliot to see him weak and wallowing in self pity . And yes a bath sounds good smelling himself yes I do stink Elliot was right Elliot looks round at Christian before he leaves the room .

" I'm gonna go and run you a bath " Christian looks up at Elliot. That would be good god why is he being so calm about this . Daniel comes out of the office before Elliot goes into the bathroom " I'm running him a bath " " Good Elliot Thanks " Elliot nods and thinks I don't understand why Daniel didn't do anything sooner besides I don't want to cause an argument with him.

Chapter 23

Bailey wheeled Senora into the icu the nurse was with the baby when they went over to him.she explained that he was ok just needed a little help with his breathing and had oxygen to help him and will be monitored. Bailey bent down in front of Senora and she looked down at him " Babe he's going to be ok " Senora nodded tears stinging her eyes Bailey wiped them away.sitting beside her laying his arm round Senora .Looking over at There son Senora leans her head against Baileys shoulder her laid his arm around her .

" Has he got a name yet " The nurse asked Bailey and Senora looked at.each other looking up at the nurse " We do Casey Roop Cambell " Bailey said the nurse went away and came back to add his name to the incubator .Bailey looks at Senora a perfect name for their son.

Baileys mum and Senora dad arrived they all hugged and went to look at Casey Harvey was pleased about the name after his late son who had passed away 5 years ago from a motorbike accident " He just needs a bit oxygen to help with his breathing " Bailey explained Catherine looking into the incubator 8 pounds 5 they said his weight was a big boy . All Senora wanted was to hold Casey, that's what Bailey thought when she said it . The nurses brought them drinks Catherine had brought some snacks in case they were hungry Senora looked a bit tired Catherine thought which is understandable.

Bailey looks into the incubator with good strong breathing. That's what the nurses said he thought to himself was ok for mummy and daddy Bailey thought please pull through buddy Bailey thought .Because when you are better we can't wait to get you home and spoil you rotten .

Christian bath was ready. He had put some bubbles in for him to relax Elliot hoped Daniel had left to let them talk he would get some work done at home Elliot helped Christian to the bathroom. He was a little shocked at the weight he had lost over the past week.Christian went into the bath sinking in it felt good he thought closing his eyes Elliot sat on the toilet seat watching him chewing his lip Thinking of what to say and not sound patronising . Bailey had texted the update on baby Casey and asked how Christian was Elliot let him know and that he would come along tomorrow Elliot looked over at Christian while he texted Bailey back .

" The baby, " Christian asked Elliot, he got up and bent down beside the bath. " He's fine, very lucky they have him on oxygen for now. " That's good Christian thought Elliot leaned against the edge of the bath Christian looked round at him . " Christian about the photo album "Christian sighed and had wondered about that to " I have no idea Elliot " .Just then Christian house phone rang whoever it would be they would call back then his own phone rang his parents maybe he hadn't the strength to talk to them yet .I just need to get through today and with Elliot's help hopefully can .

Elliot took his phone and went out to the lounge to answer it " Christisn darling are you ok " His mother asked Elliot stood at the window she sounded frantic " This is Elliot Mrs king " Oh Magda was surprised to hear another voice the Elliot Christian had told them about she thought . " Oh Elliot hello is Christian ok " .

Elliot looked at the bedroom and back out to the view " I'm looking after him Mrs King he's a little fragile at the moment he's taking a bath I think he may have a viral infection " . " Oh goodness , His father and I have been worried we have flights booked to come over in a couple of days. " Shit Elliot thought what are they gonna think when they see Christian should he stall them or will it worry them more he thought . " Um ok I'll let Christian know Mrs King " .

" THANK YOU AND GOOD to talk to you at last Elliot and please just Magda " Elliot smiled that was good of Christian mother to do that she sounded ok n the phone he thought " You to Magda and don't worry about Christian I'm looking after him " Magda was relieved to hear what Elliot said and she let him know about the flight times and to let Christian know when they would be coming over .

CHRISTIAN SAT AT THE edge off the bath taking deep breaths he had no energy to stand Elliot came into the bathroom and rushed over to him Jesus he thought he should have waited for him helping Christian up wrapping the towel round him going into the bedroom Elliot got his robe covering him up Christian looked up at him Elliot gave a faint smile sitting beside Elliot . " Your parents sound nice and they're coming over in a couple days they will text the flight times " .

Christian groaned that's all he needed and he had forgotten their plans to visit Elliot shook his head and got up went over to the drawers bringing out t-shirt pj bottoms handing them to a Christian. " Thank you " Elliot looked round at him. He stood at the dresser drawers watching Christian change into the t-shirt and pj bottoms . Elliot's phone beeped text from Carrie asking how Christian was he replied looking better he would come home tomorrow they just needed to talk it out and asked if everything was ok at home .

" Elliot the photo " Ellot looked up at Christian he sighed Christian looked at him " Christian lets talk about it tomorrow ok " " I want to talk about it now " Elliot sighed and thought wow feisty Elliot thought shaking his head while Christian sat back on the bed looking over at Elliot standing at the dresser and thought is he just going to stand there .Bloody say something Christian Elliot watching him.

Elliot went over to him sat on the edge off the bed looking round at Christian " There is trust Christian there's someone that has broken that trust and i have a feeling " " Someone close " Christian asked Elliot nodded there time apart he tried to figure out who left it out and who was out to get the both them ." Definitely not Mark and Perry there my close friends " Elliot smiled thinking back to their meeting .Its just a weird situation to be in Elliot thought I want to trust Christian it's just gonna take a while to get that back .

" Looking out for me " Christian huffed and coughed. Luckily Elliot managed to get a house call by Darians friend for tomorrow he should really go to the hospital to get it checked out . Eliot's stomach rumbled he looked up at Christian " Fancy cheesy toast " Christian screws his face up then nods Elliot stands up looks round at Christian him looking up at him with a faint smile .Elliot thought will he be able to eat something should I consult the internet about that .

" I'm glad you're here " Christian said Elliot nods at him as he taught " Me to " Elliot goes out to the kitchen into the fridge, gets out the cheese cold meat, gets the bread then turns round a lot of discussion they need to have and check online info that he will need . Maybe talk to Malcolm about it too .Bacon Elliot thought going into the fridge and bringing it out he could hear shuffling coming from the lounge he looked round at Christian he had put on a baggy jumper he looked at Elliot from the kitchen . " Do you need a hand " " it's ok I can manage it " . Christian hummed hoovers while watching Elliot in his kitchen then decided to go sit over at the lounge .

Christian went over to the lounge and sat on the couch Elliot went into the fridge brought out a bottle of water he then went over to the couch handing Christian his water he looked up at Elliot waiting for him to open it he sighed and then opened the water taking a sip . Elliot nodded and went back to sort out the cheesy toast in between looking over at Christian making sure he is ok if he is ok Elliot thought I won't push it let him talk first . That's what he learned from therapy: if you want to talk, fine . If you don't, then it doesn't get pushed to .

ELLIOT SAT THE PLATES down " cheesy toast all a carte " Christian sniggered looking up at Elliot. It did look good. He thought Elliot took a bite off his watching Christian hoovering Elliot willing him to take a bite then Christian picked up the piece of toast taking a bite then water . " I'm a big boy Elliot, you don't have to baby me " Christian said, looking over at him. " Dammit, I'm sorry. " Christian held his head in his hands. Elliot thought tears were running down a Christian face Elliot went over to him laying his arm around him .Fucking hell Elliot thought am I taking something on that I'm not capable of then thought think of it as a trial basis for his course for social work .

" JESUS CHRISTIAN IS my cooking that bad " Christian looked up at Elliot him smiling at him " And I know you're a big boy Christian " wiggling his eyebrows Christian snorted they leaned against each other then Elliot moved his plate over to take more of his cheesy toast then Christian doing the same . "It is good, " Christian said. Elliot smiled while sitting back on the couch Christian looked at him and nodded . I really appreciate his efforts Christian thought and his cheesy toast tastes good .He hoped he could keep it down don't think about that Christian thought .

" RORY SENORAS HAD THE baby " Brandon had got a text from Bailey telling him the news about Casey he and Rory had been doing the sights around San Francisco Rory looked up at Brandon coming in from the balcony off there hotel wow he thought she had seven weeks to go he hoped the baby would be ok ." Everything ok " Brandon sat on the bed beside Rory " Seems so he's in the incubator just needs help with his breathing just now emergency c section " .

" I HOPE HE WILL BE ok name " " Casey Roop Campbell after her brother " Thats nice Rory thought they are a nice couple " Rory your nose is a little red " Brandon giggled even thought they had plenty sunscreen on Rory got up went over to the mirror yes he thought a little red not that bad with a little make up on you would hardly see it . " What do you want to do tonight? Brandon asked Rory, smirking, looking at Brandon in the mirror, he shook his head .

Rory turned round cocking his head " Food babe that later " Rory came over to Brandon pouting leaned down to kiss him " when do we ever wait till later " Brandon huffed reaching up to kiss Rory he moved away Brandon wondered why he didn't want a kiss . " I'm going for a shower, want to join me " , Giving Brandon the seductive look disappearing into the bathroom . Brandon got up racing into the bathroom after Rory for a make out session .

SENORA FELL ASLEEP when she got back to her hospital bed. Poor soul was exhausted. Catherine stayed with Casey for a while so Bailey could go home to get Senora's hospital bag, clean pjs and baby stuff she wanted to take with him. Elliot updated Bailey about

Christian and that he would see him tomorrow . “ Ready “ Patrick asked while Bailey was coming downstairs he looked at him and nodded “ Did Elliot text you to “ “ He did Christian don’t sound good hopeful he will be on the mend soon “.

Bailey hoped so he thought he looked at his phone again at Brandon’s text he smiled Brandon was thinking about them he would be home in a few days Patrick looked at Bailey deep in thought he went over to him laying his arm round Bailey he looked up at Patrick . “ C'mon you, let's get you back to see your boy “ . Then Bailey thought, am I missing Brandon? That's just silly, Senora needs me right now and our son .

SENORA HAD WOKEN UP she had two hours sleep which was a miracle she must’ve needed it Bailey had texted he was on his way back Patrick was giving him a lift Harvey came into the room with the wheel chair seriously Senora thought I can walk but she was sore from the c section still and was tender . “ Baileys on his way back “ Senora said to her dad getting into the wheelchair “ still sore “ Senora nodded and they headed over to the neonatal unit . Catherine was still there. The nurse was tending to Casey when Senora arrived changing his nappy, which Senora wanted to do next time she thought .

“ HE’S HAD A LITTLE snooze “ Catherine said when Senora got closer was that a little whimper Casey was doing while the nurse tended to him “ He has a good a good pair lungs on him “ The nurse explained that’s good Senora thought she nodded “ you might be able to hold him soon to “ Really Senora thought surprised at what the nurse said Senora had tears Catherine came over to her they hugged watched by Harvey .It must be hard for her with Casey born early he can only support her and Bailey he would do anything for his daughter .

Bailey came into the room what's wrong he thought when he saw Senora crying she looked over at him when he came closer to her " what's wrong what's happened " Bending down in from off Senora she wiped her eyes and smiled " We might be able to hold him soon " Oh my god Bailey thought that's great news he looked up at his mum and Harvey smiling then stood up going over to Casey who was asleep again dummy in . " Well little man you get better for us ok " His hand placed on the incubator Senora lay her head on Bailey's shoulder Bailey lay his arm around her and kissed her head .Really happy with the news looks like things are progressing which is good the nurses have been great Bailey thought I wanna be able to hold him to .

BAILEY GOT SENORA'S cushion for her so she could be more comfy sitting beside Casey Catherine and Harvey laughed they would be back in the morning . " Bailey " " Yea " He looked down at Senora reaching for her bag he got it for her " i wondered if he would like his onesie on " Bailey bent down to Senora she looked at him bringing out the onesie Bailey nodded " Sure next time he gets changed " .

" How are we doing? " the nurse assigned to Casey asked. They both looked up " sore but fine. " Senora said the nurse whose name was Shona looked at Casey and his vitals, which seemed good . " We were wondering if next time we can put his onesie on, " Shona looked over and smiled . " Of course I was going to ask if you wanted to tend to Casey while I checked on him .

Senora looks at Bailey and nods that it would be a great thing to do. It's what Senora wants to hold Casey he does too Senora seemed a bit nervous So was he Bailey thought while Shona tended to Casey he was a little fussy at first but once he was sorted he calmed down .

Christian came out the bathroom saw Elliot sorting his bedding on the couch what's he doing that for he thought Elliot looked up he smiled at Christian " What are you doing " " i thought i'd sleep on the couch so you can rest " Christian sighed coming round to Elliots side he looked up at Christian. Christian touched Elliot's face and he leaned into Christians touch .

" No please Elliot id like it for you to be beside me " Elliot sighed sitting down on the couch Christian sat beside him " One step at a time Christian ok " Yes Christian thought one step at a time " Yes i suppose your right lots to talk about " . We don't want to push it Christian thought to talk things through .

Elliot took his hand and he got up Christian looked up at him " Let's get you to bed " Christian nodded getting up feeling a little dizzy Elliot helped him into the bedroom into the covers Elliot left water on Christian side . He then went round to the other side and sat on top of the covers Christian looked round at him . " i missed you lying next to me " Elliot took Christian hand he nodded he missed him to . " Christian " He looked round at Elliot, noticing Elliot biting his lip . "We have to try " .

Shit how can i word this he thought without sounding patronising " Elliot spit it out " " You have to talk to me Christian and " Elliot takes Christian hand they look at each other I want to open up to Elliot like he has with me it's just hard to get the words out Christian thought I don't want to lose him again . I'm too afraid to lose him again .

" I know I will " Christian lay his head against the headboard shutting his eyes " We should get some sleep " Elliot goes to move Christian opened his eyes he nodded looking round at Elliot " It started when i was 13 " Oh shit he's opening up the internet said patience and understanding is the key .Like Christian has with me from the beginning. And he has helped me heal. Could I help him through this, Elliot thought .

" I wanted to go to dance class. I was a chubby kid. I pleaded with my parents to let me. I loved to dance. My parents thought it was a faze I was going through Christian sighed leaning his head back taking a sip of water. "Were you bullied Christian " He shook his head and reached over to get his phone, bringing up a picture he handed the phone to Elliot .He had to see what he was like when he was younger .

Elliot took the phone Christian aged 13 hes not chubby there Elliot thought just normal child puppy fat he thought " Ms Greene was the dance teacher she was ok some off the time some the kids got told off most the time we even thought she had a chip on her shoulder " He sniggered looked at Elliot he looked serious Christian thought ." Christian that's not fair " " I know kids things right " . Elliot thought she had no right to tell a kid he was fat .

" Christian you don't have to tell me all right now let's sleep ok " Maybe he's right Christian thought today he didn't feel he needed to purge himself maybe it's because Elliot is around but he still had it in the back of his mind that he would sometime again . " I'll go to counselling but privately I couldn't be in a group. " Christian looks over at Elliot. Will he understand that he thought ."That's understandable Christian " .He thought because of the paparazzi prying into Christians private life we don't want that either .

Christian nodded he was so tired he coughed again it don't sound good Elliot thought should he take paracetamol Elliot thought he went to get up where is he going Christian wondered " Have you any paracetamol " " I think so " .Elliot went out to the kitchen checking a couple drawers then found a box and laxatives he won't be using them again put them in the bin he noticed a half eaten salad in there to Elliot shakes his head this eating half off the food will have to stop to .

Stop it Elliot thought you're overthinking now you have to trust him , Elliot went back into the bedroom gave Christian the paracetamol and sat them on his side " Stay with me " " Are you sure " Christian nodded Elliot got into bed settling down beside Christian .

Christian facing Elliot then hugging each other " I love you " Christian said first touching Elliot's face he took Christian hand " love you to " .Elliot watched Christian drift off to sleep until he felt sleepy himself and finally drifting off snuggled into each other .

IN THE MIDDLE OF THE night Christian had a nightmare which woke Elliot a Christian legs thrashing Elliot held him till he settled " Ella " Christian mumbled whose Ella Elliot thought Christian snuggled into Elliot he made sure he was ok rubbing Christians back he then feel asleep again was Ella a friend Elliot thought don't overthink that Elliot thought Christian will tell you whenever you ask him or he will tell Elliot who she was .

Chapter 24

Elliot opened the door to Dr Carter, the doctor that Darian knows what age he was. Elliot thought his greying hair and beard glasses and quite handsome looking that's for sure Elliot Letting him in. Gloria was doing her housekeeper jobs when Dr Carter came into the apartment oh my she thought he was handsome . " Christian is in the bedroom Dr Carter " leading him to Elliot Dr Carter went into Christians room Christian was coming out of the bathroom as Dr Carter came into the room . Elliot hoovered at the door watching them .

" Christian Dr Carter " Elliot left the room to let them have some privacy Elliot went into the kitchen to get started on breakfast ",Mr King she asked " Gloria asked Elliot to look round at her " just to check Gloria for his chest. "Gloria carried on what she was doing while Elliot stared at Christian bedroom door .Oh I hope Mr King is ok Gloria thought he has not been well for a few days now while she carried on with her cleaning .

DR CARTER SOUNDED CHRISTIAN yes he did sound crackly and thought maybe should organise an x Ray for him just incase which he can do privately at his clinic " Christian anything else " A Christian stalled I have to admit to myself that it's getting worse he thought then it all came out telling Dr Carter everything while he sat and listened to Christian rant on what has been going on .i've got to get better for myself and for Elliot for our future do we have a future together Christian thinks .

After 5 minutes Dr Carter came out of Christian room on the phone coming over to the kitchen Elliot went over to him " I have organised a car to take Christian to my clinic for a check up he is getting ready the car should be here soon " Good Elliot thought it's better he get checked over proper " Thanks Dr Carter " The door chapped Gloria went to answer it which was Christian friend Perry to take over while Elliot had to go to do some chores and go to the hospital to see baby Casey because if a don't go Bailey would be mad at me and we don't want that .

ELLIOT WAVED AT BAILEY and Senora calling them from outside Bailey came to get him they went inside going over to Casey Elliot looked at him he was out of the incubator now and in an ordinary cot he looked so tiny he thought he looked at Bailey and Senora who both looked shattered . "He is doing better, docs seem really happy with him, he might get home next week " Senora explains that's great Elliot thought " That's great Guys a tough few days huh " .

" Sure has hows Christian " Bailey asked he also thought Elliot looked really tired to they probably had a lot talking to do " Gone to the clinic to have a check up I'll see him later he's been in a bad way guys " Bailey patted Elliot's back nodding I do hope he is not taking on a lot Bailey thought .Especially with someone who has an eating disorder who would have thought that looking at Christian he looked so healthy .

Shona came over to check on Casey. He's got a right little personality she thought while she and Senora checked on him while Bailey and Elliot went to get drinks at the drinks machine and to get some snacks Bailey leaned against the wall Elliot looked at him

." Man I'm so tired " Bailey said Elliot shook his head the same he thought " What's new with Christian any update " " He opened up a bit last night he also had a nightmare too " .Elliot sighed and yawned same with Bailey they both giggled shaking their heads .

Bailey got the snack and drink he looked up at Elliot " That's good right it means he trusts you " Elliot nodded he just wished he knew how to not baby him to much they went back to the ward Alana the other nurse assigned to Casey was over at Senora patting her back what's wrong now Bailey thought he looked at Elliot . Looked back over at the cot and got a shock when Senora turned round Casey in her arms tears running down her cheeks " Holy fuck " Bailey went over to them looked down at Casey asleep in her arms they both looked at each other . " What is " " He's doing fine improving " Alanah said. I can't believe Bailey thought Elliot came over. He was happy for his friends that Casey was doing so much better than they thought .

" Your turn " Senora said shit I'm gonna break him he thought as Senora passed him to Bailey he did a little gurgle oh wow Bailey thought I can finally hold my son then there was a pump Bailey looked up Senora sniggered his face " Well we do need to take turns to change and feed him like we said we were gonna do right " Bailey looked at Elliot for reassurance looked down at Casey ok I can do this he thought . " All parents are the same Bailey you're not the only one " Alanah said Senora went into the bag for fresh clothes for Casey handing them to Bailey .Right man Up Bailey I can do this we both made him and we both did agree to joint feed him and change him better now than later .

" Dr Ellis will be doing his rounds soon " Alanah explained then going over to the nurses station to let them have their bonding time with Casey Elliot took a couple photos for them they looked so happy now that Casey was ok which was a big relief for Bailey and

Senora . Then all three of them took a photo with Casey oh gosh he is gonna be so spoiled Elliot thought .

AFTER ELLIOT WENT HOME packed some clothes and his meds to take back to Christians also Called Malcolm letting him know the update on Christian and to take some nights off till next week so he could help out Christian and that he would need him for support .Which was totally fine with Darian when he had texted Elliot not to worry about his shifts and to let him know when he would be able to come back .

Elliot let himself in Christian apartment with his spare key Christian had come back from the clinic he had texted letting Elliot know . Elliot sat his purchases on the kitchen counter and his rucksack he was about to check on Christian when he heard the bedroom door opening he looked round at Christian coming over to him Elliot thought he looked a bit better . Which was good and he had changed into jogging bottoms and a baggy jumper smiling glad that Elliot was back .

" What's that? " Christian asked at Elliots' purchases . He looked at them and said, " I got these for you, they're supposed to be healthy and give you energy, that's what the lady said in the health store " . Christian hummed his answer Elliot noticed a bottle of pills sitting on the breakfast bar " That the antibiotics " He pointed to " Yes, I have to take them 3 times a day and i start my therapy session next week ."

That's great Elliot thought he places his hand on Christians arm they look at each other should I ask him about last night Elliot thought " Who is Ella " " Ahh she was a friend from home and dance class " A cough disturbed them they both looked round at Daniel standing at the couch " Pat on the phone " Christian nods he looks at Elliot them goes into the office to talk to Pat .

" I have a few things to do be back later " Daniel picks up his rucksack Elliot nods at him and is about to go back and sort out some stuff " Oh Daniel Christians password for his emails and stuff he's forgotten it " Daniel sighs going into his rucksack bringing out a pad and pen writing down the passwords . " He is always forgetting to keep one password " .Tutting Shaking his head thinking Christian needs to try and remember passwords for stuff he is always forgetting.

Daniel left Elliot carrying on what he was doing. He picks up the piece of paper sticking it in his pocket while he sorts out the energy shake for Christian then sticks it in the fridge . Christian comes out from the office and sees what Elliot is doing watching him . Elliot looks round at Christian and smiles at him Christian coming over to him .He hoovers beside him " How was Casey " " Adorable I took some pics " . Elliot got his phone scrolling for the ones he took Christian looking at them, yes cute Bailey and Senora looked happy Christian and Elliot looked at each other . They smile at each other Christian takes Elliot's hand. I have to explain to Elliot about Ella chewing his lip looking at each other .

" REGARDING ELLA SHE died when she was 15 " Christian sat on the stool, at the breakfast bar Elliot leaned against the counter top listening to what he has to say " She got really bad towards the end of her life she eventually went into a coma " Elliot came closer to Christian placing his hand on Christians shoulder squeezing it Christian nodded tears stinging his eyes . "Elliot I'm so sorry I don't want to go through that " Elliot reached for Christian he lay his head on Elliot's shoulder giving Christian words of comfort . " Pat said to take as long as I need to recover ":" Good you need it " .Elliot wiped Christians tears he took Elliot's hand kissing it .

Christian sat up looking at Elliot he took his hands again " i'm happy you're here " Elliot nodded he brought out the password for them to check he sat out on the table . " How did " Christian asked looking at Elliot " Blamed it on you forgetting " Elliot snorted Christian shook his head . He got a burning feeling in his throat and the doctor prescribed throat spray for it and said it could be thrush or just a simple throat infection from making himself sick .

" What's wrong? Elliot asked Christian to shake his head, " Throat infection," To which they said im.ok " Elliot got up good for that cool drink ice he thought Elliot went into the freezer Christian watching him brought out a couple ice cubes and put them in a glass, handing it to Christian. " Cool your throat " Christian grinned looking up at Elliot he shook his head and his arm . " Christian King" " What " .

" When you feel better c'mon take this' ' Elliot handed Christian the glass with ice. He took it and picked it out a little bit and put it in his mouth, swirling it around his mouth. It felt cool against his throat . " How's that? "" Better cooling " Elliot made up the shake for Christian to take .Christian watching him and thought why do I deserve him? He has been so good with me. I also want to talk about Grant without Elliot getting upset .

" i'll take it later " Elliot looked at Christian didn't he want it just now he thought has he eaten while he was away am i thinking to much he thought Christian came closer to Elliot he looked up at him " You are over thinking again and I'm over thinking to " " Sorry Christian I don't mean to and what are you over thinking about " .

" US ARE YOU BACK TO help me out or are you back back " Elliot wrapped his arms round Christian shoulders looking at him " Christian stop please I told you I love you your over thinking to much " Christian wrapped round Elliot's waist moving nearer to him fuck this is hard Elliot thought but I'm here because I love him we can get through this together I hope he thought . " Sorry " Christian said Elliot sniffed looking up at him. He nodded Christian touched his face . " One step at a time, " Elliot asked Christian nodded ." Are you hungry " " What you're asking is have I eaten ":Elliot sighed, moving away from Christian he looked at him . I have to trust him and not baby him. It's up to Christian Elliot though .

" I had a yoghourt earlier " That's good Elliot thought but a yoghourt isn't enough he thought before he spoke he looked up at Christian again " Your overthinking again " Elliot cocked his head shaking his head " I think I'll go take a nap " Good idea Elliot thought it'll give him time to sort a couple things . Christian looked round before he entered the bedroom " I love you " Elliot looked round at him smiling nodding " love you to " .Then Christian disappeared into the bedroom. Elliot let out a breath he didn't realise he was holding. I should read up more, maybe ask more questions about bulimia eating disorders .

" DO I STILL LOOK SEXY " Senora asked twirling in her dotted pjs Bailey looked up while he was feeding Casey he sniggered her hair all a wiry mess " Yes babe you still look sexy " Senora sniggered coming over to them Casey was doing well with his bottle a greedy boy most the time they thought and Dr Ellis was happy with his progress he advised. For Casey to stay another few days for precautions for prem babies even though he was seven weeks early something could still happen . Senora would be discharged tomorrow thank god she thought I can have a proper shower even though hospital showers were ok " How is he doing " They both looked over at one the other mothers coming over " So far so good right babe " Senora said Bailey about to burp Casey she looked over at Rhôna and over at her husband and there daughter " what about you guys " .

Rhona looks over at her husband with their daughter who is two years old " Ok so far it's just a waiting game now isn't it " they sounded really fed up there daughter was brought in with an infection two weeks ago and has been in the unit since she seems to be improving each day which is a good thing .

" THANKS ED " ED WAVED when he went into the lift Elliot shut the door he went into the office Christian on the computer replying to his parents email regarding there flights and itinerary he looked up at Elliot coming into the office " I will have to thank Darian for his help " " I know " Christian clicked on the link for the cameras then added to the box off his email he looked at Elliot again " He doesn't say much does he " .Christian asked when Ed came to help with the cctv that's just Ed .

" Ed's Fine And Yea he doesn't say much " Christian nodded then laid out his arm Elliot went to him he kissed the top of his head then sat beside him a tap on the door they looked up at Daniel standing " Get everything done " Christian asked Daniel nodded sat his rucksack down and looked at the two of them . " About your parents Christian " " All sorted Daniel I've organised the pick up " .

" Oh you have " Elliot looked round at Daniel he looked surprised that Christian was organised " Yes Ed from the club will pick them up also there going to stay in apartment no 11 to " Elliot said looking at Christian and back at Daniel " Oh good i was gonna ask about that "

" All sorted " Christian said Daniel picked up his rucksack " Anything else i can do text call me " " Ok see you tomorrow Daniel " Daniel was about to get to the door .

The doorbell rang. Elliot checked his phone and got up to answer the door. Who could that be? Daniel thought looking over at the door a young man beanie hat in a kinda grunge style he had . Christian came out of the office looking over at Elliot with Thomas they liked round at him .Is that the boy from group therapy Christian thought . Elliot introduces Thomas to Christian he seems like a nice , polite person Christian thought Elliot let them both have a chat while he prepared dinner . Hopefully Thomas can talk to Christian about his experience with bulimia too and Thomas was doing so much better lately .

Elliot looks over at Christian with Thomas hopefully he will help Christian out any advice he can give him Elliot put the macaroni in the oven . " Thomas is leaving " Elliot looks up at them both waiting at the kitchen door Elliot stands up takes off his oven gloves going over to them Thomas hoovers Looking between them .

" All sorted " Elliot asked Christian looks at Thomas he looks at Christian nodding at him " Hope so " Thomas says " Smells good Elliot " Elliot nods going over to Christian " Thanks for coming Thomas " . Elliot pats Thomas arm he nods yes hopefully the advice he has given Christian will help .

" No problem and hang in there ok Christian " " I will thank you Thomas " Christian lays his arm round Elliot he looks up at Christian smiling those two are suited Thomas thought and he hopes things will work out between them . " I'll be going then " " Don't you want to stay Thomas made plenty " .

" Thanks but I have an appointment to see you next week " .

Thomas left Elliot and went back into the kitchen to check on the Macaroni Christian watching him " Do you want wine " Elliot looked at Christian him going into the fridge . " Sure " .Elliot sits the wine on the table he stares at it looks at Christian .

" What is it love " Christian reaches for Elliot's hand they look at each other " I couldn't bare to lose you to Christian " Damn

Christian thought a tear in Elliot's eyes Christian got up went over to Elliot bending down in front of him " Elliot you won't I promise you I am determined to get better please believe me " .

" I DO BELIEVE YOU CHRISTIAN and I'm here aren't I and well " " Elliot please let's just have tonight and we can work out the rest ok " Elliot nods Christian wipes his tear away he reaches up to kiss Elliot and they bump heads I really don't want to lose him after Leyton it had taken a long time to be with anyone Elliot thought and Christian is amazing . He didn't think he would meet anyone like him Christian went back to his seat and poured some wine into Elliot's glass and water for himself . " Don't you want any " " best not since the meds " .

Elliot forgot can't take alcohol when taking antibiotics which is fine while they tucked into their meal Elliot thinking I will not stare while Christian tries eating them chatting away about most things .

Chapter 25

There's nothing like having your own bath Senora thought she had been in there 20 minutes with Baileys help after they would go to the hospital to see how Casey is doing Bailey was sorting out the bag off clothes and stuff to take his phone beeped he looked to see who it was a text from Brandon he was back home Bailey smiled hearing from him . " Bailey I'm ready to get out now " " coming " He went into the bathroom picking up the bath towel, helped Senora out the bath, wrapped the towel around herself, then sat on the toilet seat .

" Thats tired me out a bit ",Bailey looked round at he emptied the bath " You didn't sleep good ":Bailey bent down in front off Senora she looked down at him " why don't I go to the hospital first you rest a bit come later " " we'll I guess we could do that " it would be a great help Senora thought .Because at this moment I could just curl up in bed .

Bailey stood up Senora got changed into her lounge wear yea it best we do it that way Bailey thought Senora slowly walked into the bedroom Bailey fluffed her pillows got her blanket Bailey sat beside her . " Who would have thought having a baby can be exhausting " Bailey snorted Senora looked over at him then her phone rang Bailey handed it to her it was her dad calling .

" Hey dad " " What is the plan today " Senora looked up at Bailey while he got ready she smiled while watching him " Baileys going to go first to the hospital we can go this afternoon " Harvey stirred the two pots nodding while his staff took orders out " Ok that's fine what time " " say 1sh " .

" ok honey need anything " " No dad I'm fine see you later " .He is definitely gonna be a great grandad Senora could tell Harvey was itching to get hold of Casey and same with Bailey's mum too.

SENORA WAVED FROM THE door while Bailey sped off to the hospital his phone pinged. When he got off the bike Senora went into the kitchen and put the kettle on thinking about Casey and Bailey. He is besotted with him already which is a good thing Smiling to herself at the beginning of the pregnancy not so much but he had worked up to it .

Bailey parked the bike at the usual spot at the motel. He took a deep breath. He hadn't seen Brandon for two weeks. Suddenly he felt nervous because he thought Bailey got off the bike and was about to walk over to the room when the door opened, Brandon was standing there smiling . Bailey stopped looking at him all tanned Brandon smiled when Bailey got closer they went inside Bailey went closer to Brandon reaching up to kiss him both smiling .

" Hi " Brandon said Bailey snailed went for his jeans " Hey not even a hello " Bailey looked up " Hello " Bailey kissed him again lifting up Brandon's t shirt his ring gleaned he stopped taking Brandon's hand looking at the ring " I didn't congratulations did I " Bailey looked up at Brandon again he gave a faint smile

" Thanks how's Casey " Bailey huffed them went over to the bed sitting on it Brandon stood then Bailey flopped back on the bed and sighed " Bailey " " He is ok thankfully " Brandon came closer to the bed hoovered over Bailey " That's good right " " Mmm" Bailey reached up to Brandon bringing him closer to him they kissed Bailey reaching for Brandon's fly Brandon bent to kiss him while Bailey stick his hand inside Brandon's jeans spring free his cock .Jesus Can't he wait Brandon thought biting his lip while Bailey stroked him .

Bailey looked down at his length pushed Brandon onto his back lifting up his arm stroking Brandon with the other kissing Bailey then straddled him taking off his t shirt Brandon took off his Bailey noticing a new nipple ring he grinned touching it when did he get that Bailey thought bending down licking his nipple . Brandon hissed while Bailey tugged at his look up at Brandon and then reached over to get the condoms and lube Brandon sat up and they looked at each other . " I want to " Bailey sad taking out one condom picking up the lube Brandon opened it while Bailey squirted some lube onto his finger Brandon lay back Bailey flicked his finger inside Brandon he arched up for better access he started stroking Bailey took looking at each other while pleasuring each other .

Bailey slipped on the condom lifting up one off Brandons legs easing himself inside him holding onto Brandon's hand getting into a rhythm fuck Bailey thought I've missed him then thought shit why am I being like this he thought he stilled for a minute Brandon looked up at him . " Bailey " He looked down at Brandon bending down to kiss him, getting him not in rhythm again " Just fuck me " Bailey said . It didn't take long for them to come Bailey lay beside Brandon he looked round at Bailey he was being weird he thought .Bailey had his arms over his head Brandon staring at him Bailey looks round at Brandon he wiggles his eyebrows Bailey sniggers Shaking his head .

Later after their second shot of sex Brandon lay on his arm while Bailey got dressed doesn't he want to stay longer? Bailey zipped up. His jeans looked over at Brandon watching him . " Are you not gonna stay a bit " " Cant too many things to do and the hospital which I'm late going back to " Bailey already had a missed call from Senora and a text too . " I gotta go " Bailey went to the door and looked round at Brandon him laying half naked on the bed looking delicious Bailey smiled . " See you soon," Bailey nodded. Yes hopefully he will, he thought man he is so sexy lying there right now Bailey thought but I gotta go .

WHERE IS HE SENORA thought flicking through her phone again Harvey sighed shaking his head noticed by Catherine she should give the boy a break Harvey thought it has been full on since Casey a" Honey Bailey will be here soon try not get to anxious about it ok " Harvey said Senora looked over at her dad maybe he's right Bailey hasn't had a minute to himself past week Senora nodded and looked down at Casey who was asleep .Maybe I shouldn't be so anxious it's not good for Casey or mum .

" Sorry sorry I'm late " Bailey apologising when he arrived he went over to Senora who was with Casey he went to hug her she shrugged him away what was that about he thought " Baby what's wrong " " What took you so long " Bailey signed sat his stuff down Senora looked round at him " Stuff to do remember and I had to go into work to organise time off to " .Senora sighs again Jesus I can't help being late Bailey thought .

HARVEY CAME OVER GUIDING Senora to the door to take her out for a breather Catherine came over to Bailey `` What was that about mum " " She is just feeling overwhelmed that's all son " " And I'm not it's a lot mum all we want is for Casey to be home " .Catherine pulled Bailey close to her patting his back tears stinging his eyes . Senora saw them when she came back immediately, going over to them and joining the huddle " I'm sorry " Senora said they looked at each other. Bailey nodded at Senora thinking he's doing it again, leaving her thinking where he is .No I need to stop this overthinking Senora thought I will just make myself ill if I do and it won't be good for Casey either .

" Your both exhausted now is not the time to argue ok " Catherine said to the both of them Nurse Shona came over to them to see if they were ok and noticed a little tension with the family most probably feeling overwhelmed like most families are a This point .

CHRISTIAN HAD TEXTED his parents about getting picked up at the airport when they got off the flight after collecting their bags they went through the arrivals looking around for the driver and noticed someone rather tall and bulky holding up a sign off there name they went over to him . " Mr , Mrs King " " Yes that's us are you

Ed " Ed nodded and went to take Magda bag " Thank you Eric said looking at Magda " Ed guided them outside to the range and looked over at Eric as they walked to the car and got inside .

Eric sat in the front Magda the back " Do you work in security Ed " Ed nodded looked at Eric " i do i work for Darian Longstrome at his club " : Ahh the the one that Christian told us about darling " Magda explained Eric nodded he thought silent type while they drove off to Christian apartment .Yes Christian had mentioned about this club and that Elliot works in it part time .

CHRISTIAN HUGGED HIS parents. It was good to see them. They both got a shock when they saw he looked too thin so Ed put their cases in their apartment Elliot stood back watching them Ed chapped came in letting them know their cases were in their apartment and gave them the keys .Nice chap Eric thought looking between his wife Christian and Elliot .

" Elliot lovely to meet you at last " Magda said coming over to him " You too " Christian snaked his arm round Elliots waist smiling at him " He is amazing " Christian said looking at Elliot smiling at each other Elliot snorted, shaking his head . Magda took Christian arm leading him.to the veranda Eric watching them they are going to have mother son chat good he thought .

" How's he been? " Elliot looked round at Christian with his mum hugging " Good days bad days the antibiotics are helping though " Eric nodded they went over to the couch Elliot wondered if Christian parents were tired from their flight . " Do you want a drink Mr King " " Don't be formal, call me Eric i'm ok son thanks " .

" The view is amazing Eric " Magda came inside with Christian sitting beside him on the couch " What is your plans dad " Eric looked at Magda and back at Christian he sat forward looking at Christian. " Well we're here for a week. I want to spend time with you and get to know Elliot. " Eric looked over at Elliot Christian looked at him smiling. It's nice to know they want to get to know Elliot. He was happy to hear that .

" Obviously we have to talk Son " " Dad I'm getting help " Magda came over to Christian taking his hand looking over at Eric ' Darling we were very worried we should have known what was going on " .Christian nods tears stinging his eyes Yes he should have been honest with his parents and not bottle it up . And keeping it from them they must have been frantic .

" Magda, now we can discuss more. All we want to know is if your relationship is stable " Christian took Elliots hand and they smiled at each other then looked at Christian parents . " I love him " Christian said Elliot nodded Magda looked at Eric they both nodded. " Please don't worry Mr , Mrs King, I'm not going to leave Christian at this difficult time " " We understand that " . Eric said, looking at his wife and back at Christian and Elliot .

" Eric let's not dwell on this right now, why don't we all have dinner tonight and go out for a treat? " . That would be lovely to have a family meal together Elliot thought Christian takes Elliot's hand and mouthed thank you Elliot nods his silent understanding squeezing Christians hand I so love him right now Elliot thought .

MELINDA ANSWERED THE phone to Bailey while he stood outside to get air. Is everything ok? She thought " Bailey " " Mel please do me a favour " Melinda shook her head she had done a lot of favours for him she thought " Sure what is it " . Melinda asks, sighing leaning against her worktop .

" I think Senora needs girl time. Could you and Lyndsay take over? I think she needs it . Sure, I can do that. Leave it with me . Great Bailey thought it's the only thing can think of, Bailey thought a girly pamper is just what Senora needs he sounded exasperated they were both bound to be exhausted since Casey arrived .

After the call her phone beeped a text from someone who she had met on a dating app and had been chatting with for a month and decided to meet up soon. Finally she thought they had been chatting on and off for some time now and they now decided to arrange to meet up .Melinda smiled blushing looking at her text. She likes him and he likes her and they have been chatting for the past month .

SENORA WAS CHANGING Casey he was being a little fussy today which was understandable I would be fussy to being cooped up in the hospital she had put on his bottoms and was about to put on I'm mummy's best boy top on when Melinda and Lyndsay appeared what are they doing here she thought the nurses looked over at the balloons they had brought in with them to .They were cute she thought blue and congratulations on them which made her smile all three hugged it was good to see her friends .

" What is going on " Senora asked while Melinda got Casey buggy " We are here to pamper you Off course " " And by the looks of it you need it missy " Senora sniggered she didn't look that bad did she " But " " But nothing it's all arranged us four are having a bonding time let Bailey have a timeout today hun ok " Lyndsay said what had he said she thought .I guess they are right he does need a time out and well doesn't she Senora thought .I guess I've been hard on Bailey lately and yes he needs his downtime to which is totally fine they just needed to have a chat .

" Senora seriously don't overthink things it's not good for you and Casey will pick up on that and it won't be god for you and Bailey either " Good point there that Melinda made she nodded " He is doing it again though " Lyndsay huffed honestly she shouldn't be doing this to herself she went over to Senora " Hun stop it you both need time out go have a shower because honestly you need it and here change into this and take you time " .

" But " " Go " Melinda pointed to the bathroom then Senora picked up her summer dress toiletries and went to get a shower Melinda texted Bailey with an update .

Melinda " operation pamper is a go ⍰😊"

Bailey checked his text while in the pub with Patrick and Ellie, good he thought which he was relieved about .

" Bailey " Thanks Melinda ⍰" .

"Mate that was a good idea you came up with " Patrick said Bailey looked at him and nodded. He also needed to chill out, have a couple beers with his friends then go to the hospital later . " Yea she needed it especially not able to have her baby shower which we were gonna do when we came home " .

" That will be good ":Ellie said Ivy was happily drawing beside her. Bailey looked over. She was a good kid well mannered so he thought " Bet you can't wait to get him home " Ellie asked Bailey he nodded then the waitress came with their food .Yea it would be better when we get Casey home Bailey thought and get into a routine for the little guy ." Mummy " " Yes Honey " Ivy whispers in her mum's ear Ellie looks over at her and nods Ellie whispers back .

Ivy gets up going over to Bailey, he looks down at her and lifts up her drawing off a mum dad holding a picture. Bailey smiles while taking the picture " Wow Ivy is that for Casey " Ivy nods looking at her mum Ellie nods at Ivy " U huh " Thank you " . Ivy giggles and goes back over to Ellie sitting on her knee . That is the cutest thing to do. Bailey thought checking out the picture he was overwhelmed Patrick thought looking at Ellie " Bailey Mate you ok" " Yea just unexpected " .

" THERE HAVE A LOOK " Lyndsay held up the mirror for Senora wow she thought she did a good job while Melinda had Casey on her lap happily asleep " I have a date " Melinda announced the girls looked over at her she blushed " The guy you've been talking to past month " Lyndsay asked Melinda nodded blushing Yea finally they could meet because of each other's jobs was difficult to set up a date to meet .

They went out to the garden and Senora made sure Casey was well strapped in his buggy while Melinda and Lyndsay sorted out the table with the buffet and mocktails. This was really nice of them to do. Senora was so thoughtful and also very good and it was good that Melinda and her guy can finally meet up. She looks happy about it now .

ELLIOT AND CHRISTIAN parents went to dinner Christian was being weird. Elliot thought he may have thought for the first time going out with his parents he had progressed over the few days before their arrival . A couple people in the restaurant recognised Christian from going to his past shows he did say that would happen sometimes and cheered him up a bit too much to Elliots delight .Sometimes he liked being recognised and sometimes it irritated him but tonight Christian seemed irritated . Elliot touches Christians leg he looks over at Elliot, smiles at him and nods probably just nerves with coming out Elliot thought .

While looking through the menu chatting between Eric and Magda discussed there itinerary where they would be visiting other family members roundabout scotland and England also .Elliot looked at Christian again he looked tense again he thought he squeezed his leg again to reassure him Christian looked up at Elliot he nodded he took his hand from under the table .Also squeezing his hand for reassurance Christian smiles and nodding letting Elliot know he was still ok .

“ What does everyone wanting to drink " Eric asked looking round the table noticing Elliot and Christian interaction he looked at Magda she shook her head “:Why don’t we share a bottle wine dear “ “ Beer for me “ Elliot said Christian opted for a water then the conversation flowed Eric mentioning his business Magda ran a flower shop business which were both doing well . Elliot mentioned starting college doing social studies he had changed over from engineering and working at the club part time .

Eliot felt he was getting on with Christians parents. He made him feel welcome. There was no animosity between them even though Christian and his parents had to talk things out when he’s not around .They chatted about South Africa and the many places they visited previously it made Christian a bit homesick Magda took Christian hand . “ I’m ok Mom, just talking about Home got me “ .

“ I know honey hopefully you can come home for Christmas “ Christian smiles thinking back to the past christmases they had he looks at Elliot “ Hopefully you can have time off Elliot and come over “ Elliot looks at Christian smiling at each other “ We have talked about it haven’t we “ Christian Looking at Elliot again he nods that would be amazing spending time with Christians parents for Christmas “ That would be great “ .

Bailey came back from the toilet something had come up online to about Christian and Elliot it didn't look good he and Patrick looked through the post obviously someone had sold their story about them and mentioned the cousin off Christians Patrick went outside to call Elliot he knew he was out with Christians parent but he had to know what was going on .He will go ballistic when he finds out it's not great whoever did this and with Christian how he is right now won't do him good either .

ELLIOT GOT HIS PHONE out from his jacket Patrick calling him two missed calls Christian looks over at Elliot wondering what's happening he excuses. Himself to call Patrick back " Is everything ok Christian " Magda asked looking at Eric " Not sure mom his friend Bailey had their baby early I'll go see " .Christian gets up and goes to find Elliot who is outside on the phone pacing up and down god I hope it isn't the baby .

" There's what " Elliot asked when he called Patrick back Patrick told him about the online article regarding him Christian and his cousin and a couple private things Patrick forwarded it to Elliot holy shit he thought who or what had done this . " Elliot " he looked round at Christian while he read the article " it's bad " Elliot handed him his phone reading the contents Christian was enraged as to who could do this he thought and why . His personal stuff and his struggles and something about Elliot .

BACK AT THE APARTMENT Christian went into his office going over emails Calling Gloria also getting in touch with his friends Pat and the rest of the group he also got in touch with a couple ex's to Daniel had arrived to help out Patrick to see if he could help with the online articles . Elliot was getting a vibe from Daniel which he had ever since they met and Christian knew this when Elliot told him .

Elliot called Darian regarding security and his friend Darren to see if he found any info he asked Darian for Darren to feel and our Christians parents were not happy about what's going on and had also got in touch with people they knew also to see if any reporters had contacted them.

CARRIE CALLED ELLIOT regarding a couple reporters hanging around outside. He told her what's going on and not to worry Darian had his security coming over to them soon. She was not happy people were invading their privacy Elliot promised it would get sorted .

Bailey stopped before into the neonatal unit Senora looked great in her summer dress hair all done makeup on. The girls did a Great job. He smiled as she was holding Casey rocking back and forth with him signing to Casey which was cute. It was a good sight to see .

Senora looked round at Bailey coming in he kissed her cheek " Do I look sexy still " " You will always look sexy baby " Bailey rubbed Casey head he gave a little whimper and a pump they both laughed Senora handed him to Bailey for daddy cuddles ." So what's the latest on the news " " Sorting it out it's a mess Senora who would do that "

.

" I know some people would do anything for money " " Ahh miss Roop Mr Campbell " They looked round at Mr Ellis the consultant smiling his notes in hand " Dr Ellis anything wrong " Dr Ellis came over as Bailey put Casey in his cot he looked down at Casey Senora and Bailey looked at each other Dr Ellis locked up at them . " Casey results came back from the other tests all clear "

Senora and Bailey looked at each other and back at Dr Ellis `` Really he's ok we can take him home " " Yes depending on what the nurses opinions he should be able to get home the weekend " Senora Started crying Bailey lay his arm around her shoulder she moved nearer to him she couldn't believe what she had just heard they may take there boy home . " All his other tests, hearing and responsive are all ok to " .Dr Ellis explains .

" Dr Ellis we cant thank you enough right Bailey " Bailey nodded yes he thought he has been brilliant " Now i will give you a number for support if needed and how are you feeling in yourself " Senora did feel overwhelmed by everything the only thing was Casey she wanted him to be ok .

" Well i'm not gonna lie a bit overwhelmed my scar is healing all we want is Casey to be ok " " Understandable " .

" NO NO MR KING I WOULD not do that " Gloria said poor woman looked terrified Elliot thought when she arrived Christian was frustrated and was still puzzled by who would do this Leo and Ivan turned up for security incase any paparazzi turned up Ed and Frank went to his sisters the paparazzi disappeared once they arrived there and reassured Carrie they would stick around for a bit which she was grateful for . Christian also spoke to Pat and the rest of the crew by facetime and she reassured Christian she would sort things her way. In a couple days they would meet to sort some business out .

Christian also spoke to one his ex Martin who was on holiday with his partner he would let him know if any journalists approached him while talking to Martin Elliot answers the phone to another ex Scott they had a brief chat and the same what Christian spoke to Martin about . " Thanks for letting me know Elliot damn reporters huh " " No problem Scott yea he's mad about it and Daniel is trying his best to sort the situation " .Huh Scott thought Daniel is still doing his PA he had thought long ago Daniel and Christian would have parted ways by now often they had butted heads .

“ DANIEL MASON " SCOTT asked Scott " Yes is something up “ Should he mention before Scott thought maybe let Christian tell him he thought “ Christian will send you an email Scott and we're onto a couple things to” Christian came out to the balcony Elliot handed the phone to him he went inside for to let them talk . Magda and Eric had called the family to let them know what was going on so they were in the kitchen making drinks when Elliot appeared . “ Coffee or tea Elliot " Magda asked Elliot sat on the stool exhausted “ Coffee please “ “ is your sister ok “ Eric asked Elliot nodded he will go over there tomorrow Christian appears sitting beside Elliot poor soul looked tired Elliot thought Eric Patted Christians back he nodded . "Mom ,Dad , Sorry “ .Christian sighed and scrubbed his face. I don't have much energy for this, he thought .

“ SORRY FOR WHAT DARLING “ Christian sighed looking between his mum and dad Eric lay his arm round Christians shoulder “ All this mess “ Elliot took Christians hand he looked at Elliot “ Christian we're here for you this isn't your fault ok the person who did this only wants publicity and once we find out who it is they will be punished “ .Yes they should be Elliot thought Christian doesn't need this right now .

“ Maybe we should let the police know about this “ Christian said looking at his parents for advice Daniel overheard the conversation when he came out the office going over to them “ We shouldn't just yet Christian “ Everyone looked at him maybe he's right they all thought . “ I'll be back in the morning, hang in there ok “ Christian nodded, then Daniel left after a while Christian parents went to their apartment. It had been a tiring day for everyone .

Elliot and Christian went into the office, opened the computer to the cctv scrolling to see for anything until it came up. He was talking to someone while doing an email. They angled the CCTV to see what it was Elliot looked at Christian who couldn't believe what they saw . Elliot got out his phone to call Darian when they found Christian checked for other footage .

" I'll tell Darren to come over in the morning with Ed "Poor sods Darian thought what a damn mess he hopes it will die down soon " Thanks Darian " .

CHRISTIAN FLOPPED ONTO the bed he was exhausted Elliot stood shaking his head he went over to Christian bending over him " I'm so tired " Christian reached up his arms sitting up Elliot went to him hugging into him " Christian will this affect your work " " I shouldn't think so besides I had already let the principle at the school know I wouldn't be doing any work for them Pat said she will work something out " "Good " Elliot went to move Christian held him Elliot looked at him Elliot cocks his head what is wrong with Christian he thought .

" What are you worried about " Christian asked Elliot got up got his pjs to change into Christian watching him " incase you get dropped by other company's that you had plans to work with " Christian brought Elliot closer to him Elliot looked down at him " Please don't worry about that ok " Elliot nodded and went to move again Christian holding him again . " Christian " " What " Elliot sniggered he kissed Christian cheek " is that all I get " Elliot snorted again he said he was exhausted earlier . " I thought you were exhausted " " well I am but ."

Christian wiggles his eyebrows and pinches Elliot backside Elliot giggles again " Raincheck " Christian pouts then shakes his head wrapping his arms round Elliot's waist laying his head on his stomach Elliot rubs he head " Let's get into bed ok " Christian grunts looks up at Elliot " I love you " "love you to " .We shouldn't be to quick in having sex just yet Elliot thought Besides Christian is healing right now it's not that I don't want to Elliot thought .We just need for al, this business sorted first and for Christian to get stronger .

ELLIOT GETS INTO BED the other side shuffles over to Christian they snuggle into each other they kiss Elliot lays his arm over Christians stomach " Christian " " Mmmm " Elliot looks up at Christian " I do want to have sex but it's You I'm thinking about you know " Which is perfectly fine Christian thought no rush he bends to kiss Elliot then snuggling into each other . " I know it's fine " .He is such an adorable Christian thought and yes we shouldn't rush into things since their Reunion .

LATER THAT NIGHT CHRISTIAN threw up twice Elliot heard him and got up shit he thought he was doing great past few days he went into the bathroom Christian was splashing his face with water he looked pale " I'm sorry " Elliot went over to him felt his head maybe it's the antibiotics Elliot thought getting a cloth for Christian to put over his head " C'mon let's get back to bed I think it's the antibiotics Christian " .

Christian went into bed Elliot went into the lounge to the kitchen and got a bottle of water from the fridge. Could it be the antibiotics or did he not think about that Elliot thought going into the bedroom he gave Christian his water . He took a couple sips lay his head back Elliot went back into bed looked at the time after 3 " I didn't make myself sick Elliot " Elliot looked round at Christian he looked at Elliot `` like I said could be the antibiotics let's get back to sleep "

Christian lay his head on Elliot's shoulder and kissed his head wrapping his arm round Christian I've jumped the gun Elliot thought thinking Christian had made himself sick and Yea some antibiotics can make you feel woozy.

Chapter 26

The day had come for Bailey and Senora to take Casey home Bailey's mum waited at the house for them while Harvey drove them home they both decided. To have the baby shower in a couple weeks since Senora didn't get to have one before Casey was born ." Honey he's strapped in stop worrying " Harvey said making sure Casey was ok in the carrier Bailey shook his head she's stressing again he thought " Sorry dad " Harvey patted her back then Senora got in the back Shona came to see them off and told them any worries they know what to do .

MRS CRANTHAM FROM NEXT door from Senoras came out when they arrived home with a gift for them which they were both grateful for she was a sweet woman they had no problems with her " Thanks Mrs crantham " Bailey said she looked down at Casey he was tiny she thought full head off hair " How is he doing " " Mrs crantham come in I've made the tea " Catherine stood at the front door would they all piled in to the house .Bailey took Casey upstairs laying him in his cot with his dummy in .Bailey looks round at him before he goes back downstairs good he is sleeping smiling to himself .

Senora appeared Bailey lay his arm around her Senora leaning into Bailey kissing her head " It's going to be ok isn't it Bailey " Senora asked looking up at Bailey " Yes Babe he's doing great look at him he's here and healthy " Baileys right I should stop worrying so much and enjoy motherhood .The little man is quite content in his cot she thought .

" c'mon let's have tea " .Bailey said taking Senoras hand to go back downstairs into the kitchen where their parents were making the tea and had also brought some messages for them which they were grateful for .

Elliot chapped the office door at the club then went inside Darren Darians pI was there on his computer Darian beside him Elliot looked at Christian before they went in they had both had been to Christian first therapy session Darian looked up and came over to them shaking Christians hand he and Elliot sat on the couch they both looked tired Darian thought . "Your parents ok Christian " " Yes they're fine, gone to meet friends and thanks for the security much appreciated " .

" No problem, it's been a couple weeks for yourselves and Bailey, " He called earlier. Darren came round to them holding his computer and an envelope of information for them " We are going there after " . "That's for you Christian no doubt you already know what I'm gonna say " Darren said handing Christian the envelope " Thanks for your help Darren Elliot and I appreciate " .Christian looks round at Elliot smiling at him noticed by Darian those two are definitely in love he could see that .And it as good to see Elliot a lot happier it has been a tough few months for him and they seemed good together .

" No problem, now you have a bug in your phone. " Elliot looked at Christian and shook his head. Incredibly, he thought, "I don't understand how. " How would that happen Christian thought, looking between Darren and Elliot .And how do I get rid of it? That means some of his email messages have been hacked . Not that there was anything on the emails to be worried about thankfully .

""You've heard about the celebrity bugging cases. I can sort that for you " Shit Elliot thought the messages texts between them Christian looked at Elliot he took his hand " We can definitely go to the police about this can't we " Elliot asked looking at Darren and Darian . "You'll need a confession " Darren said Elliot looked at Christian they nodded at each other .Yes they definitely will need a confession but how and when .

" We can do that, " Christian said as Ellot looked at him . He thought " I have a friend in the police that can help. I'll call him tonight ``.Darren explains that's good news Christian thought we need to get on with our lives. All I want is Elliot and I to live a private life if we can and not be all over social media for the wrong things .

PATRICK LOOKED DOWN at baby Casey in his cot. He had brought a gift for him, a teddy that he and Ellie bought. He looked up at Ellie. She looked at him and smiled. Ivy came over to the cot looking at baby Casey . " Mummy " " Yes honey " Ellie picked up Ivy so she could see Casey " i like him." Ellie snorted, kissing her head . " Tea is ready, " Bailey shouted from the kitchen .The front door chapped and opened with Elliot and Christians arrival with takeaways . " Finally " Bailey announced Elliot tutted shaking his head taking the bag " So has anything calmed down yet " Senora asked while Elliot checked on Casey `` kind of " Christian said coming into the kitchen Bailey dished out the takeaway on the table Senora got the plates .

" You little man just wants to see your mummy and daddy " Elliot bending down to Casey who was fast asleep Senora came over she smiled at Elliot's interaction with Casey Elliot looked up at her and over at Christian helping out in the kitchen " How is he "Senora asked while they look down at Casey asleep " Getting there wants me to go in with him next session " .Wow Senora thought that could be a lot for the both them but if Christian is willing for Elliot to be with him for his therapy it means he trusts him .

Senora nodded looking over at Christian and back at Eliot `` Time and patience and the other thing "That's true Elliot thought which they are both doing " Getting sorted " Patrick came into the lounge handing Elliot a bottle of beer then they all huddled round the table tucking into their take away just as Melinda arrived . Eliot squeezed Christian leg , he looked at him and smiled a silent understanding between them that Christian was comfortable then

Casey made himself heard Bailey went over to pick him up and brought him into the kitchen . " He is a hungry boy huh buddy " Elliot and Patrick looked at each other knowing the change in their friend since the arrival of Casey Senora was proud of him for stepping up to his father duties .Also Elliot and Patrick were proud of their friend especially with Casey coming early .

" we're going to have his baby shower in a couple weeks, " Senora announced to everyone, humming their approval while they ate and drank. Afterwards everyone took turns to have cuddles with the baby until it was time to go .It was good of everyone coming round and helping out for a little while, Senora thought . Especially Christian with his problem and it didn't bother him being around people and the food situation too .She did notice Christian didn't eat much maybe with being around other people she thought maybe a bit much .

Senora tidied up while Bailey took Casey up to his room to change into his night onesie she could see from the monitor they bought and another gadget to hear if he was awake . Bailey's phone pinged twice Senora locket round probably from the others thanking them for the take away she noticed it was a text from Brandon Senora glanced at it which had said . " Hope Casey is doing ok. and don't worry and let him know what day is ok " .

What day is ok she thought maybe to do with work she thought Melinda came not the kitchen giggling she had been speaking to the guy she was seeing Senora shook her head she's smitten Senora thought Bailey came back downstairs with Casey came over to Senora gave her a kiss. Then took his phone and went into the lounge . " Hey " , Melinda asked Senora, looking at her " What is up "Melinda asked, cocking her head, had it been too much today she thought " Nothing What about you when you see him again " .Melinda smiles and lays her arm round Senora .

“ Soon “ Senora sniggered and then carried on cleaning up with Melinda's help; she hoped Melinda had found someone nice; she sounded keen on the guy and they had been chatting online by the sounds of it she really likes him to and him with her . Senora looks over at Bailey with Casey while checking his phone Melinda notices Senora staring at Bailey. I think she is worrying over nothing going over to her handing Senora a glass of wine . “ Hun drink up and stop worrying about stuff “ “ Sorry Yes I know “ Melinda is right I should stop worrying I’m going to make myself ill and it won’t be good for Casey and Bailey .

Molly hugged her uncle it had been a couple days since she saw him Jack was in the garden playing footy with his friend Ben he waved at his uncle and Christian Elliot took Morag from Carrie he missed them past two days " Are you better now Christian " Molly asked looking up at him Elliot looked at Christian and Carrie " Getting better Molly "Christian looks at Elliot him watching there interaction " Mummy always has the best medicine don't you mummy " .

" yes I do darling " Elliot snorted what a girl he thought while bouncing on his knee she started giggling Christian went into the lounge where Carrie was fixing Morag's cot " Sorry about the mess Carrie " Carrie looked over at Christian she sat on the sofa and patted the other side for him to sit beside her . " it's calmed down now onto another story as long as you're ok that's what matters " .

" Thanks I will be " " He is happier " Carrie nodded over at Elliot with Morag and Molly " He has helped a lot which I'm grateful for " That's good Carrie thought hopefully things will calm down soon for the both them even thought Darian sorted out security for them which was great they checked in to see if they were ok no journalists have been around the past day thankfully .

ELLIOT AND CHRISTIAN go into his room to get some more clothes to take to Christians , Christian closes the bedroom door watches Elliot taking stuff out his drawer he shakes his head goes over to Elliot wrapping his arms around his middle Elliot smiles Christian gives him a kiss on the cheek oh Elliot thought someone has a hard on Elliot wiggles to try get free . " Christian I have to get some clothes " " You don't have to, we're staying here tonight' ' .

Elliot snorts and moves round facing Christian " We are " Christian nods goes to kiss Elliot `` Woo wait don't we " " Elliot some normality tonight away from the apartment can we do that besides my parents are meeting up with friends " .He is right Elliot thought they do need to have chill out time he thought which they hadn't had since reuniting . " I love you " Elliot said Christian touching his face they kissed Elliot wrapped his arms round Christians shoulders " love you to and I've it with Carrie " Elliot shakes his head sneaky he thought.Elliot grinning he can be so sweet that's why I love him Elliot thought .

They kissed again Christian laying back on the bed Elliot hoovered bet him he should lock his door Elliot thought about to get up a Christian stopped him " Already locked it "Christian grinned He did wow Elliot thought bending down to kiss Christian sliding his hand under his t shirt " Thats sneaky " Elliot giggled going for Christians fly he didn't stop Elliot while he pulled down his jeans and boxers Elliot bent down taking Christian in his mouth .

Christian held onto Elliot's head while he licked his inside leg while massaging his balls. That's good Christian thought then stroking him taking his time and taking him in his mouth again Christian arched up and didn't want to come just yet he thought . Elliot sat up crawled up straddling Christian he looked up at Elliot while he took off his t-shirt Christian reached up pulling Elliot towards him kissing him chasing tongues . Christian licking Elliot's nipples that's so good Elliot thought grinding into him " shhh " Elliot said trying to be quiet he reached over for the condom Christian watching him also pick up the lube . " Let me go on top, " Christian nodded. Elliot got up stripped and looked round at Christian watching him. Elliot grinned, picking up the lube, squirting some on his hand coming over to Christian slicking him and Christian before Christian slid on the condom .

Elliot eased himself on Christian wrapped his arms round Elliots waist he bent down to kiss Christian stifling their moans Elliot put one hand on the wall while getting into a rhythm biting his lip Christian touched his mouth at this moment all Elliot wanted to do was scream while they made Love Christian kissing Elliot him moaning into Christians mouth .So they were not to noisy in there lovemaking then the kids would wonder what they are doing .

"MUMMY UNCLE ELLIOT'S doors locked "Molly said with a sad face Carrie was giving Morag her bottle and hadn't realised Molly had gone upstairs she looked round at Molly standing at the door pouting " They will want some privacy honey did you get your pjs " Molly held them up then Jack came into the lounge holding his phone talking to Micheal on FaceTime then handing it to Carrie . " Ok " Micheal asked Carrie, holding the phone down to Morag, Micheal giggled " Ok so far Elliot and Christian are staying over " .Good Micheal thought and he hoped Christian was ok although he had a long road ahead of him .

" THAT'S GOOD, HOW IS he? " " Seems ok " . Carrie says while they Carried on chatting while the kids hung around to speak to their dad and Micheal chatting to Morag while on FaceTime she giggled Carrie pinching her cheeks Molly sitting beside he

ELIOT COLLAPSES ONTO the bed beside Christian he looked round at him taking off the condom and that reminded him to get tested soon Christian looked round at Elliot lifting up his arm Elliot went nearer to him kissing Elliot's head " Ok " " mmm " Elliot felt good sleepy but good he was where he wanted to be beside the person he loved . " I was thinking " Christian eventually said, always with the thinking Elliot thought " What about " " GoGoto Spain for a holiday hire a villa " Elliot looked up at Christian that sounded so good he thought just the two of them together in the sun perfect to get away from all the troubles .

“ I’d so like that when “ “ soon once we sort things " Elliot kissed Christian then lay on his chest “ that be perfect Christian “ Elliot yawned and sat up Christian took his hand they looked at each other Elliot yawned again “ are you tired “ “ been an exhausting few days " They kissed again Christian slid his hand down under the covers feeling Elliot . “ Fuck Christian you got your appetite back “ .Christian sniggers “ We Have Making up to do “

They kissed again Christian pulling harder Elliot nuzzling Christian neck he’s gonna come soon Christian lay Elliot down kissing all the way down to his cock and taking him in his mouth Elliot put his hand to his mouth while Christian head bobbed up and down he lifted one leg up to get better access sticking a finger inside Elliot arched up tingles down his back he was close to coming . “ Christian I’m “;At that Elliot orgasmed oh my god he swallowed Christian sat back up wiping his mouth wow that’s sexy Elliot thought . "I'll be back “ Christian pulled on Eliot’s robe and went to the bathroom Elliot lay back feeling good smiling . Christian came back a few moments later jumping back into bed snuggling together . “ Wanna go for round 3 “ Christian asked Elliot giggled, dundunting him on the side they kissed again Christian facing Eliot holding each other till they fell asleep.

Chapter 27

Darren had got more information for Christian as well as getting his phone sorted Christian and Elliot checked more footage that they checked before confronting Daniel Elliot was making Pasta with Sausage for him and Christian over the past week Christian had went to his therapy sessions he had suggested he seek more professional help which he did which they suggested he should try rehab which Christian insisted he didn't want to do .Possibly an alternative a counsellor that can come see him or he go see the other counsellor regarding his bulimia .

There was a professional that had come to see Christian they discussed his meal habits etc Christian also spoke to Pat regarding coming back into the troupe. They all missed him. The journalists weren't as intrusive anymore onto the next story thankfully because they would not be getting any Christian also confided in Pat, which she was grateful for; she would support him whenever he needed it which he was most grateful for .

ELLIOT'S AND CHRISTIANS phone beeped Christian came over to the kitchen. The pasta smelled good. He thought Elliot looked at him. He wrapped his arms around Christians shoulders. " Be brave , ok " Christian nodded, taking Elliot's hand, leading him to the couch ." Christian " They look at each other " I'm ok " .Christian kisses Elliot's head this has to be done Elliot thought .

Christian chapped the office door before going in. Daniel looked up from his computer " Can we talk " " Sure " Daniel closed the computer followed Christian out Elliot was sitting on the couch Christian sat beside him Daniel on the chair what's going on Daniel thought looking at them both . " Is something wrong? Daniel asked Christian Daniel to look at Elliot .

" Daniel can you explain this ":Christian handed Daniel he envelope he took it opened it up looking at the contents at everything he and Elliot Darren found Daniel looked up at Christian and Elliot " I thought Scott was being paranoid about you but after talking to him and he told me what you guys had said " Daniel read the contents he looks up at Christian chewing his lip .

" Christian he made a pass at me " " Bullshit " Elliot said he huffed Christian lay his hand on Elliot's leg shaking his head Elliot nodded Christian looked back at Daniel " Daniel I'm grateful bringing Elliot back to me but leaving the photo album out for him to find was pretty Shiitty don't you think " . Dammit Daniel thought looking at Elliot he could tell he was not happy . But he thought in his own way he was trying to help and that Elliot had to know that Grant was his cousin .

": I am really sorry about that I really am please believe me " Elliot huffed shaking his head he got up to sort the pasta taking it off the heat then went back ' Did you ever think you would get caught " Elliot asked Daniel shook his head then Christian handed Daniel the other folder off evidence they found . "It was you that alerted the journalists, it's all in there and the emails I had investigated to why on earth did you want my phone hacked Daniel what have I ever done to you tell me " .Daniel picks up the envelope reading the contents again tears stinging his eyes reading through the contents .

Christian was getting angry now Elliot could tell he held Christians arm he looked round at Elliot letting him know he was ok and looked back at Daniel he was close to tears again " it wasn't my idea he manipulate me even now Christian Grant we meet before I became your PA I didn't realise the connection we were on off and when he mentioned you . I had nothing to do with the rapes Christian I didn't want anything to do with him but he kept on at me I told him it was wrong " . Tears ran down Daniels cheeks shaking his head . Holy shit Elliot thought Daniel was involved with Grant before that is a revelation .

" How the fuck did he know about Christian and I Daniel " Elliot couldn't believe what he was hearing Daniels confession he started crying again bloody hell Elliot thought he's not getting sympathy from me Christian looks at Elliot " I didn't tell , him I think from his parents or friends " .Christian looks at Elliot and back at Daniel he better be telling the truth .

" You're lying Daniel " Elliot said seething Christian taking his hand to calm Elliot he didn't want him upset again " You nearly ruined Christians life Daniel what for a rapist what satisfaction are you getting from it " . Daniel huffed Shaking his head and all Elliot thought I wanted to punch him right now .

" I don't get any satisfaction. I have tried to sort the mess out Christian please believe me " Elliot shook his head " Grant wanted me to help.him with his appeal i told him no Christian he threatened to kill himself " Elliot tutted asshole he thought maybe he should have died .

" He should have "Then Elliot immediately regretted what he said Christian glared at Elliot and after but it's what he felt at that point " i think i've heard enough " Christian said looking at Elliot he nodded " Did you get all that " Daniel was puzzled at what Elliot said .The door Chapped Darren with his police friend and another policeman came into the apartment. Christian and Elliot stood up Christian looked around at Daniel " I am sorry it's come to this Daniel " .

Elliot handed Darren friend the info as the other put Daniel in cuffs " Daniel you're fired " Christian said tears rolling down Daniel's face Daniel was given his rights before they took him away . Christian sat on the couch and he felt a weight come off him while Daniel was taken away .What a mess he thought shaking his head .

Elliot sat beside Christian taking his hand watched by Darren " You guys did great " Elliot looked over at him and nodded " will keep you updated Christian " alli said then left with Darren . " Am i supposed to feel relieved " Ellot looked at him Christian gave a faint smile Elliot reached over to kiss him . " I know it's hard but it's over hopefully "Christian said taking Elliot's hand " I hope so I can't take any more crap "Elliot said sighing leaning back on the couch .I'm tired Elliot thought .

Elliot sniggered and got up to see to dinner Christian came over to him wrapping his arms round Eliot's waist " Thank you " " You are welcome now sort the plates " Elliot looking round at Christian smiling . " Also no more surprises mr ok can we just get on with " Christian bent over Elliot and kissed him " Yes we can hopefully now I have to get a new PA " . Eliot sighed he didn't need a PA he thought bad enough having a housekeeper but a guess it would be helpful he thought .

Chapter 28

2 weeks passed the day off Caseys baby shower arrived thankfully the weather was to be warm Senora's dad and Catherine helped with the catering they decided to have it at home saved expense Lyndsay and Melinda organised the baby shower end which was helpful for Senora and Bailey Casey was now a month old and thriving no after effects from m being born premature.

Christian and Pat meet to discuss the group ; he also wasn't interested in doing an interview about what happened to give his side. Elliot thought it was a crazy idea but he wanted to since the media sometimes gives out false information.It is his life after all why should the media pry into his private life he is perfectly happy the way things are .

Everyone arrived for Caseys baby shower everyone thought he looked handsome in his little suite that he grew into people thought he looked like Bailey a mini me they joked Darian , Malcolm and Cameron with Philip came along to the kids played together now that Greece was home Brandon and Rory came along with him Catherine had Casey on her lap Harvey pulling funny things faces at Casey he giggled .Senora and Bailer were thankful that her dad and Catherine chipped in to help with Casey whenever her and Bailey needed a break .

Senora thought Melinda looked pissed off while they sat around talking while Senora and Bailey opened the presents they got for Casey, some clothes for him, toys and teddy's money for him and for Bailey and Senora which they were both grateful for . Pamper sessions at one of the local spas which will definitely get used. Casey was so spoiled today which was great .

Bailey went inside to get food followed by Brandon Bailey looked at him then carried on what he was doing " He has got so big hasn't he " Brandon asked Bailey hummed his answer while stuffing his mouth with a sandwich " Bailey " Is he pissed of at me about something Brandon thought " Daddy I'm starving " Reece announced coming into the kitchen Brandon sighed helping Reece with what he wanted.Looking over at Bailey while he helped Reece to get what he wanted .

" Someone has done a whoopsie " Catherine came into the kitchen taking Casey upstairs " You want another beer " Bailey asked going into the fridge bringing some out handing one to Brandon they went outside Brandon handing Rory his plate .He didn't look happy Rory thought he had been a bit of fish since they arrived .And wondered what was up with Brandon didn't he want to come Rory thought .

" What's up? " Senora asked Melinda she lifted her glass of wine while taking a sip " I thought Eddie could be here today but he's got to work today " Is that all Senora thought maybe she wanted to show him off Senora thought maybe next time whenever they decided to have a night out. He can come along or maybe he isn't great with strangers Senora thought which would be a shame .

" When do you guys go to Spain " Malcolm asked Elliot who looked at Christian " Couple weeks we can't wait can't we " Elliot says looking at Christian " We need it after the month we have had " Christian taking Elliot's hand he looked happy Malcolm thought which was good he deserved to be happy Malcolm looked over at Cameron he winked at Malcolm . " Daddy " Malcolm looked round at Philip. He brought him closer. " What is it buddy? "" Can I join a football team? " Malcolm snorted. Cameron rolled his eyes. It was always something different every week with this boy, he thought . Also a bit random he wants to join Everything Which he doesn't have to .

" Maybe let's get the taeKwondo a go first ok " Philip pouted then went of to play with the other kids " it never stops doesn't it " Carrie announced Bailey sitting down beside her with Casey " What doesn't " Bailey asked looking round the table " You have that to look forward to Bailey constantly asking for stuff " Carrie explained bouncing Morag on her knee .She giggles And that is totally fine if Casey wants to join anything he can .

CHRISTIANS PHONE RANG a call from Pat he excused himself to take her call inside Elliot watched him go inside and wondered who the call was from Carrie noticed his worried look " Pat what's wrong " " Sorry Christian nothing serious honey but I think I may have a new Pa for you " Patricia looked round at the person who was with other people . Pat hoped that Christian would agree to see her; he does need a bit of organisation; he can't do it himself or get Elliot to help him .

" I know what your going to say you would rather I would but it's my niece Anna who I mentioned before " " Ahh yes I remember well there's no harm in talking to her give her my details and we can sort something out " Patricia was pleased to hear that Anna would do a good job for him she can vouch for that .

" I'D LOVE TO DO A SHOW for you Darian " Rory was pleased that Darian had asked him to do his drag show at the two clubs whenever he was available Darian was pleased he was such a lovely person he thought and he and Brandon are a lovely couple. Rory noticed Bailey and Brandon with baby Casey he smiled at Brandon looking over at Rory he had a gooey look on him . Bailey got up and handed Casey to Rory he was shocked until he looked down at him Casey gurgling sucking on his dummy oh my this little guy is sure cute " Uncle Rory turn " Bailey looked over at Brandon smiling then went into the kitchen to help Senora tidy up .

Brandon Came over to Rory sitting beside him. They look at each other " Suits you " Brandon teased Rory huffed looking down at Casey he is cute and someday I would like a kid my own or our own . Brandon lays his arm round Rory " Someday we couldn't we " Brandon asked they look at each other Brandon smiling " That would be a good look at options " Brandon nodded and looked down at Casey who had fallen asleep Yea he could see him and Rory with a family someday .

" Can I just say you look exceptionally gorgeous today? " Bailey whispered in Senora's ear as she sniggered, batting him away. " You two got a room, " Patrick said, passing them going up to the toilet ." Mmm that be fun " " Bailey i'm not properly healed yet " Senora turned round to face Bailey he cocked his head grinning " Other ways " He whispered Senora tutted " i know i better go rescue Rory and Brandon " . Senora leaves Rory will be fine with Casey Bailey though carrying on what he was doing .shaking his head Yea he knows she isn't quite healed yet eventually they would get round to having sex again .

BRANDON BROUGHT SOME plates and bottles into the kitchen while Bailey washed up some dishes. Brandon picked up the tea towel and started drying the dishes. Bailey looked over at him and sighed . " We are on the same shift friday " Bailey looked over at Brandon did he change his shift " Rory has his drag show Saturday " Bailey hummed his answer passing the plates to Brandon `` Are you able to " " Let you know ``.Bailey replies handing Brandon the dishes to dry .While Senora rescues Rory taking Casey and putting him in his pram Brandon watching there interaction .

" A new Pa that's good right " Elliot was pleased to hear Pat was able to let him know about Christian new potential Pa. He was a nightmare trying to organise things and eventually Elliot had to help him out till Pat could check out people she knew .

AFTER EVERYONE LEFT Bailey checked on Casey he was asleep he smiled putting his dummy back in lifting his cover over him Bailey went into the bedroom Senora was in bed asleep already it was a good day everyone spoiled them his phone beeped off a text which was from Brandon saying it was a good day and he would see him soon . Bailey replied then went into the bedroom stripped down to his boxers and went into bed moving over to Senora's side lay his arm over her stomach he kissed her cheek . " Casey ok " " Asleep " Senora moved round facing Bailey and she reached over to kiss him . " Love you " Bailey said first " love you to give it another month ok then we can try " .Senora said feeling Bailey's face he kissed her hand .

" Sure we can do that " Bailey moved up the bed Senora moving up with him leaning her head against his shoulder Bailey lay his arm round Senora kissing her head " Good day "Senora asked looking up at Bailey " Yep it was a good day" it was good to see everyone and they all got a proper chance to see Casey he was certainly loving the attention and everyone was so generous with the gifts .

" I WAS THINKING WE should do a rota system " Senora says Bailey sighs always with the thinking Bailey thought but I guess we could do that " Senora let's think about that in the morning ok " .Does there have to be a rota system Bailey thought scrubbing his face .

To go ahead myself Senora thought but it would be a good idea if we did the rota system although they both took it in turns to get up for Casey bottle feeds and nappy changes which was a challenge for Bailey sometimes it's just something we have to work through together Senora thought .

Chapter 29

Christian meet with Anna a couple days later at a local eatery he frequented in previous she seemed nice enough while they chatted away Anna told him she previously worked for an author for a few months to do promotion for her that was her second Pa job she also worked reception at a local London hotel and did Pa for that hotel to . Christian was impressed with her CV work the waiter came over with more tea coffee for them " Anna I'll be honest i wasn't gonna get another Pa let your aunt Pat do the business side but see the guy inside grey hoodie" Anna looked over at who Christian was talking about she saw the blonde guy in a grey hoodie he waved smiled giving a thumbs up at them Anna smiled at nodded looking at Christian .

" I take it that's Elliot " " It is if he's happy with the way things are going today then i am " Elliot came over sat beside them he reached over to Christian whispered in his ear " I like her " They both looked over at Anna " When can you start " Anna giggled wow she thought she didn't expect to be hired she thought .Christian and Elliot looking at each other and back at Anna well Anna thought they certainly are a cute couple .

" I got the job " " You have " Christian smiled he looked at Elliot " Just make sure he has his coffee in the morning he's a total bear in the morning " Elliot teases Christian sniggers shaking his head Anna looks between them " Totally not like that I'm glad to have you on board Anna " " Me to " .Hopefully we will get on working together

Anna thought .And I think we will get along and they seemed a solid couple to very much in love she noticed .

SENORA INSPECTS HER work she had spent most the morning sorting and out a rota system for her and Bailey even though they took turns to get up for Casey Bailey was grumpy for work which wouldn't do they had to compromise on something she thought Bailey can check it out when he comes home after there chat she wanted to have with him first . They were both tetchy and tired but that's not gonna be all the time Senora thought once Casey is a bit older things will get better .She hoped she was tired of having to get up also to tend to Casey and also tend to the house .

RORY IS IN THE CAFE drinking his second cup of tea waiting for Bailey to come. He had texted him that he wanted advice on something he had a gut feeling about Brandon and wanted to talk to Bailey about it. First, seeing it from his side, The cafe door opened. Bailey looked round for Rory . Rory waved he was over at the corner. Bailey came over and sat down. He ordered tea from the waitress. Bailey looked over at Rory. He seemed sad because he thought he and Brandon were having problems . " Rory what is it, talk to me " .

Rory looked over at Bailey he's such a sweet boy he thought I'm not gonna get angry with him " Brandon doesn't know I'm here with you I wanted to talk to you first " Rory took a deep breath looking at Bailey no I'm not gonna cry I'll be brave he thought " I never thought I would meet a person like Brandon he's accepted the way I am I know I can be a bit much for people " . " Rory you be yourself you don't need to change for no one you guys are amazing together I can see that" .What the hell is this about Bailey thought .

" You think so I thought having a three way would bring us closer we both suggested it Club only though just the twice " " Has it not " Bailey asked Rory shook his head looking down " I haven't told him I quit drag Uk " Fuck sake Bailey thought why did he go and do that it's his dream to be on the show ." Rory why " " Many reasons Bailey can ask me how much do you care about Brandon " .What the hell Bailey thought looking down at his hands What do I say.

Shit thought Bailey he knows and figured it out Bailey cleared his throat shifted in his seat he felt hot all of a sudden " Rory he's just a friend nothing else he's with you isn't he " Rory wondered what that meant Brandon is with him he snorted looking at Bailey again " is it curiously Bailey " " Not even sure myself to be honest " Rory looked down at his ring twirling it round Bailey watching him . " The day he picked the ring you went with him right" " For advice Rory he picked a good one " Rory snorted, nodding his head that it was a good day and holiday to Rory locked back up at Bailey. "You were careful I hope " Bailey nodded. Rory thought " You know there are support groups online "Rory suggested maybe Bailey needs to talk to someone how he is feeling Bailey held his hands up waving and shaking his head " No no can't besides I don't think I'm not remotely attracted to guys could that be a pan sexual or whatever it is " . Maybe it could be that I haven't found any other guy attractive, Jesus what am I thinking that for.

Rory snorted shaking his head he smiled " You have responsibilities Bailey you have a beautiful girlfriend and son don't throw that away ok " Yep she is awesome Bailey thought and he was surprised Rory wasn't mad at him which was weird he thought " Rory you're not mad " " Bailey honey I'm terrified it's a good thing I like you or I wouldn't have been so nice " Bailey giggled Rory reached for Baileys hand they looked at each other . " Dont worry ok and whatever happens between Brandon and I it's not your fault ok and you and Senora should talk " Bailey nodded yes they both had to have a chat about stuff." I felt safe with him " . Bailey announced felt safe with Brandon Rory though he did not feel like he would be safe with anyone else .

" I think Brandon and I are just going through stuff right now Bailey don't think it's because of you " That's a relief Bailey thought he didn't know he and Rory were going through stuff not his business and yes I love Senora and my son I wouldn't change that Bailey thought .

SENORA PINNED UP THE week's schedule planner on the board in the kitchen not a bad job she thought smiling into herself the front door opened the arrival of Bailey he went over to the Moses basket Casey was asleep when looking down at him he looked up at Senora in the kitchen sorting out dinner Bailey smiled he went into the kitchen looked up at the board she's been busy he thought . " What's this? " Senora looked round while Bailey inspected it " A planner like I mentioned was gonna do what you think " .Senora leaned against the sink watching Bailey check out the board .

BAILEY LOOKED AT SENORA and back at the board. Yes, great idea but some bits were blank " why are days blank " Bailey pointed To the board " our free days you pick what day to have your day out same with me and when you're working you don't have to get up overnight . Also we alternate mornings and get up with Casey while the other has a lie in . And pick a family day out " . Well I guess that could work out Bailey thought we gotta compromise on some things . I like this idea he thought and it's something on the family days out they can plan to do and yes I have been a bit tired going to work which everyone has noticed .

BAILEY MOVED CLOSER to Senora wrapping his arms round her waist he kissed her which surprised Bailey " You are amazing great idea " Senora giggled shaking her head " Thank you " Senora went to move he gave her a peek on the cheek then let Senora go to go over to Casey for daddy time " I was wanting to talk to you about something else " Senora asked from the kitchen Bailey looked over at her then Casey pumped thanks son Bailey thought jeez that's a smelly pump " Sure " . " Do you want chicken wraps for dinner? " .

" That be great c'mon little man, let's finish off the episode huh " Senora snorted. He's only a month old, she thought and what's the big deal with the show he had started watching anyway she couldn't get into it .But that was ok it's his thing Senora grinned at the both of them Casey on his dads chest it was so cute ." Now little man where were we " Bailey switching on Netflix for the show he had started which was getting good .

RORY SAT ON THE COUCH twirls his ring he had thought about leaving a note but that would be just to cruel he thought they should just talk it out that be reasonable thing to do Rory wiped his eyes from crying he didn't want Brandon to see him al, eyes blotchy the apartment door opened off Brandon's arrival home he noticed the bags in the hallway had Rory brought more stuff he thought . " Hey " he said coming into the lounge Rory sitting on the couch he went over to him bending down to give Rory a kiss " Hey yourself " Had he been crying Brandon wondered" The bags Rory " .Brandon pointing to them at the door what's going on he thought .

" Brandon sit for a minute " Brandon sits beside Rory he takes Brandon's hand they look at each other " I quite drag Uk " " Rory why " Jesus he's been upset because of it why didn't he call him " Not the right time but at least I got regular work at the clubs right and the kids still need me " Brandon tutted the outreach kids would've been fine he thought that is no excuse. It was his dream to do Drag Uk Maybe reapply hopefully Brandon thought .

" Brandon am I enough for you " Rory asked what a weird question is this to do with the couple threesomes they had at the club " Baby your enough for me we only tried it out if you don't want to anymore we won't " was he being serious Rory thought that's another discussion for later to " I need a break Brandon " Brandon snorted they've just come back from a holiday . " I don't know what's happened to us lately Brandon, it's like we're going through the motions we use to talk for hours stupid stuff like we did, maybe I'm overthinking too much " . What the hell Brandon thought? Why is he acting like this? Brandon thought this isn't like Rory .

Rory stood up going over to the window Brandon watching him Rory looked round at him tears stung his eyes " I talked to Bailey " Shit Brandon thought how did he guess what was going on " Did you forget what we talked about my ex Brandon " Brandon got up went over to Rory he tried to hug him he pulled away " Don't leave me " Rory huffed glared at Brandon "He said he felt safe with you " " I was helping him Rory we decided not to anymore how else can I explain it " .

" YOU CAN'T BRANDON I can't stay here I do love you I just need space right now " the door chapped Rory guessed it was Kenny come to pick him up Brandon wondered who it was Rory going to the door letting Kenny in " ok " Kenny asked Rory shook his head he looked at Brandon standing in the hallway . " Can you take the bags Kenny I'll be down soon " Kenny took Rory's bags while he went into the lounge Brandon followed him . Rory took off his engagement ring sitting on the table looking round at Brandon . " Brandon just for now ok we can talk in a couple days ok " This is killing me Rory thought but I have to I just need space right now to think things over .

" Brandon, I think Bailey is confused right now. I don't know how else I can explain it. Maybe he is just curious at the moment . "

Brandon couldn't talk everything felt like a whirlwind he didn't want to lose Rory he went over to Brandon took his hand they looked at each other " I'm sorry " Rory went to walk away Brandon grabbed his arm he looked at Brandon prizing himself away until he got to the door looking back Brandon flopped onto the chair why is this happening he thought hearing the front door shut . Tears rolled down Rory's cheeks. He had to do this to get some space for each other for a few days leaning against the wall his heart was breaking .

BAILEY CHANGED CASEY'S nappy before his bed time oh boy that's a stinky one he thought he's a little wriggler he thought his phone beeped of a text while he lifted Casey up the text was from Brandon and Rory .Bailey was shocked to read the text from Brandon and Rory .

Brandon " Rory left me "

Rory " look after him for me "

Shit Bailey thought what's he gone and done that for he lay Casey in his cot lifting the cover then quickly texted them back and went downstairs into the kitchen put the kettle on " Can we talk about something " Senora asked from the door bringing through the washing for folding Bailey looked up at her she looked at him . " What about " Senora sat down while Bailey stood she looked up at him " We are going through the motions right now aren't we "What the hell does that mean he thought Senora was looking up at him again . " You know how we talked about having a three way sometime Club only " Senora asked while she carried on with sorting the washing " Yea just exclusively to the club " .

" Bailey are you confused " " About what exactly " Senora sighed Bailey went over to her sitting beside Senora " Do you think I'm controlling "Senora looks at Bailey , Bailey snorted taking Senoras hand kissing it she smiled " No baby I don't think your controlling your just particular in your ways that's all " .Maybe I am in a way she thought but I have to be or Bailey wouldn't be doing half the stuff for her in her opinion .

" Do you want to be here with us " Bailey cocked his head she's acting weird again is this the baby blues he thought " Of course I do what do you mean am I confused " " Guys Bailey " Tears stung her eyes Bailey took her hand kissing it he reached for her Senora moving away . ",Senora " " Bailey you told me it was a mistake checking the porn that time I know I had a gut feeling you and Brandon "

Bailey moved to kneel in front of Senora he went to hug her she didn't want a hug " Were you careful why do this to us Bailey " " All time baby we haven't for a while I don't understand it myself " Casey started crying they heard though the monitor " I'll go " Bailey went to get up and went upstairs his dummy came out and lifted his blanket back up then went back down stairs Senora was holding onto the sink he went over to her she turned round Bailey went onto his knees holding her . " We will get passed this Senora please I love you and our son please don't make me go "

" Bailey I'm not we will " They heard a car door shut who was that Bailey thought the door opening he looked round at Patrick fuming " You called Patrick " Senora nodded looking at Patrick " I think you should stay at Patrick's tonight Bailey " what the hell he thought no he should stay here talk it over with her . " Senora we should talk about this " " Bailey c'mon get in the car .Bailey looks between Senora and Patrick we have to talk it out tonight " We can talk about it tomorrow, ok I just need some space tonight ok " .

WOW ELLIOT THOUGHT was he dreaming or did he just hear Patrick explain what's happened between Bailey and Senora Elliot looked over at Christian going through some notes regarding the police report he got about Daniel " I'll be there in a while Patrick " Elliot went over to Christian sitting beside him he looked up at Elliot ." What's happened " " Bailey and Senora had a huge fight. I won't be that long ok apparently he's been sleeping with Brandon " .Elliot sighed shaking his head this is just a weird situation he thought .

Wow Christian thought that's a revelation Elliot did look worried he came over to Christian gave him a kiss " I'll. be ok I'm a big boy now " Elliot wiggled his eyebrows smiling I know he will be ok he is getting better which was good Elliot thought .But be Go to go and sort out Bailey has he gone insane who knows .

ELLIOT PATTED BAILEY'S back listening to him rant and cry Patrick was too dumbstruck he just sat and watched him cry and rant at one point he did want to punch him but that would have made it worse . " Bailey you haven't been remotely attracted to guys before " Elliot said Bailey looked at him he was right he wasn't but Brandon was different he liked him as a friend only though " I know Senora asked Brandon that time to ask talk to me Elliot , Patrick I felt safe with him I don't want to lose Senora and Casey help me " .Bailey clung to Patrick crying he looks over at Elliot what can they do he thought we just got to support him .

" Jesus Bailey you're being dramatic get a grip of yourself " Elliot Bailey looked over at Patrick that's not like Patrick he did look pretty pissed off " Your my best friends what can I do " " Well for a start give Senora space tonight sleep here tonight then talk to her tomorrow " . Maybe that would be better . I just don't want to be a part time dad to my son like Brandon is with Reece .Bailey wiped his eyes god I'm exhausted he thought .

" I think you should stay away from Brandon for now to " Patrick also mentioned shit how am I gonna do that Bailey thought " Patrick's right Bailey " How am I gonna manage that when I work beside the guy Elliot handed Bailey a bottle beer was still mad at him but all he and Elliot could do was support him when needed it . It's possible Bailey could be just curious about guys Elliot thought or is it something else .

" MEN THERE ASSHOLES " Melinda said comforting Senora when she was venting to them Yep definitely she thought wiping her eyes Melinda comforting Senora " Should Bailey and I have a threesome with Brandon " .Wow Melinda thought I can't believe she has just come out with that maybe or maybe not a good idea they both got to work it out between them ." Well he is quite attractive " Melinda confesses they both laugh Melinda dunts Senoras arm " Thanks for coming over Mel " .

" No problem hun you guys just need to sort out boundaries right " Melinda was right they do need to do that I can't think right now Senora thought I need to sleep on it then decide what to do in the morning.

Later Elliot left Bailey went to bed in Patrick's spare bed god he was dog gone tired when his head hit the pillow Brandon had texted a couple times Bailey answers Brandon had wanted to see him Bailey told him not a good idea at the moment let things die down then he could see him he did let Brandon know that Senora knew about them .Patrick let Ellie know what was happening with Bailey hopefully he and Senora could work it out .

BRANDON SAT UP IN BED texting Bailey. It didn't sound good between him and Senora Bailey and he talked previously about stuff before he had said he wasn't bi it was just a curiosity thing which most men are at first . Brandon looks round at the empty side of the bed missing Rory and he had thought they should've talked about stuff more he thought. He hopes that he and Rory can talk in a few days and he also hopes Senora and Bailey could work things out; she will be mad at Brandon for a while .

Chapter 30

Brandon sat at the end of his bed he hardly slept most the night the sun was coming up now that it was after six in the morning he read over Baileys text how sorry he was that things turned out this way Rory's text god he so missed him they will talk eventually he hoped Brandon then decided fuck it I'm not going into work and texted his dad that he wasn't feeling well he couldn't face work anyway he thought . He got back into bed lifting the covers up to his head and just shut out the world today. I will deal with stuff tomorrow. Today I just want to be alone .

SENORA HEARD THE BIKE engine off Baileys arrival home Catherine had called her asking if she was ok after Senora ranted about Bailey last night he was lucky he didn't go home or Catherine would have had a go at Bailey Melinda had left an hour ago for work Senora lay Casey in his cot putting his dummy in and lifting up his cover . Senora was tired. She didn't sleep well and with Casey being grizzly most the night so he had sensed something was wrong the front door opened. She heard Bailey going into the kitchen and heard him on the phone to whoever it was .

SENORA WENT DOWNSTAIRS Bailey was coming out the kitchen when Senora came downstairs shit she looks tired he thought a bit off an awkward silence between them " I'm glad your home Caseys Been up most the night " Bailey looked upstairs and looked at Senora he nodded tears stung Senoras eyes shut Bailey thought . He held out his arms Senora went to him wrapping her arms round his middle " I'm sorry " Bailey whispered Senora looked up at him " I thought I'd lost you " Bailey sniggered smoothing her hair away from her face she still looked beautiful even though her face was blotchy from crying .Silly woman he thought them hugging Senora clung to him tighter .

" You haven't lost me baby " " There are things we need to talk about Bailey " They went into the lounge Bailey held Senoras hand " Where is my boy " " sleeping Bailey we need a holiday I need it we both need it " She was right Bailey thought the three of them could go on a few days away somewhere which would be good for them .Away from there troubles together and enjoy family time with there boy .

" WE CAN DO THAT ANYWHERE you want to go " " is your passport up to date because Christian and Elliot have asked we go with them so your mum can look after Casey. We can take him somewhere else when we get back later in the year we need this Bailey " .

Wow Bailey thought so thoughtful of Christian to do that yeah why not he thought it would be good for the two of them to go something with his best friend " Also the club and if you're wanting a threeway with another guy or female we can do that Club only though and we have to have boundaries right talk about that another time " .

Bailey touched Senoras face he nodded he brought her closer to him kissing her head " We can talk about that why don't you go and lie down for a bit I'll take Casey out in the car for a bit " Senora looked up she nodded good idea she thought she was tired Senora got up locked down at Bailey ` ` We have to be honest with each other Bailey " Bailey nodded then Senora went up to bed following her. He went into Caseys room and when he was awake Bailey picked him up ." Hey you " Bailey kissed Casey's head, took him over to the chair, got his all in one jacket to put it on him . " Let's give mummy some space ok ""His bottle is ready in the fridge " Senora shouted. Bailey shook his head always one step ahead .

Bailey strapped Casey in the back of the car double checked he was strapped in if he wasn't he would get hell Bailey giggled a little that woman her sassiness But he wouldn't have it any other way I love that woman looking up at the window before he got into the car driving off .

I SHOULDN'T REALLY answer the door Brandon thought not in the mood to chat to anyone wrapping the blanket around him answering the door getting a shock Bailey standing there with the baby carrier smiling " Bailey " " You look like shit I brought a little person to see you " Bailey said walking into the apartment which was a mess an empty vodka bottle sat on the table Bailey tutted sitting down the baby carrier he looked up at Brandon standing watching him .Bleary eyed Brandon looks over at Casey in the carrier asleep Brandon gives a faint smile .

" LOOK I KNOW IT'S HARD right now Rory told me to make sure your ok and by the looks of it and drinking isn't gonna solve it is it " Bailey took out Casey from his carrier went over to Brandon handing Casey to him Brandon looked down at him and smiled Brandon sat on the couch Casey on his lap . Bailey looked at him interacting with Casey " Senora and I had a fight. I stayed at Patrick's last night".

Brandon looked up at him he nodded Bailey got up started collecting the rubbish that was around Brandon had tears reminded of Rory tidying the apartment " Senora knows I'm here Brandon " He looked round at him putting Casey's dummy back in he looked up at Bailey " Is she mad "He asked Bailey sat on the couch " Yea she's mad I'm mad at Rory but you gotta pick yourself up Brandon for me for Rory I know it's a shitty thing he's done we've done I " .They look at each other Brandon nods yea it's a shitty thing he thought .

" I KNOW BUT I LOVE him it hurts " Bailey got up started tidying up again he looked round at Brandon again " Go and have a shower I'll make us coffees ok " Brandon nodded he got up put Casey back in his carrier making he was secured while Bailey put the rubbish at the door . He got out his phone and sent a text to Rory and David Brandon's friend . Rory was at work at the outreach centre when his phone beeped the kids were making up posters Rory read the text from Bailey good that he went to check on him then a picture message Casey saying hi so cute Rory thought . He texted back thanking Bailey for checking in on him David also texted Bailey back he would go and see Brandon later .

BRANDON FELT BETTER after his shower and changed he came out the bedroom going into the kitchen Bailey giving Casey his bottle all he had to do was add water to his cup he sat on the other side the table Bailey looked at him " Better " Bailey asked Brandon grunted his answer looking at Bailey `` Thanks " Bailey sat Casey's bottle which he had finished on the table " You must've been hungry little man “ Casey burped Bailey and Brandon sniggered looking at each other .” What are you doing on Sunday? “ “ Not sure why “ .

“ SENORA SAYS TO COME over for Sunday dinner “ “ Really it won’t be weird “ What the hell Brandon thought bit of a weird situation but maybe they just want him to feel ok “ Patrick’s mad at me Elliot thinks it’s hilarious and don’t worry about Patrick he won’t be mad at you for long “ That's another person he might have to avoid to whenever he goes to work I can deal with that Brandon thought .But I guess we just have to get on after things settle down .Brandon sighed taking a drink his tea Bailey watching him chewing his lip thinking is he gonna be ok .

LATER BRANDON WALKED Bailey to the door he looked better Bailey thought Brandon was glad he came Brandon took Baileys arm they looked at each other “ Brandon we agreed “ “ I know I just well thanks " Bailey touched Brandon’s face he leaned into his touch “ I’m here for you Brandon ok aren’t we little man “ looking down at Casey Brandom smiled Bailey opened the door looking round at Brandon . “ Talk to Rory Brandon" " I will and thanks again see you Sunday " .

Brandon shut the door leaning against it yea talk to Rory see where they stand but give it a couple days Bailey stared at the door before he walked off .Then thought I could have stayed longer but it’s gonna be hard for Brandon right now I gave him advice and hopefully take it on board .Bailey shakes his head looks down at Casey you little guy have all this to come when you grown up .

BAILEY WAS ABOUT TO get out the car his phone rang his mum he answered the call with her shouting down the phone to him " Mum Senora and I are sorting stuff out " " You had better that girl is good for you " I know that Bailey thought " Mum Senora and I are talking through stuff " They had better be Catherine thought what the hell was he thinking . Bailey took Casey out of the car, disconnecting his call from his mum. He was about to go into the house when Harvey came out of Senora standing at the door . " Harvey " Harvey looks round at Senora and back at Bailey " Good job I like you Bailey one more chance boy" " Dad " .Senora tuts Shaking her head Harvey looks between them and nods. I like this boy but if he hurts her again I won't be so calm .

" I KNOW I KNOW WORK it out you two ok " " We will " Bailey said Harvey left as Bailey took Casey out his carrier handing him to Senora " How was he " " Not great had to tidy his apartment he drank a whole bottle vodka " That's not good Senora thought Bailey also telling her Brandon wants him back he was gonna text him in a couple days to meet for a coffee . He had better talk it out with Rory when they meet up, Bailey thought .

Senora took Casey upstairs, laid him in his cot for a sleep then she heard the shower come on she bit her lip and looked down at Casey lifting up his cover making sure he had his dummy in .Senora smirked chewing her lip looks down at Casey and then the door grinning .

BAILEY LET THE WATER flow over him soaping himself was about to get the shampoo when the shower door opened Senora coming inside holy shit he thought they hadn't showered together in a while is she mad at me or not he thought Senora wrapped her arms round Baileys waist from the back kissed his back sliding her hand down he was hard . Bailey turned to face Senora. She looked up at him smiling looking down, biting her lip then slid down taking his cock in her mouth. Bailey thought bobbing her head up and down he held onto her head leaning against the tile .Fuck me he thought biting his lip while Senora carried on sucking him off .

SENORA LOCKED UP AT Bailey she could tell he was close while she massaged his balls to she went to stick a finger inside he clenched again while still sucking him off tingles off pleasure up his back " Shit baby I'm gonna cum "Bailey held onto Senora hair Then he Came Senora stood up wiping her mouth smiling . " Better " She asked Bailey wrapped his arms round her " Mmm Thank you what about you " Senora kissed him " I'm good " she was about to leave the shower he stopped her " Are we ok " " jury's still out on that " Senora smirked then got out why that's sneaky he thought was that revenge she had just done not fair that's what Bailey thought .He got out the shower dried and wrapped the towel round him shaking his head .

BAILEY WENT INTO THE bedroom stood at the door while Senora tidied up " That wasn't fair you know " Senora smirked turned round ahh his little face she thought " What isn't fair " " What you just did " Senora sniggered Bailey shook his head she went over to him cocked her head " Hurdles Bailey and trust " " I know " Casey made himself heard they both sighed " I love you " Senora said first was about to leave to get Casey when Bailey held Senora guiding her to the wall he kissed her grinding into her holding her hands Senora groaned they kissed then Casey made his presence Senora went to move " I'll get him " Bailey said Senora was breathless and hot oh my that's the hottest thing he's done she thought smiling to herself .

" HEY MISTER WHAT'S the fuss about " Bailey bending down to pick up Casey he stopped crying " That wasn't fair either " Senora said from the door Bailey smirking he looked round shrugging his shoulders Senora tutted " I'll get his bottle "Bailey left the room Senora watching him go downstairs shaking her head .Bloody asshole she thought well it was my fault for teasing him she thought looking down at Casey again kicking his legs .

Chapter 31

Rory waited in the cafe for Brandon it had been 3 days since they last spoke Rory was nervous he still missed Brandon so much Bailey had texted him couple days ago he had been to see him he was ok but upset he hated to hear that he thought ."Rory " Rory looked up at Brandon standing there he gave a faint smile " Hi " He looked ok Brandon thought sitting down across from him the waiter came over took there order " You ok " Rorry asked " I will be you " .Rory cocked his head smiling be brave he thought let's talk it out .

" Been tough but Debs helped " " Good " .

The waiter brought there drinks and left again all Rory wanted to do was to go over and hug Brandom tell him no Rory thought stand your ground and be brave " Reece ok " " He is I've not said Anything about us yet " That's understandable Rory thought he loves that boy it would be shame not to see him again . " Rory, let's not lose our friendship. I couldn't bear it . " He didn't want that either, Rory thought Brandon hadn't judged him. Maybe over time they could get back what they had before and they should definitely stay friends whatever the outcome .

" I agree, " Brandon nodded. He looked at Rory, he just looked sad, he thought " Bailey said you guys talked " .

" We did I tried to think why he would want to experiment with you he said he felt safe with you ": Brandon thought back at the time when Bailey said it at times they talked about stuff and other times he didn't " it's crazy I ruined it with us " Rory reached his hand over to Brandon he looked down at Rory's hand then looked up at him smiling at Brandon . " Don't think about that right now hun " " I fucked up Rory " .

AFTER THERE CHAT THEY decided to take a walk in the park like they normally did and with Reece who Rory thought about " I have the possibility of a summer holidays job next year " Brandon stopped walking Rory looked round at him " where " " Benidorm Wesley you know Wesley he's over there right now living and working at a new show bar he contacted me asking if I'm interested I'm thinking about it " Brandon thought well if it's what he wants to do why not he should . He gave up Drag Uk which he shouldn't have and the offer of this job will be good for him .

RORY STOPPED WHEN THEY had come across the kiosk he looked at Brandon he smiled and knew Rory would want one he went over got himself and Brandon an ice lolly they walked along the path chatting and eating their ice lollies . It felt good to talk to each other again chatting about stuff while they walked along the path at the park . Which they normally did with Reece taking him to the park. This is good Rory thought of two friends meeting for a coffee and along the park Brandon chatting away normally about Reece and his antics .

Elliot and Christian walked into Edinburgh airport followed by Bailey a week later , Senora , Patrick , Ellie , Lyndsay and Paul with Melinda who was looking miserable. Senora tried to get her to open up. It was something Eddie couldn't make because of work schedule . They went to the check in first class which Elliot thought was a bit extreme " Ed's on his way " . Christian said looking at his phone looking up at Elliot who thought again why do we need security when Callum is around to other security bodyguards Elliot got annoyed about it . Christian got round that with him by making up in the shower this morning when Christian sneakily surprised him cheeky bugger Elliot thought .

" Mr King good to see you again " The lady at the desk politely smiled while checking everyone in Calum helping everyone with the bags after checks they went through to VIP area fancy everyone thought so much better to "champagne anyone " The lady in the vip section asked wow fancy Elliot thought taking his glass going over to the food area . Nice Elliot thought I could get used to picking up what he wanted. I wonder if Christian wants anything looking over at him chatting to the lady from vip .

AFTER PICKING OUT WHAT the everyone wanted Ed arrived going over to Christian to go over plans Melinda looked over did a double take and couldn't believe what she saw her Eddie so this is the gig he was doing she thought " Thats Ed " Senora explained Melinda nodded and carried on eating her sandwich Ed noticed Melinda he will have to talk to her at some point he thought .Maybe a bit awkward with the job but he wasn't allowed to say which job it was to her he noticed she didn't look happy .

" ARE THOSE TWO GONNA be ok? " Christian asked Eliot about Senora and Bailey. He looked over at them chatting and eating. He hoped Elliot thought this time away which they needed would do them good. " They will be " . Elliot wraps his arm around Christians looking up at him and taking a sip of his champagne " Are you ok love " Christian asks " More than ok " They kiss, noticed by the others cute Senora thought watching Elliot and Christians interaction .

ON THERE WAY OUT TO departures Ed stopped Melinda she looked up at him he didn't look happy she thought " Mel if I'd known I wouldn't have taken on the job " Melinda huffed the job she thought shaking her head "A job Eddie " Melinda huffed again and walked off to get the others to check in .Dammit she is mad at me what can I do he thought I'll have to try and talk to Melinda later .

After their three hour flight Callum got the suvs and he and Ed drove to the villa which was twenty minutes away everyone got out and looked up at the villa wow amazing a pool lounge outside area perfect and hot too .Callum and Ed each took the cases into the villa for everyone nice they both thought great view .

CHRISTIAN AND ELLIOT got to their room in an en suite . Nice Elliot thought of inspecting the room Christian standing watching him. He opened the balcony window to a great view of the pool area and the view was amazing Christian wrapped his arms around Elliot's waist and he leaned into Christian . " Happy " " mmm yes " Christian kissed his neck " Good ' Elliot looked round at Christian smiling Christian cocked his head . "What are you thinking " Elliot looked over at the pool then looked at Christian he sniggered , shaking his head ." Later maybe Elliot smirks, shaking his head Christian giggles .

" Are you guys coming down " Patrick asked beside the pool while he and Ellie sorted the sun loungers then Bailey and Senora appeared looking up at Elliot and Christian "Be down soon ":Elliot shouted over going back inside leaving the window open Christian started to unpack his phone beeped he picked it up looking at it . A text from his parents on their cruise around the med " Are they having a nice time? " Elliot asked while putting away his clothes' ' They are " .That's good that Christians parents are having a good holiday. He looks over at Christian typing away his reply while putting away his clothes .

SENORA STARTED PUTTING on sunscreen just as Lyndsay and Paul arrived where was Melinda she thought Patrick and Bailey were sorting out the drinks " where's Mel " Senora asked " she will be down soon she said " She has better be in a better mood because she isn't happy right now regarding Ed while Senora sorted herself out .

MELINDA HAD PUT ON a shirt over her swimming costume she was coming out her room when Ed appeared she wasn't happy he could tell Ed thought she looked up at him " You ok " Ed asked Melinda she nodded she looked amazing he thought she smiled " Eddie " Ed lays his hand against the wall she moves nearer to him " Come to my room tonight " Smiling up at him Melinda walks off just as Callum appeared noting that Ed watching Melinda walking down the stairs to the poolEd looks over at Callum . " I was wanting a word about the cameras" " sure' ' .

" THERE'S A SOUND SYSTEM to " Elliot asked while Christian sorts out the music system at the bar " just here in there " Christian pointed to a box he looked sexy in his white linen shirt and shorts Elliot thought Patrick came over to them " Amazing place Christian your friend certainly has good Taste " .That was nice of Patrick to say Christian thought while he sorted out the sound system .

" TAYLOR AND HIS WIFE built this Taylor is an architect " " Wow amazing I can see why they picked the place with the view " Patrick took a couple soft drinks and a couple beers over to the others I hope they won't drink too much Elliot thought since they are going to the local restaurant tonight ." What's wrong? " Christian asked Elliot to look round at him " Nothing babe " .Elliot lay his arm round Christian giving him a peck on the cheek .Cuddling into each other I'm loving this place already Elliot thought .

THAT NIGHT THEY ALL descended on the restaurant Christian recommended which was at the marina, an amazing view everyone thought afterwards they took a walk along the Marina every now again Melinda looked over at Ed who was engaged in conversation with Callum . They spotted a pub which they all decided to go into an Irish pub which was even better .Everyone thought it was busy then after an hour they all descended. Back to the villa and have more drinks there .Scattered around the pool area for a bit .

PATRICK CAME OUT THE bathroom he looked over at Ellie standing at the window it was open a breeze coming in she looked beautiful he thought Ellie looked round she smiled " What " " You look amazing " Ellie huffed Patrick went over to her wrapping his arms round her waist she looked up at him Patrick bent down to kiss her moving her back against the wall lifting up her arms up kissing her neck “ We should come back here again bring Ivy “ Patrick said Ellie hummed her answer he looked down at her again while Ellie unzipped his shorts sliding her hand inside “ Sneaky “ They kissed again Ellie carrying on stroking Patrick he closed his eyes they kissed again then moved to the bed kissing while tearing at each other’s clothes .

Patrick got out the condoms sitting them on the bed Ellie say he went over to her bending over her she looked up at him they kissed again Patrick gently pushed her onto the bed sliding down her shorts and pants kissing her leg then the inside leg Ellie squirmed as Patrick looked up at her he moved up kissing her stomach and stuck a finger inside her . Ellie groaned while Patrick flicked his finger in and out her sex she was wet he moved down kissing licking all the way till he got to her sex Ellie groaned .

LICKING INSIDE OFF her leg lifting her leg up while he licked her sex Ellie arched up flicking a finger inside again tingles off. Pleasure coming from everywhere he licked her sex again still flicking his finger in and out Ellie put her hand up to her mouth to stifle her moans .Patrick slid on the condom he guided himself inside Ellie holding onto her hand getting into a rhythm they kissed .Ellie tasting herself Patrick getting into a rhythm “ Fuck you tasted good “ . Ellie’s face was flushed and Patrick rammed back in.

ELLIE MOVED ONTO PATRICK easing herself on him he wrapped his arms around her she bent down to kiss him holding onto his hand getting into a rhythm again Patrick moving up kissing each other Ellie wrapped her arms round Patrick’s shoulders his arm around her waist . " mmm you look so good " Ellie smiles she bounced fuck that's amazing when she does that .

Patrick lay Ellie on her back kissing her neck, flicking a finger inside her she gave a whimper Patrick then moved and slid inside Ellie again she held onto his back he took it slowly lifting up Ellie's leg and pushed inside one more time before they Came . Patrick stilled until he stopped coming Ellie moved onto her back bringing the sheet up to her Patrick reaches over to her bringing Ellie closer to him they kiss " I love Spain " Ellie says looking over at Patrick " me to ".

MELINDA KNOCKED ON Ed's door. Within a few minutes he smiled and glad to see Melinda he took her hand leading her into his room. The door shutting while Bailey passed was that Melinda thought wow that's sneaky he thought grinning to himself , shaking his head and going into his room . Senora was out on the balcony sitting Bailey stood for a moment. She looked beautiful in the moonlight, he thought the right picture moment he thought .

" Did you get the ice? 'Senora asked. Bailey went out to the balcony with the bottle of water and ice in the ice bucket. " I did. " Senora looked up at him and smiled. " Ok, " Bailey asked. Senora nodded. Bailey sat on the other chair. Bailey's nose and cheeks were a little red, she noticed . " Casey's Fine Your mum is having a great time with him" " Great see I told you it will be ok " . They heard moans coming from Patrick's room. They both looked at each other and sniggered good on them they thought , Then they decided to go inside; they giggled again, good on him, Bailey thought smiling to himself at least someone is getting laid he thought .When Senora is ready to have sex again they look at each other he is deep in thought Senora thinks but they are having a nice time so far no rushing things right now .

Elliot and Christian lay in bed Elliot holding onto Christians hand snuggled into each other Christian kissed Elliot's shoulder after there love making Elliot hummed moving closer to Christian "What do you want to do tomorrow " Christian asked at this point Elliot didn't care what they did he even thought about staying in bed with Christian all day . " I could stay here all week " Christian snorted, not happening he thought but a good idea too .Kissing Elliot's head he is so adorable too .

" There is lots to explore " Christian said Elliot smiled he sat up his arm on his head hand on Christians chest " mmm nice " Christian shook his head Elliot moved round straddling Christian he looked up at Elliot who trailed his finger down his chest " Lots to explore you say interesting " Elliot bent down to kiss Christian grinding into him then slowly worked his way down his chest kissing licking all the way . He looked up at Christian looking down at him . Elliot flicked a finger inside Christian he arched up still slick from the lube earlier Elliot bending down taking Christian in his mouth Christian squish's his face into the pillow while Elliot fingered and gave him a blow job at the same time .So good Christian thought his face still squished into the pillow it didn't take them both long to come .

Christian movies Elliot onto his back kissing his neck his chest he looks up at Elliot watching him and lifts his leg up looks at Elliot who hands him a condom " Again " Christian asks Elliot smirks " What can't keep up old man " Christian snorts he is only five years older than Elliot Christian bends to kiss Elliot " Enough the old mister I am not five years older " Elliot giggles and gives Christian a peck on the cheek " That you are " then they heard giggling coming from the hallway and wondered what was going on they look at each other .

Then heard the girls outside at the poolside hearing Melinda , Lindsay , Ellie and Senoras voices Christian got up looking out the window the girls were over at the chairs sharing a bottle of wine Elliot Came behind Christian looking out good on them he thought . Christian looks round at Elliot smiling at him Christian looks down at Elliot naked “ I’m feeling a shower “ Elliot suggests Christian grins good idea he thought Elliot lays out his hand Christian taking it and they go off to the bathroom for another make out session .

Chapter 32

The next day they had hired cars for the week Christian , Elliot , Bailey and Senora in one followed by Ed and Callum in another Patrick , Ellie , with Lyndsay Paul and Melinda on one the other cars they drove to one the other towns for lunch and shopping which only took them twenty minutes to get there the girls walked along together looking at the shop windows they eventually went into a couple to look around as well as the boys to .Browsing the aisles Melinda looks over at Ed whenever no one is looking .

After an hour of shopping looking around the area they descended into one of the restaurants, a lovely little place they all thought while looking through the menu and ordering drinks . " Christian " Christian looked up the same with Elliot at the couple who spoke to him. He looked surprised. Elliot thought " Aunt Meg Uncle Liam " The couple looked over at Elliot and nodded. Christian looked shaken, Elliot thought . " Ahh you're with friends' ' His uncle said Christian got up, going over to his aunt and uncle looking round at the table . " Yes we are at a villa 20 minutes away my parents have gone on a cruise" " We heard " His aunt mentioned looking at her husband and back at Christian.Who are they Elliot thought Christian didn't look too happy to see them .

They looked sad Elliot thought and shocked after a couple minutes they left, smiled and nodded. As Elliot Christian sat down Elliot took his hand Christian looked at him " I'm sorry" "What you sorry for " Bailey and Patrick looked at each other. Then Elliot and Christian “ it’s Grant's parents “ Elliot nodded and thought that’s why they were giving him strange vibes Elliot nodded and took Christians hand . " Mate, are you ok? “ Patrick asked. They both looked round at everyone. Elliot smiled and nodded looking round at Christian . " Do you want to speak to them? "" Elliot out of respect for you . Besides, my parents haven’t spoken to them since Elliot nodded shame but understandable .

“ Christian it’s not there fault go talk to them it’s fine “ “ Are you sure “ Elliot nodded then Christian left the table Ed and Callum were about to get up Christian told him it was ok “ That is brave mate “ Bailey said Elliot nodded he and Patrick came over to him all three them hugged . “ Guys I’m ok. " Elliot sniggered, pushing them off him. It's hard for Christian to and his side of the family .But as they say you can’t pick your family .

“ Aunt Meg uncle Liam “ Christian shouted to them just as they were about to get into their car they looked at each other at each other “ Everything ok Christian “ His uncle asked “ Yes fine it was just a surprise to see you both that’s all Elliot don’t worry about him he’s ok and I’m ok “ . Oh Meg thought that’s the boy she hopes that one day Grant will stop his nonsense and hopefully Jail will fix his problem .

“ THAT IS GOOD TO KNOW Christian it was lovely to see you isn’t it Liam “ Liam nodded smiling at his wife “ Would you both come to the villa for dinner “ Meg looked at Liam should they , They both thought “ it would mean a lot for Christian if you could “ Elliot asked Christian looked round at him surprised at what he had just said he took his hand that is really brave of Elliot to say he thought .
“ Ok we will be there when we go back on Sunday “ .

CHRISTIAN AND ELLIOT held hands on the way back to the table and sat down Bailey looked over Eliot gave him a thumbs up he was ok Bailey nodded and thought he was awfully brave off him " Thank you " Elliot looked at Christian putting his hand on his knee " it's ok I kinda guessed the rest the family don't really talk to them " " Just a couple of the family " . Elliot hugs Christian and lays his arm round Christians shoulder. Those two should just get a room Bailey thought watching .

AFTER LUNCH THEY WENT back to the villa to rest and hang around the pool. Elliot , Bailey and Patrick sat on the lounges sunbathing while Christian sorted out the barbecue with Paul they decided to cook for tonight and had bought things at the local supermarket. " How's he doing? Patrick asked while they watched them sort out the barbecue. Elliot looked at Patrick and Bailey " Doing better his therapy sessions are helping " . " You shouldn't worry too much mate " Bailey was right he shouldn't but he does look over at Christian " He is still a bit self conscious but not with me he isn't " . Patrick did notice that Christian keeps his shirt or T shirt on but that was understandable .

Patrick looked at Bailey, he nodded , Then the girls appeared as if they had made cocktails. Lyndsay wondered where Melinda had gone to look around. Maybe she went up to her room to rest. She was still a bit peeved off about something . She thought she decided to go get her and noticed two people down the bottom off the veranda . Lyndsay looked over and there was Melinda and Ed all over each other " Mel what are you doing " Melinda and Ed parted looking up at her Melinda giggled taking Ed's hand " Lyndsay its Eddie " . Melinda and Ed look at each other smiling .

they both look up st Lyndsay what the hell she thought Ed Eddie from the club well that's something Ed's phone beeped a text from

Callum he looked up at Melinda " I'll see you later "Ed looks up at Melinda gives her a kiss on the cheek " You sure will " Ed went off Melinda watching him smiling " Mel " "What " Melinda looked at Lyndsay shaking her head " Lyndsay I'm an adult I know what I'm doing I really like him " .Seriously Lynda's thought shaking her head Melinda giggles .

" LIKE WHO " SENORA asked when she came looking for the girls she looked between Lyndsay and Melinda " mel's Ed from the club " Thanks Lyndsay for spoiling it for me Melinda thought Senora looked at Melinda then sniggered what's that about Lyndsay thought " it was so obvious Mel c'mon let's make more cocktails " . Lindsay was gobsmacked; she wasn't bothered who Ed was and Melinda was being sneaky with him here .

SENORA WHISPERED TO Bailey about Melinda and Ed he couldn't believe what he had just heard he sniggered Senora shushed him he just couldn't get the image of the two off them out his head Patrick wondered what was going on while they did the barbecue everyone chipped in getting plates etc taking them out to the patio to eat . Setting up the table for them to eat and placing the drinks on the table chatting away about most hints while they had their drinks and barbecue .

AFTERWARDS EVERYONE retreated to their rooms Elliot and Christian decided to go into the jacuzzi and with the bubbles on they felt relaxed drinking his beer Elliot his wine Elliot closed his eyes Christian looked at him he smiled Elliot looked relaxed Christian sipped his wine . " I know you're looking at me " Elliot said, opening his eyes looking over at Christian he cocked his head and smiled at Elliot . " What are you thinking? " Elliot sat his bottle down and moved closer to Christian he kissed him then whispered " A first in the jacuzzi. " They looked at each other Christian smiled " A first for me too " . Elliot hummed, raising his eyebrows and grinned ." Have you not had enough of me yet" Elliot said Christian touches Elliot's face " I'll never have enough of you Elliot " soppy Sod Elliot thought .

HE SLID HIS HAND DOWN feeling Christian over his shorts Elliot facing Christian kissing his neck Christian wrapped. His arms round Elliot's shoulders while he carries on. Stroking him he groaned while Elliot carried on kissing his neck chin and the other side off his neck sucking lightly they looked at each other . " I'll bruise you know " Christian said Elliot grinned "I'm leaving my mark he thought " Marking what's yours are you " " Yup ``.Elliot grins you get I am Making my Mark .

CHRISTIAN KISSED HIM started to move to the other side this time Elliot leaning against the jacuzzi they kissed again this time christian stroking Elliot and kissing him on his shoulder a light suck there to leave his mark " Christian I want you " He looked at Elliot nodding about to get out the jacuzzi Christian stopped him . " Here " Elliot asked Christian nodding. He moved over to his wallet bringing out a condom. Elliot thought of a sneaky thing to do Christian ripping it open and putting it on .

Elliot moved up a bit Christian guiding himself inside him Elliot holding onto Christians shoulders while he got into a rhythm Elliot bit his lip wrapping his legs round Christians waist Christian going faster Elliot tried to be quiet kissing Christian in the crook of his neck to stifle his moans .While Christian pounded into him so good Elliot thought holding onto Christian .

BAILEY STOPPED JUST as he was about to go round the corner to the jacuzzi shit Elliot and Christian were there having sex he leaned against the wall so not to disturb them shit what do I do now Senora came over Bailey lead her away to the pool " Are we not having a jacuzzi tonight at " "No baby it's occupied "Occupied Senora thought Bailey went red then it clicked ahh someone is making out there good on them she thought Bailey lead Senora to the pool with his two bottles beer her glass wine .Oh he is embarrassed Senora thought sniggering to herself Bailey glares at her not funny .

Senora sat at the edge of the pool dangling her feet. The air was still warm. Bailey sat beside her " Are you cold? " Bailey asked Senora to look at him " I'm ok still warm " They heard giggling as they looked over. At Elliot and Christian arms round each other they stopped to look over and waved then went inside the villa Bailey shook his head. Those two are just unbelievable. " They certainly had fun " Senora said Bailey looked round at her luck then he thought sighing they have been at it since they Came to Spain .

" BAILEY " "WHAT " HE looked at her taking a sip his beer " You ok " " Yes babe I'm ok " Senora reaches over to kiss Bailey then she took a sip her wine she's doing it again giving him sexy vibes Bailey shifted taking another sip his beer " wanna swim " Bailey looked at Senora wide eyed not here he thought Senora sniggered not funny Bailey thought . Senora got up and picked her to sit on one of the loungers Bailey came over sitting on the other lounger . "It's still early so we could go to that club " .

Senora looked at Bailey looked at the time 9.30 yes it's still early she thought looked at Bailey again " I'm tired Bailey can we go another night besides I'm not dressed for it " Bailey snorted not dressed for it she's gorgeous he thought she didn't need to doll herself up he reached over to take her hands `` Baby your fine believe me " Senora smiled shook her head then Melinda appeared in a blue mini dress all dolled up with Ed . "We're going out, c'mon hun get yourself changed, come with us ."

Ahh Senora thought they've planned this Bailey smirked, Senora looked at Melinda " Ok ok I'll go get sorted " Melinda whooped took Senora's hand and they went up to the bedroom to get changed .Good Bailey thought they needed it. A night out things were kinda getting back to what they had before Bailey hoped . It's been a good couple days so far Bailey thought I love this woman. She is amazing and a good mother too .

THE NIGHTCLUB WAS BUSY with the tourists Senora and Melinda danced and giggled while the boys watched from the tables Bailey was right she would have a good time. He looked over at Ed sipping his beer while scanning the room Bailey shook his head, typically he thought never off duty . " Ed you're not at Nero's Mate " Ed looked over at Bailey habit he thought " Just habit " Ed smiles Bailey nodded and noticed a girl blonde hair very pretty watching the girls " So you and Mel " Bailey nodded his head towards the girls Ed looks over and smiles Melinda waves at him .

" Yep we have Been talking for a couple months now she's something else that girl " oh he is smitten Bailey could tell it was nice to see a different side from Ed instead of his stoic usual self at the club " Eddie come dance with me " Melinda grabbing his arm he protested until he eventually got up with her to dance . Senora sat beside Bailey taking a sip of her wine. She was starting to feel the effects from drinking so much wine now. " He is smitten " Bailey says to Senora she sniggers and reaches over to Bailey to kiss him .

Senora wrapped her arms round Baileys shoulders while they danced Melinda came over laying her arm round Senora pointing to the bar the same girl Bailey noticed earlier " Her name is Aria from Sweden she thinks you two are cute " Senora looks at Bailey they both look over at Aria with Ed chatting then Melinda goes back over to them .Cute Bailey thought these Swedish people are not shy he had heard .

SENORA FELT QUITE FLATTERED. A girl thought she was cute. She blushed, but noticed by Bailey he moved closer to her. " No harm in taking her right. " Senora nodded. Bailey took her hand and they went over to the bar to introduce themselves to Aria from Sweden .

What's the noise Patrick thought that woke him up he checked his phone four am Ellie sat up wiping her eyes wondering what was going on Patrick got up to look outside Bailey , Senora , Melinda and a stranger at the poolside lounges hell no that's not happening he thought Ed appeared. " Patrick what's going on? " Patrick put on his t-shirt and shorts while giggling .Looking between everyone and who is this female they have brought back .

" JESUS' ' ELLIOT THOUGHT who was the female they brought back with them Christian got up and looked out the window. Just as Patrick appeared down at the pool " looks like they had fun " Christian said sniggering " I must be getting old but that's normally what I would a done " .Elliot said giggling well at least they have had fun tonight " Let's get back to bed let Patrick deal with it " Maybe he's right Elliot thought .

“ HEY PATRICK, THIS is Aria from Sweden. Bailey announced Aria waves ` ` Hello Aria . From Sweden guys it’s four am don’t you think you should go to bed “ bed great idea right baby “ Bailey kisses Senora as Aria watched " Uber is on its way “ Ed said Melinda , Bailey and Senora pouted Elliot appeared to help after all Christian watched from the balcony while Ed and Callum helped Aria into her Uber .

“ I WANNA MOVE TO SWEDEN do you know they have free love over there are call Swedish women like that “ Bailey said holding onto Senora “ C’mon you let’s get you to bed “ Elliot said helping Bailey up “.Bed good idea I’ve had the best night haven’t we baby “ “ we have “ .Senora snorted shaking her head he is gonna feel it in the morning she thought .

Bailey put his hand to his mouth he felt sick running into the kitchen throwing up into the sink Patrick coming over to Bailey patting his back Oh no Senora thought he has definitely had too much to drink she went over to them patting Bailey's back . Patrick held his nose Wow he shouldn’t have drunk so much “ Sorry Guys “ .

“ Come On You let's get you to bed “ Bailey grins Patrick goes over to Bailey laying an arm round him helping him upstairs to their room helping Bailey onto the bed he flops down “ Thanks Patrick “ “ No problem not the first time goodnight “ . Goodnight Patrick “ .

Patrick goes to the door looks round at Bailey and Senora her helping to take off Baileys shoes Patrick shakes his head and shuts the door just as Elliot appears “ He ok “ “ Fine Mate Senora is dealing with him “ Good Elliot thought cause I really didn’t wanna deal with drunk Bailey so many times in the past they have helped him get home after a night out he can be such a lightweight sometimes .

“ See you in the morning “ Elliot says they hugged and parted “ Love you “ Elliot shouts Patrick giggles shouting his love you back and they went back to their rooms .

Chapter 33

The next day Bailey and Melinda didn't get up till one in the afternoon Senora had gotten up earlier in the day and let Bailey sleep he had put on his sunglasses jugged a bottle water watched by Elliot sitting at the breakfast bar Bailey looked over at him jeez my head hurts Bailey thought " I'm sorry mate " Elliot sniggered shaking his head . " How do you feel? " Bailey leaned on the table, his head in his hands. " I just want to die. " " Well, did you have a good time? " .

" I THINK SO SHIT THE Swedish girl " " All taken care off " Bailey drank more water Christian appeared laying his arm round Elliot " Sorry Christian " He looked at Elliot who shrugged his shoulders " it's ok no need to apologise " Bailey got up goes over to Elliot and Christian to hug them Elliot pats his back . " I'll just go die in the shade now " Bailey goes off over to Senora they hug and kiss and he moves his lounger into the shade Senora just shakes her head at him .Its best he get over his hangover himself she thought as long as he drinks plenty water he will get over it. And best be in the shade so once he drinks more water and something to eat he will feel better .

BRANDON COULDN'T BELIEVE the texts he got from Bailey last night drunken rambles when he checked his phone that morning and.a selfie when out in a club unbelievable Brandon thought while he drank his coffee while taking a break at his dads business he missed Bailey to more Rory to he had texted him the other day telling him about the adventure outreach they were going to for the week . The kids loved going there. Reece was missing Rory so they arranged to meet up whenever he got back he wouldn't be out there living for Good they did agree to that . What was going on in Baileys mind when he sent the texts I'm definitely gonna say something to him when he gets back from Spain .

ELLIOT AND CHRISTIAN arrived at his aunt uncle's holiday home which only took them a half hour to get to the lovely place Elliot thought great views to Christians aunt brought out lemonade she had made for them. They talked about their last few days exploring and what Christian had planned and Elliot going to college to do his social studies . His aunt had mentioned their daughter Rhea was doing well, was engaged, they were living together and planned their wedding for next year . Her fiancé was lovely Mark, he was a teacher and they both were besotted with each other.that was good to know Christian thought .

" I made chicken for lunch with salad and potatoes, that 's ok " " sounds lovely " Christian said Elliot excused himself to go to the toilet Meg looked at Liam while they ate. They did notice Christian was thinner since they last saw him a year ago and had wondered if things were ok with him . " Christian about Grant " Christian looked up at his aunt and uncle " What about him " Meg looked at Liam then looked at Christian .

" How are things with Elliot " Liam asked " He is doing ok going to therapy sessions which are helping have his moments " Elliot did overhear the conversation when he came back from the toilet Christian lay his hand on his knee Elliot nodded his way saying he was ok . “ You can talk about your son while I’m here, “ Elliot said, looking at Christian smiling and then looking at Meg and Liam . “ We were being respectful to you Elliot “ “Understandable “ .Which it was their son but it seemed that Liam didn’t want to know anything about him and Meg just seemed sad about her son .

AFTER LUNCH LIAM TOOK Christian round the garden while Elliot helped clear up chatting away “ Elliot is Christian ok “ Elliot leaned against the sink looking out the window watching him and Liam chatting “ Christian has bulimia Meg “ “ Oh because I thought there was something is he getting help “ .So sad to hear about Christians condition Meg thought but at least he has Elliot to help him through it .

ELLIOT EXPLAINED HIS treatment he had been having and the therapy he was getting and had said it had come as a bit of a shock to him but they were working through it together and their plans for the future together Christian wanted to take Elliot to visit his home in South Africa . “ That's good! “ Elliot sat the dish towel down and was about to go outside when Meg stopped him. Elliot looked round at her .

“ GRANT WAS ALWAYS GETTING into trouble his father and I did our best with him but he got into the wrong crowd “ Elliot took a deep breath he knew this was coming they had to mention him sometime “ We can’t choose our family right “ Meg nodded she had a tear in her eye shit Elliot thought please don’t cry . “ I’m ok it’s just so hard when we hear from him you know his sentence he was up on court again a couple weeks ago his sentence added trouble in the jail and added another year " .

Elliot didn't know what to say it's her son after all he thought but he didn't feel pity for Grant it's his own fault then Christisn and Liam came back in Liam went over to his wife to comfort her Christian slid his arm through Elliot's waist he looked at Christian and back at Meg and Liam . " It's hard, you know, " Liam said. Looking at his wife it must be hard for them Elliot thought .But he couldn't find the words and just didn't say anything Elliot looked at Christian they smiled at each other .

" Gosh What you must think of me " Meg Said Christian went to his aunt hugging her watched by her husband and Elliot they must be going through a hard time right now Elliot thought .

They said their goodbyes at the gate, got into the car and drove back to the villa Christian took Elliot's hand and he looked round at him " I'm ok. Christian " Christian kissed his hand and held it all the way back to the villa .Why is he so adorable Elliot thought .But it was a lovely lunch even though it was a bit tense at times. It was good for Christian to spend time with his aunt and uncle. They did seem nice .

Meg cleared the table wiping it down Liam Came into the villa he went over to Meg wrapping his arms around her waist Meg looks round at Liam he kisses her cheek " I thought lunch went pretty well " " Yes I agree " Liam helped with the dishes while Meg washed he dried . " Christian Elliot said he was getting therapy " " He did Elliot seemed a nice chap " Meg looks at Liam they smile at each other Liam touches Meg's arm " You need to stop worrying " Meg sighs she can't help worrying it has been at least a month since they visited Grant at the prison . " I'm sorry I know " " C'mon love let's have another glass wine out on the veranda " Good idea Meg thought Liam picked up the bottle wine Meg got the glasses he is so wonderful she thought and has been a total rock since her son got into trouble what would she do without him .

THAT NIGHT AFTER DINNER they danced to Lewis Capadi someone you loved Callum watched them all dancing it was a lovely sight to see he thought in two days they would all be going home Ed got a beer from the fridge handing one to Callum Melinda sat beside Callum at the breakfast bar drinking her wine watching the rest dancing she smiled great sight to see . " Have you a girlfriend , boyfriend at home Callum " Jesus Ed thought straight to the point of no messing about . " Neither and I'm straight " " Really a good looking guy like you shame " .Callum giggled Yea it's not as if he is fighting them off since he has had no action for at least a couple months .

" Christian " "Mm. " Christian looked down at Elliot " Take me to bed and love me forever " Christian snorted Elliot smirked kissed Christians cheek " What it's the line from a classic movie Top Gun " Elliot wrapped his arms round Christians shoulders again and thought don't tell me he hasn't heard off Top Gun " Babe you have watched it right " Christian looked at Elliot he smirked he's teasing him Elliot thought " Off course I have seen it " Good Elliot thought then thought they haven't skinny dipped in the pool yet he smiled into himself . " Christian " .

" I WANT TO DO ONE THING before we leave." They looked at each other again. Elliot looked down at the rings hanging from his neck, leaving a little bit of mum's ashes Christian smiled, touching Elliot's face. What a nice thought " We can do that " . Christian brought Elliot closer to him, kissing Elliot's head, hugging him tight and thinking of Elliot's suggestion .Yes it's him he now let go of the past he was his present now and I won't let anyone hurt him Christian thought .

" Senora " She looked up at Bailey while they danced " What is it " Bailey kissed her wrapping his arms around her waist " is the jury still out " Senora huffed shaking her head while they danced " Maybe " Bailey smiled they looked at each other Senora smirked he's still in the dog house for now but she might give him something later .I do love him really Senora thought he has been trying and maybe they could try a three way sometime Club only that's something they need to talk about when they get home .Which won't be all the time and they would have to have clear boundaries to she thought maybe write up a contract or something like it .

⁂

“ I LOVE YOU “ PATRICK whispered in Ellie’s ear she looked up at him smiling “ Love you to “ Patrick smiles pulling Ellie closer he bends to kiss her this is just perfect Ellie thought he is so good with Ivy and Ivy loved him around too .And it has been a few months now who knows what There future will bring one thing is for sure Ellie thought I am definitely in love with this man hugging Patrick .

The next day Elliot picks a spot in the Villa Garden to place the little box off his mother's ashes they carve out a hole deep enough to lay the box inside Elliot goes into his pocket and brings out the chain with the two rings Christian is surprised does he want to do that it's sentimental to Elliot . Christian takes Elliot's arm he looks at him " Elliot are you sure they mean a lot to you " Elliot looks down at the chain yes it means a lot but I'm moving on he thought . Christian is his future, Leyton is his past he has to let it go sometime and the time is now .

" I HAVE TO CHRISTIAN to move on with you I have to and whenever we come back I know mum will be watching over us and Leyton will be with her " . Christian hugs Elliot with tears running down his face " It's ok please don't cry I'm here " They look at each other Christian wipes Elliot's tears and gives him a kiss " I love you " Christian whispers Elliot nods his understanding .

FUCK BAILEY AND PATRICK thought watching Elliot and Christian over at the garden Patrick lay his arm over Baileys. He nodded then they went over to Elliot and Christian watching over Elliot while he put the box and the chain into the flower bed . Elliot's shoulders moved, wiping his eyes Christian went to him again , wrapping his arms around him, giving him words of comfort, Elliot nodding .

They stood up Patrick and Bailey moved closer to Elliot and Christian all four of them hugging just a perfect moment. It felt right Elliot thought they didn't need any words . He just needed his boyfriend and friends at this important moment .

" Love you guys " Senora wiped her eyes. What a beautiful moment she thought while watching all four boys laying Elliot's mom's ashes. Bailey looked round at her and smiled , mouthing love to her. Senora nodded . Bailey laid out his arm for her to come to them which she did .Tears stinging her eyes and they all hugged again . Bloody hell Senora thought it's certainly been an emotional morning for everyone she was pleased for Elliot deciding to bury his mum's ashes and the rings that Leyton kept .

THEY LOOKED OUT TO the mountain Elliot looked round at his friends. This has been the best week he thought and with the best people and the love of his life .All of them interlinked their arms around each other looking out to the mountain and thinking about happy times and their future .Elliot looks up at Christian he looks at Elliot smiling at him and all Elliot wishes was for Christian to get over his eating disorder and for Bailey and Senora to make up he can tell they love each other a lot like he does with Christian .

THE END

Club Nero Series Will Return

Epilogue

1 year 5 Months Later

If I've to taste another bottle of wine or visit another winery I'm gonna kill him, Elliot thought but I love him just the same way Christian had brought Elliot to South Africa, Cape Town, his hometown. They were into their second week. Visiting his parents and travelling around South Africa Christian wanted to show Elliot his home country he was loving it so far Christians friends and family were welcoming .And had been so kind to him he was liking the country a lot . They did most of the touristy things and learned about South African culture .

" Babe honestly I don't think I can drink anymore wine " Elliot certainly wasn't a wine drinker more a beer person but at weddings he would take the of glass Christian snorted and lifted up a packed bottle " Love please this one for me you will like it " Elliot rolled his eyes he always says that he thought opening up the box taking out the bottle from the box . Elliot thought another box he looked at Christian who was smiling. Elliot was puzzled is it a gift he thought because their anniversary passed a couple months ago lifting out the box .

ELLIOT STARTED UNWRAPPING it coming across a red box he looked at Christian then opened it up revealing two white gold plated rings holy fuck Elliot thought he looked at Christian who was down on one knee holding his hand out for Elliot to take " Elliot Mattheson I love. You are so amazing I never thought I would meet anyone like you will marry me " .

TEARS ROLLED DOWN ELLIOT'S cheeks when the hell did he get these damn rings he thought Christian took out one of the rings placing it on Elliot's finger Elliot moved towards Christian kissing him he threw his arms round him " Yes yes I will marry you " Elliot sniffed they hugged he's made me the most happiest man then Elliot got out the other ring placing it on Christians finger . They hugged again and the waiter appeared with Champagne for them Elliot inspected his ring while it gleamed in the sun he certainly had good taste Elliot thought .

ELLIOT'S PHONE RANG facetime by Bailey he connected the call " Congrats Mate " Elliot looked at Christian ahh so they planned this did they Senoras face appeared smiling then Casey tried to get in on the call Elliot laughed that boy wants in on everything he thought . "We have news' ' Bailey said that's right they had their sonogram appointment Bailey and Senora found out they were having twins five months ago but not the sex until now . "We're having girls' ' Senora shouted. Bailey rolled his eyes. Elliot snorted Christian lay his arm round Elliot .Wow amazing Elliot thought looking at Christian would he and Christian have kids in the future he thought .

" THAT'S GREAT NEWS guys congratulations " Christian said certainly was good news he thought " is it I'm gonna be overrun by women can you imagine " Elliot snorted it was bad enough they were having twins it freaked him out but in the end accepted it twins on Senoras side of the family, They had found out previously well it's something they will just have to deal with Elliot thought .Bailey better not complain when he gets back .Especially having twin girls and wondered if they would be identical wouldn't that be something if they were .

" GOODBYE BAILEY " Elliot disconnected the call. Christian couldn't believe what he had just done Elliot looked at him " I'll call him back later let's continue our celebration " Christian smiled Elliot reached over to kiss him . And wrapping his arms round Christian shoulders they kissed again " Do you think they will give us champagne for free " Elliot asked Christian sniggered, then the waiter came over with a bottle of champagne that's sneaky, Elliot thought . Inspected his ring god I can't believe I'm a fiancé now I so love that man drinking their champagne.

" WHAT THE HELL? " BAILEY couldn't believe it. Elliot disconnecting their FaceTime calls he looked at Senora she shrugged her shoulders while Casey ran round the table with his toy tractor Bailey giggled while he picked him up kissing his head he looked at Senora she smiled . " we're gonna have to get a bigger house " Bailey announced she nodded and tickled Casey he giggled . That's true Senora thought they had been thinking about moving for a while now . And since they found out Senora was pregnant again they definitely thought about a bigger place especially now they know that they are having twins .

" We sure are " touching her stomach she looked up at Bailey " I still look sexy right " Bailey sniggered Shaking his head off course she still looks sexy " Yes baby you still look sexy " .kissing her belly and rubbing it fuck he thought I'm gonna have twins looking up at Senora . " Bailey are you freaking out " Bailey shakes his head he is freaking out she thought patting his head " We will be fine there are loads couples that have had multiple births ok " .

" Ok " Bailey reaches to kiss Senora I wonder if she would still have sex nearer her due date and with Casey being early the hospital said they would keep a close eye on her Senora did opt for a caesarean nearer her due date .

The Prison door opened Grant walked out looking up to the sky finally out of that awful place a car door shut he looked over at Daniel standing at the car hands in pockets he came Grant thought . Grant picks up his bag going over to Daniel Grant smiles Daniel moves round to the other side opening up his side of the car . " Daniel " Daniel looks over at Grant " I'm only doing you and your mum a favour Grant " .

" I know Thanks " They both get into the car Daniel looks over at Grant he looks tired he thought while Grant buckles up Daniel's phone beeps he picks it up on the dashboard checks it and quickly sends a text . I have work later you can help yourself to whatever you need for food wise and rules " .

" Yea I know I've learned my lesson Daniel " I hope so he thought looking over at Grant then his phone goes off his mum ringing Grant answers " Mum " Darling how are you " Meg asks standing out in her garden while Liam is out Grant looks over at Daniel Who is concentrating while driving " Fine mum " " Good now please this time for us try and not get into trouble ok " .

Grant looks down at his leg with the tag on it Well I'm not likely to since I have the tag on since I was released early but with the tag for monitoring " Well I'm not likely to am I Mum since I have the tag on " Daniel huffs Shaking his head Grant looks over at him " I know Darling at least Daniel had kindly opened His house to you keep your nose clean I will speak to your father I love you " .

" Love you to Mum " They disconnect their call Grant places his phone between his legs and looks out the window chewing his lip " I'm not gonna get into trouble Daniel " Grant looks over at Daniel good to hear he thought if he does he is out and back in jail again . " Don't you believe me " " I want Grant and as for Blair " .

" I know and I really appreciate this I really do " He had better be true to his word and stick to what they agreed Especially for his parents to trust him again he had to go to counselling and be seen actively looking for a job and the police would do regular checks regarding his tag and check in each night . If he was to relapse and stay out longer he will be back in Prison. It wasn't the best situation but he would try and make it work Daniel thought .

The End

BY

Dale V Mcfarlane

Club Nero Series Novel
Club Nero (Vol 1)
Club Nero Series (Vol 2)
New Beginnings (Vol 3)
A New Start (Vol 4)

STANDALONE NOVEL
The Réunion (Sam's Pov)

His Cold Heart Series Novel
His Cold Heart (Vol 1)
Warm Heart (Vol 2)
The Warmest Heart (Vol 3)

The Little Coffee Shop On The Corner (Vol 1) coming January 31st 2025

Linktree
https://Linktr.ee/dalevmcfarlane[1]

PATREON
Patreon.com/dalevmcfarlane

1. https://linktr.ee/dalevmcfarlane

Don't miss out!

Visit the website below and you can sign up to receive emails whenever Dale v Mcfarlane publishes a new book. There's no charge and no obligation.

https://books2read.com/r/B-A-WMJU-ZISMD

Connecting independent readers to independent writers.

Also by Dale v Mcfarlane

Little Pretty Things - Vol 1
A Club Nero Series Novel - Little Pretty Things- Vol 1

The Little Coffee Shop On The Corner - Vol 1
The Little Coffee Shop On The Corner- Vol 1

Vol 1
Club Nero
His Cold Heart
Club Nero Series Novel - Little Pretty Things - Vol 1

Vol 2
His Cold Heart - Warm Heart - Vol 2
Club Nero

Vol 4
Club Nero Series - The Next Chapter - Vol 4

Vol one

Club Nero - Vol 1

Standalone

Club Nero Series - New Beginnings vol 3

His Cold Heart - The Warmest Heart - vol 3

Club Nero Series - The Reunion

About the Author

Hi i am Dale i live in scotland writting is my passion i also write fan fic to please check out my socials

Milton Keynes UK
Ingram Content Group UK Ltd.
UKHW031458231024
450082UK00001B/46